Alexander Hieke, Hannes Leitgeb
Reduction
Between the Mind and the Brain

Publications of the
Austrian Ludwig Wittgenstein Society.
New Series

Volume 12

Alexander Hieke, Hannes Leitgeb

Reduction

Between the Mind and the Brain

ontos

verlag

Frankfurt I Paris I Lancaster I New Brunswick

Bibliographic information published by Deutsche Nationalbibliothek
The Deutsche Nationalbibliothek lists this publication in the Deutsche Nationalbibliographie;
detailed bibliographic data is available in the Internet at http://dnb.ddb.de

Gedruckt mit Förderung des
Bundesministeriums für Wissenschaft und Forschung in Wien
und der Kulturabteilung der NÖ Landesregierung

North and South America by
Transaction Books
Rutgers University
Piscataway, NJ 08854-8042
trans@transactionpub.com

United Kingdom, Ire, Iceland, Turkey, Malta, Portugal by
Gazelle Books Services Limited
White Cross Mills
Hightown
LANCASTER, LA1 4XS
sales@gazellebooks.co.uk

Livraison pour la France et la Belgique:
Librairie Philosophique J.Vrin
6, place de la Sorbonne ; F-75005 PARIS
Tel. +33 (0)1 43 54 03 47 ; Fax +33 (0)1 43 54 48 18
www.vrin.fr

©2009 ontos verlag
P.O. Box 15 41, D-63133 Heusenstamm
www.ontosverlag.com

ISBN 13: 978-3-86838-046-0

2009

Printed on acid-free paper
ISO-Norm 970-6
FSC-certified (Forest Stewardship Council)
This hardcover binding meets the International Library standard

Printed in Germany
by buch bücher dd ag

Introduction

The investigation of the *mind* has been one of the major concerns of our philosophical tradition and it still is a dominant subject in modern analytic philosophy as well as in science. Many philosophers in the scientific tradition want to solve the "puzzles of the mind"; but many philosophers in the very same tradition do regard these puzzles as puzzles of the *brain*, or to put it differently, they suggest we should avoid the reference to the mind altogether. So, whilst the former think of mental entities as something independent and of our speaking about them as irreducible to talk about physical entities, the latter deny that philosophy of mind has to do with anything else but the brain (or related physical entities) and thus rather want reference to mental entities to be eliminated altogether. And then there are those who think that *reduction* is the way to go: even if the language of the mental can not be translated into some language referring to physical entities only, maybe mental entities are still brain-dependent and hence reducible to physical entities in some ontological way.

This volume collects contributions comprising all those points of view. The articles originate from the 31st International Wittgenstein Symposium, August 2008, Kirchberg am Wechsel, which was devoted to *Reduction and Elimination in Philosophy and the Sciences*. We want to thank the authors for their great support, and we are confident that their work will stimulate further philosophical progress in this area of research.

Alexander Hieke & Hannes Leitgeb
Spring 2009

TABLE OF CONTENTS

I. BETWEEN THE MIND...

II. ... AND ...

III. ... THE BRAIN

I.
BETWEEN
THE MIND ...

ENOUGH WITH THE NORMS ALREADY!

JERRY FODOR
Rutgers University

This isn't really a paper. It's more of a temper tantrum. Perhaps it will make up in vehemence what it lacks in arguments.

Everybody goes on about norms. Well, I am fed up with norms. If I never see another norm, that will be soon enough for me. Enough with the norms already. I am not, of course, antithetic to *every and all* norms. To the contrary, there are many norms with which I absolutely concur. For example, Flanders and Swann famously remarked that 'eating people is wrong' (In 'The reluctant cannibal'). Well, eating people *is* wrong (except, perhaps, in the most dire of emergencies.) Speaking for myself, I simply can't imagine eating a person. I honor this norm and I wish it well.

By contrast, the norms with which I am fed up are the kind that are alleged to block certain philosophical projects of naturalization to which I am professionally committed. In particular, I'd very much like there to be a naturalized account of the kinds of concepts (or terms, or constructs, or properties, or predicates, or whatever) that figure centrally in semantic and in intensional psychological explanations. Among the former, I tentatively Include 'is true', 'is false', 'is necessary', 'entails', 'means', 'refers to' and so forth. Among the latter, I tentatively include 'believes', 'intends', 'desires', 'acts', 'thinks', 'sees as' and so forth. In neither case do I know exactly what belongs on the lists; suffice it that the notions I would like to see naturalized include all the ones that occur ineliminably in such psychological explanations as we take to be true (or will take to be true.when/if we finally arrive at reflective equilibrium).

In particular, I'm interested in the prospects for constructing a naturalistic propositional attitude psychology. The idea is that believing, intending, and other states that figure in typical explanations of cognitive phenomena, informal or in the laboratory, would be treated as relations to a certain class of mental particulars ('mental representations'); and mental processes would be defined over these. This approach has been around, in one form or other, at least since Hume, according to whom mental representations are 'Ideas' (something like mental images), and mental processes are causal (associative) relations among Ideas.

But a lot of philosophers think, on the one hand, that all the concepts, properties,..., whatever that such an account of cognition would require (for economy's sake, I will henceforth call them all 'whatevers' because that avoids having to decide about just what ontology a naturalistic theory of cognition might be supposed to postulate), are, as it were, quasi- or crypto-normative. And these philosophers also think that practically as a point of definition, that what is normative can't be naturalized. So, because of the normative character of whatevers, the naturalization project can't but fail in precisely the areas where I most want it to succeed. In a nutshell, the norms I'm fed up with are the ones that are supposed to be incompatible with a naturalistic account of the psychology of cognition.

I strongly suspect that all the issues about the naturalization of whatevers have to do, in one way or other, with questions about symbols. I shall therefore assume that any explanation that is remotely plausible in the psychology of cognition will have to endorse (not just some notion of mental representation but also) some notion of 'mental representations'. In the core cases, mental representations are discursive (non-iconic) symbols. That's to say that their tokens must be susceptible of semantic evaluation and they must have causal powers. Except for the 'discursive' part, this would come as no surprise to Hume, for whom Ideas are typically *of* something (in effect, they have referents) and association is a process of (mental) causation. Unlike Hume, however, I doubt that mental representations are anything like images. The reasons for denying that they are are familiar in both the philosophical and the psychological literatures, so I won't rehearse them here.

In short, I want there to be a language of thought. I may, of course, be ill advised to want this; but, if so, I want to be ill advised on empirical grounds; I do not want to be ill advised a priori. So, assuming that what's normative can't be naturalized, I don't want accounts of mental symbols or mental processes to be ipso facto normative.

Where did all this normative stuff come from? Some of it must surely be blamed on Hume, who claimed (or, at least, is claimed to have claimed) that you can't derive 'ought' from 'is'. But I imagine that its modern incarnations started with, on the one hand, G.E. Moore's formulation of the 'open question' argument and, on the other hand, Wittgenstein's suggestion that the use of symbols is a kind of rule-governed behavior. The open question argument went something like this: Whatever naturalistic account you propose for goodness (or for 'good'), the question will remain intuitively open whether something that is good according to that account is, in actual fact, good. I think this is plausible because I suppose (and so, I take it, did Moore) that any account that doesn't leave the open question open would have to be not just *necessarily* true but a priori; and that got such an account to be a priori, it would have to be true by definition (hence analytic). Unlike Moore, however, I very much doubt that there are *any* definitions or analyticities, normative or otherwise. And even where there is definitional equivalence between a naturalistic expression and a normative expression, the two might nonetheless differ in their pragmatics, which may or may not count as a parameter of their 'use'. (As far as I know, no one has any serious proposal on offer as to what aspects of the use of an expression constitutes its 'use' in the technical sense where, we're told, use either is meaning or is what meaning supervenes on. That being so, issues like whether perlocutionary force is a parameter of use are moot as things stand.)

Anyhow, the open question argument is one plausible source of the notion that theories of whatevers are ineliminably normative. Another is Wittgenstein's suggestion that using symbols (mental or otherwise) is a species of rule-governed behavior. If that is granted, then the question arises whether, on a certain occasion, a symbol is used correctly or incorrectly. The idea is roughly that the semantics of symbols emerges from conventions for using them properly. And it seems plausible that notions like *proper* and *improper* are normative and ipso facto incapable of naturalization.

It's easy enough to tell a story that makes this seem true for natural languages (English, as it might be). Natural languages are vehicles of communication, and there is no communication without synchronization. If, for example, you and I are to communicate in English, you must mean by 'giraffe' and 'blue' what I mean by 'giraffe' and 'blue' and vice versa; otherwise we won't understand one another when either says that giraffes are blue. It's natural enough to gloss this as 'we must both be following the same rules for using 'giraffe' and 'blue'', where the normative force of the 'must' is instrumental; it means something like 'on pain of failing to communicate.'

But then, it would seem that the sort of story that seems plausible enough for English breaks down if you try to apply it to mental representations (unless mental representations are expressions in natural languages; a question that I also wish not to be settled a priori). For one thing, we don't *use* the language of thought (hereinafter 'LOT' or 'Mentalese'). Not, at least, in the sense in which our using it would involve our having intentions with respect to how we use it. We mean to refer to giraffes when we say 'giraffe'. But (supposing that 'swiggle' is the word that refers to giraffes in Mentalese), we don't use 'swiggle' to refer to giraffes with the intention of so doing. In fact, we have no intentions at all in respect to 'swiggle'. Tokenings of expressions in Mentalese don't count as *actions*; they're things that just happen; presumably as a causal consequence of prior thoughts or of perceptual promptings. Least of all do we use 'swiggle' with the intention of acting in accord with norms for its use.

So, to gather all this together, English and LOT may well be different in that here are norms in accordance with which we use English, but (so far at least) none in accordance with which we use Mentalese. And maybe (*maybe*) a normless language is a contradiction in terms.

Notice, however, that here the normativity comes from the (instrumental) demands that *communication* makes, not from any demands (instrumental or otherwise) that *reference* makes. And there is, nothing so far, that shows that an expression's being used for communication is, as it were, *constitutive of* its being a referring expression. So, suppose that there aren't any *rules* for using a Language of Thought; psychology might still be naturalizable even though it claims that 'squiggle' refers to squiggles.

So now the question whether it is possible to naturalize Mentalese comes down to the question whether Mentalese is used as a vehicle of communication. Which, of course it isn't. Nobody ever used 'squiggle' to communicate anything to anyone; not even to themselves. Rather, the assumption is that Mentalese is used as the vehicle of *calculation*, (which, according to the kind of psychological theories I have in mind, is what many mental processes consist of). So, finally, the question about naturalization comes down to whether or not there can be a language that is used to calculate but not to communicate; a *de facto* private language. Or at least I shall assume that it does in the rest of this discussion.

I suppose that the burden of proof is on anybody who argues: 'no language without norms; no norms without communication; hence no de facto private languages', hence no Mentalese. I assume that, in any such argument, questions about normativity and questions about de facto publicity are inextricably tangled together: either normativity is inferred from publicity or that publicity is inferred from normativity, and both are taken to be essential properties of languages. It would be nice to have a reason to believe that this sort of argument is sound, but it's remarkably hard to find

4

one in the literature. What follows is a sketch of some of the candidates that have occurred to me. I don't claim that these exhaust the options; but I do claim that all of them are, in all likelihood, fallacious.

First Try: Nothing is a symbol unless there is a difference between using it correctly and using it incorrectly. But if E is an expression in a de facto private language, then there is no difference between using it correctly and using it incorrectly. So the expressions of Mentalese aren't symbols. So Mentalese isn't a language.
Reply: Who says there's no difference between using its expressions correctly and not using them correctly?

Second try: Excuse me, I misspoke. What I meant was that, if a language is *de facto* private, then there must be a *verifiable* difference between using its expressions correctly and not using them correctly; there must be 'criteria' for their use.
Reply: I'm not a verificationist. Assuming that 'squiggle' is an expression that refers to giraffes, it is wrong (mistaken, incorrect) to use it to refer to trees. But nothing *epistemological* follows as far as I know.

Third try: The normativity of the rules of English is instrumental. It derives from the use of Engllish as a vehicle of communication. Since Mentalese is de facto *not a* vehicle of communication, its putative rules have no normative force. So there's an essential difference between Mentalese and English.
Reply: Strictly speaking, this begs the question whether normativity is an *essential* property of rules of language. But put that aside. The story is that the normative force of the rules of English derives from the use of English to communicate, which is a project in which we have an interest. But it seems perfectly possible that there is some *other* project in which we are likewise interested, and that the normativity of the rules of Mentalese derives from it. For example, we're interested in having true beliefs, so the instrumental value of Mentalese may derive from its *de facto* necessity for our doing so. It's one thing to say that there must be norms. It's quite another that to say that the norms must derive from the exegencies of communication.

Fourth try: Our acquiescence in the rules of Mentalese is merely tacit.
Reply: So too is our acquiescence in the rules in English.

Fifth try: Equivalence is defined for the rules of Mentalese only up to extensional equivalence. Whereas there can be a matter of fact about which of two extensionally equivalent rules a speaker of a natural language is following.
Reply: Maybe there is no choosing between extensionally equivalent rules for using Mentalese even if the extensions of counterfactual tokenings are included (which they should be). But I can't think of any reason for believing that, and some such reason is owing.

Actually I *can* think of a reason; but it presupposes that rules of natural languages are, as it were, 'written down' in the heads of its speakers. If they are, then the choice between extensionally equivalent rules might be a choice between intensionally distinct ways of mentally representing them. On pain of a Lewis Carroll regress, however, nothing like this could be true of the rules of Mentalese, so this line of argument is unavailable to anyone who denies that Mentalese expressions are symbols (and hence have no referents).

Sixth try: Expressions in Mentalese have no perlocutionary force. For a symbol to have perlocutionary force is for its tokens to be intended to have a certain effect on their hearers. Expressions in a private language (even expressions in a merely de facto private language) don't have hearers and its users don't have intentions with respect to them.
Reply: But this begs the question whether its being used with perlocutionary intent is an *essential* property of something a symbol. I deny that it is; or, anyhow, that it has been shown to be. (See above)

Seventh try: Languages have to be learned. Learning requires instruction by someone. So, de facto, Mentalese can't be learned; so it's not a language.
Reply: It's true that English has to be learned (or, anyhow that it has to be 'picked up'); and that Mentalese can't be (again on pain of a Lewis Carroll regress.) This shows that anyone who posits a language of mental representation will have to be, to some very appreciable extent, a nativist. What's wrong with that?

6

Eighth try: Languages have to be translatable from the epistemic position of a radical translator. Since Mentalese is de facto private, it is not so translatable. So it isn't a language.

Reply: I know of no reason to suppose that a language must be translatable from the epistemic position of a radical translators. Come to think of it, I know of no reason to suppose that English is.

Ninth try: Tokenings of a language have to have (or any how, to be capable of having) interpreters. Since Mentalese is de facto private, there is no interpreter of its tokenings. So Mentalese can't be a language.

Reply: The premise needs arguing for (on some grounds other than the assumption of verificationism. See the reply to *second try*). But suppose we pass that. Still, the question remains why a *counterfactual* interpreter ('If there *had been* an interpreter, he would have taken the token to mean such and such') wouldn't meet the specifications. Is there some reason why there shouldn't be counterfactual interpreters of Mentalese? (In particular, counterfactual interpreters who know about the causes and effects of its tokenings.) See Fodor 2008 for a sketch of how 'triangulation' (which, at least according to Donald Davidson, is par excellence what interpreters do for a living) might be worked out in terms of such counterfactuals.

I'm out of candidates. I have no proof that the only possible normativity/privacy arguments against the naturalization of Mentalese are of the kind that I've been surveying. But, I can't think of any others, and these do all seem to be to be distinctly dubious. I intend, therefore, to proceed on my way, assuming that there aren't any good arguments against a de facto Mentalese that turn on issues of privacy/normativity. If you think of one, do please let me know right away. I have an email account at which I can almost always be reached.

REFERENCES

Fodor, J. *LOT2: The Language of Thought Revisited.* Oxford University Press, Oxford, 2008.

INTENTIONALITY, INFORMATION, AND EXPERIENCE

JOHANNES L. BRANDL
University of Salzburg

INTRODUCTION

Descartes claimed that the essence of the mind is thinking (*cogitare*), to which Brentano added that the essence of thinking is to be mentally directed at objects of some kind.[1] These are controversial assumptions about the nature of the mind. A more modest starting point would be to say that intentionality is an important feature of a large class, but not necesarrily of all mental phenomena. Though this claim too has been challenged in the behaviourist tradition, it is now widely accepted that having a mental life involves mental states with a mental content. Cognitive scientists call it the representational power of the mind. Like Descartes and Brentano, we therefore face the task of explaining this important feature of the mind. Where does its representational power come from?

It is also widely agreed today that the project of reducing intentionality to language has failed. The representational power of the mind does not derive from our capacity to speak a language. It is rather the other way round: linguistic expressions derive their meaning and their referential power from the mental states of speakers and hearers which guide their linguistic behaviour. Mental representation is the foundation of linguistic representation. The foundations on which the power of mental representation rests must lie elsewhere. Can we dig here any deeper? Sceptical philosophers like Quine have resisted that demand. That, however, is not a comfortable position, if one has agreed that intentionality is a real feature of thought. How could there be no further explanation of how the mind acquires its representational power?

---

[1] Brentano gives credit here to the scholastic doctrine of "intentional (or mental) in-existence", i.e. the existence of objects "in" psychic phenomena (see Brentano 1874/ 1973, p.88). Though the term "intentionality" derives from Brentano and therefore still echoes these historical roots, the term "object" no longer denotes what exists "in" mental acts but has been replaced by the term "mental content".

Fortunately, there is a better option available. In fact there are *two* broadly conceived programs for explaining intentionality that compete with each other. One of them is *informational semantics*.[2] It takes the category of information to be fundamental and tries to explain how intentional mental states arise in cognitive systems from tracking the information that is available in their environment. Theories that propose to naturalize intentionality typically follow this program. The other project might be called *phenomenological semantics*.[3] It rests on the claim that intentionality is founded in conscious experience. Accordingly it tries to explain how conscious experience generates a phenomenal content from which the conceptual content of thoughts can be derived. This too might be seen as providing intentionality with a natural foundation, but it is clearly a very different form of "naturalization". Thus we face a difficult choice: where should we put our money?

The goal of this paper is modest in several ways. First, I will not argue for the claim that informational semantics and phenomenological semantics are the only two games in town. I do think, however, that on a broad understanding of these terms most theories of intentionality may be regarded as belonging to one of these frameworks.

Secondly, I cannot rule out the possibility that there is a deeper level of explanation at which informational semantics and phenomenological semantics might be reconciled with each other. There are theories, like Castañedas guise theory, that might be interpreted along these lines.[4] However, I think that such an integrative theory, if it is successful, would be more like a third approach that shares some features with the others but also gives up some of their basic assumptions.

---

[2] I use the label 'informational semantics' here in a broad sense to include any theory that assigns a fundamental role to natural meaning. This holds for informational theories that emphasize causal relations, like the semantics 'Wisconsin style' of D. Stampe, B. Enç and F. Dretske, as well as for other naturalistic accounts of mental representation by A. Denkel, R. Millikan, D. Papineau, K. Sterelny, and others (see Macdonald & Papineau 2006).

[3] I use the label 'phenomenological semantics' here for any theory that assigns a fundamental role to experience in the constitution of mental content. This includes Husserl's theory of meaning constituting acts, but also a conceptual role semantics that starts with phenomenal intentionality, and other recent contributions to the 'phenomenal intentionality research project' by T. Horgan, U. Kriegel, B. Loar, G. Strawson, and others (see Bayne & Montague, forthcoming).

[4] More recently, Edward Zalta has suggested that his theory of abstract objects might allow for a similar reconciliation; see Zalta 2000.

Thirdly, I am not going to suggest a method or criterion of how one might rationally choose between informational semantics and phenomenological semantics. Clearly, both programs have their advantages and disadvantages, and it would take considerably more space than is available here to evaluate them and weigh their respective pros and cons.

The modest task I set myself here is to show how the conflict between informational semantics and phenomenological semantics *cannot* be resolved. It cannot be resolved, so I shall argue, by demonstrating that one of these programs is "deeply flawed" or perhaps even inconsistent. Arguments that try to find such a flaw in informational semantics have been proposed by Jonathan Lowe (1995/97) and Uriah Kriegel (2007). These arguments, so I shall argue, are ultimately question-begging.

In sections 1 and 2 I do the stage-setting by introducing the main ideas and the attractive features that one finds in informational semantics and phenomenological semantics respectively. In section 3 I present and criticize Lowe's argument against informational semantics. A brief summary of the core of Kriegel's argument is given in section 4, followed by my criticism of this argument in section 5. In the final section I indicate how these results may be helpful – even if not decisive – in finding the right method for explaining intentionality.

1 FROM INFORMATION TO INTENTIONALITY

Information is a commodity of our daily life. We continuously receive, transmit and store information of all kinds. Although this information processing is very familiar to us, it is hard to say exactly what this comes to. What is this curious thing called 'information' that exists in our brains, in books and on TV, in our computers, and in many other places?

An answer to this question has been offered by Fred Dretske in his book *Knowledge and the Flow of Information* (1981). This seminal work launched the project of informational semantics in explaining the foundations of cognition. Dretske's conception of information takes its lead from Claude Shannon's probabilistic notion of 'amount of information' that a signal can carry in a communication process. It diverges from Shannon, however, by also appealing to the semantic notions of 'meaning' and 'content'. Thus Dretske arrives at a definition of *informational content*. It defines the content that a signal s carries, relative to the knowledge k of an agent who receives that piece of information. The definition says: "A signal r carries the information that s is $F =_{df}$ The conditional probability of s's being F, given r (and k), is 1 (but, given k alone, less than 1.)" (Dretske 1981, p.65).

This technical notion seems at first sight to be far removed from our commonsensical understanding of information. We take it that a piece of information can be more or less accurate and that a person can have misleading or even completely wrong information. This is not compatible with Dretske's definition. It is therefore a bit surprising when he claims that his notion of informational content "corresponds strikingly well with our ordinary, intuitive understanding of information: [...] it enables us to understand the source [...] of the semantic character of information; and it reveals the extent to which, and the reason why, the information one receives is a function of what one already knows." (Dretske 1981, pp.81f.) Where do we find the correspondence that Dretske is speaking of here?

The intuitions that fit Dretske's proposal can be found in the veridical usage of terms like 'perception', 'remember' and 'know'. This usage is constrained by the condition that a subject S can perceive an object O, or perceive that O has a certain property F, only if O exists and actually has that property. Equally, one can remember that something happened only if it really happened, and one can know something only if it is true. In these contexts we use the notion of informational content (or simply 'information') in the way in which Dretske defines it. We say, for instance, that in perceiving something we pick up information, that in remembering something, we retrieve information from our memory, and that a person who is thus informed about a subject matter knows something about it.

The point here is that perception and memory bring us in contact with reality. This contact becomes more elusive when we consider mental operations in general, not just cognitive operations like veridical perceptions and successful cases of memory retrieval. The faculties of perception and memory can also deceive us. They may deceive us about being in contact with reality. In this case we still have thoughts and these thoughts are about reality, but in a different sense: they merely *purport* to bring us in cognitive relation with real objects and states of affairs. They create an appearance of contact that is not actually there.

Informational semantics requires acknowledging the fact that mental states can deceive us, while also respecting the veridical usage of epistemic terms. In this way the Dretskian notion of information can be sustained. The insight here is that carrying information (in the Dretskian sense) is not essential for a mental state, just as it is not essential for it to bring us in contact with reality. This insight gives rise to an important question: Why is it that cognitive systems are necessarily fallible? Why is it that any system that has the power to receive and store information by perceiving and remembering things, also has the power of forming false beliefs and false memories about reality?

This question takes us beyond the notion of information, as Dretske defines it. The central term now becomes 'representation'. With this notion we enter the familiar territory of a theory of intentionality. The fallibility of mental operations is their central feature from an intentional point of view. There are three aspects to it that may be distinguished:

(1) Thoughts can represent existing objects as well as objects that do not exist.
(2) Thoughts can represent some object O that has property F without representing the fact that O has F.
(3) Thoughts can represent some object O although the subject of this thought does not believe to have thoughts about O.

How does informational semantics explain these features? That question is too complex to be answered succinctly. There are several attractive ideas that one may pursue here. I can only mention some of these ideas without offering any details.

First, there is the idea of *teleological function* and *cognitive fitness* championed in the work of Ruth Millikan (see Millikan 1989/93). According to this idea, thoughts have the power to represent because in doing so they enhance the cognitive fitness of the system in which they occur. For instance, it is of great importance for an organism to know when an enemy is near. It is therefore part of the proper function of its cognitive apparatus to make the system aware of the presence of enemies. Yet objects may appear to be dangerous for the system without actually being so. When the system is thus deceived, its cognitive system still performs its proper function of indicating the presence of a dangerous object. This is, in a nutshell, the teleological explanation how our thoughts can come to represent non-existing objects.

A second idea is "nomological control". Jerry Fodor has proposed this idea for explaining which properties enter the content of a concept and thus become part of the thoughts we have about objects having those properties (see Fodor 1990). For instance, why do we think of an animal with a tail when we think of a dog? This cannot be explained by saying that all dogs that we have seen actually had tails since we may have seen dogs without tails. Yet we might try the following explanation: a concept C refers to objects with a certain feature F iff C is under the nomological control of F, i.e. if there is a counterfactual-supporting causal relation between tokens of C and instances of F. This might explain why "having a tail" is part of our concept of dog and why other features, like their color, are not. This is, very briefly stated, the nomological explanation of how we can represent objects without also representing all the properties they have.

A third idea that plays an important role in informational semantics is *etiology*. This idea may be used to explain why our thoughts can represent objects different from those that we believe them to represent. Such cases have become prominent with the Twin-Earth thought-experiments. My twin on Twin-Earth may believe that he is drinking water and that he has thoughts about water, while in fact he is drinking and thinking about a quite different substance. Causal theories of reference explain this possibility along the following lines: A concept C refers to objects of kind K iff an object of kind K has been the incipient cause for forming the concept C. That explanation is useful also in cases of real life. We all have many false beliefs about the environment we live in. This need not prevent us from having thoughts about the real substances we interact with. Only etiology, so it seems, can explain this peculiar aspect of intentionality.

These ideas have often been taken to be in competition with, or even opposed to informational semantics (see Fodor 1990; Millikan 1990/93). If one thinks of it as a project that addresses a number of different problems, however, these ideas may also be fruitfully combined with each other. Explanatory power can thus be gained by combining a teleological background theory with the facts of nomological co-variation and incipient causation. This certainly looks like a highly promising research program for a reductive explanation of intentionality.[5]

But doubts remain. These doubts do not just concern the details of the program. There are reasons to think that informational semantics might be completely on the wrong track. Before I consider some of these objections, however, I want to introduce the main alternative approach to explaining intentionality, namely phenomenological semantics.

---

[5] For a recent example of such a combined approach see Jesse Prinz 2002.

Phenomenological semantics takes its inspiration from the work of Brentano. As I mentioned at the beginning, Brentano claimed that to be directed at an object is an essential feature of all mental phenomena. He therefore conjectured that even the most primitive experiences that we find in a human mind already exhibit a form of intentionality. This prompted him to take the notion of "being directed at an object" in a very broad sense. These objects may be common things like an apple that we see or a doorbell that we hear ringing. We should also include in the class of objects, however, such entities as colors and sounds. One might call them "objects of appearance" that we encounter in experience.[6]

In this way Brentano made the simplest experiences – he calls them 'simple presentations' – the starting point for a theory of intentionality. There was a special reason for him to take this approach. Brentano was interested in psychology as a discipline that could play a fundamental role for scientific inquiry in general, including philosophy. This could not be a psychology that relied on observations of behaviour and brain functions. Hence, Brentano began to develop what he later called a *descriptive* psychology that operates from a first-person perspective. Its task is to give a comprehensive description of the presentations that form the basis of our consciousness and also to provide an account of how complex mental phenomena are founded on simple experiences. If this is done strictly from the first-person perspective, Brentano thought, it will lead to descriptions of mental phenomena that are immediately evident. These descriptive truths can then be taken as a starting point and as background knowledge that is needed in philosophy as well as in the experimental sciences.

What exactly is the role that intentionality plays in this project? There are two ways in which we might interpret Brentano's project. One reading would be that intentionality is for Brentano an irreducible feature of experience that cannot – and need not – be explained any further. It is an immediately evident truth of descriptive psychology that experiences are object-directed by their very nature. Intentionality would thus be given to us as a fundamental feature of experience. It would make no sense here to ask where this power of representing objects comes from. Intentionality is

---

[6] Brentano calls these objects "physical" phenomena thereby indicating that they belong to the physical world at which our mind is directed (see Brentano 1874/1973, pp.79f.).

simply "there" as part of the experience and thus has to be *presupposed* in every explanation of mental phenomena.

Another possible interpretation, however, opens up when we add a distinction that one might make between the content of experience and the content of a thought that results from "processing" the experience in a certain conceptual framework. Such a distinction has been commonly made in the Kantian tradition, and it may have been Husserl who first seized the opportunity of connecting this distinction with Brentano's ideas. The pay-off is that intentionality now can – and even needs to be – reductively explained. Conscious experience is not itself intentional by nature, but only provides the foundation for intentional content. It is from experience that our thoughts derive the power for mental representation.

This move beyond Brentano also creates a new problem however. How can we describe what an experience is like without describing it as object-directed? Consider, for example, the visual experience of a blinking red light. There is no way how I could articulate what that experience is without saying that it is an experience *of* a red light that is blinking. I must describe the experience by describing the object at which the experience is directed. How else could I make clear what I am talking about?

Husserl found a congenial solution to this problem. In his *Logical Investigations* (1901) he draws a firm distinction between the *content* of an experience and the objects that such an experience may or may not represent. This allows us, Husserl claims, to say that a perceptual experience has a certain phenomenal content without mentioning the fact that it directs the attention to an (external) object. We can bracket the external world in describing the nature of our experiences from a first-person perspective.

Since Brentano also used the term 'content', however, this term now becomes highly ambiguous and much caution is in order here. Following a contemporary usage, one might distinguish between the narrow (phenomenal) content of an experience that is not yet intentional, and the wide (intentional) content of mental states that have a representational function. Unfortunately the term 'wide content' is also used for the target objects that are represented in such states. Alternatively, one might adopt a proposal that distinguishes between the 'intentional content' of experience and the 'cognitive content' of thought (see Prinz 2002, pp.3ff). Given this multitude of usages, I think we need another term here that we can contrast with the term 'content'. The term 'character' comes in handy at this point. One might say that experiences have a phenomenal character that is somehow too basic to be described in representational terms. It is a feature of experience that we can access from the first-person point of view, and it is different from intentional content (of all sorts).

How could this appeal to phenomenal character help in a reductive explanation of intentionality? A plausible suggestion here is to draw on insights from developmental psychology. We might learn how phenomenal character is turned into intentional content by studying how children learn to identify and recognize objects in their perceptual field. Jonathan Lowe has endorsed this approach:

> The intentional content of a perceptual experience is, in a certain sense, *grounded* in its phenomenal character, but that grounding relation here is a complicated one, which arises at least in part through the subject's individual history of perceptual learning. (Lowe, 1995/97, p.118).

Lowe takes the intentional content of an experience to be the result of our *conceiving* of objects in a certain way. This is something we learn in infancy, and we do so on the basis of how objects *appear* to us. Therefore, Lowe concludes, it is a plausible assumption that "how we conceive of physical objects is inextricably bound up with how they appear to us in perception." (ibid.)

This "inextricable" connection between phenomenal character (how things appear to us) and intentional content (how we conceive of them) poses a problem for informational semantics, as Lowe argues. I will deal with this objection shortly. First, however, I want to make explicit what the alternative is. How does a phenomenological explanation of intentionality work?

Phenomenological semantics, too, is a large-scale project. In carrying this project out, three steps need to be taken:

(1) First one has to give a description of appearances as such, i.e. a pure description of their phenomenal character.
(2) Secondly, one has to explain how the intentional content of these experiences is grounded in their phenomenal character.
(3) And thirdly, one has to explain how the conceptual content of thoughts is grounded in the intentional content of perceptual experiences.

The enormous range of this task can be seen from the attempts that have been made to execute such a program in Husserl's constitution systems, or in Carnap's *Aufbau*-project. One also must not overlook the complication that Lowe mentions in the quotation above. The explanation steps here can only be very local since they may be different from concept to concept, and even from subject to subject. For instance, my concept of dog may be grounded in real encounters with dogs, while my concept of a sea gull may be grounded in experiences with picture books. For other subjects it may be just the other way round. This could be a serious difficulty in systematizing the approach and in defining a hierarchy of concepts depending on how closely they are related to experience. But if informational semantics fails, this may be the only way to go.

3 A "FUNDAMENTAL FLAW" IN INFORMATIONAL SEMANTICS?

I have now described two different large-scale projects of how the intentionality of mental states may be explained in a reductive manner. According to the first project, intentionality is founded on the faculty of tracking information by cognitive systems that causally interact with their environment. According to the second project, intentionality is founded on the phenomenal character of experience that is accessible to subjects even when they disregard the objects in their environment. The task before us now is to find a way how one can rationally decide between these projects.

Advocates of both projects may point out the specific advantages of their approach. The information-theoretic approach is usually advocated by saying that it naturalizes intentionality (see Loewer 1987). It takes into account that intentionality comes in degrees and exists at different levels. We therefore need to compare simple minds that exhibit only a low grade of intentionality with more complex systems – such as the minds of human beings – that reach a much higher level of intentionality. It also takes into account that intentionality can be found in unconscious mental states, as they occur at a sub-personal level, and that it might be found even in artefacts, like robots, that compute information and thereby adapt to their environment.

This has raised doubts that mental features are here confused with non-mental features. Critics of the information-theoretic approach have thereby turned an alleged advantage of the program into a serious objection against it. Intentionality cannot be found at the biological or computational level, they say. Therefore informational semantics commits a fatal mistake when it tries to explain the intentional content of mental states in terms of the functioning of devices for information processing as they can be found in biology or computer science. Much hinges here on the question where to draw the line between an organism that performs certain biological functions and a cognitive system that is capable of having genuine thoughts with intentional content. But why should this be such a decisive question? Why should an advocate of informational semantics not simply reject this question and say that no sharp line can be drawn here?

Jonathan Lowe has therefore tried to strengthen the argument that informational semantics commits a fatal mistake in taking intentionality to arise in simple minds. The mistake here is, Lowe argues, that the project of informational semantics ignores the question whether simple minds have any phenomenal experiences in the first place. If such experiences are missing, no amount of information processing can provide such systems with genuine intentionality.

The point that Lowe is trying to make here is clearly a fundamental one. It is a mistake, Lowe argues, that philosophers have started to separate the problem of explaining intentionality from the problem of explaining phenomenal consciousness. These problems cannot be detached from each other:

> The upshot is that it is quite erroneous to suppose that we can ascribe genuine thoughts, with conceptually articulated structure, to creatures or machines lacking altogether the capacity to enjoy conscious experiences with phenomenal or qualitative character. Whatever a computer can do by way of information processing, storage and retrieval is not by any means to be confused with what a thinking human being does who reasons, remembers and recalls. (Lowe 1995/97, p.119)

If Lowe is right, it would be a decisive advantage of the phenomenological project that it takes the subjectivity of mental states to be fundamental. It would be decisive since we are living in a world of appearances that determines all our thinking and reasoning. All thinking takes place from a certain perspective that is defined by how things appear to a single subject. Hence, no explanation of the intentional content of thought can succeed from an objective point of view that transcends our subjective experience.

But like before, this alleged advantage of phenomenological semantics also has a downside. Critics of phenomenology can try to counter this objection by pointing out that their program *shows* how intentionality can arise from informational processes that do not presuppose a subjective point of view. The phenomenological objection thus takes subjectivity *too* seriously. It is true that within a certain realm subjectivity reigns, namely in the realm of sensory experience. But there is also the realm of representations that are publicly available and not subjectively grounded. Symbolic systems, like languages, are such public symbol systems that allow us to form thoughts whose content is accessible to everyone. It is therefore simply false to claim that *all* intentional content has to be tied to the perspective of individual subjects.

This dialectic shows, I think, that it is very unlikely to reach a rational decision along these lines. The arguments that are used here all turn out to be question-begging. They do not rely on standards of evaluation that are generally accepted. They are based on premises that are itself part of the debate. One cannot refute the program of informational semantics by taking for granted the premises on which phenomenological semantics is based. And conversely, one cannot refute phenomenological semantics on premises that are central to informational semantics. Such debates will necessarily end in a stale-mate.

In the next section I will consider a different argument that tries to avoid this dialectical impasse.

4 A NEGLECTED PROBLEM OF ONTOLOGY?

In a recent paper Uriah Kriegel proposes to evaluate theories of intentionality with respect to their ability to solve a fundamental problem of ontology which he calls "the perennial problem of intentional inexistence" (Kriegel, 2007). This problem has been widely discussed in the tradition of Brentano, but it has played hardly any role in the "mainstream research into intentionality" as it has been pursued since the advance of informational semantics (ibid, p.312). It seems that the problem is no longer considered to be a serious and important problem for a theory of intentionality. But that is a mistake, Kriegel argues, because it is a truly perennial problem that needs to be solved.

Kriegel thus sets aside the debate about naturalizing intentionality. One may subscribe to this goal, he suggests, without agreeing on the *way* in which it can be achieved. The way in which informational semantics tries to achieve this goal, Kriegel says, "is to identify the natural (broadly causal) relation that holds between x and y when, and only when, x *represents y*." (ibid.) That is where the problem of intentional inexistence can teach us a lesson. It shows that this attempt is ontologically confused and that we need a "reconceptualisation of how we are to go about naturalizing representation" (ibid, p.331, fn.13).

So, let us consider the problem of intentional inexistence. Kriegel describes it as a problem that arises from three propositions each of which have a certain *prima facie* plausibility:

(P1) One can think of (represent) non-existents.
(P2) One cannot bear a relation to non-existents.
(P3) Thinking of (representing) something involves constitutively bearing a relation to it.

Proposition (P1) is plain common sense since we can think of dwarfs and monsters that we hope to be non-existent. It is less obvious that we cannot stand in relation to such creatures by imagining them or by fearing them. But one might argue for the plausibility of proposition (P2) by pointing out that some relations clearly cease to obtain if one of its relata ceases to exist. For instance, a person is no longer married but becomes a widow or widower when his or her spouse dies. Examples like this can be interpreted in different ways, however, and the relation of being married to somebody may be different from the relation of thinking about him. We still seem to be related to people that no longer exist when we stay emotionally attached to them. Thus it seems that proposition (P3) too expresses something that we intuitively accept as true.

Now the problem of intentional inexistence arises as a problem of logical consistency. There is no obvious way of consistently subscribing to all three propositions. Once we accept two of them, we seem to be committed to denying the third proposition in this triad. Hence, we must face the question as to how we can best save our intuitions here without sacrificing our logical consistency.

Kriegel spends some effort on showing how implausible it would be to reject propositions (P1) or (P2), and he assumes that no serious attempt at reconciling all three propositions can be made. The only option remaining is therefore to deny proposition (P3). The intuition that supports this proposition seems less strong and might therefore be outweighed by the stronger intuitions in favour of the two other propositions. This is the general strategy we must pursue in solving the problem of intentional inexistence.

But this is *not* the strategy of the information-theoretic approach, Kriegel tells us. The goal in this approach has been, as mentioned above, to *identify* representational facts with the obtaining of a relation that can be described in causal terms. If one accepts that goal, one is committed to "the claim that representing something involves constitutively bearing a relation to it." (ibid, p.312).

This is how far Kriegel develops his argument against informational semantics. In the remainder of the paper he proposes his own solution to the problem of intentional inexistence. This solution I will not discuss here any further, except to mention two important assumptions that Kriegel adds to the intuitions for which he has argued so far. He accepts as a fundamental premise the claim of phenomenological semantics that all intentional content is grounded in the structure of consciousness. And he defends an adverbialist analysis of the intentional content of conscious representations.

These two assumptions are important for the following reason. They are not only fundamental to Kriegel's proposal how we can legitimately reject the idea that representing something involves constitutively bearing a relation to it, i.e. how we can get rid of proposition (3). The two assumptions just mentioned also are needed to complete his argument against informational semantics. The argument, in its completed form, runs as follows:

K1) Information-theoretic explanations of intentionality assume that such explanations must appeal only to natural (broadly causal) relations.

K2) Thinking of non-existing objects cannot be explained by appealing to natural (broadly causal) relations.

K3) The only way to avoid relations to non-existing or merely possible objects is to opt for an adverbialist analysis of conscious representations.

K4) Accepting an adverbialist analysis of conscious experience means to give up the research project of informational semantics in favour of the program of phenomenological semantics.

Once the argument is set out completely in this form, one sees how much depends here on giving a proper solution to the problem of intentional inexistence. Initially it was a logical puzzle that required some adjustment in our intuitions. Now, it seems that in making these adjustments we are driven to a fundamental decision about the general form that a semantic theory can take.

But the argument fails, I think, both in its initial stage as well as in its completed form. Information-theoretic semantics is not committed to accepting proposition (P3), and therefore the adverbialist analysis of conscious representations is not the only way for a theory of intentionality to avoid relations to non-existing objects. This is what I shall argue for in the next section.

5 INFORMATIONAL SEMANTICS REMAINS UNDEFEATED

Advocates of informational semantics have not been much concerned about the problem of intentional inexistence. In Kriegel's view this has been a dangerous neglect. Reflecting on this problem can show us that it is a misguided attempt to combine a naturalistic ontology with a relational treatment of intentionality. These two goals are simply incompatible. One will either miss the first goal, because one must tacitly accept in one's ontology non-existent or possible objects; or one will fail the second goal because one must give up the relational view inherent in informational semantics in favour of what he calls "phenomenal adverbialism". [7]

This dilemma opens up, however, only if one interprets the relational view of intentionality in a highly unfavourable way. Kriegel describes this view as saying that there is a certain relation R that holds if and only if an item x represents an object y. It should therefore be possible to *identify* the obtaining of a representational fact with the obtaining of a relation that can be described in broadly causal terms. But the claims that are actually made by informational semantics are considerably weaker. The relational analysis applies only to signals that carry and transmit information about some object O, not to all processes or states with a representational function. Therefore, there is an additional explanatory job to be done here. One needs to explain how the representational power of a mental state can be grounded in the informational relations that are taken as fundamental. It is to be *grounded* in such relations, but not to be *identified* with them.

A proper description of informational semantics therefore has to distinguish two levels on which this theory operates: there is (a) the level of relations that enable cognitive systems to pick up and transmit information,

---

[7] This is not strictly correct since adverbialism could also be developed in a non-phenomenological manner, for instance in terms of conceptual role semantics. Kriegel mentions this possibility on another occasion, but does not discuss it further (see Kriegel 2008).

and there is (b) the level of cognitive functions that enable such systems to represent objects, properties, and facts. At the bottom level, information can be transmitted only if certain (broadly causal) relations obtain. At the cognitive level systems can perform cognitive functions even if the objects that they represent do not exist. Those functions may not be "proper" functions in the biological sense of serving a biological purpose. There may be other purposes that make it useful for a system to have representational powers that transcend the realm of what actually exists.

If one conceives of informational semantics in this way, how should one respond to the logical puzzle that arises from the problem of intentional existence? The solution will be just what Kriegel suggests, namely to give up proposition (P3) in his depiction of the puzzle. This proposition (P3) says that thinking of (representing) something involves constitutively bearing a relation to it. Kriegel argues, as we have seen, that informational semantics is *committed* to the truth of this proposition. But he can claim this only by ignoring the two levels on which informational semantics operates. It would be perfectly correct to say that perceiving an object or remembering a certain event involves constitutively bearing a relation to the perceived object or the remembered fact. It would be correct because perception and memory are veridical in nature. They require that information is transmitted from the objects and events to the subject who perceives or remembers them. It is the *veridicality* of those states, not their representational function, that needs to be explained in relational terms. Since mental states are often non-veridical, however, proposition (P3) cannot be true as it stands.

We can see now why informational semantics has not been much concerned with the puzzle of intentional inexistence. If one takes the distinction between veridical and non-veridical states to be fundamental, it becomes difficult to see why there should be a problem here in the first place. When the puzzle is formulated, one immediately suspects that there is something "fishy" about proposition (P3). This proposition is much too general and needs to be restricted in the following way:

(P3*) Perceiving and remembering something involves constitutively bearing an information-transmitting relation to what is perceived and remembered.

While informational semantics is committed to (P3*), it can safely reject the much stronger claim (P3). Thus we may conclude that informational semantics remains undefeated by the problem of intentional inexistence.

This result also undermines the more elaborate argument against informational semantics that I have tried to reconstruct from Kriegel's paper. This argument starts out from claiming (K1) that only natural relations should be used in explaining intentionality, and (K2) that thinking of non-existent objects cannot be explained by appeal to such relations. Properly understood, these premises should not be in dispute. A proper understanding of these premises, however, would allow for an appeal to the level of cognitive functions in explaining intentionality. It would be an unreasonable constraint to require that informational semantics has to explain intentionality exclusively on the level of informational relations. Admittedly, there is no way how one could explain at that level how one can think of non-existent objects. But there is also no *need* to restrict oneself to that level. Thinking of objects – existing or non-existing – may be explained by cognitive functions that are grounded in informational relations. The goal of informational semantics is to explain how this "grounding" of cognitive functions in informational relations gives rise to intentional mental states. The general idea, as we have already seen, is this:

> The cognitive function of mental states is grounded in the processing of information in the following way: (a) the intentional content of perceptions and memories is grounded in information-transmitting relations, and (b) the intentional content of all other mental states derives from the intentional content of perceptions and memories.

Does Kriegel's argument provide any reason against pursuing *this* goal? The argument, as I have reconstructed it, continues with the claim (K3) that the only way to avoid relations to non-existing or merely possible objects is to opt for an adverbialist analysis of conscious representations. With this claim, one simply denies that there exists an alternative project here, namely informational semantics. This project does not take conscious representations to be fundamental, nor does it require an adverbialist analysis of such representations. At this point, Kriegel's argument simply *assumes* that intentionality has to be grounded in conscious experience. If one takes this basic presupposition of phenomenological semantics on board, however, the objection to informational semantics becomes question-begging again.

6 CONCLUSIONS

In this paper I have tried to make explicit a basic conflict between two large-scale projects concerning how intentionality might be explained. Both projects agree that there are basic facts about the mind that may serve as an explanatory basis, but they disagree what these basic facts are. For informational semantics these foundational facts are given with the cognitive functions of the mind and the information-transmitting relations on which these functions are based. For phenomenological semantics the basic facts are given with conscious experience, with its phenomenal character and with an intentional content that arises from these phenomenal features.

I then considered the problem of deciding which of these programs one should adopt. Here my conclusions have been exclusively negative. I have examined arguments that claim to find a fundamental "flaw" in the project of informational semantics. Examination of these arguments, however, reveals that these arguments either misconstrue the project of informational semantics, or simply assume the truth of some controversial phenomenological premise. No rational decision can be based on such question-begging arguments.

How should one proceed then? A pessimistic conclusion at this point would declare the sceptic to be the winner in this conflict. If we are unable to decide the conflict on rational grounds, the most reasonable thing to do might be to reject some of the premises on which both sides agree. Perhaps we should give up the idea that intentionality is an important feature of the mind, or perhaps we should resist the idea that it can be explained by appeal to certain basic facts about the mind.

My own view is less pessimistic and more pragmatic. I think that we have reason to pursue a semantic project as long as it raises interesting questions and objections that can be answered. This test has been applied here to informational semantics, and so far the project has passed this test. But one must not forget that it is large-scale project. If one asks, for instance, how our thoughts about abstract objects or fictional characters are grounded in perceptual processes by which we pick up information from the environment, an advocate of this project will have a hard time proving his case. Advocates of phenomenological semantics might claim that it is much easier and therefore more reasonable to ground such thoughts in the phenomenal qualities of our imaginatory experiences. That however remains to be seen.

ACKNOWLEDGEMENT

This paper was written as part of the European Science Foundations EUROCORES Programm CNCC, and was supported by the Austrian Science Fund (FWF), project I94-G15.

REFERENCES

Bayne, Timothy and Michelle Montague (eds.) forthcoming. *Cognitive Phenomenology*. Oxford: Oxford University Press.

Brentano, Franz 1874/1973. *Psychology From an Empirical Standpoint*. Engl. transl.: London: Routledge.

Dretske, Fred 1981. *Knowledge and the Flow of Information*. Cambridge Mass.: MIT Press.

Fodor, Jerry 1990. *A Theory of Content* I & II. In: J.A. Fodor, *A Theory of Content and Other Essays*. Cambridge: The MIT Press, pp.89–136.

Kriegel, Uriah 2007. "Intentional Inexistence and Phenomenal Intentionality", *Philosophical Perspectives* 21: pp.307–340.

Kriegel, Uriah 2008. "The Dispensibility of (Merely) Intentional Objects" *Philosophical Studies* 141: pp.79–95.

Loewer, Barry 1987. "From Information to Intentionality," *Synthese*, 70: pp.287–317

Lowe, E. Jonathan 1995/97. "There Are No Easy Problems of Consciousness", reprintetd in: J. Shea (ed.): *Facing Up to the Hard Problem of Consciousness*, Cambridge Mass., pp.117–123.

Macdonald, Graham and David Papineau (eds.) 2006. *Teleosemantics. New Philosophical Essays*. Oxford: Oxford University Press.

Millikan, Ruth G. 1989/93. "Biosemantics", reprinted in R.G. Millikan: *White Queen Psychology and Other Essays*. Cambridge Mass.: The MIT Press, pp.83–101.

Millikan, Ruth G. 1990/93. "Compare and Contrast Dretske, Fodor, and Millikan on Teleosemantics", reprinted in R.G. Millikan: *White Queen Psychology and Other Essays*. Cambridge Mass.: The MIT Press, pp.123–133.

Prinz, Jesse J. 2002. *Furnishing the Mind. Concepts and Their Perceptual Basis.* Cambridge Mass.: The MIT Press.

Zalta, Edward N. 2000. "The Road Between Pretense Theory and Abstract Object Theory", in: A. Everett and T. Hofweber (eds.), *Empty Names, Fiction, and the Puzzles of Non-Existence*. Stanford: CSLI Publications, pp.117–147.

ACCEPTANCE AS CONDITIONAL DISPOSITION

FABIO PAGLIERI
Istituto di Scienze e Tecnologie della Cognizione – CNR, Roma

Abstract
The notion of acceptance has a checkered history in philosophy. This paper discusses what version of acceptance, if any, should qualify for inclusion in epistemology. The inquiry is motivated by van Fraassen's invitation to be more liberal in determining basic epistemological categories (section 1). Reasons are given to avoid extending this liberal attitude to include van Fraassen's acceptance of scientific theories (section 2) and Bratman's pragmatic acceptance (section 3): both notions are showed to be reducible to combinations of simpler constitutive elements, and thus useful only as a shorthand. Other cases of divergence between action and belief, due to automatic sub-personal routines, are also not liable of being interpreted as acceptances (section 4). Only acceptance of conditional statements is argued to have something solid to offer for epistemological purposes: in particular, discussion on accepting conditional statements serves as a springboard to develop a new understanding of acceptance in general (section 5). It is proposed to consider acceptance as a *conditional disposition*: the consequences of this view for epistemology are discussed (section 6).

1 INTRODUCTION

Bas van Fraassen recently urged us to be more liberal in our epistemological explorations: "Epistemology has in the past been guilty of a really big sin of omission. There is in fact an enormous variety of epistemic attitudes, with many nuances and distinctions to be drawn. Prior to epistemological controversies we should have had a descriptive epistemology, to canvass this variety. What we have instead at this point is a patchwork, to which items are proposed for addition or deletion from time to time. [...] But traditionalists were and are guilty of the opposite extremism. They write as if belief, disbelief, and neutrality are the only epistemic attitudes there are" (2001, p.165). There are two ways to go, if we are to endorse van Fraassen's invitation: atomism and molecularism. An *atomist epistemology* is one in which new *primitive* epistemic attitudes are considered for inclusion, on a par with more traditional notions such as belief and knowledge. In a *molecular epistemology*, new epistemic attitudes are conceived as *molar* notions, defined as stable combinations of more primitive elements that present specific functional properties, possibly not reducible to those of their parts. As far as epistemology is concerned, these alternatives are not mutually exclusive: epistemic categories can be expanded both by defining new primitives, and by describing stable and relevant combinations of them. However, when considering a single attitude as a candidate, a decision need to be made: Is it a primitive notion or a molar one?

A prime candidate for van Fraassen's descriptive epistemology is the notion of *acceptance*, that over the past decades cropped up in many philosophical fields, each with its own variety: in philosophy of science, defining acceptance of a scientific theory is a basic concern of constructive empiricism (van Fraassen 1980; 2001); in philosophy of action, pragmatic acceptance is proposed as a cognitive attitude guiding practical reasoning and action (Bratman 1992); in philosophy of mind, acceptance is a key concept in the debate on collective mental states (Tuomela 2000; Wray 2001; Gilbert 2002); and in philosophy of language and logic, acceptance of conditional statements is the crux of the Ramsey Test and its subsequent elaborations (Ramsey 1929; Stalnaker 1968; Lewis 1976; 1986; Gärdenfors 1986; Leitgeb 2007). More in general, insofar as acceptance is broadly conceived as a *cognitive* attitude, determining its exact status is a chief concern for philosophy of mind, with ancillary benefits for other fields where the notion plays a role.

This paper addresses two questions on the status of acceptance: "Is acceptance either a primitive or a molar notion?", and "Is acceptance a truly epistemic attitude?". The answers to these questions are intertwined: it is argued that acceptance can be conceived either as a molar attitude with both epistemic and conative components (in which case it is not particularly heuristic), or, more interestingly, as a *primitive transformational attitude*. Depending on what definition one endorses, acceptance is either reducible to a finer epistemological grain or not. This clearly requires qualification, in light of the various meanings of "acceptance". Indeed, part of the challenge is to identify significant connections among some of these meanings, in spite of their apparent heterogeneity.

2 ACCEPTANCE IN CONSTRUCTIVE EMPIRICISM

In *The Scientific Image*, van Fraassen suggests that accepting a scientific theory as valid does not coincide with believing it to be literally true, but rather *empirically adequate*: "A theory is empirically adequate if what it says about the observable things and events in this world is true – exactly if it 'saves the phenomena'. A little more precisely: such a theory has at least one model that all the actual phenomena fit inside. I must emphasize that this refers to all the phenomena; these are not exhausted by those actually observed" (1980, p.12). The implication is that whatever the theory says about events or processes that are not (and never will be) observable need not be believed by those who endorse the theory. But this is not the whole story: "Acceptance of theories [...] is a phenomenon of scientific activity which clearly involves more than belief. One main reason for this is that we are never confronted with a complete theory. So if a scientist accepts a theory, he thereby involves himself in a certain sort of research programme. [...] Thus acceptance involves not only belief but a certain commitment [...] to confront any future phenomena by means of the conceptual resources of this theory. [...] A commitment is of course not true or false: The confidence exhibited is that it will be vindicated" (ibid., pp.12–13). This commitment is what van Fraassen calls the pragmatic dimension of acceptance.

Let it be noted in passing that doing justice to van Fraassen's constructive empiricism is not the purpose here: it is enough to assess whether his notion of acceptance is primitive or molar, and whether it is purely epistemic or not. In this respect, the verdict is easy to reach: theory acceptance combines a general belief in empirical adequacy (which entails several specific beliefs on concrete instantiations of that adequacy), plus a pragmatic commitment to perform certain actions, given the appropriate conditions (e.g., confronting new data with the theory's predictions, striving to further detail the theory itself, being open to controversy on it, etc.). This defines acceptance as a molar notion, which combines both epistemic and conative ingredients.

A more subtle issue is whether this concept deserves hospitality in descriptive epistemology, and why. It certainly serves as a useful shorthand, because the notion (assuming van Fraassen is right) elegantly captures our attitude towards a large class of phenomena, i.e. scientific theories, and being reducible to simpler ingredients does not diminish this practical value. But is this enough to justify relaxing the traditional austerity of our epistemological categories? After all, another way of putting van Fraassen's proposal is to say that (i) belief in the empirical adequacy of a theory generates a certain commitment to vindicate it, but (ii) such a belief does not imply belief in the truth of the theory or in the reality of the entities it postulates, whereas the converse is true. This characterization, plus the psychological hypothesis that belief in empirical adequacy is what matters in assessing scientific theories, approximates well the basic tenets of constructive empiricism, with no need to mention acceptance. We can still use it for the sake of brevity, of course, but this seems pretty much the whole extent of its heuristic value.

Moreover, there are good reasons to consider van Fraassen's notion of acceptance as specifically tailored to scientific theories, and to reserve its use for that purpose – which further limits its general significance. Imagine in contrast to extend the scope of application of van Fraassen's acceptance beyond scientific theories to factual statements. The suggestion would be to conceive factual statements like "Barack Obama is a smart man", or "The brain is the seat of the soul", as *theories-in-a-nutshell*, so that accepting them (as opposed to believing them) would consist of believing in their empirical adequacy and having a commitment to vindicate them: e.g, the subject would believe that Obama will not be outsmarted by political adversaries, or that dualists are mistaken on the nature of consciousness, and will be ready to confront any future phenomena by means of the conceptual resources derived from the accepted statements.

The problem with extending the notion this way, and the reason why van Fraassen would probably not subscribe to it, is that in general it is very hard to justify the claim that accepting a factual statement does not also implies believing it to be true, rather than just empirically adequate. Is it possible to accept that "Barack Obama is a smart man" without believing it to be true? With the exceptions of few limiting cases (discussed in the next section), the answer seems to be negative. This is because factual statements usually do not involve appeal to unobservable postulates and are not inherently incomplete, contrary to what happens with scientific theories. Since factual statements can typically uphold the stronger standards of belief, there is no reason to invoke the weaker attitude of acceptance.

To sum up: acceptance in constructive empiricism is a molar notion of spurious composition, including both epistemic and conative elements, i.e. beliefs plus commitments. While quite handy for easiness of reference, it does not add anything specific to the alchemy of its primitive components, and its significance is best confined to discussion of scientific theo-

ries: thus its limited appeal for inclusion in a general descriptive epistemology.

3 DECONSTRUCTING BRATMAN:
WHY PRAGMATIC ACCEPTANCE IS NOT AN EPISTEMIC PRIMITIVE

Stalnaker (1984) introduced the notion of acceptance as a technical term, in
the context of his analysis of inquiry, to identify a broad class of propositional attitudes of which belief is just a member.

> Acceptance, as I shall use this term, is *a broader concept than belief*; it is a ge-
> neric propositional attitude concept with such notions as presupposing, presum-
> ing, postulating, positing, assuming and supposing falling under it. [...] To ac-
> cept a proposition is *to treat it as a true proposition* in one way or another – to
> ignore, for the moment at least, the possibility that it is false. [...] To accept a
> proposition is *to act, in certain respects, as if* one believed it (Stalnaker 1984,
> pp.79–80, my emphasis).

Two points deserve special consideration: first, this notion is linked, by
definition, with the practical usage of a representation (the accepted proposition is *treated* as true; the individual *acts* in certain respects as if it were
indeed held to be true), and thus it is usually labelled "pragmatic acceptance"; second, the notion is deemed to be broader than belief, so that the
class of acceptances encompasses the class of beliefs as one of its subsets.
While the former claim is largely uncontroversial, the latter is a matter of
debate. According to Stalnaker, to believe something would imply accepting it as well, because the first notion is just a specification of the second.
This view, however, is at odds with cases where the agent's beliefs are not
acted upon, i.e. are not pragmatically accepted. In certain situations it may
be prudent to behave in accordance with a conception of the world that de-
viates from the agent's beliefs in two ways: accepting something without
believing it, and refusing to accept something that is believed. Consider the
following example, due to Bratman:

> I plan for a major construction project to begin next month. I need to decide
> now whether to do the entire project at once or instead to break the project into
> two parts, to be executed separately. The rationale for the second strategy is that
> I am unsure whether I presently have the financial resources to do the whole
> thing at once. I know that in the case of each sub-contractor – carpenter,
> plumber, and so on – it is only possible at present to get an estimate of the range

of potential costs. In the face of this uncertainty I proceed in a cautious way: In the case of each sub-contractor I take it for granted that the total costs will be at the top of the estimated range. On the basis of these assumptions I determine whether I have at present enough money to do the whole project at once. In contrast, if you offered me a bet on the actual total cost of the project – the winner being the person whose guess is closer to the actual total – I would reason differently (Bratman 1992, p.6).

Similarly, in certain neighbourhoods of large metropolitan areas it may be prudent to act *as if* any passer-by is a potential bag snatcher, even if one does not really believe that this is likely – i.e., you would not be ready to denounce any of them to the police without further evidence. In such situations, subjects seem to accept something which they do not believe, and also (against Stalnaker's claim) to believe something that they do not accept, i.e. that they are unwilling to use as a basis for action. In the construction example, the subject forms an estimate of the most likely total cost of the construction work, but he does not act on the basis of this estimate. In order to account for cases of "believing without accepting" and "accepting without believing", some authors (Cohen 1989; Bratman 1992; Tuomela 2000) argue that, contrary to the view of Stalnaker and others (Engel 1998; Wray 2001), beliefs and acceptances are closely related but *mutually independent* concepts, neither of which entails the other. The rest of this section is devoted to discuss such view, while Stalnaker's position will be considered in section 5, on the acceptance of conditionals.

An independentist view of pragmatic acceptance invites to consider this notion as an *epistemic primitive*, on a par with belief but distinct from it. Bratman (1992) championed this proposal, indicating in the *sensitivity to context* the main difference between belief and acceptance, and the reason for including the latter in his analysis of practical reasoning. Whereas what we rationally accept can change across contexts, belief is supposed to be context-independent: it is not typically considered reasonable to have belief p relative to context X but not with respect to context Y (Bratman 1992, p.3). To further show that acceptance is not reducible to belief, Bratman discusses a garden variety of cases where actions and beliefs part ways, and argue that similar cases require us to make use of the notion of acceptance to analyze the agent's practical reasoning. All the examples are gathered under five categories: (1) simplification of one's reasoning; (2) asymmetries in the costs of errors; (3) needs of social cooperation; (4) special relations to others; (5) pre-conditions for any practical reasoning at all. For reasons of space, here only examples in categories (2), (4), and (5) will be discussed, with the aim of showing that all these situations can easily be explained without making use of the notion of acceptance, thus they fail to justify treating acceptance as a genuine epistemic primitive, contra Bratman. Similar considerations apply also to cases under (3), whereas instances of (1) do not provide any conclusive reason for the distinction between belief and acceptance to start with, as Bratman admits (1992, p.6).

The construction example mentioned above is a typical case of acceptance motivated by asymmetries in the costs of error. But is it possible to explain similar cases (i) without invoking any independent notion of acceptance, and yet (ii) saving the intuition that here the subject is acting sensibly, regardless any apparent divergence between beliefs and actions? Indeed, the construction example is clearly amenable of an alternative reconstruction: we could argue that here the subject is simply acting on a *complex set of beliefs*, in view of *several intertwined goals*. More precisely, he believes it to be unlikely that the costs will be at the top of the range, and yet he also believes it to be *possible* (although remotely) for them to skyrocket to that height – in fact, if he did not believe possible for such a thing to occur, he would have no reason to act as he does, and our intuition on his rationality would waver.[1] Moreover, he believes that, if the costs should levitate too much, then he would be in deep financial troubles, and he wants to avoid that, even if he intends to realize the construction project within a reasonable amount of time. Given these motives and these beliefs, he acts as he does, and we consider him to be rationally justified in doing so. This seems a reasonable explanation of this case, one in which acceptances do not feature at all.

The same reasoning applies to any kind of behaviour dictated by prudential reasons. In the bag-snatcher example mentioned before, my overly suspicious behaviour towards passer-bys does not need to indicate that I am accepting that each of them is a potential bag-snatcher, although I do not really believe it. Instead, I am simply acting on the belief that it is at least possible to be robbed in certain metropolitan areas, and since I have a strong desire to avoid that happening to me, I stick to a 'better-safe-than-

---

[1] Alternatively, the case could be construed as involving a general belief to the effect that "Shit happens!", so that being prudent whenever something very important is at stake is rational as a general policy, rather than as a specific strategy for this particular problem. Even so, there is no need to invoke any notion of acceptance: the situation can be explained in terms of the interplay between specific and general beliefs, modulated by the agent's concerns, i.e. how much he cares about, respectively, quickly finishing the construction project and avoiding the risk of bankruptcy.

sorry' policy. Given that prudential strategies are usually coupled with some uncertainty on future outcomes, they can be easily explained by bringing into the picture *beliefs on possibilities* and the desire of avoiding the most bleak of those possibilities, rather than acceptances.

Similar considerations apply also to different cases. Take two other examples from Bratman, concerning, respectively, *special personal relation* with someone, and *precondition to any further practical reasoning*:

> My close friend has been accused of a terrible crime, the evidence of his guilt is strong, but my friend insists on his innocence. Despite the evidence of guilt, my close friendship may argue for assuming, in my ordinary practical reasoning and action, that he is innocent of the charge. In making plans for a dinner party, for example, such considerations of loyalty might make it reasonable for me to take his innocence for granted and so not use this issue to preclude inviting him. Yet if I find myself on the jury I may well think that I should not take his innocence for granted in that context for reasons of friendship.
>
> A soldier in a war zone has his doubts that he will make it through the day and expresses these doubts in a letter he writes in the morning. Nevertheless, after writing his letter he proceeds to make plans for his daily tour of the battlefield; and in so doing it takes it for granted that he will be around to execute these plans. After all, how else could he plan for the day? Since he needs to make such an assumption in order to get his planning off the ground, such acceptance may be reasonable even in the face of his doubts (Bratman 1992, p.8).

Both examples can be convincingly explained without mentioning acceptance. In the first case, different standards clearly depends on different motives: while planning the dinner party, my main concern is towards my friend, and I want to be fair and loyal to him, not being completely sure of his guilt; whereas, once I am called upon to pass judgement on his conduct in a court of law, I feel compelled to assess the matter as objectively as I can, since my goal is to reach a true conclusion on the charge against him. My beliefs concerning the possibility of his guilt can be the same in both contexts; it is enough that I am driven by different motives, to account for the apparent incongruence in my behaviour. As for the second case, here the soldier's decision to carry on with his routine for the day, despite bleak prospects for survival, appears rational to us precisely because of the system of beliefs and goals that supports this choice. He seems convinced that giving in to despair would prevent him from performing his duty, and he may well be determined to avoid this disgrace. In fact, if he had a different set of mind, he should act differently: if he was insensitive to the call of duty and inclined to depressive brooding, it would be reasonable for him not to make anything and simply lay low in some trench, waiting for the worst to happen. The proper way of understanding his behaviour is not to contrive a stipulative notion of acceptance, but to look more carefully at the complex set of beliefs and goals that makes his conduct reasonable.

In the end, many alleged examples of the independence of acceptance from belief have an alternative explanation, one that is *equally heuristics, more general*, and *more economical* – insofar as it avoids introducing an additional epistemic item. Following van Fraassen's advice, we may wish to be more liberal in epistemology, but certainly we do not want to be careless, introducing a new primitive when there is no apparent need for it. This said, it remains possible to keep the label "pragmatic acceptance" as a shorthand for indicating a structure of beliefs and goals such that the agent seems to act in violation of some other beliefs. But this label would be of dubious value. For start, we lack a precise definition of what structures of beliefs and goals would qualify: it is one thing to show that Bratman's examples are liable of intuitive explanations in terms of beliefs and goals, it is another matter to extrapolate a common pattern out of those explanations. Moreover, in some cases talk of acceptance is not only unnecessary, but even counter-intuitive: in the construction example, is it really helpful to say that the subject accepts that the costs will skyrocket, but does not believe so? It seems much more perspicuous to say that the subject does not want to take any risk that the costs will skyrocket, even if he believes unlikely that this will happen.

To sum up: pragmatic acceptance, as discussed by Bratman, does not qualify either as an epistemic primitive (because more economical explanations are viable) or as a molar notion (because it lacks a precise definition of its structure in terms of primitive components). Hence the suggestion that we should not include in epistemology a notion of acceptance conceived along these lines.

4 AUTOMATICITY: WHY ROUTINES ARE NOT ACCEPTANCES

Before moving to consider acceptance of conditional statements, another case of potential divergence between belief and action needs to be briefly discussed: *behavioral routines*. Imagine you are driving towards a new restaurant: at some point along the road, you realize that for some time you have been actually driving towards your home, 'as if' that was your destination. However, you did not believe anything of the sort – indeed, you always knew your destination was the restaurant. Similar occurrences, which are quite familiar to all of us, are not amenable of reconstruction in terms of beliefs and goals, as it was the case with Bratman's examples. However, should they count as acceptances? Would it make sense to say that, while driving, you are accepting your home to be the destination, even if you believe to be headed towards the restaurant?

The answer is "No", because there is a better explanation available: here *cue-sensitive sub-personal processes* take control of the behavior, with little or no role of conscious awareness at the personal level. In the driving example, the behavioral routine happens to jeopardize the agent's conscious plans, and this is why we consider the driver's behavior defective, i.e. somehow sub-par, in contrast with the cases discussed by Bratman. But the question is whether the notion of "normative rationality" should have legislation over such cases: the driver's action is not determined by some defective practical reasoning (e.g. a mistaken inference), but it is rather the result of a sub-personal process gone awry: a partial overlapping between the road to the restaurant and the road to home, or the time of day when the driving was taking place, triggers an automatic response that is inadequate to the present context. If this happens frequently enough, the adaptive value of the agent's automatic responses may be questioned: but this has little to do with the issue of normative rationality, that simply does not apply in the absence of explicit reasoning.

This is why framing similar cases in terms of acceptance vs. belief sounds so odd: these categories apply to practical reasoning, and serve to make sense of the subject's actions in terms of *reasons*. When reasons do not play any role to start with, as it happens with behavioral routines, talk of acceptance and belief is beside the point. It is worth noting that psychological research on automaticity (Bargh, Chartrand 1999; Gollwitzer 1999; Wegner 2002; Gollwitzer, Bargh 2005) suggests that behavior is frequently controlled at such implicit, sub-personal level. On this ground, it would be easy jumping to the conclusion that a reason-based explanation is rarely (if ever) appropriate for the analysis of human behavior. This conclusion is, however, largely unwarranted by current evidence on automaticity. What is warranted, instead, is careful consideration of the appropriate explanatory level and action granularity for reason-based explanations: in the driving example, the action of driving towards home is not reason-based and should not be assessed as such; but the realization that this is a mistake, and your consequent U-turn, are based on reasons, thus perfectly liable of analysis in terms of mental attitudes (see also Koriat 2007; Pacherie 2008).

To sum up: acceptance is not a useful concept to explain cases where behavioral routines lead the agent to act in spite of some beliefs. Reference to automatic or semi-automatic processes of action control is much more adequate to explain both the observed behavior, and its divergence from some of the subject's beliefs. So there is nothing in behavioral routines that support inclusion of acceptance in descriptive epistemology.

5 ACCEPTING CONDITIONALS AND CONDITIONAL DISPOSITIONS

The traditional way of connecting acceptance of conditional statements to belief systems is in terms of the Ramsey test. According to Ramsey, "if two people are arguing 'If p will q?' and are both in doubt as to p, they are adding p hypothetically to their stock of knowledge and arguing on that basis about q [...]. We can say they are fixing their degree of belief in q given p" (1929, p.155). Stalnaker offers the following, more precise formulation: "This is how to evaluate a conditional: First, add the antecedent (hypothetically) to your stock of beliefs; second, make whatever adjustments are required to maintain consistency (without modifying the hypothetical belief in the antecedent); finally, consider whether or not the consequent is then true" (1968, p.102).

Broadly speaking, two formalizations of the Ramsey test are possible, depending on whether belief states are modeled as closed sets of propositions, e.g. in AGM belief revision (Alchourrón et al. 1985; Gärdenfors 1988; Rott 2001), or as subjective degrees of probabilities, e.g. in Bayesianism (Howson, Urbach 1993). These approaches propose, respectively, a qualitative and a quantitative version of the Ramsey test, as follows (Leitgeb, in preparation):

Qualitative Ramsey test:
For every belief set K, for all sentences A, B:
    "If A then B" is acceptable (in K) if and only if $B \in K*A$
where belief sets are deductive closed sets of sentences and the belief revision operator * obeys the AGM axioms (Gärdenfors 1988).

Quantitative Ramsey test:
For every subjective probability measure P, for all sentences A, B (with $P(A) > 0$):
　　The acceptability of "If A then B" (in P) equals $P(B|A)$
where P obeys the standard axioms of the probability calculus, and conditionals probabilities are defined by the ratio formula.

In short, the Ramsey test rules that a conditional "If A then B" is rationally acceptable (with degree x) in a belief state if and only if, were the belief state revised with A as a new piece of evidence, then it would be rational to believe B (with degree x). The relevant question for present discussion is how this acceptability should be interpreted: in particular, does acceptance of a conditional statement consists in believing the corresponding conditional? In pseudo-formal terms:

(1)　$Acc(A \rightarrow B) = Bel(A \rightarrow B)$

If this was the case, then two other facts would follow, by applying (1) to both versions of the Ramsey test:

(2)　$(A \rightarrow B) \in K$ iff $B \in K^*A$
(3)　$P(A \rightarrow B) = P(B|A)$

It has been argued (Leitgeb 2007) that interpreting acceptance of a conditional as a belief in that conditional is not a viable option, due to impossibility results in AGM belief revision (Gärdenfors 1986; 1988) and in probability theory (Lewis 1976; 1986). These results prove that (2) and (3) are incompatible with, respectively, basic rationality assumptions in AGM belief revision and the standard axioms of probability theory, under minimal non-triviality assumptions.[2] Hence accepting a conditional cannot be reduced to believing the corresponding conditional statement: in other words, (1) is false. This leaves open the possibility that acceptance of conditionals

---

[2] These results are very robust in probability theory, since they hold also for various "naturally" restricted classes of probability measures (Lewis 1976; 1986; Hájek, Hall 1994; Milne 1997; Bradley 2000). It remains to be seen whether triviality results in AGM belief revision are equally robust: it would be interesting to check whether Gärdenfors impossibility theorem holds also for belief revision operators which obey to only some of the standard AGM postulates, e.g. in non-prioritized belief revision (Hansson 1999).

may constitute a genuinely independent epistemic attitude, worthy of inclusion in our epistemology.

Leitgeb (2007) proposes a different solution: acceptance of conditionals is taken to indicate *conditional beliefs*, as opposed to beliefs in conditionals, where the former are defined as *higher-order single-track dispositions*. The fact that subject X accepts the conditional "If A then B" says something about the cognitive dispositions of X: roughly speaking, it is equivalent to saying that, were X to believe A (with a certain degree), then he would also believe B (with a certain degree). This analysis is restricted to indicative conditionals, whereas subjunctive conditionals (to which the Ramsey test does not apply) are taken to represent regularities in the world and thus be endowed with truth values (Leitgeb in preparation). Conditional beliefs are considered higher-order dispositions because they express the disposition of the subject to acquire mental states that are in turn amenable of dispositional analysis, e.g. a belief that B. Moreover, whereas simple beliefs are multi-track dispositions, i.e. they constraint the subject's behavior in various ways, conditional beliefs entail "a so-called single-track disposition, i.e., a disposition to show one particular type of manifestation in one particular type of circumstance" (Leitgeb 2007, p.124; on the single-track/multi-track distinction, see Ryle 1949). Finally, conditional beliefs, as opposed to simple beliefs, have more than one propositional content and lack truth conditions (ibid., pp.122–123), and their communicative purpose is to express, as opposed to represent, the mental dispositions of the subject (Leitgeb in preparation; on the need for distinguishing metacognition from metarepresentation, see also Proust 2007).

Leitgeb is aware that some might resist his proposal of considering conditional beliefs as a species of the genus "belief": the obvious alternative would be to abandon any talk of belief in relation to the acceptance of conditionals, and claim that what we are dealing with in these cases is a different kind of attitude altogether (for suggestions in that vein, see Levi 1988; 1996; Mellor 1993). Leitgeb regards this issue as largely terminological, and thus not worthy of too much attention (2007, p.120), albeit he endeavors to show that conditional beliefs present some typical features of belief (namely, intentionality, influence over action, representational structure, and justification), while lacking others, i.e. uniqueness of content and truth-aptness (ibid., pp.122–131). I agree with Leitgeb that the issue is largely terminological, in the sense that it does not matter much whether we label our attitudes on indicative conditionals as either "acceptances" or "conditional beliefs", provided we have good reasons to distinguish them from beliefs simpliciter. Nonetheless, in what follows I will refer to Leitgeb's conditional beliefs as acceptances, since I agree with Mellor and Levi that truth-aptness is paramount in determining our intuitions on belief, so that labeling "beliefs" some attitudes that admittedly lack that feature is, to my mind, rather counterintuitive. Moreover, acceptance is a vague notion in search of a precise definition, possibly one that does not reduce it to a mere shorthand. In the attitude expressed by assenting to indicative conditionals we have, at last, a suitable candidate.

The suggestion is thus to consider acceptances as *conditional dispositions*: accepting a certain state of affairs X means being disposed to believe X and/or act on X, but only when certain conditions occur. In cases like those considered by Leitgeb, both condition and disposition concern beliefs: accepting "If A then B" means being disposed to believe B, on condition that one believes A. But it is now possible to extend this definition to cover also cases of pragmatic acceptance a la Bratman: here the disposition is to *use* a certain propositional content in guiding one's action, on condition that certain circumstances obtain. What these circumstances are depends on the situation: in the construction example, the risk of facing bankruptcy is the key factor in making the subject disposed to act on the worst possible scenario; in the suspected friend example, loyalty and friendship are the condition that justify an inclination to grant the benefit of doubt in certain contexts (but not in others); in the war zone example, the soldier's belief that giving in to despair is useless and even despicable is the precondition for his disposition to bracket the worst possible scenario in his daily deliberation, regardless the fact that he sees that scenario as highly probable. In other words, what Bratman conceived as atomic instances of pragmatic acceptances are revealed to be the *consequents* of a series of conditional acceptances, where the antecedent is either left implicit or described as "context".

In fact, analyzing acceptances as conditional dispositions gives us a precise understanding of their characteristic *context-sensitivity*: the reason why we accept something (i.e. the consequent of a conditional acceptance) in certain contexts and not in others is because only those contexts satisfy the preconditions upon which our acceptance is based (i.e. the antecedent of a conditional acceptance). The mental attitude of acceptance per se is not context-dependent, but its application is: the subject, if rational, accepts "If a dear friend is in legal trouble and you are planning a social event, then do not ostracize him/her" in all contexts, but this (conditional) acceptance modifies the subject's behavior only when some dear friend is indeed in legal trouble and only as far as social events are concerned – it does not apply in a court of law, and yet this is no reason to claim that the subject no longer has the same conditional acceptance of what is appropriate to do when your friends are accused of a crime.[3]

So this view has the merit of reconciling the context-sensitivity of acceptances with a decent level of *cognitive stability*: rational agents do not change their mindset from one context to another, but part of their mindset is intrinsically conditional, thus it invites certain responses only in certain contexts. The implication is that all pragmatic acceptances worth considering can be understood as conditional dispositions where the antecedent is left either implicit or vague: this strategy works fine with Bratman's examples, as discussed. The difference with Leitgeb's view is that, in accepting conditional statements, the disposition expressed by the consequent concerns belief, whereas with pragmatic acceptance the disposition is directly tied with action. But of course a disposition towards action entails also a disposition to believe that such action will occur, assuming the antecedent of the conditional disposition is believed – and assuming the agent is minimally rational.[4] In the accused friend example, believing that my friend is accused and that I am planning a social event has two consequences: I will not ostracize him/her, and I believe I will not ostracize him/her. The second consequence is precisely what is required by Leitgeb's analysis of conditional beliefs: hence extending a similar analysis to pragmatic acceptances is not in contrast with Leitgeb's proposal,[5] but it provides yet an-

---

[3] Notice that acceptance here refers to *mental attitudes*, not linguistic behavior. Take a subject who is, as a matter of fact, disposed to act on B when A is believed: it is immaterial whether or not the subject is ready to linguistically assent to the corresponding conditional "If A, then act accordingly to B". Indeed, the subject could well be unaware of having such a conditional disposition, thus being incapable of assenting to the corresponding conditional: nonetheless, as long as the disposition is present, it correctly describes the mental attitude of the agent, and thus we are justified in saying that the subjects accepts "B, if A".

[4] Ceteris paribus conditions may also be needed to ensure that the implication is carried through. For the sake of brevity, I do not discuss the issue here: see Leitgeb (2007, pp.121–125) for some considerations on ceteris paribus conditions in the context of accepting indicative conditionals.

[5] This means that Leitgeb's argument against interpreting acceptance of a conditional as a belief in that conditional applies also to pragmatic acceptances, once conceived as conditional dispositions. Given a pragmatic acceptance of the generic form "If A, then act according to B", this is an indicative conditional, to which Gärdenfors' and Lewis' impossibility results still apply: it cannot be the case that having such a conditional

other reason to use the label "acceptance" rather than "belief" in this context.

Stalnaker's intuitive definition of acceptance resonates with the current proposal: "To accept a proposition is to treat it as a true proposition in one way or another – to ignore, for the moment at least, the possibility that it is false. [...] To accept a proposition is to act, in certain respects, as if one believed it" (Stalnaker 1984, pp.79–80). Some vague expressions in this characterization ("in one way or another", "in certain respects") hint to the conditional nature of acceptance: only when certain conditions apply the corresponding disposition (to act and/or to believe) is elicited. But to insist that only the latter constitutes an acceptance, without appreciating its conditional nature, would undermine the heuristic value of this notion, and leave it open to the criticisms discussed in section 3. Moreover, conceiving acceptances as conditional dispositions gives them a clear place in a dispositional epistemology, where beliefs are rather conceived as dispositions simpliciter, i.e. unconditional dispositions.[6] Believing p means being ready to act according to p *no matter what*. In contrast, accepting p (i) is just a shorthand for "accepting (p if q)" and (ii) means being ready to act according to p only when q is believed – where q stands for any proposition of arbitrary complexity that serves to capture the circumstances upon which being disposed to p is conditional.[7]

---

disposition is tantamount to believing the corresponding conditional, unless we want to forsake minimal rationality.

[6] It would be tempting here to postulate a straightforward connection with Ryle's distinction between multi-track and single-track dispositions: the claim would be that what makes a disposition multi-track, i.e. manifest across different contexts and in a variety of ways, is its being unconditional, whereas conditional dispositions are necessarily single-track, i.e. tied to specific conditions for their manifestation. This, however, would misrepresent Ryle's distinction, which is about the ways in which a disposition manifests itself (see for instance 1949, pp.43–44), and not so much about the conditions that trigger its manifestation. In short, single-track/multi-track is about *how* a disposition is manifested, whereas unconditional/conditional is about *when* it manifests. If there is a relationship between these couples of notions, it is not in terms of identity or implication.

[7] A formal consequence is that believing p entails having an infinite number of acceptances of the form "If X, then act on p", where X is an arbitrary statement. Since believing p means being disposed to act on p no matter what, it is true that I am disposed to act on p given whatever circumstances X might obtain, hence I can be said to be in a conditional state of acceptance of the form "If X, then act on p". In short: an unconditional disposition to p is equivalent to having an infinite number of conditional disposition to p with whatever you like as antecedent. Should we be alarmed by such profli-

The strong claim that characterizes this view is that there is no such thing as "unconditional acceptance" of a given proposition: *all acceptances are conditional* by definition, whether the relevant conditions are spelled out or left implicit. This is not mere stipulation, but rather an appeal to intuition: give me a single example of acceptance that is neither conditional to specific circumstances nor reducible to belief, and the definition of acceptance as conditional disposition will be falsified. But no such counterexample is in view: none of Bratman's cases qualifies, and I honestly cannot think of any other that would. If a proposition is endorsed with no strings attached, then it is believed, and there is no reason to invoke the weaker notion of acceptance for it – as discussed in section 2, to reject the view of factual statements as "theories-in-a-nutshell". If, on the other hand, my endorsement is conditional upon certain circumstances, then the proposition cannot be said to be believed, because belief has no such qualms: as Bratman would say, it is not context-dependent in that way.[8] In this case, and only in this case, it is useful to apply the notion of acceptance. Finally, when the proposition is never endorsed, regardless the circumstances, then it is simply disbelieved, that is, neither believed nor accepted.

Given this view of acceptance, let us see how it fares as a candidate for inclusion in epistemology. The first question is whether this kind of acceptance is a primitive or a molar notion. At first sight, it may seem a molar concept, since belief figures as part of its definition: accepting "p, if q" means being disposed to p (and to believe you p) if you believe q. But the role of belief in this definition is not that of a constitutive element: acceptance, thus conceived, is not reducible to belief, or to belief plus action. Belief is not a necessary condition for acceptance: it remains true that I accept "p, if q" (i.e. I am disposed to p on condition that q) even if q never

---

gacy of acceptances? Not at all, because acceptances describe what a given cognitive system is geared to do under certain circumstances, but they do not represent mental content. If we decide to be needlessly byzantine in how we describe the workings of the system, this is a problem for our description, not for the system itself. The fact that X believes p, i.e. X actions are guided by p in all contexts, has the same degree of complexity whether you choose to describe it as X having a single unconditional disposition to p or as X having an infinite number of conditional dispositions to p. Since profligacy of acceptances is a threat only for theoretical reconstruction, it can be handled at that level, e.g. forbidding translation of unconditional dispositions as infinite sets of conditional dispositions.

[8] An obvious corollary of this view is that Leitgeb's "conditional beliefs" are actually a specific class of (non-pragmatic) acceptances. The reasons for this terminological disagreement have already been discussed.

comes to be believed and so my disposition is never realized. Instead, believing q and thus doing p is a sufficient condition for acceptance, in the sense that it provides an instantiation of it: but acceptance *qua* conditional disposition does not require such instantiation for being correctly attributed to the subject. So I propose to conceive acceptance as a primitive notion, albeit quite different in nature from belief: whereas acceptances are conditional dispositions that express the cognitive potentialities of the subject, beliefs are unconditional dispositions that mirror the subject's understanding of reality.[9] The former tell us something of how the subject's mind works, the latter refer to how the world is supposed to be, according to the subject.

But what kind of primitive notion is acceptance – epistemic, conative, or a mix of both? Part of the answer depends on the kind of acceptance being considered. Pragmatic acceptances, like those dear to Bratman, have a clear conative element, insofar as their consequent specifies an action policy: being cautious in allocating money for your construction project, being supportive of your friends, etc. Acceptance of indicative conditionals in general, however, determines what the subject would believe, if the antecedent of the conditional was also believed: as such, it seems to qualify as an epistemic attitude and not a conative one, since believing is traditionally conceived as an event rather than an action. However, the whole distinction epistemic/conative may be largely misleading here, since it refers most naturally to mental states, whereas acceptances refer instead to *mental transitions* – or, more precisely, predispositions to realize a given transition in the appropriate circumstances. Can a transition be described as either "epistemic" or "conative", and what purpose would this serve? At best, we can say that the conditions triggering such transitions are epistemic (beliefs), while the end result can be either conative (an action) or epistemic (a belief), or both. None of this, however, seems sufficient to characterize the transition itself and the corresponding conditional disposition as either epistemic or conative.

In conclusion, it seems better to abandon the distinction between epistemic and conative attitude, and characterize acceptance rather as a primitive *transformational* attitude, i.e. a notion that describes how a cognitive system is expected to react, in the presence of specific inputs. If so, should we grant it admittance in our descriptive epistemology, on the grounds of van Fraassen's initial invitation? This time the answer is positive, but with

---

[9] This distinction is different from, but largely compatible with, Audi's notion of *dispositions to believe* (1994).

a proviso: as soon as acceptance *qua* conditional disposition is given credit in our epistemology, on a par with belief, this forces us to expand the boundaries of that epistemology beyond merely epistemic attitudes, at least as they are traditionally conceived. Acceptance is not just a slightly different way of endorsing a given proposition: it is rather a different matter altogether, a principle of organization (and functioning) of the cognitive system to which it refers. Among other things, it invites us to embrace a dispositional epistemology, for both beliefs (as unconditional dispositions) and acceptances (as conditional dispositions). This has important consequences for the scope and purposes of epistemology, which will need to be carefully considered in future works on this topic.

6 CONCLUSIONS

After critical scrutiny, two well-known versions of acceptance, van Fraassen's acceptance of scientific theories and Bratman's pragmatic acceptance, had to be denied the status of primitive epistemic notions. What they can be, for partially different reasons, is a shorthand for naming complex structures of beliefs and goals. The usefulness of such shorthand, however, is questionable. Along the way of this critique, we noted also that cases where actions and beliefs differ due to automatic sub-personal routines do not count as instances of acceptance either. On a more positive note, acceptance of conditional statements gave us more epistemological leverage, helping to reconsider also pragmatic acceptance in a new light. This led us to define acceptances as conditional dispositions, and to study their properties and their place in a dispositional epistemology.

This may have far-reaching consequences for epistemology in general: in particular, a conditional view of acceptances naturally invites adopting a dispositional epistemology also for beliefs. The morale is that the step from open-minded descriptive epistemology to radical re-description of traditional epistemology may be short. Is this move justified by the arguments produced so far? Should the pebble of acceptance start an epistemological avalanche? Answering this question requires considerations that go beyond the aim of this essay. But a conditional conclusion is offered for that debate. If we want to have a meaningful notion of acceptance, then embracing a dispositional view of epistemology seems to be the only way to go. If, on the other hand, we are not yet ready to bring our dispositions out of the closet, then we are left with an impoverished notion of acceptance, one that at best qualifies as a shorthand of dubious value. According to the line of reasoning presented in this paper, these are the options. Whatever we pick, we must know (and accept) the consequences.

ACKNOWLEDGMENTS

This work was supported by the CNR and the EC 6th Framework Programme as part of the ESF EUROCORES Programme CNCC. I am grateful to Hannes Leitgeb, Mehmet Cakmak, and Cristiano Castelfranchi for extensive discussion of the ideas presented here, and to participants of the CNCC workshop on "Representations: Perspectives from philosophy, psychology and neuroscience" at the 31st International Wittgenstein Symposium (Kirchberg am Wechsel, 11 August 2008).

REFERENCES

Alchourrón, C., Gärdenfors, P., Makinson, D. (1985). "On the Logic of Theory Change: Partial Meet Contraction and Revision Functions". *Journal of Symbolic Logic* 50, pp.510–530.
Audi, R. (1994). "Dispositional Beliefs and Dispositions to Believe". *Noûs* 28 (4), pp.419–434.
Bargh, J., Chartrand, T. (1999). "The Unbearable Automaticity of Being". *American Psychologist* 54, pp.462–479.
Bradley, R. (2000). "A Preservation Condition for Conditionals". *Analysis* 60 (3), pp.219–222.
Bratman, M. (1992). "Practical Reasoning and Acceptance in a Context". *Mind* 101, pp.1–15.
Cohen, L. (1989). "Belief and Acceptance". *Mind* 98, pp.367–389.
Engel, P. (1998). "Believing, Holding True, and Accepting". *Philosophical Explorations* 1, pp.140–151.
Gärdenfors, P. (1986). "Belief Revisions and the Ramsey Test for Conditionals". *Philosophical Review* 95, pp.81–93.
Gärdenfors, P. (1988). *Knowledge in Flux: Modelling the Dynamics of Epistemic States*. Cambridge: MIT Press.
Gilbert, M. (2002). "Belief and Acceptance as Features of Groups". *Protosociology* 16, pp.35–69.
Gollwitzer, P. (1999). "Implementation Intentions: Strong Effects of Simple Plans". *American Psychologist* 54, pp.493–503.
Gollwitzer, P., Bargh, J. (2005). "Automaticity in Goal Pursuit". In: A. Elliot, C. Dweck (eds.), *Handbook of competence and motivation*. New York: Guilford Press, pp.624–646.

Hájek, A., Hall, N. (1994). "The Hypothesis of the Conditional Construal of Conditional Probability". In: E. Eells, B. Skyrms (eds.), *Probability and Conditionals. Belief Revision and Rational Decision.* Cambridge: Cambridge University Press, pp.75–111.

Hansson, S. (1999). "A Survey on Non-prioritized Belief Revision". *Erkenntnis* 50, pp.413–427.

Koriat, A. (2007). "Metacognition and Consciousness"s. In: P. Zelazo, M. Moscovitch, E. Thompson (eds.), *The Cambridge Handbook of Consciousness.* Cambridge: Cambridge University Press, pp.289–325.

Leitgeb, H. (2007). "Beliefs in Conditionals vs. Conditional Beliefs". *Topoi* 26, pp.115–132.

Leitgeb, H. (in preparation). "Metacognition and Indicative Conditionals". Draft manuscript.

Levi, I. (1988). "Iteration of Conditionals and the Ramsey Test". *Synthese* 76, pp.49–81.

Levi, I. (1996). *For the Sake of the Argument. Ramsey Test Conditionals, Inductive Inference, and Nonmonotonic Reasoning.* Cambridge: Cambridge University Press.

Lewis, D. (1976). "Probabilities of Conditionals and Conditional Probabilities". *Philosophical Review* 85, pp.297–315.

Lewis, D. (1986). "Probabilities of Conditionals and Conditional Probabilities II". *The Philosophical Review* 95, pp.581–589.

Mellor, D. (1993). "How to Believe a Conditional". *The Journal of Philosophy* 90 (5), pp.233–248.

Milne, P. (1997). "Quick Triviality Proofs for Probabilities of Conditionals". *Analysis* 57 (1), pp.75–80.

Pacherie, E. (2008). "The Phenomenology of Action: A Conceptual Framework". *Cognition* 107 (1), pp.179–217.

Proust, J. (2007). "Metacognition and Metarepresentation: Is a Self-directed Theory of Mind a Precondition for Metacognition?". *Synthese* 159, pp.271–295.

Ramsey, F. (1929). "General Propositions and Causality". In: D. Mellor (ed.), *F. Ramsey, Philosophical papers.* Cambridge: Cambridge University Press, 1990, pp.145–163.

Rott, H. (2001). *Change, Choice and Inference: A Study of Belief Revision and Nonmonotonic Reasoning.* Oxford: Oxford University Press.

Ryle, G. (1949). *The Concept of Mind.* London: Hutchinson.

Stalnaker, R. (1968). "A Theory of Conditionals". In: N. Rescher (ed.), *Studies in Logical Theory.* Oxford: Blackwell.

Stalnaker, R. (1984). *Inquiry.* Cambridge: MIT Press.

Tuomela, R. (2000). "Belief versus Acceptance". *Philosophical Explorations* 2, pp.122–137.

van Fraassen, B. (1980). *The Scientific Image.* New York: Oxford University Press.

van Fraassen, B. (2001). "Constructive Empiricism now". *Philosophical Studies* 106, pp.151–170.

Wegner, D. (2002). *The Illusion of Conscious Will.* Cambridge: MIT Press.

Wray, K. (2001). "Collective Belief and Acceptance". *Synthese* 129, pp.319–333.

II.
... AND ...

"SUPERVENIENT AND YET NOT DEDUCIBLE": IS THERE A COHERENT CONCEPT OF ONTOLOGICAL EMERGENCE?[*]

JAEGWON KIM
Brown University

Abstract
Formulating a concept of emergence that is intelligible and prima facie coherent is a significant issue not only because emergence concepts continue to proliferate, attracting a great deal of positive attention from scientists and philosophers, but also because the idea of emergence is closely related to some of the concepts of central importance in the current debates on the mind-body problem. Most early emergence theorists, like C.D. Broad and C. Lloyd Morgan, intended emergence to be an objective phenomenon in the world and considered emergent properties as real and causally potent characteristics of objects and events of this world. This classic conception of emergence, now called "ontological" or "metaphysical", or "strong", is standardly contrasted with an "epistemological", or "weak", conception according to which properties are emergent in case they are "surprising" or "unexpected", or unpredictable and unknowable from information concerning base-level phenomena. But what is ontological emergence? On Broad's characterization, shared by a number of other writers, ontologically emergent properties are properties that are *determined by,* or *supervenient on, their base-level conditions and yet not deducible from them.* This paper explores some issues arising from the notion of ontological emergence so conceived, and uncovers what appears to be a possibly damaging incoherence. This raises the question whether there is a workable notion of ontological emergence.

I

C. Lloyd Morgan, one of the leading British emergentists of the early 20th century, describes the "emergent evolution" of the world, or how we got where we are and where we are headed from here, in these words:

> "From [the ultimate basal phenomenon, space-time] first emerged 'matter' with its primary, and, at a later stage, its secondary qualities. Here new relations, other than those which are spatio-temporal supervene.[1] So far, thus supervenient on spatio-temporal events, we have also physical and chemical events in progressively ascending grades. Later in evolutionary sequence life emerges – a new 'quality' of certain material or physico-chemical systems with supervenient vital relations hitherto not in being. Here again there are progressively ascending grades. Then within this organic matrix, or some highly differentiated part thereof, already 'qualified' ... by life, there emerges the higher quality of consciousness or mind. Here once more, there are progressively ascending grades. ... As mental evolution runs its course, there emerge ... 'tertiary qualities' – ideals of truth, of beauty, and of the ethically right... And beyond this, at or near the apex of the evolutionary pyramid of which space-time is the base, the quality of deity – the highest of all – emerges in us ..."[2]

It is plain that Morgan is presenting "emergent evolution" as an actual history of the world, though perhaps more than a little speculative. The sequential emergence of matter from space-time, life in inorganic systems, and mind from biological processes is a historical fact about this world. For Morgan, as well as many other emergentists, emergent phenomena like life and mind are genuinely novel features of reality which make their distinctive causal contributions to the subsequent evolution of the world. There are bridges and building, works of art and electronic gadgets, nuclear bombs and ozone holes, because minds and consciousness have emerged. Emergence is an objective feature of the world, with powers to change,

---

[1] As Brian McLaughlin and Karen Bennett note in their entry "Supervenience" in the *Stanford Encyclopedia of Philosophy* (http://plato.stanford.edu/), Morgan is using "supervene" and "supervenient" in this paragraph in their vernacular sense, something like "occur later" or "follow upon", rather than in the philosophical sense now commonly associated with these terms (as in the title of this paper).

[2] C. Lloyd Morgan, *Emergent Evolution* (London: Williams and Norgate, 1923), pp.9–10. Here Morgan represents himself as reporting Samuel Alexander's views in *Space, Time, and Deity* (London: Macmillan, 1920). But there is little doubt that Morgan accepts the picture he presents.

create, and destroy. In the fullness of time, Morgan assures us, if things continue to go right, we humans will achieve divineness.[3]

In his classic *The Mind and Its Place in Nature*,[4] C.D. Broad distinguished three types of theories concerning biological ("vital") phenomena: "Biological Mechanism" (what we would now call physical reductionism), "Substantial Vitalism" (Broad had in mind Hans Driesch's neo-vitalism which posited "entelechies" to account for biological phenomena), and his own "Emergent Vitalism" (which takes biological phenomena as emergent from, but not reducible to, physicochemical phenomena). These were clearly intended as three possible views making contrasting claims about the nature of biological organisms and their distinctively biological capacities, functions, and activities. These theories stake out disparate and mutually exclusionary positions on the nature of biological entities and processes. Unquestionably, the emergent nature of biological phenomena, for Broad, is an objective fact about them; it does not concern what anyone knows or believes about them.

This conception of emergence as an objectively real fact about the world is now standardly called "metaphysical" or "ontological" emergence; some call it "strong" emergence. This is contrasted with an "epistemological", or "weak", conception which seems more common among the burgeoning ranks of emergentists on the current scene, especially those from scientific fields. Unlike metaphysical emergence, the epistemological conception focuses on certain supposed epistemic aspects of emergent properties and phenomena, emphasizing such features as their novelty, unpredictability, and our inability to calculate, or "compute", them from information concerning the basal conditions from which they emerge. The main point then is that we, as cognizers, cannot get there from here – that is, get to higher-level emergent phenomena from information about the lower-level base phenomena. On the metaphysical conception, it isn't just that emergent phenomena are unpredictable for us; that may be more of a commentary on our cognitive powers than the phenomena themselves. More importantly, the point is that they are objectively new, extra additions to the ontology of the world. Their newness, or novelty, does not consist in their ability to "surprise" us, or our inability to "predict" them;

---

[3] Most emergentists seem incorrigible optimists; they are blissfully unmindful of the glaring fact that if good things have emerged, so have many unspeakably bad and evil things!

[4] C.D. Broad, *The Mind and Its Place in Nature* (London: Routledge and Kegan Paul, 1925), p.58.

rather, their newness is meant to be metaphysical in import: before these emergents came on the scene, there had been nothing like them in the world and they represent net additions to the world's furniture. And what could be the point of these extra entities if it isn't their bringing with them *new causal powers*, powers that go beyond the powers of the lower-level conditions in their emergence base?

I don't know when the distinction between the two types of emergence was explicitly recognized, although of course there have been weak and strong emergence theories and theorists for a long time. In their entry "Emergent Properties" in the *Stanford Encyclopedia of Philosophy* (http://plato.stanford.edu/), Timothy O'Connor and Hong Yu Wong say that the emergence concept in J.S. Mill and C.D. Broad was the strong ontological variety, whereas Samuel Alexander's emergence concept, though still metaphysical, had considerably weaker ontological significance[5] (they liken Alexander's position to contemporary nonreductive physicalism). In his "Weak Emergence" (1997), Mark Bedau introduces an epistemological notion of emergence; and a distinction between ontological and epistemological emergence is explicitly drawn in Silberstein and McGeever's "In Search for Ontological Emergence" (1999). Following Silberstein and McGeever, Van Gulick recognizes a similar distinction between epistemic and metaphysical emergence in his useful 2001 survey article on reduction and emergence. In "Strong and Weak Emergence" (2006), Chalmers' main theme, unsurprisingly, is the difference between the two kinds of emergence he distinguishes.[6] This list is not intended to be exhaustive.[7]

---

[5] See also Philip Clayton, "Conceptual Foundations of Emergence Theory", in *The Re-Emergence of Emergence* (Oxford: Oxford University Press, 2006), ed. Philip Clayton and Paul Davies.

[6] Mark Bedau, "Weak Emergence", *Philosophical Perspectives* 11, pp.375–399; Michael Silberstein and John McGeever, "In Search for Ontological Emergence", *Philosophical Quarterly* 49 (1999): pp.182–200; Robert Van Gulick, "Reduction, Emergence and Other Recent Options on the Mind-Body Problem: A Philosophical Overview", *Journal of Consciousness Studies* 8 (2001) pp.1–34; David J. Chalmers, "Strong and Weak Emergence", in *The Re-Emergence of Emergence*, ed. Philip Clayton and Paul Davies.

[7] Carl Gillett distinguishes three concepts of emergence, "strong", "weak", and "ontological", in his interesting paper "The Varieties of Emergence: Their Purposes, Obligations and Importance", *Grazer Philosophische Studien* 65 (2002): pp.95–121. All of these seem to be metaphysical notions of emergence in our sense, and Gillett's distinction does not straightforwardly relate to the standard ontological/epistemological distinction.

II

We will assume that the metaphysical emergentist would want to include supervenience as a component of his emergence concept; that is, if a property emerges from a set of basal properties, it supervenes on the latter. To put it another way, if the same basal conditions recur, the emergent property will necessarily recur as well (we will return to the question what the sort of necessity is involved). C.D. Broad clearly recognized this; he writes:

> "No doubt the properties of silver-chloride are completely determined by those of silver and of chlorine; in the sense that whenever you have a whole composed of these two elements in certain proportions and relations you have something with the characteristic properties of silver-chloride ... But the law connecting the properties of silver-chloride with those of silver and chlorine and with the structure of the compound is, so far as we know, an *unique* and *ultimate* law."[8]

And again:

> "And no amount of knowledge about how the constituents of a living body behave in isolation or in other and non-living wholes might suffice to enable us to predict the characteristic behavior of a living organism. This possibility is perfectly compatible with the view that the characteristic behaviour of a living body is completely determined by the nature and arrangement of the chemical compounds which compose it, in the sense that any whole which is composed of such compounds in such an arrangement will show vital behaviour ..."[9]

Supervenience, or "upward determination", may ultimately turn out to be detrimental to the emergence program; and yet, without supervenience, it would be difficult to explain the "from" in "property P emerges *from* basal conditions C".[10] David Chalmers says that an emergent phenomenon "arises (in some sense) from"[11] lower-level phenomena, but says nothing further about just what sense of "arising from" is involved here. Superven-

---

[8] *The Mind and Its Place in Nature*, pp.64–65.

[9] *The Mind and Its Place in Nature*, pp.67–68.

[10] For more on this, see my "Emergence: Core Ideas and Issues", *Synthese* 151 (2006): pp.547–559. In his "From Supervenience to Superdupervenience" (*Mind* 102 (1993): pp.555–586), Terence Horgan has an interesting footnote (fn.7) in which he quotes Arthur Lovejoy as countenancing a form of emergence which excludes supervenience.

[11] "Strong and Weak Emergence", p.244.

ience supplies a clear and robust sense to Chalmers' "arises from". We can explore whether some weaker relation might be able to serve the purpose,[12] but it is clear that if the emergent phenomenon occurs randomly when its purported basal conditions are realized, it would be difficult to make sense of the claim that the phenomenon emerges "from" these conditions, or that the lower-level phenomena are its "basal conditions". Besides, this would likely allow cases of emergence to proliferate beyond what even the most lavish and bountiful emergentist would want. In any case, it is quite certain that major early emergentists accepted the supervenience of the emergents as a condition of emergence.[13]

What else do we need to characterize ontological emergence? Some writers (for example, Silberstein[14]) cite the capacity for "downward causation" – that is, the power to causally affect the events at the basal level – as a condition of ontological emergence. But I think this is not a wise move; downward causation is highly controversial and building it into the very concept of emergence will make it more difficult to defend the claim that there are any real cases of emergence. A better course would be to define emergence, or ontological emergence, in less contentious terms, postponing the issue of downward causation to be threshed out another day. The most important and widely used strategy, which goes back to Morgan and

---

[12] The idea of probabilistic supervenience is clearly coherent and deserves consideration. But we will presumably need stable lawlike probabilities grounded in the laws at the basal level. Details of this approach need to be worked out. I hope it is obvious that the condition that the basal conditions are merely "necessary" for the occurrence of an emergent property will not do.

[13] It is interesting to note that several current philosophical advocates of emergence reject supervenience, for apparently different reasons, as a component of emergence; see, e.g., Paul Humphreys, "How Properties Emerge", *Philosophy of Science* 64 (1997): pp.1–17; Timothy O'Connor and Hong Yu Wong, "The Metaphysics of Emergence", *Noûs* 39 (2005): pp.658–678; Michael Silberstein, "In Defense of Ontological Emergence and Mental Causation", in *The Re-Emergence of Emergence*. In the current post-classical period of neo-emergentism, the idea of emergence has become very fluid, plastic, and variegated. Since "emergence" is a term of art, one is free to define it as one wishes, the only constraint being that the resulting concept is a philosophically or scientifically useful one. However, in rejecting supervenience, these writers are making a radical (and, in my view, unwise) departure from the core concept held by the classic British emergentists like C.D. Broad and C. Lloyd Morgan. I believe that one should stay at least in the vicinity of these writers in order to justify the claim that one is dealing with "emergence".

[14] Michael Silberstein, "In Defense of Ontological Emergence and Mental Causation", p.203.

Broad, has been to add the condition that an emergent, even though super-venient on, and determined by, its basal conditions, is *not deducible* from them. When Broad first introduces the idea of emergence in *The Mind and Its Place in Nature*, this is what he says:

> "Put in abstract terms the emergence theory asserts that there are certain wholes, composed (say) of constituents A, B, and C in relation R to each other; that all wholes composed of constituents of the same kind as A, B, and C in re-lations of the same kind as R have certain characteristic properties; that A, B, and C are capable of occurring in other kinds of complex where the relation is not of the same kind as R; and that the characteristic properties of the whole R(A, B, C) *cannot, even in theory, be deduced* from the most complete knowl-edge of the properties of A, B, and C in isolation or in other wholes which are not of the form R(A, B, C). The mechanistic theory rejects the last clause of this assertion."[15]

So the difference between emergentism and its principal rival, mecha-nism/reductionism, consists precisely in that, on reductionism, "the charac-teristic properties" of a whole are *deducible* from the facts about its parts and their relationships, whereas emergentism holds them to be *not so de-ducible*. Or, to put it another way, let F be a property of a whole which is determined by, or supervenient on, properties and structural relations char-acterizing its constituents: F is emergent if and only if F is not deducible from these facts about its constituents.[16] Emergentism, in its broadest form, would be the claim that there are properties like F, while reductionism would deny that such exist. (There are also specific emergentist theses concerning selected classes of phenomena; notably, biological phenomena in relation to physicochemical phenomena, and mentality and conscious-ness vis-à-vis the domain of the neural/biological sciences.) It is widely as-sumed that there is an important connection between logical deduction on one hand and explanation and reduction on the other. Thus, we might add: F is mechanistically, or reductively, explainable, or reducible, just in case F is deducible from facts about the constituents of the whole. In the quote above, Broad speaks of "the most complete knowledge" of the facts about the whole's constituents, but this seemingly epistemological aspect of his

---

[15] p.61. Emphasis added.

[16] In speaking of "deducing" properties we follow the usual practice. When we say "F is deducible from conditions C" what is meant is that the fact, or proposition, that something has F, or that F is instantiated in something, is deducible from the proposi-tion that conditions C hold for that thing. Similarly, when we speak about deducing a property from other properties.

characterization is easily eliminated: instead of "the most complete knowledge", we can refer to "all the facts" or "a complete set of truths". In fact, this replacement would be appropriate because whether or not anyone "knows" these facts about the constituents is irrelevant. Further, we should understand "all the facts", or "the most complete knowledge", to include *all the laws* operative at the basal level. So, when we say biological phenomena are emergent from physicochemical phenomena, the latter is understood to include physicochemical laws as well as individual facts at this level. In any case, a property's nondeducibility from base-level facts is what separates emergent from nonemergent properties.

Broad is not alone in this. When C. Lloyd Morgan talked about nonemergent properties as "additive and subtractive only, and predictable",[17] he is naturally taken to be referring to something similar to deducibility. In a paper published in 1926, shortly after Morgan (1923) and Broad (1924), Stephen C. Pepper describes emergentism thus:

> "The theory of emergence involves three propositions: (1) that there are levels of existence defined in terms of degree of integration; (2) that there are marks which distinguish these levels from one another over and above the degree of integration; (3) that it is *impossible to deduce* the marks of a higher level from those of a lower level ..."[18]

Later writers who have invoked nondeducibility as the pivotal criterion of emergence include Carl G. Hempel, Ernest Nagel, James Van Cleve, and David Chalmers.[19]

Broad, like many other writers, often resorts to epistemological terms to explain emergence. We have noted this in regard to Broad's statement that "no amount of knowledge" about the micro-constitution of a living thing is sufficient for the "prediction" of the biological features of the organism. Similarly, an emergentist about consciousness would sometimes put his emergentist claim by saying that a complete physical, physiological, and computational knowledge of our brain at a given time does not

---

[17] *Emergent Evolution*, p.3.

[18] "Emergence", *Journal of Philosophy* 23 (1926): pp.241–245. (The quote is from p.241; emphasis added).

[19] Carl G. Hempel and Paul Oppenheim, "Studies in the Logic of Explanation", *Philosophy of Science* 15 (1948): pp.135–175. Ernest Nagel, *The Structure of Science* (New York: Harcourt, Brace, and World, 1961). James Van Cleve, "Mind-Dust or Magic? Panpsychism versus Emergence", *Philosophical Perspectives* 4 (1990): pp.215–226. Chalmers, "Strong and Weak Supervenience".

suffice to give us any knowledge about our consciousness – whether or not we are conscious at the time and if we are, what sort of consciousness is being experienced. There is also Frank Jackson's Mary,[20] the famous superstar vision scientist confined to a black-and-white room: we are to suppose that she has complete physical information about the physical/neural processes involved in the workings of our visual systems but, before her release from the room, she has no knowledge of color qualia. One could take such talk as referring to an epistemological conception of emergence, but I believe that would be premature. I think that the epistemological relationships being talked about are best explained in terms of deducibility. If, as Broad thought, physicochemical knowledge of an organism doesn't yield knowledge of its biology, that would be so because biological truths are not deducible from physicochemical truths. If only truths about visual qualia were deducible from physical/neural truths, Mary could know, before her release, what it would be like to see a ripe tomato. In this way, metaphysical emergence characterized in terms of nondeducibility would appear to offer an explanation of epistemological emergence. We will soon see that the notion of deducibility is itself fraught with problems but, at least on a first pass, it seems like just what we need to characterize metaphysical emergence.

Deducibility can fail on two levels. First, there is the idea that the novelty of an emergent property consists precisely in the fact that the property is beyond our conceptual reach before it makes its first appearance and we have a chance to observe or experience it. The pre-release Mary seems often taken to be in a situation of that sort in regard to color qualia (though I don't believe she has to be, for Jackson's purposes). According to Thomas Nagel,[21] our epistemic position vis-à-vis the experiences of a bat is precisely like that: we have no idea, no conception, of what a bat's phenomenal experiences are like, and as a result we cannot even entertain propositions about their qualitative character. This would mean that we don't even know just what propositions we should try to deduce about bat phenomenology from truths about bat physiology. Second, deducibility can fail even though we know what the supposed emergent properties are and know just what propositions are being considered for deduction. I believe a situation of this kind is what figures primarily in the emergentists' claim that propositions involving emergent properties are not deducible from truths about the base-level processes. This is the sort of situation Broad

---

[20] "Epiphenomenal Qualia", *Philosophical Quarterly* 32 (1982): pp.126–136.
[21] "What Is It Like to Be a Bat?", *Philosophical Review* 83 (1974): pp.435–450.

considers in regard to the deducibility of biological truths from physico-chemical truths. The availability of biological concepts is not at issue.

To sum up, then, deducibility, or the absence thereof, is the key to the standard traditional conception of metaphysical emergence. Properties of a whole are emergent just in case they are not deducible from properties and relations characterizing its constituent parts, even though they are determined by and supervenient on them.

III

So then, do we now have a properly characterized ontological concept of emergence, a conception that makes emergence something objective in the world, not a phenomenon that has to do with our cognitive resources and powers? We have reached a concept that takes nondeducibility as the mark that distinguishes emergent properties from the rest. Now the critical question arises: Is deducibility, or nondeducibility, itself a wholly nonepistemic concept? If biological properties are emergent from physicochemical properties, we cannot deduce truths involving the former from those that only involve the latter – that is, we cannot deduce biological truths from physicochemical truths. But whom does this "we" refer to? Who is doing the deduction? How adept a logician is Jackson's Mary supposed to be? No human person, we may assume, has unlimited logical powers. Although "we" cannot deduce biological truths from physical truths, why couldn't a cognizer with vastly greater logical and mathematical powers produce the required deductions? Mustn't we fix the level of deductive or logical competence we have in mind to give a clear meaning to "deducible"? If so, is there a "right" level to pick, and what makes it "right"? But, more importantly, don't these questions show that the idea of deducibility, or nondeducibility, threatens to turn into an epistemic notion, making Broad's emergence epistemic rather than metaphysical?

Think about how we go about making deductions – how we reason from premises to a conclusion in practice. I believe we have something like the following picture in mind: we start off with a list of premises, and proceed from there, step by step, where each step is seen as obviously and directly implied by selected earlier steps (in the best cases, in accordance with simple formal rules known to guarantee implication, like modus ponens), and, with luck, finally reach the proposition to be deduced. In his *Rules for the Direction of the Mind*, Descartes described deduction as "a continuous and uninterrupted movement of thought in which each individual proposition is clearly intuited". [22] Further, he says, "the self-evidence and certainty of intuition is required not only for apprehending single propositions, but also for any train of reasoning whatever."[23]

More recently, Gilbert Harman has given a similar characterization of reasoning. According to him, we have a fundamental disposition, or power, to recognize "immediate implications" and "immediate inconsistencies", and this capacity is what guides us through a process of reasoning. Harman recognizes that all this is relative to individual cognizers, saying "I suggested that certain implications and inconsistencies are 'immediate' for a given person."[24]

It is clear that the problem with this picture of deduction, or deducibility, is that it makes the notion of deducibility relative to the cognitive powers and dispositions of the deducers and thereby makes the concept of emergence defined in its terms both epistemic and relative, whereas what we are seeking is an objective, ontological conception of emergence. To his credit, Broad was well aware of this problem. Observant readers have surely noticed that in the last quoted passage above, he says that the emergent properties of a whole "cannot, *even in theory*, be deduced" (emphasis added) from those of its constituents. Clearly in a similar spirit, Chalmers writes that "truths concerning [emergent phenomena] are not *deducible even in principle*" from truths about lower-level phenomena.[25] But what does this mean? Here is where Broad summons his "mathematical archangel":

"If the emergent theory of chemical compounds be true, a mathematical archangel, gifted with the further power of perceiving the microscopic structure of atoms as easily as we can perceive hay-stacks, could no more predict the behavior of silver or of chloride or the properties of silver-chloride without having observed samples of those substances than we can at present. And he could no more deduce the rest of the properties of a chemical element or compound from a selection of its properties than we can."[26]

---

[22] *The Philosophical Writings of Descartes*, vol.1, tr. John Cottingham, Robert Stoothoff, and Dugald Murdoch (Cambridge: Cambridge University Press, 1985), p.15.
[23] Ibid. pp.14–15.
[24] *Change in View* (Cambridge: MIT Press, 1986), p.19.
[25] "Strong and Weak Emergence", p.244. Italics added to "even in principle".
[26] *The Mind and Its Place in Nature*, p.71.

The mathematical archangel,[27] we may presume, is logically and mathematically omniscient. If a proposition is deducible, "in principle" or "in theory", from a set of premises, it will know that it is, and be able to construct a step-by-step proof. If the archangel cannot produce a proof, it's because there is no proof and the proposition is not deducible, in an absolute sense, from the premises. Thus, if a property is emergent from a set of basal conditions, there is no deduction of it from those conditions; and our cognitive limitations have nothing to do with it. This idealization of deduction is Broad's attempt to purge any epistemic and relativistic aspects from the notion of deduction and thereby objectify deducibility, or nondeducibility. For him, there being no deduction of an emergent property from its basal conditions is not an epistemological fact. It is not because we are not smart enough, or don't have enough time or inclination, that we cannot deduce, say, geological truths from the truths of macroeconomics, or facts about the surface composition of the moon from facts about neurotransmitters in the human brain; not even the mathematical archangel can do that, and that is because there are no deductions between these sets of truths. This surely seems like an objective fact about the relationships between sets of truths, or facts. Broad's idealization strategy appears to remove from the notion of deducibility an apparent epistemic relativity, and the characterization of emergence as supervenience *plus* nondeducibility appears to stand as an ontological conception of emergence. At least, so it may seem at this point.

IV

Thus, there being a deduction or proof is an objective matter independent of epistemological facts about us or anyone else. Does this solve the problem with Broad's conception of emergence? There remains one more issue to deal with: deduction or proof makes sense only relative to a specific set of rules of inference, or a proof system, which specifies permissible trans-

---

[27] Achim Stephan calls the mathematical archangel "a colleague of the Laplacian demon" in his "Emergence – A Systematic View on its Historical Facets", in *Emergence or Reduction?*, ed. Ansgar Beckermann, Hans Flohr, and Jaegwon Kim (Berlin: de Gruyter, 1992). For interesting discussion of some issues formulated in terms of Laplace's demon that are relevant to our concerns in this paper, see Terence Horgan, "Supervenience and Cosmic Hermeneutics", *Southern Journal of Philosophy* 22, Spindel Supplement (1984): pp.19–38.

formations of sentences in constructing proofs. That is to say, a sequence of sentences is a proof only relative to a system of deduction. Should we say, following Descartes and Harman, that the relevant system must include only those rules that give us "immediate implications"? No; that would bring back epistemic relativity. Evidently, what the mathematical archangel sees when it recognizes a sentence as "deducible" from a given set of premises is a proof in some proof system. But what proof system does the archangel use? Does it matter?

The answer is that it does matter – and matters very much. The proof system must be a *correct* system in the following sense: If there is a proof of Q from $P_1,\ldots, P_n$, then $P_1,\ldots, P_n$ must logically imply, or entail, Q. That is, the premises of a proof in a correct system must guarantee the truth of the conclusion proved. We are assuming that the language in which the issues of emergence are considered is provided with a semantics and that semantic notions like validity and implication are available for sentences of the language. What matters from a metaphysical point of view is semantics, more specifically logical implication, not syntax – proofs are relevant only if they are proofs in a correct system, and that is so because that guarantees these proofs will have the right semantic property, that of preserving truth from premises to conclusions. Does it matter which correct proof system is used by the archangel? Some proof systems are more intuitive and perspicacious than others; the usual deduction systems we find in logic textbooks are formulated, we may assume, with an eye toward simplicity and perspicuity – that is, for the typical student. But that is epistemology; the archangel is hardly a typical student, and any system is as perspicuous to it as any other. Remember: the archangel was expressly called into service in order to cancel out epistemological considerations and get unalloyed metaphysics reinstated, untainted by cognitive limitations and relativity. There also is a formal reason why for first-order logic (with identity), arguably the core of what we call "logic", the choice of a system does not matter – because this is a "complete" system, that is, there are formalizations of this logic that are complete. A proof system is complete in the technical sense just in case there is a proof of a sentence from a set of premises *if and only if* the premises imply, or entail, that sentence. In consequence, it doesn't matter which one of these complete deductive systems we use to define deducibility; for they are all equivalent in that something is provable in one system from a given set of premises if and only if it is so provable in each of the rest. The only thing that matters is the fact that there being a proof guarantees implication, or logical entailment. And if there is no proof in the system, then there is no logical implication; that is, nondeducibility amounts to the absence of implication in languages whose logic is amenable to complete formalization.

So the relativity of proofs to proof systems cancels itself out as cause for concern for us. Does this mean that we are finally home free with Broad's metaphysical conception of emergence as supervenience plus nondeducibility?

Unfortunately, the answer is no, at least not yet; in truth, we are now in far worse trouble than before. For look where we are: we have just seen that in speaking of deducibility and nondeducibility, what matters turns out to be logical implication, or entailment, or the absence of thereof. Deducibility in a complete system of proof, or deducibility as the mathematical archangel sees it, is nothing but logical entailment; similarly, nondeducibility amounts to logical nonentailment. With this in mind, look again at Broad's attempt to combine supervenience with nondeducibility to obtain a metaphysical relation of emergence. An emergent property supervenes on basal-level conditions (including basal-level laws); this means that certain basal conditions, namely those that constitute a supervenience base for it, necessitate, or entail, the emergent property. We have just seen that the net effect of nondeducibility comes to the absence of logical necessitation. Consequently, metaphysical emergence, as conceived by Broad and others, comes to this: Emergent properties are entailed but not logically entailed by their basal conditions. Or, to put it another way, emergent properties supervene, but do not logically supervene, on their basal conditions.

On the face of it, this seems like a coherent conception, because we think that logical supervenience is not the only kind of supervenience. There is another recognized variety that is weaker than logical supervenience, what is called "nomological", or "natural", supervenience: the bases of supervenient properties do not logically entail them but when combined with prevailing laws of nature, the entailment holds. Thus, the necessitation is nomological, not logical or metaphysical. As nomological supervenience appears to be the only alternative to logical supervenience, the Broad-style conception of emergence has now taken the following form: Emergent properties supervene nomologically, but not logically, on their basal conditions. And this may seem to fit in well with certain current forms of dualism, in particular, Chalmers' "naturalistic dualism", which consists in the claim that consciousness is naturally (that is, nomologically), but not logically, supervenient on physical phenomena.[28] On the present construal, therefore, the classical British emergentism of Broad and others might seem to be an almost exact anticipation of Chalmers' naturalistic dualism.

But not so fast! We must at this point look a bit deeper into the nature of nomological supervenience that may be involved in the Broad-style metaphysical emergence. When we refer to the "basal conditions" of an emergent property, as we have noted more than once, these conditions are taken to include not only particular facts – events, states, and processes – at the base level but also *laws operative at that level*. So as regards the emergence of mental properties on biological/physical properties, the appropriate basal conditions include all biological/physical laws – all laws applicable to biological, neurological, and physicochemical systems and phenomena. Recall the iconic emergentist question: Knowing all about the biological, neural, and physicochemical facts about the brain, can we predict, or know, what conscious experience, if any, will be present in that brain? Obviously, "knowing all about what goes on at the neural level" should be taken to include knowing the laws that hold at that level.[29]

This means that when we say that an emergent property is not logically implied, or necessitated, by its basal conditions, the latter include not only particular basal facts but also all basal laws, laws holding at the base level. So in a sense the logical supervenience we are talking about is a form of nomological supervenience, where the laws involved are base-level laws (we may assume that these laws include all laws holding at still lower levels). It is crucially important to keep in mind that *the laws assumed to be included in the basal conditions are* not *all the laws of nature; they are only laws that hold at the basal level*.[30] Thus, when we say emergent properties are not logically but only nomologically necessitated by the basal conditions, the *additional* laws needed to yield the necessitation are not

---

[28] *The Conscious Mind* (New York and Oxford: Oxford University Press, 1996). Chalmers says: "In general, B-properties supervene naturally on A-properties if any two *naturally possible* situations with the same A-properties have the same B-properties", where a situation is naturally possible if "it could actually occur without violating any natural laws", p.36. On naturalistic dualism, see pp.168ff.

[29] Chalmer's notion of logical supervenience on physical facts is similar; the physical facts are stipulated to include all physical laws. See *The Conscious Mind*, p.33.

[30] I believe it should be assumed – and this is what I assume – that laws operative at a given level include all laws that hold at the lower levels as well. Thus, for example, laws at the biological level include all physical and chemical laws.

base-level laws (we have them already) but laws that connect the emergents with specific basal conditions, namely those that Broad calls "trans-ordinal laws", laws connecting events and states at different levels, or "orders". These are also sometimes called "laws of emergence" or "supervenience laws",[31] and take the following form:

> When conditions C at the base level hold for system S at t, S instantiates, at t, emergent property E.

These laws are the auxiliary premises we need to deduce statements about facts involving emergent properties from statements about their basal conditions. Trans-ordinal laws, like the bridge laws in Nagelian theory reduction,[32] are not exclusively about the base level; they concern the relationships between the base-level phenomena and the phenomena at a higher level. In the case of the mind-body relation, these are psychophysical laws telling us under what neural/biological conditions, a given type of conscious experience occurs. On emergentism,[33] every conscious state will be connected by such an inter-level law with its underlying neural basal conditions; and there can be multiple emergence bases for a given type of conscious state. As these laws involve higher-level phenomena, they cannot be part of the basal conditions from which the deducibility of an emergent is considered.

These considerations bring to light a deep difficulty – in fact, what may well be an incoherence – in Broad's characterization of emergence as supervenience *plus* nondeducibility. For this combination threatens to turn into an outright contradiction: supervenience says that basal conditions entail, or imply, the emergent phenomenon; however, nondeducibility, which, as we saw, comes to nonentailment, or nonimplication, says that the basal conditions do not entail or imply the emergent phenomenon. Or equivalently, the emergent phenomenon both supervenes and does not supervene on its basal conditions. We tried to defuse this potentially disastrous situation by construing the combination as nomological supervenience *plus* the denial of logical supervenience; that is, emergent properties

---

[31] Chalmers' term in *The Conscious Mind*, p.127.
[32] See Ernest Nagel, *The Structure of Science* (New York: Harcourt, Brace, and World, 1961), chapter 11.
[33] Obviously, an assumption of this kind is shared by many physicalist theories of the mind.

are nomologically, but not logically, supervenient on their basal conditions. We can now see that this rescue strategy fails. The reason is that nomological supervenience as it is usually understood, for example, Chalmer's "natural" supervenience, fails to capture Broad's concept of supervenience, or determination. Look at an earlier quote from Broad again:

> "No doubt the properties of silver-chloride are completely determined by those of silver and of chlorine; in the sense that whenever you have a whole composed of these two elements in certain proportions and relations you have something with the characteristic properties of silver-chloride ... But connecting the properties of silver-chloride with those of silver and chlorine and with the structure of the compound is, so far as we know, an unique and ultimate law."[34]

What Broad is claiming is that when we have fixed the base-level conditions and laws, that determines what phenomena will, or will not, emerge, even though the latter are not deducible from the former. So an emergent property supervene on its basal conditions plus basal laws but not deducible from them. It is crucial here that *the supervenience base and deduction base are held identical.* When we speak about nomological supervenience, we usually have in mind *all laws* prevailing in this world, which will include Broad's trans-ordinal laws, or Chalmer's "supervenient laws", or Nagel's "bridge laws" – that is, laws connecting phenomena at different levels. Broad will cheerfully admit that if trans-ordinal laws are admitted as part of the deduction base (that is, among the premises), emergent properties or phenomena are easily deduced from the basal conditions. His point is that when we are limited to base-level laws and conditions, no deduction is possible, since there is none. And yet he maintains that the emergents supervene on, or are determined by, the base-level phenomena and laws. And this supervenience is logical or metaphysical supervenience. There is a nomological aspect to that because the supervenience base includes basal laws. But once these laws are considered as part of the base, the supervenience relation becomes the logical/metaphysical variety.

This apparently puts Broad and his like-minded colleagues in an untenable position. He has been reduced to saying that emergent properties logically supervene on basal conditions and laws and yet they are not deducible from them. To repeat, nondeducibility, on Broad's idealization, turns into the absence of logical entailment. So Broad's conception of emergence turns into an apparent incoherence: logically supervenient on

---

[34] *The Mind and Its Place in Nature*, pp.64–65.

basal facts but not logically entailed by them – that is, to be brute, both logically supervenient and not logically supervenient on basal facts! I think the source of the problem is rather obvious: to avoid an epistemic interpretation of "deducible", Broad tries to idealize it in terms of the mathematical archangel, as Laplace tried with his logically all-powerful "demon" (who, like the mathematical archangel, is also microphysically omniscient), but idealized deducibility turns into entailment, contradicting the first component of his metaphysical emergence, that is, supervenience. Is there a way out for Broad from this apparently incoherent situation?

V

One point to consider is the following. We have been assuming that the language in which emergence issues are considered is a first-order language with a complete proof system. Without completeness, we cannot equate nondeducibility with nonentailment, or the absence of implication. So what about languages for which there are no complete proof systems? Elementary number theory, or arithmetic, is famously incomplete; that is, there is no consistent formalization of number theory in which all and only number-theoretic truths are provable. Surely, it might be said, number theory must be taken to be part of the deductive system when we consider the deducibility of emergent phenomena.

However, it doesn't seem to me that the emergentist can exploit the incompleteness of arithmetic to dispute our claim that nondeducibility boils down to nonentailment. The reason is that we can happily let the emergentist add *all mathematical truths* (including of course arithmetic truths) to her deductive system and ask her whether this would help her deduce the emergents from their basal conditions. I believe the emergentist would have to say no. After all, the mathematical archangel is mathematically omniscient and it has at its disposal all mathematical truths. Its deductive system has to be complete. If a truth is not deducible from another in such a system, it must be because the former is not implied by the latter.

There is another concern we should address briefly. One might point out that "x is a male" is not deducible in first-order logic from "x is a bachelor" and yet obviously "x is a bachelor" logically implies "x is a male". The reply is that definitions are free in deductions and don't count as additional premises; one is entitled to use them at any point in a proof.

So the deduction goes through with the definition "x is a bachelor iff x is an unmarried adult male".

But this may not put away the concern entirely. For one might continue: Even so, "x is water" is not deducible from "x is H_2O" since there is no conceptual definition linking "water" and "H_2O". And yet the proposition that Lake Michigan is filled with H_2O entails that it is filled with water. Therefore, we cannot say that nondeducibility, even with the proviso concerning definitions, amounts to nonentailment. This point touches on various controversial issues currently debated in the philosophy of mind, philosophy of language, and metaphysics – issues arising from (supposed) cases of a posteriori necessities and entailments. I will simply state here my own response without detailed explanation or justification (this response derives from – and, I believe, is consistent with – the views of philosophers like David Chalmers and Frank Jackson[35]). True, there are no direct conceptual links between "water" and "H_2O", but this doesn't mean appropriate deductive links cannot be forged between statements about water and statements about H_2O. What do we mean by "water"? We reply: it means something like "the local watery stuff", where "watery" is short for a conjunction of predicates designating the observable properties by which we ordinarily recognize and identify water – properties like transparency, the power to quench thirst, the characteristic viscosity (the way it "flows"), its freezing and boiling temperatures, its power to dissolve sugar and salt but not butter, and so on. We take this to be a conceptual fact grounded in meanings. Now consider the following array of statements:

(i)   Lake Michigan is filled with H_2O
(ii)   The local watery stuff = H_2O
(iii)   Water = the local watery stuff
(iv)   Therefore, Lake Michigan is filled with water

We assume that (ii) is deducible from physical facts – physical laws as well as particular facts. Physical theory, we may assume, can show that the local stuff that is transparent, can dissolve sugar, and flows in a certain way is made up of H_2O molecules; and it can explain why quantities of

---

[35] See, e.g., Chalmers, *The Conscious Mind*; Chalmers and Frank Jackson, "Conceptual Analysis and Reductive Explanation", *Philosophical Review* 110 (2001): pp.315–360. For views critical of the present approach, see Ned Block and Robert Stalnaker, "Conceptual Analysis, Dualism, and the Explanatory Gap", *Philosophical Review*, 108 (1999): pp.1–46.

H$_2$O molecules behave in the way water behaves. Step (iii) is a meaning-based definition; so it comes free. And (iv) can be deduced from the preceding steps in any first-order logic. Note that the use of physical laws is appropriate since, as we have repeatedly emphasized, the base of deduction for the emergence debate is taken to include base-level laws as well as particular conditions. In any case, other cases of a posteriori entailments hopefully can be dealt with in a similar fashion.

There are more issues and problems to be discussed, but that would have to wait for another occasion. However, our provisional conclusion stands: We are still in need of an intelligible and coherent metaphysical characterization of emergence, one that does not involve ineliminable references to our, or anyone's, cognitive situations or powers. So there is work to do – not only for the emergentists bent on defending emergentism as a metaphysical thesis about the world but also for those reductionist physicalists who think that although metaphysical emergentism is false and refutable, it is an intelligible thesis.

NON-REDUCTIVE PHYSICALISM, MENTAL CAUSATION AND THE NATURE OF ACTIONS

MARKUS E. SCHLOSSER
University of Bristol

Abstract

Given some reasonable assumptions concerning the nature of mental causation, non-reductive physicalism faces the following dilemma. If mental events cause *physical* events, they merely overdetermine their effects (given the causal closure of the physical). If mental events cause only other *mental* events, they do not make the kind of difference we want them to. This dilemma can be avoided if we drop the dichotomy between physical and mental events. Mental events make a real difference if they cause *actions*. But actions are neither mental nor physical events. They are realized by physical events, but they are not type-identical with them. This gives us non-reductive physicalism without downward causation. The tenability of this view has been questioned. Jaegwon Kim, in particular, has argued that non-reductive physicalism is committed to downward causation. Appealing to the nature of actions, I will argue that this commitment can be avoided.

1 INTRODUCTION

Non-reductive physicalism about the mental appears to be an attractive position. It is compatible with the widely held assumption that mental properties are multiply realizable (Putnam 1967). It can accommodate the plausible claim that intentional explanations and attributions of mental attitudes have "no echo" in the physical domain (Davidson 1970). And it claims to be compatible with physicalism and a broadly naturalistic worldview. So it is no surprise that non-reductive physicalism has been a standard view in the analytical philosophy of mind, where the commitment to naturalism is widespread and usually taken for granted.

The most important internal objection to non-reductive physicalism is the causal exclusion argument (also known as the supervenience argument). This argument is the topic of a vast amount of literature. It has shaped the mental causation debate and the development of different forms of non-reductive physicalism. Jaegwon Kim (1991, 1998 and 2005) has been the most influential and the most persistent proponent of the causal exclusion challenge.

In this paper I will focus on Kim's most recent formulation of the argument, and I will defend non-reductive physicalism by way of a detour to the philosophy of action. First, I will give a brief outline of the basic notions and I will identify an apparent dilemma for non-reductive physicalism that is closely related to the causal exclusion problem. Then I will outline the standard causal account of the nature of actions, which will provide the basis for my response to Kim's challenge. The focus will be on the first stage of Kim's argument, in which it is argued that non-reductive physicalism is committed to downward causation. I will show that this commitment can be avoided for the most important variety of mental causation; namely, the causation of actions by mental events.

2 NON-REDUCTIVE PHYSICALISM

It is controversial how, exactly, non-reductive physicalism should be formulated. The following rough characterization, however, is widely accepted and it is sufficiently precise for a fruitful discussion of the view. The two main kinds of reduction are ontological and theoretical reduction. The former concerns concrete entities and properties, the latter is about theories. Non-reductionism about the mental is non-reductionism about mental properties and psychological theories. I will assume that this entails, firstly, that mental properties are not identical with physical properties, and that, secondly, psychological theories are not reducible to physical and other non-mental theories (in the traditional sense of theory reduction).[1]

Physicalism has the following two main components. It holds, firstly, that the physical domain is causally closed. That is to say, roughly, that every physical event that has a sufficient cause has a sufficient physical cause. The second component can be characterized, for our purposes, with a view towards non-reductionism about the mental. It holds that mental properties are ontologically dependent on physical properties: mental prop-

---

[1] The traditional view of theory reduction says, roughly, that a theory T is reducible just in case there is a lower-level theory T^* and a set of bridge-laws L such that the laws of T can be derived from the laws of T^* in conjunction with the laws in L. For a more detailed outline and discussion see, for instance, Kim 1998.

erties exist only if the right physical properties exist, and they are realized and determined by them. This relation of dependence and determination is usually construed in terms of supervenience (we will turn to this further below). Given all this, we can characterize non-reductive physicalism as the conjunction of physicalism and non-reductionism about the mental.

3 WHAT IS MENTAL CAUSATION?

All standard versions of non-reductive physicalism are committed to the claim that mental entities are causally efficacious, and it is widely assumed that mental causation is event-causation. Events may be construed as particulars or as instantiations of properties, and it is common to use the terms "events" and "event-causation" as umbrella terms for events and states and for causation by events and states, respectively. Given this, we can say that there is mental causation only if some mental events are causally efficacious in the sense that they stand in event-causal relations with other events. Further, it is often claimed that there is genuine mental causation only if mental events are causally efficacious in virtue of their *mental* properties (in virtue of instantiating mental properties). And it is usually assumed that genuine mental causation requires that mental events do not merely overdetermine their effects. Given all this, we can begin with the following three necessary conditions on mental causation:

(1) Mental events are causally efficacious: mental events cause events.
(2) Mental events are causally efficacious in virtue of their mental properties.
(3) Mental events do not merely overdetermine their effects.

One important question has been left open. What *kinds of things* must mental events cause for there to be *genuine* mental causation? Are the conditions (1)–(3) jointly sufficient for genuine mental causation, or do we need to impose further restrictions on what kinds of events must be caused?

The contemporary mental causation debate, it is sometimes claimed, has its roots in Donald Davidson's seminal paper "Mental events" (1970). One of the basic assumptions in this paper says that there is *interaction* between mental and physical events: some physical events cause mental events and some mental events cause physical events (p. 208). Damage to muscle tissue, for instance, causes pain, and intentions cause behaviour. Most philosophers have followed Davidson on this. They have assumed, in particular, that mental causation requires what we can call *mental-to-physical* causation: the causation of physical events by mental events.[2]

However, most philosophers would also acknowledge that mental events can be causally efficacious by causing other *mental* events. So why insist on interaction with physical events if there can be mental causation within the domain of the mental itself? We can identify two closely related reasons for the insistence on mental-to-physical causation. If there is mental-to-mental causation that satisfies our conditions (1)–(3), then the mental is causally efficacious. Nevertheless, we tend to think that this alone falls short of genuine mental causation, because we tend to think that the mental is truly efficacious only if it causes also physical events. We tend to think that mental events make a *real* difference only if they make a difference in the physical world. This, in turn, is motivated by the very plausible intuition that an agent's mental events make a real difference only if they make a difference to the agent's overt behaviour. We tend to think that there is *genuine* mental causation only if mental events cause bodily movement.

4 A DILEMMA FOR NON-REDUCTIVE PHYSICALISM

Let us assume, for the sake of argument, that non-reductive physicalism is true: psychological theories are not reducible, mental properties are not identical with physical properties, but they are dependent on, realized and determined by them. Most philosophers, as just pointed out, think that there is genuine mental causation only if some mental events have physical effects. But mental-to-physical causation leads to the following well-known problem for non-reductive physicalism. If mental events cause physical events, then they merely overdetermine their effects due to the causal closure of the physical. Assume, for instance, that an agent's decision causes the execution of a bodily movement. Given that this is a physical event, and given the causal closure of the physical, the movement has a sufficient physical cause. The decision, it seems, is neither identical with nor a part of this sufficient cause, as it is not identical with any physical

---

[2] To name only a few, see Kim 1991, 1998 and 2005, Crane 1995 and Menzies 2003.

event. So it seems that the decision merely overdetermines (or "over-causes") the movement.[3]

Given all that, non-reductive physicalism appears to face the following dilemma. If mental events cause physical events, they merely overdetermine their effects, and if they cause only other mental events, they are not truly efficacious. So, either way, the efficacy of the mental falls short of *genuine* mental causation.

This dilemma is based on a dichotomy between mental-to-physical and mental-to-mental causation. It is based, in other words, on the assumption that mental causation is either mental-to-physical or mental-to-mental – there is no further possibility. I will now argue that this is a false dichotomy.

5 ACTIONS AND MOVEMENTS

The causation of *actions* is, arguably, the most important variety of mental causation. Given this, we can say that there *is* genuine mental causation if mental events cause actions in a way that satisfies the conditions (1)–(3): there is genuine mental causation if mental events cause actions in virtue of their mental properties and without overdetermination.

Actions can be distinguished from bodily movements. This distinction is familiar within the philosophy of action. But in the philosophy of mind it is often overlooked or neglected, and it is frequently blurred by talk about *behaviour*. So, what are actions? Are they physical or mental events?

Most philosophers of mind presuppose, implicitly perhaps, an event-causal theory of action. According to this view, actions are constituted by events with a certain causal history. Certain events, that is, constitute actions *in virtue of* being caused by the right antecedents (and in the right way).[4] The right antecedents are mental events that *rationalize* the action (such as desires, beliefs and intentions). So, on this view, an event constitutes an action only if it is caused by rationalizing mental events, and if it

---

[3] This is, basically, the causal exclusion problem. The causal sufficiency of the physical excludes the causal relevance of the mental. Compare, again, Kim 1991, 1998 and 2005, Crane 1995 and Menzies 2003.

[4] The right way of causation is *non-deviant* causation. It is widely believed that it cannot be specified what non-deviant causation consists in, and many philosophers think that this is a very serious problem for the causal theory. I do not share this pessimistic assessment, and I have proposed an account of non-deviant causation elsewhere (Schlosser, 2007).

does constitute an action, it does so in virtue of being caused by them. The causal history is therefore part of an action's essence or identity. Actions, in other words, are etiological phenomena, just like banknotes, sunburns or Picasso's paintings.[5] (A perfect copy of a banknote, for instance, is not a banknote because it has not been printed in the right way, by the right institution. Its causal history is part of its identity.)

It is very plausible to think that some actions are *mental* actions. On the causal theory, mental actions are realized by and perhaps token-identical to mental events. But they are not type-identical with mental events, because being of a certain mental event-type does not determine whether or not the event is an action. The formation of an intention, for instance, may be an action. We form some intentions actively, but others are formed passively. Whether or not a mental event is or constitutes an action depends on its causal history. It is an action only if it is caused by desires, beliefs and intentions in the right way.

The same holds for *overt* actions (actions that involve bodily movement). Consider the basic action of raising one's arm. Actions of this type are physically realized by bodily movements (arm risings), and perhaps every particular action of this type is token-identical with a particular movement. But they are not type-identical. It is not the case that you are raising your arm whenever your arm rises. The occurrence of the particular type of movement does not determine whether or not the event constitutes an action. The movement, rather, is an action only if it is caused by the right antecedents and in the right way.

What is the rationale behind thinking of actions in etiological terms? Consider the following two widely accepted doctrines. According to the first, all actions are intentional under some description. In particular, something is an action, or counts as an action, only if it is something that is done intentionally under some description (compare Anscombe 1957 and Davidson 1963). According to the second, something is done intentionally only if it is done for reasons (in the minimal sense of being motivated by mental states and events that rationalize its performance). Proponents of the causal theory have argued that the best explanation of the fact that an action is done *for* reasons is provided by the assumption that it is *caused* by the mental antecedents that rationalize it (Davidson 1963). Given all this, we can see why the causal history enters into the essence of actions. Some-

---

[5] This point is not often made explicit, but it is part of the causal theory of action. Compare Mele 1997.

thing *is* an action, or *counts as* an action, in virtue of being caused by rationalizing mental states and events.

A further reason for thinking that actions are not type-identical with the physical events that realize them is given by the fact that most of our non-basic actions are multiply realizable. Suppose that I give someone a signal by raising my arm. In this case, I perform the non-basic action of giving a signal by performing the basic action of raising my arm. Clearly, there are many different ways in which I can give someone a signal. The act-type of *giving a signal* is in this sense multiply realizable, and therefore not identical with a certain type of movement.

To summarize, according to the standard causal theory, actions are neither mental nor physical events. Given this, there can be genuine mental causation that is neither mental-to-physical nor mental-to-mental causation; namely, mental causation of *actions*. On this view, actions are caused and causally explained by mental events, and both mental events and actions are realized by physical events. Given, however, the irreducibility of the mental, mental events are not type-identical with physical events, and given the etiological nature of action, actions are not type-identical with physical events. In particular, overt actions are not type-identical with bodily movements. Given further that mental events cause actions in virtue of their mental properties, we obtain a view according to which the mental is causally efficacious in a way that avoids the mentioned dichotomy. Mental events cause *actions* in virtue of their mental properties and without overdetermination. This is non-reductive physicalism *without downward causation* (without, that is, mental-to-physical causation).

In the following sections, I will turn to Kim's challenge, according to which non-reductive physicalism is committed to downward causation. But before that, let me add a few brief remarks concerning the interaction between mind and body. I suggested that there is genuine mental causation if mental events cause actions, and that actions are neither mental nor physical events. But what are they? Actions are realized by physical events, and it is plausible to assume that particular act-tokens are identical with physical event-tokens. Despite that, they belong to the domain or level of intentional explanation and mental state attribution. Actions are explained in terms of the agent's reasons (or in terms of rationalizing mental states and events), and we recognize or identify something *as an action* only under its intentional description.

What about the other direction? Is pain, for instance, caused by physical events? This appears to be undeniable. But consider the following alternative. It seems plausible to suggest that damage to muscle tissue, for instance, causes certain physical events in the brain that realize the mental event of being in pain. On this view, no physical event *causes* pain. Physical events cause other physical events, which *realize* pain. If something like this holds for all mental events, and if the proposed view of mental causation is correct, then there is *no causal interaction* between the mental and the physical. Nevertheless, epiphenomalism is false, because mental events do cause actions.

6 OVERDETERMINATION AND DOWNWARD CAUSATION

One apparent advantage of the suggested non-reductive view is that it avoids the causal exclusion problem. Mental events do not cause physical events. Hence there is no problem of overdetermination and causal exclusion. But it has been argued, most prominently by Jaegwon Kim, that non-reductive physicalism is committed to downward causation. This argument constitutes the first stage in Kim's most recent statement of the causal exclusion argument (2005, pp.39–41). In this first stage, Kim considers the case of mental-to-mental causation. Assume that the mental event M causes another mental event M^*. According to any version of non-reductive physicalism, M and M^* are realized and determined by physical events (their supervenience bases). Assume that P is the supervenience base of M and that P^* is the supervenience base of M^*.

What, Kim asks, explains the occurrence of M^*? There are two candidates: the occurrence of M and the occurrence of P^*. Both explain the occurrence of M^*, and together they overdetermine M^*, albeit not causally. M determines M^* in virtue of being its cause, and P^* determines M^* in virtue of being its supervenience base. This, Kim argues, creates a *prima facie* tension between two competing explanations, and he suggests that the best way to resolve this tension is to assume that M causes M^* *by causing its supervenience base P^**. This shows, according to Kim, that "mental-to-mental causation entails mental-to-physical causation – or, more generally, that 'same-level' causation entails 'downward' causation" (p.40). This is represented by the following figure, where the arrows stand for causation and the vertical lines for the relation of realization:

Fig. 1 Mental-to-mental

It would seem obvious that the same reasoning can be applied to the view that I have proposed. If actions are caused by mental events, and if they are realized by physical events, then the resulting tension and overdetermination appears to commit us to downward causation: we must assume that mental events cause the physical events that realize actions.

But this line of reasoning is mistaken. According to Kim, the occurrence of the supervenience base of a certain mental event realizes, determines and necessitates the occurrence of the mental event. So, in the example, the occurrence of P^* realizes, determines and necessitates the occurrence of M^*. P^* by itself necessitates M^*, as Kim says, "no matter what happened before" (p.39); in particular, no matter whether M occurred or not (unless, that is, M is a cause of P^*). Putting aside the question of whether non-reductive physicalism is in fact committed to this, the same reasoning does not hold for actions.

Actions, we assume, are realized by physical events, such as bodily movements. But the occurrence of a certain bodily movement does neither necessitate nor determine the occurrence of a certain type of action, for the reasons given above. A certain physical event, such as a certain bodily movement, realizes an action only if it has the right causal history. Let us replace the mental event M^* by an action of type A:

Fig. 2 Mental-to-action

Given the assumptions, A is caused by M and realized by P^*. But given the causal account of the nature of action, it is not the case that the occurrence of P^* necessitates or determines the occurrence of A. Whether or not P^* realizes A depends on the causal history.

Given that an action is performed, we can assume that M is a rationalizing cause of A. Had there been no rationalizing cause, there would have been no action performed and P^* would not have realized an A-ing. So, in this particular case, whether an A-ing is performed or not depends on whether or not M occurs and on whether or not M causes A. Hence, P^* alone neither necessitates nor determines the occurrence of A. Subsequently, there is no *tension* due to overdetermination that has to be resolved, and so there is no need to assume that the mental event M must cause A *by causing P^**. The argument, in other words, collapses if the effect of mental causation is an action.

One possible objection to this goes as follows. Given the standard view of the nature of actions, it is not P^* alone that necessitates and determines A, but P^*'s being caused by P. So, P's causing P^* is the causal history that makes P^* an action. In that way, the occurrence of A is realized and determined by the occurrence of physical events and physical causation, and the problem of overdetermination reappears: M merely overdetermines A, as A is determined by P's causing P^*.

This objection overlooks the important point that P's causing P^* realizes and determines the performance of A only if it realizes and determines M's causing A. Non-reductive physicalism is motivated by the thought that rationality and reason-explanation have "no echo" in the physical domain. P does not rationalize P^*. P cannot rationalize anything, because only *mental* events can possibly rationalize other events and actions. And mental events, we assume, are not reducible to physical events. Moreover, the fact that P's causing P^* realizes and determines M's causing A does not raise a problem, as it does not result in the overdetermination of A's occurrence. If P had not realized M and if P's causing P^* had not realized M's causing A, then P's causing P^* would not have realized and determined the occurrence of A. In other words, P's causing P^* does not by itself determine A. Whether it does depends on whether it also realizes and determines M's causing A. So, M and P's causing P^* do not overdetermine the performance of A – not in any clear and familiar sense of overdetermination. (To be sure, the fact that P's causing P^* realizes and determines M's causing A is not a problem, because this is precisely what non-reductive physicalism says: the mental is realized and determined by the physical.)

The objection, however, highlights a more serious issue. Mind-body supervenience is at the core of Kim's characterization of non-reductive physicalism. For the case of mental-to-mental causation Kim assumes, with non-reductive physicalism, that P is the supervenience base of M, and that P^* is the supervenience base of M^*. The argument is based on the assumption that non-reductive physicalism shares this commitment to mind-body supervenience. But the response that I have offered appears to violate this presupposition. It claims that the occurrence of P^* alone does not determine the occurrence of the effect (on the basis of considerations concerning the nature of actions). This means, firstly, that the response does not share one of the background assumptions that Kim assumed with non-reductive physicalism (and for the sake of argument). And it shows, secondly, that the response is based on the further assumption that the supervenience base of an event may be distinct from the *realization base* of that event. This assumption appears to be in need of justification. It is not shared by Kim's challenge, nor is it made by standard versions of non-reductive physicalism.

First of all, the distinction between the supervenience base and the realization base of a higher-level event is not entirely implausible or unmotivated. If externalism about mental content is true, for instance, then the supervenience base of some mental events includes the agent's environment and causal history. Despite this, it would still seem plausible to think that the instantiation of a mental event of this kind is realized by the instantiation of some of the agent's intrinsic physical properties. It would seem plausible, in other words, to distinguish the supervenience base from the realization base of the mental event. This distinction, however, raises a host of difficult and controversial issues. I shall therefore propose the following reformulation of my response, which does not presuppose the distinction between the supervenience and the realization bases of mental-level events.

Let us return to our schema, where a mental-level event M causes a mental-level effect, and where both events have a physical supervenience base P and P^*, respectively. According to Kim's construal of mental causation, the physical-level and mental-level events occur simultaneously: P occurs exactly when M occurs, and P^* occurs exactly when M^* (or A) occurs. In particular, P^* determines the effect no matter what happened before. I argued that it does matter what happened before, when the mental-level effect is an action. But we do not have to put it that way. We can, instead, assume with Kim that P^* is the supervenience base of the effect, no matter what the effect is, and that the occurrence of P^* determines the effect's occurrence, no matter what happened before. We can say this, because we can construe P^* as *containing* the supervenience base of the action's mental antecedent. We can, in other words, think of P^* as encompassing both the physical event that realizes and determines the mental antecedent and the bodily movement.[6] This is represented in the following figure:

Fig. 2.1 Mental-to-action

Reconstructed in this way, the bodily movement P' is *part* of the action's supervenience base, and so we can say that it *partly* realizes the action. If we think of it this way, we do not violate the initial assumption that P is the supervenience base of M and that P^* is the supervenience base of the mental-level effect that is caused by M.

Construed in this way, the response is now in conflict with different presuppositions of Kim's argument. Most obviously, P, the supervenience base of the mental antecedent, is not a cause of the effect's supervenience base P^* anymore. But this is not problematic as we focus exclusively on the first stage of Kim's argument. The occurrence of P does not play any role in this stage, as its dialectic stems from the purported overdetermination of the effect by M and P^* alone. The assumption that P causes P^* does not enter Kim's argument before the second stage (compare p.41).

More importantly, though, the reformulation of the response is now in conflict with Kim's definition of mind-body supervenience, which goes as follows:

---

[6] An alternative is to identify the action with the causal *process* rather than with the *effect* or *product* of this process. There are, to my knowledge, no decisive arguments for or against this process view, but I do not want to presuppose this non-standard view of agency here.

Supervenience: Mental properties strongly supervene on physical properties. That is, if any system s instantiates a mental property M at t, there necessarily exists a physical property P such that s instantiates P at t, and necessarily anything instantiating P at any time instantiates M at that time. (With minor alterations from Kim, 2005, p.33)

According to Kim, mind-body supervenience is a crucial component of non-reductive physicalism. Above, we agreed with this when we assumed that the kind of dependence and determination that holds between physical and mental properties can be captured in terms of supervenience. But whether or not we can agree with Kim's more specific claim depends on how supervenience is defined.

Given the standard causal view on the nature of action, it is clear that we cannot accept Kim's definition of supervenience – at least not for mental-to-action causation. First of all, we need to interpret the definition in a way that covers both mental events and actions. This is not problematic. According to the offered causal account, actions are realized by, dependent on and determined by physical events, just like mental events. Although realized by physical events, actions belong to the mental level, as explained above. In the light of this, Kim's definition of supervenience could be interpreted as covering mental events and actions. It could be interpreted as a claim about the supervenience of mental event-types, mental act-types, and overt act-types (this will be made explicit below).

The problem with Kim's definition is that it presupposes a *synchronic* occurrence of mental-level events and their corresponding physical supervenience bases. Given the offered account of action, we have good reason to reject this. On that view, a mental or overt action is realized and determined by a physical process that begins *before* the performance of the action. This just means that the physical supervenience bases of actions begin to occur before the actions begin. (In many cases the time lag may be very short – so short, perhaps, that it cannot be noticed consciously.)

Both mental and physical events take some time to occur. Let us say that a time interval t^* *includes* the interval t just in case t begins at the same time or after t^* and ends at the same time or before t^*. We can then reformulate Kim's definition as follows:

Supervenience*: Mental-level properties (mental event-types, mental act-types, and overt act-types) strongly supervene on physical properties. That is, if any system s instantiates a mental-level property M at t, there necessarily exists a physical property P such that s instantiates P

at t^*, where t^* includes t, and necessarily anything instantiating P at a time t_P instantiates M at a time t_M that is included in t_P.

Is this move justified? Can we simply define supervenience in a way that suits the response? This move, I think, is justified, and there are no obvious reasons to think that it is begging the question against Kim's objection.

Firstly, there is no obvious reason to think that non-reductive physicalism is committed to Kim's definition of supervenience. The debate on the different notions and definitions of supervenience is complex and intricate. One of the main questions in this debate is how the different definitions of *individual* supervenience relate to *global* supervenience. Kim's definition is a version of strong individual supervenience. It concerns, that is, the correlation between the properties of individuals (agents or systems) rather than the global correlations between families of properties within possible worlds. Some philosophers have argued that physicalism can be characterized in terms of global supervenience (Lewis 1983 and Jackson 1998, for instance). Kim argued, at one point, that global supervenience and strong individual supervenience are equivalent (compare Kim 1991). But this is controversial. Arguably, strong supervenience implies global supervenience. But it has been argued that global supervenience does not imply strong individual supervenience (see McLaughlin 1995, pp.37–38, for instance). If this is correct, and if physicalism can be characterized in terms of global supervenience, then non-reductive physicalism is not committed to any version of strong individual supervenience (neither to Kim's *Supervenience*, nor to *Supervenience**). If, on the other hand, the characterization of physicalism requires a form of strong individual supervenience, it still remains to be shown that it requires Kim's *Supervenience* (rather than the proposed *Supervenience**). In connection with that it should be noted that supervenience is not necessarily a *synchronic* relation, and that the general debate on supervenience does not provide direct support for Kim's time-indexed version of strong individual supervenience, as the versions of strong supervenience discussed within that debate are usually not time-indexed (compare McLaughlin 1995).

Secondly, the question of how the timing of mental events is related to the timing of their neural correlates is largely an empirical question. Benjamin Libet, for instance, argued on the basis of empirical evidence that unconscious brain processes precede both bodily movements and their conscious mental antecedents. In fact, Libet argued that conscious awareness occurs in general a short time after the onset of the corresponding neuronal processes (Libet 1996, for instance). Now, even if this is correct, it does not show that all mental events occur after the onset of their neural correlates (because it does not show that *unconscious* mental events occur after the onset of their neural correlates). Nevertheless, the experimental findings remind us that processes of realization usually *take time*, and they lend some credibility to the assumption that all mental events may be preceded by their neural correlates. Given all this, Kim's definition of supervenience, which stipulates a strict synchronic relationship between mental events and their supervenience bases, may well turn out to be false.

Thirdly, and most importantly, Kim's definition of supervenience, together with his schema of mental causation, is incompatible with the etiological nature of action. The outlined account of the nature of action is an integral part of the widely accepted causal theory of action, and it is, as I have suggested, plausible on independent grounds. Given this, the proposed revision of the definition of supervenience (*Supervenience**) is well motivated and justified.

8 CONCLUSION

The argument of this paper leaves us with a somewhat awkward position. According to Kim, non-reductive physicalism is committed to downward causation. I argued that this does not hold for the case of mental-to-action causation. Given my arguments, non-reductive physicalism is not committed to downward causation, if we assume that mental causation is mental-to-action causation. But why would we make this assumption? The causation of intentional actions by mental states and events is perhaps the most important variety of mental causation. But mental events cause other mental *events* as well as actions, and it seems clear that not all instances of mental-to-mental causation constitute mental agency. The formation of a judgement, for instance, may or may not be a mental action; the occurrence of a memory may cause the formation of a belief without the agent's *doing* anything; and so on.

So, the argument of this paper provides only a partial defence of non-reductive physicalism. This argument, it should be noted, might hold for essentially etiological properties in general (it might hold, that is, for all higher-level properties with a historical identity or nature). But this seems to be irrelevant, as mental events do not in general fall under this category. It has been suggested that all higher-level properties, and hence all mental-level properties, are functional properties (properties that can be individuated in terms of their characteristic causes and effects. Compare, for instance, Shoemaker 1980). But functional properties are not necessarily etiological properties. Consider the mental property of being in pain. If this is a functional property, then it can be characterized in terms of its causes and effects, and it can, presumably, be multiply realized. It can, that is, be realized by any physical event that can play its characteristic causal role. Assume, then, that being in pain is realized in humans by physical events of type P (firings of certain patterns of neurons, for instance). Given this, the instantiation of P in humans is sufficient for the instantiation of the mental property of being in pain. That means that a particular instantiation of pain does not necessarily have to be caused by one of the characteristic causal antecedents of pain. Given this, being in pain is a functional, but not an etiological property.

To conclude, the scope of my argument is restricted to mental-to-action causation. Nevertheless, it highlights some interesting and important features of the problem of mental causation. It shows that an abstract and general treatment of the causal exclusion problem is problematic, and that there are important differences between mental-to-physical, mental-to-mental and mental-to-action causation. And it highlights the fact that it is important to distinguish clearly between bodily movements and actions.

REFERENCES

Anscombe, G. (1957) *Intention*, Cambridge: Harvard University Press.
Crane, T. (1995) "The mental causation debate", *Proceedings of the Aristotelian Society,* Supplementary Volume LXIX, pp.211–236.
Davidson, D. (1970) "Mental events", reprinted in his *Essays on Actions and Events*, Oxford: Clarendon Press (1980), pp.207–227.
Davidson, D. (1963) "Actions, reasons, and causes", reprinted in his *Essays on Actions and Events*, Oxford: Clarendon Press (1980), pp.3–20.
Jackson, F. (1998) *From Metaphysics to Ethics*, Oxford: Oxford University Press.
Putnam, H. (1967) "The nature of mental states", reprinted in D. Chalmers (ed.) *The Philosophy of Mind*, Oxford: Oxford University Press (2002), pp.73–79.
Kim, J. (2005) *Physicalism, or Something Near Enough*, Princeton: Princeton University Press.
Kim, J. (1998) *Mind in a Physical World: An Essay on the Mind-Body Problem and Mental Causation*, Cambridge: MIT Press.
Kim, J. (1991) *Supervenience and Mind*, Cambridge: Cambridge University Press.
Lewis, D. (1983) "New work for a theory of universals", *Australasian Journal of Philosophy*, Vol.61, pp.343–377.

Libet, B. (1996) "Neural time factors in conscious and unconscious mental functions", in S. Hamerhoff, et al., (eds.) *Toward a Science of Consciousness*, Cambridge: MIT Press, pp.156–171.

McLaughlin, B. (1995) "Varieties of supervenience", in E. Savellos, and U. Yalcin, (eds.) *Supervenience*, Cambridge: Cambridge University Press, pp.16–59.

Mele, A. (1997) "Agency and mental action", *Philosophical Perspectives*, Vol.11, pp.231–249.

Menzies, P. (2003) "The causal efficacy of mental states", in S. Walter and H. Heckman, (eds.) *Physicalism and Mental Causation*, Exeter: Imprint Academic, pp.195–224.

Schlosser, M. (2007) "Basic deviance reconsidered", *Analysis*, Vol.67, No.3, pp.186–194.

Shoemaker, S. (1980) "Causality and properties", in his *Identity, Cause and Mind*, Oxford: Oxford University Press, 2003, pp.407–426.

SORITICAL SERIES AND FISHER SERIES

PAUL ÉGRÉ
Institut Jean-Nicod, Paris[*]

1 INTRODUCTION

Little empirical evidence has been discussed so far in the philosophical literature in order to shed light on the phenomenon of vagueness, despite the existence of a large body of psychological literature on categorization and discrimination.[1] Most often, vagueness is discussed from the standpoint of a single thought experiment, namely the *sorites paradox*. Indeed, philosophical treatments of vagueness can be classified depending on which stance is taken on the sorites paradox and on the status of the main premise of the sorites in particular. My aim in this paper is not to object to the methodology which consists in finding the best logical treatment to the sorites, for ultimately, I consider that such a treatment is needed, and that logical matters cannot be evaded. Nor would I recommend discarding normative intuitions about vagueness, for here as elsewhere they must guide philosophical thinking. However, I am of the opinion that new and potentially fruitful hypotheses for our understanding of sorites series can be gathered from the experimental literature, and more generally that thought experiments themselves can be emulated by the consideration of actual experiments.

In this preliminary essay I thus wish to discuss an intriguing set of stimuli originally designed by psychologist G. Fisher (see Fisher 1967), bearing a striking analogy to a soritical series. The specificity of Fisher's figures is that they combine two phenomena: vagueness and ambiguity. In the literature on vagueness, the two phenomena of vagueness and ambiguity have been mostly opposed, and rightly so in my opinion, but mainly in relation to the phenomenon of lexical ambiguity (see Fine 1975, Keefe

[*] Institut Jean-Nicod (ENS-EHESS-CNRS), Département d'Etudes Cognitives de l'ENS. E-mail: paulegre@gmail.com.
[1] Numerous exceptions ought to be mentioned, of course. What I mean is that few empirical data have been discussed by philosophers in proportion to the vast amount of theoretical work accumulated on vagueness.

2000, Bromberger 2008). Despite this, Raffman has made the suggestion that within soritical series, borderline cases typically pattern as ambiguous stimuli (see Raffman 1994. For instance, Raffman considers a series of color shades making a smooth transition from red to orange and notes that "borderline cases are cases for which looking red and looking orange are very much alike". One observation she makes – presumably on the basis of her introspection in this particular case – is that while the color's quality appears to change as the judgment flips, there is also a more basic sense in which the stimulus remains constant. Her conclusion is that "such an effect may amount to a kind of Gestalt switch: there is a similar respect in which (for example) the duck-rabbit 'looks the same' while yet 'looking different' as it species fluctuates" (Raffman 1994: 53).

Though highly suggestive, Raffman's comparison between the kind of instability experienced in sorites series and the sort of multistability experienced in ambiguous stimuli has not received close attention. In this paper, I want to suggest that further evidence might be adduced in favor of her hypothesis from the consideration of Fisher series. Prima facie, what Fisher series may reveal is only that ambiguity is a gradable notion, at least when it comes to perceptual ambiguity, and therefore that ambiguity itself is a vague concept. However, I propose to examine the symmetric and more interesting hypothesis, according to which standard sorites series may share structural features with Fisher series. To the extent that this analogy can be sustained, I shall argue that it is at odds with one understanding of the epistemic conception of vagueness, on which a vague predicate must have a sharp boundary along a sorites series. At the same time, the analogy will allow us to give a precise articulation of the idea that borderline cases are cases for which contradictory judgments are permissible (see Wright 1994).

2 SORITES SERIES AND HYSTERESIS EFFECTS

Sorites series are series of stimuli that are gradually altered in such a way that the first stimulus in the series clearly and unambiguously instantiates a given category A, while the end stimulus clearly and unambiguously instantiates a distinct and exclusive category B. Adjacent stimuli in the series are assumed to be hard to discriminate when taken pairwise. The puzzle raised by sorites series is that although the first individual and the last individual in the series are very distinct when taken pairwise, there seems to be no way to draw a non-arbitrary boundary between the categories *A* and *B* along the series.

When exposed to a sorites series and forced to categorize one way or the other (a situation T. Horgan called *forced march*), however, subjects do draw a boundary, as can be expected on logical grounds. What is interesting is how subjects tend to do this. In recent work (see Lindsey, Brown and Raffman 2005 and Raffman forthcoming), Raffman and colleagues have undertaken a series of experiments on color perception showing that soritical transitions between two color categories give rise to *hysteresis* effects, namely to the longer persistence of one judgment over the other, depending on which color category one is coming from. Thus, within subjects and across subjects, the point at which subjects switch their judgment from "blue" to "green" is significantly displaced relative to the point at which they switch their judgment from "green" to "blue".[2] In other words, the direction of the sorites matters to the way people draw the boundary between the two categories. Hysteresis effects are interesting from a theoretical point of view because they suggest that there is a range of cases for which subjects can equally respond in two ways.

Several interpretations of this phenomenon are conceivable, however. Standardly, vagueness is seen as a phenomenon of semantic *indefiniteness*, such that central shades in a soritical series instantiate neither of the categories that are instantiated at the end of the series. Alternatively, vagueness has been described as a phenomenon of *ignorance*, namely as a form of uncertainty regarding the location of a precise boundary. On both of these interpretations, one may expect subjects who are forced to categorize one way or the other to adopt a conservative strategy for the range of cases that are indefinite relative to the categorization task, or to maintain their previous classification as far as possible for the range of cases for which they are uncertain.[3]

---

[2] See Raffman (2009) for details. In their experiment, subjects were given the choice between three answers, "blue", "green" and a "?" answer for where they would feel dissatisfied with the "blue" and "green" answers. Lindsey, Brown and Raffman's data show clear instances of a range of stimuli on which the "blue" and "green" judgment overlap, or so that the switch to "?" is shifted depending on the order of presentation. In her interpretation of the data, Raffman suggests interpreting "?" as meaning "borderline". But if borderline cases are seen, as C. Wright suggests, as cases where subjects can judge either way, one may be tempted to characterize the borderline area more broadly as the whole overlap area on which hysteresis occurs.

[3] See Raffman (2009), for a detailed discussion of the hypothesis that hysteresis might be evidence for the epistemic theory of vagueness.

This, however, may fall short of explaining on what grounds subjects would choose to be conservative. Another interpretation for the phenomenon is that along a sorites series, the central shades might bear cues that support *both* interpretations rather than neither. Not only would subjects be conservative for those cases, but arguably they would exploit cues that favor the category from which they come until cues to the contrary become more prevalent. This view of the hysteresis phenomenon, arguably, may be more readily compatible with a general conception of vagueness either as the outcome of an overlap between categories (as in glut theories of vagueness, or degree theories) or as a form of boundarylessness (see Sainsbury 1990).

Interestingly, hysteresis effects have been reported independently in the psychological literature on the perception of bistable stimuli (see Hock et al. 1993, 2004, Gregson 2004), which help to clarify this issue. Hock and colleagues discuss in particular the case of motion quartets. Motion quartets consist of imaginary rectangles whose opposite corners along the diagonals are materialized by dots that twinkle alternately (imagine a rectangle whose corners are Top Left, Top Right, Bottom Left, Bottom Right: TL-BR get illuminated together, then BL-TR together, and so forth; see Hock et al. 1993, 2004 for figures). Motion quartets are bistable stimuli, since one can perceive the opposite points either as moving vertically along the left and right edges of the rectangle, or as moving horizontally along the top and bottom edges. Which of these two percepts is seen first depends in large part on objective cues, namely on the ratio of the vertical path length to the horizontal path length of the rectangle (also called the *aspect ratio*). When the aspect ratio is near 1 to 1.25, namely when the rectangle is a square, both percepts appear equally likely to be first perceived (see Hock et al. 1993: 66). When the ratio is less than 1, the vertical path motion is more likely, and conversely for the horizontal path motion. Thus the motion perceived appears to depend on a "shortest path" principle. In series of trials in which the aspect ratio gradually increases from 0.5 to 2.0, or gradually decreases from 2.0 to 0.5, hysteresis effects are observed. This indicates, once again, that confronted with an ambiguous stimulus, subjects categorize not directly as a function of the aspect ratio statically presented, but also as a function of their previous choices and of the dynamics of the presentation of the stimuli.

It would be well beyond the scope of this paper to investigate the nature and origin of hysteresis effects in general (see Kelso 1995 and Raffman 2009 for extensive discussions). However, one relevant question posed by Hock and colleagues for our own inquiry is whether hysteresis effects can be considered properly perceptual, or whether they are rather "judgmental", namely to be imputed to a higher level of representation such as a judgment bias in the presence of uncertainty. The conclusion they reach in the case of motion quartets is that, because subjects are never uncertain of what they see in motion quartets (they clearly see either horizontal motion or vertical motion, exclusively), hysteresis can be said to be properly perceptual, rather than grounded in a judgmental bias (see Hock et al. 1993, p.70).

The situation may be different in the presence of borderline cases of an arbitrary sorites series, however. When confronted with a series of colors, for example, each individual color presents a particular quale. Borderline cases are characterized by the fact that they give rise to a form of judgmental uncertainty, so that classifying some of these qualia is more difficult than classifying others. Hysteresis effects may therefore reflect only a judgmental or response bias in those cases, rather than be the expression of a perceptual dynamics. If so, this may contradict the second hypothesis we put forward above, which is that in the case of standard sorites series, hysteresis would not simply be the persistence of the recent history of a category for uncertain cases across some unknown boundary, but rather the expression of a competition or rivalry between overlapping categories. In the rest of this paper, however, I shall attempt to make a case for the latter hypothesis, namely for the view that for soritical series in general, hysteresis effects arise from more than simply ignorance of a sharp boundary. To do this, I turn to a closer examination of series of ambiguous stimuli of the kind originally designed by G. Fisher.

3 FISHER SERIES

The stimuli to be discussed in this section were originally designed by G. Fisher in order to measure perceptual ambiguity. Fisher wanted to question the assumption that in a two-way ambiguous figure, such as the Necker cube, or Jastrow's duck-rabbit, the two percepts are always equally likely to be perceived. In order to challenge this view, Fisher designed several sets of ambiguous figures in which individual features are altered so as to gradually favor one percept over the other. He then asked individual subjects to report which percept they first saw when presented with a given figure.

3.1 Fisher's "Gypsy and Girl"

For instance, Fisher's "Gypsy and Girl" set of cards comprises 15 cards, each of which represents an alteration of the same ambiguous figure, which can be seen either as representing a Man's profile (percept A, "the Gypsy") or as representing a Girl holding a mirror (percept B, "the Girl") (see Fisher 1967, Figure 1, here reproduced in the Appendix). The cards are designed in such a way that card 1 strongly favors the perception of a man's face, while card 15 strongly favors the perception of a woman's figure. As in a sorites series, adjacent cards in the series are hard to discriminate when considered pairwise, and the difference between adjacent pairs is made to be "approximately the same" (see Fisher 1967: 542); but each card $n+1$ is designed to make percept B slightly more salient than percept A relative to card n.

Indeed, what Fisher found is that the central figures in his series (Figure 7 in the case of the "Gypsy-Girl" set) are those for which the subjects' responses come closest to the mean value of the corresponding binomial distribution for two equally probable events. For such central figures, not only is the split between subjects statistically the greatest in comparison to other figures, but it therefore comes closest to the theoretical maximum of ambiguity.[4] For the end figures in the series, on the other hand, subjects' judgments converge in a proportion of more than 80%, and the corresponding percept is reversed between the first and the last figure. Indeed, as expected, the proportion of answers reporting percept A (the Man's face) as first percept decreases monotonically from its maximum in Figures 12 until it reaches a minimum in Figure 15 (see Fisher's Table I, reproduced in the Appendix). As a consequence, each card in Fisher's set of cards appears to determine a different objective probability for any of the two percepts to be seen first, as reflected by the changing distribution of answers along the series.

---

[4] See Fisher 1967, p.545, who writes: "It may be considered justifiable to accept a figure as being ambiguous, in the sense that the appearance of each of its two alternative aspects is equally probable, if the number of responses indicating one of them to become apparent falls within the range plus or minus two standard deviations about the mean of the sampling distribution."

3.2 Connection with the sorites

An aspect we must emphasize is that Fisher presented his stimuli in random order, as is customary in categorization and discrimination experiments, precisely to minimize order effects. A second aspect that deserves emphasis is that Fisher was not concerned with the investigation of vagueness or with sorites phenomena. Fisher's focus, once again, was the phenomenon of perceptual ambiguity. Nevertheless, Fisher's study is undeniably of interest when thinking about vagueness and sorites phenomena.

The first respect in which it turns out to be relevant is the idea that perceptual ambiguity can be graded, in such a way that a figure is more or less likely to be perceived as ambiguous. In the case of lexical ambiguity, for instance, we usually consider that an ambiguous word has the same potential of conveying two distinct meanings in principle. Of course, it remains possible that the word "bank" has a most salient meaning, namely that out of the blue, it will tend to convey one of its meaning first (for instance the meaning "money bank" might come to mind more readily than "river bank"). It is reasonable to think that the relative salience of each concept relative to an ambiguous word is furthermore different from one ambiguous word to the other, as a function of uses and contexts of use. Still, a difference between ambiguous words and ambiguous figures is that it is hard to imagine how one would modify the acoustic or written form of the word "bank" so as to modulate the perceived ambiguity between its two conventional meanings. Pinkal (1995: 76), for instance, opposes lexical vagueness and lexical ambiguity on considering that a vague word usually has a continuous range of potentially distinct extensions, while an ambiguous word only has a finite and discrete range of possible meanings. Fisher's experimental design, on the other hand, suggests that a tighter connection between vagueness and ambiguity can be conceived when considering perceptual, rather than lexical ambiguity, precisely because perceptual ambiguity seems compatible with a fine-grained and even continuous modulation of the stimulus itself, in a way that simply does not happen with words.

The second main element of connection one can see between Fisher's framework and the vagueness phenomenon concerns the analogy one may establish between Fisher's stimuli, when considered in ascending or descending order, and an ordinary soritical series. At this point the ingredients of the analogy should be obvious, but they are worth repeating. As in a sorites series, a Fisher series makes a smooth transition of a given figure into a different figure, by means of small alterations. As in a sorites series, adjacent pairs in the series are hard to discriminate. More crucially, these changes are such that when focussing one's attention only on pairs of adjacent figures, the same percept seems to come to mind, whichever it is. Finally, the first figure and the last figure in the series appear sufficiently distinct when considered pairwise, in such a way that the first figure and the last figure elicit quite distinct percepts.

3.3 Limits of the analogy

One should carefully qualify the scope of the analogy we are drawing. One element of disanalogy is that in a paradigmatic soritical series, such as a series of homogeneous color shades gradually altered, for instance, shades are not ambiguous when seen in isolation. At any rate, they do not seem to be ambiguous in exactly the way Fisher's figures are. Individually and in normal lightning conditions, a homogeneous color shade gives rise to only one percept, whatever its quality. If ever there is ambiguity in a series of such color shades gradually altered, this ambiguity seems to be contextual rather than internal to the stimulus, and to be constrained primarily by the similarity *relation* of a given shade to the surrounding shades.

This does not necessarily mean that the color's ambiguity is not perceptual in this case, and that it should be purely "judgmental". For instance, the same red-orange shade can appear more red than orange when seen next to only redder shades, and more orange than red when seen next to shades that are all more orange.[5] By talking of contextual ambiguity, however, what I have in mind is that a color shade seen in isolation does not appear to pattern as a bistable stimulus. Even if the color would be described as "orange-reddish" when seen in isolation, there is reason to doubt that what that means is that the same color would be perceived alternatively as red and then as orange while the subject keeps her attention fixed at the stimulus. Nevertheless, depending on the context, the same orange-red shade can be perceived as slightly more red than orange, or as slightly

---

[5] In many cases, context will enhance contrast rather than similarity between colors. The case of assimilation I have in mind is one in which a set of 13 shades gradually going from clear red (#1) to clear orange (#13) is presented in two sub-series ending in the same intermediate shade (#7). In one occasion, only shades 1-7 are simultaneously presented from left to right; in the next, shades 13-7 are simultaneously presented in place of 1-7. While both series end in the same rightmost shade #7, the quality of that shade appears to change from one environment to the next: in my experience the shade tends to appear rather red in the first series, and rather orange in the second.

more orange than red (we return to this point below). But prima facie an orange-reddish color is more accurately characterized as a fusion of red and orange, or as intermediate between a clearly red shade and a clearly orange shade, rather than as something that flickers alternatively between a clear orange and a clear red.

A second element of disanalogy between Fisher's series and a standard sorites series is that, as we said earlier, the ends of a sorites series are supposed to clearly and unambiguously instantiate categories that are distinct and exclusive. In the case of Fisher's series, on the other hand, each card in the series is such that both percepts remain available in principle, even for the end cards. Thus, in Fisher's experiment, 7 subjects out of 200 still report a Man's face as first percept seen on card 15, and 29 out 200 first see a Woman on card 1. The same phenomenon would most likely be evidenced if Fisher had made repeated trials within subjects. For instance, individual inspection of Fisher's stimuli is enough to see that both percepts remain available in principle. When I look at Fisher's Figure 1, which more readily presents a Man's face to me, I can nevertheless strain my attention to see an imperfectly drawn Girl holding a mirror. When looking at Figure 15, I can likewise still see the contours of an imperfectly drawn face. Some of the cues, in particular, remained constant from Figure 1 to Figure 15 (such as the shadow under the Girl's arm on Figure 15, or the left contour of the Man's nose in Figure 1). The invariance of these cues, combined with the memory of the most salient percept, appears to be sufficient to make the percept available in principle.

3.4 Discussion

The two elements of disanalogy we emphasized between Fisher's series and an ordered series of color shades do not necessarily compromise the project of building a tighter analogy between Fisher's series and sorites series. Both elements of disanalogy concern the notion of ambiguity. Thus we saw (i) that in a Fisher series, individual stimuli can be perceived ambiguously to various degrees, and (ii) that the end stimuli in the series too have this property.

Regarding (ii), however, we may easily imagine to extend Fisher's set of stimuli on both ends in a way that would make the probability of perceiving a Man's face higher than what it is for the first card and even close to 1, and similarly for the probability of perceiving a Girl's figure on the last card. In other words, in principle we can imagine to extend Fisher's series so as to reach stimuli that are unambiguously perceived, or very unlikely to be perceived ambiguously. Seen in this light, feature (ii) of Fisher's series may therefore strengthen rather than weaken the analogy we are seeking. Thus, if the penumbral area of a sorites series can be characterized as the area in which a subject is likely to categorize one and the same stimulus in two opposite ways, though possibly to different degrees, then what we are saying is that an analogy can be established between a series of ambiguous figures like Fisher's and the penumbral area of a more extended sorites series.

Objection (i), on the other hand, is directly relevant to assess the validity of Raffman's 1994 suggestion that within soritical series, borderline cases might pattern as bistable stimuli. Let us consider Fisher's series again. There, each figure in the series can be seen either as a Man's face or as a Girl holding a mirror, alternatively. Raffman's claim is that in the case of a series of color shades, the shades that are borderline can be seen as red or as orange in a similar fashion.[6] The content of objection (i) is that when looking at a particular shade in isolation, we do not have the impression that two percepts overlap. There is a single percept, even though this percept can be referred to two distinct categories, "red" or "orange".

I think this objection is correct, but I surmise that it does not undercut Raffman's point, it only forces us to make it more precise. For one thing it could be that although the percept is relatively stable upon a single occasion, the underlying stimulus might elicit distinct percepts and therefore distinct judgments upon sufficiently distant occasions.[7] Besides, we acknowledge that a distinction must be made between a stimulus being ambiguous when seen in isolation, and a stimulus being ambiguous due to contextual effects. Once that distinction is made, however, it remains that contextual ambiguity can be properly perceptual. Again the same red-orange color shade, seen next to only redder ones, will look congruent and sufficiently so to be seen as red. When seen next to only more orange shades, it will look congruent too and sufficiently so to be seen as orange. The hypothesis I am making is that this "seeing as" is indeed a matter of perception, and not merely of the decision to categorize one way rather

---

[6] Raffman subsequently rejected this view of borderline cases, and now considers borderline cases as instantiating neither of the other categories, rather than both (Raffman, p.c.).

[7] As suggested to me by J.-L. Schwartz, one would need to check, then, whether the categorization dynamics would or not pattern like the perceptual dynamics of bistability evidenced for more rapidly alternating stimuli (see Pressnitzer and Hupé 2006).

than the other. Hence, although the rivalry between categories may not be directly present in the stimulus in this case (because "orange-reddish" here designates a shade of its own), the assumption I am making is that in a series of shades that go from clear red to clear orange, each shade has a different potential of being classified as red or as orange because ultimately it has a different potential of being seen as congruent to either of the two end colors.

Incidentally, one may wish to reflect more thoroughly on the very status of semantic categories such as "orange-reddish", "blue-greenish", and others of this kind. If indeed we can make sense of such categories, this also suggests that some such colors bear cues that are simultaneously congruent with more "pure" instances of categories like "red" or "orange". The consideration of Fisher's stimuli is interesting in this particular respect. When looking at Figure 1 in Fisher's series, I almost inevitably see a Man's profile. When looking at Fisher's Figure 15, I likewise see first and foremost a Girl holding an object. When looking at Figure 7, I feel that I am switching between either of these two interpretations. Now, if I look at 1 and then at 7, I will indeed tend to see clearly a Man's profile in 7. If I go the other way, I will tend to see clearly a Girl's face in 7. Still, I am aware that Figure 7 is different from both Figure 1 and Figure 15. While entirely self-administered, this small experiment seems to exemplify both the kind of hysteresis phenomenon we discussed in section 1, but also the potential for Gestalt switch that Raffman talks about.

Now, my own impression is that the same is true to a significant extent of color shades. If I happen to consider a fine-grained series of 13 color shades that go from a specific quality of red to a specific quality of orange by similarly small shifts, which seem to make no difference for pairwise adjacent pairs: when I look at shade 1 first, and then at shade 7, I perceive a form of "color echo" in 7, and then a different color echo when I then look at shade 13 and then at shade 7. In that particular case, shade 7 may be described as "orange-reddish", and indeed, despite the fact that it is homogeneous, it bears a resemblance to the other two shades. Of course, when I look at 7, I can discriminate it from either of shade 1 or 13. But in fact the same is true of Figure 7 in Fisher's series, which I can discriminate from Figure 1 and 15 respectively, and which is such that I could learn to memorize it distinctively.

The upshot of these considerations, therefore, is that neither of the disanalogies we pointed out seems to run against the project of using Fisher's series as a template for the analysis of soritical series more generally. Of course, there are as many sorites series as there are varieties of stimuli to start from, and as we saw, colors and structured figures are different kinds of objects with different psychophysical properties. The purpose of the next section, however, will be to draw general consequences about the nature of sorites series, based on the idea that the analogy with Fisher series is sufficiently safe.

4 CUT-OFFS AND TOLERANCE IN SORITICAL SERIES

The aim of this section is to cast light on the nature of sorites series, reflecting on features that we find in play in Fisher's particular series. On the one hand, we propose to raise and discuss an objection to what appears as a consequence of the epistemic solution to the sorites paradox. On the other, we shall argue that the paradox-inducing principle at the heart of the sorites cannot be literally correct. Both objections, ultimately, are grounded in the consideration of the phenomenology of Fisher's series.

4.1 Epistemicism

As is well-known, the sorites paradox results from the assumption of a particular premise, commonly referred to as the *tolerance principle* (see Wright 1976), which states that if an arbitrary individual n in the series instantiates property A, and if $n+1$ is indiscriminable from n, then n *ought to* instantiate property A as well. I here put emphasis on "ought to" because the normative aspect conveyed by this expression is usually not reflected in the way the premise is formalized, no more than the intended meaning to be given to "ought" (should it mean "must", "is likely"?). Indeed, usually this principle is formalized as a standard induction principle, of the form $\forall n(A(n) \rightarrow A(n+1))$. A more abstract version of the principle is $\forall xy(A(x) \land R(x, y) \rightarrow A(y))$, where R is a relational predicate intended to express a specific similarity relation (such as indiscriminability), but here too the normative component is left implicit.

Let us temporarily set aside the normative intent of the tolerance principle and focus on its standard form, namely $\forall n(A(n) \rightarrow A(n+1))$. As is well-known, a contradiction results from the tolerance principle if it is assumed that $A(m)$ and $\neg A(n)$ hold for some n and m with n greater than m. One way to envisage the strength of the paradox is to present it in the form of a dilemma. One horn of the dilemma is that the tolerance principle seems entirely plausible: two objects that differ imperceptibly are such that if one is categorized one way, the other should be too. Yet we see that accepting the principle leads to contradiction. The other horn of the dilemma is that if we reject the tolerance principle, and keep our reasoning classical, then we should endorse its negation, namely $\exists n(A(n) \wedge \neg A(n+1))$. In that case, we must endorse the view that there is a sharp cut-off in the series, a demarcation between the last object n to which A applies and the first object m to which A does not. But the problem is that, in general, we do not see such an n and find it very hard to imagine that there is such a demarcation.

Faced with the dilemma, epistemicists like Sorensen and Williamson go for the second horn (see Williamson 1994, Sorensen 2001). On the epistemic view of sorites series, there is such a sharp cut-off point, but we are simply ignorant as to its precise location. The epistemic solution suggests that if classical logic is to be preserved, then it is more sensible to revise and explain away our intuition that the tolerance principle is plausible and true, rather than to end in contradiction. Of course, several other ways out of the paradox are conceivable if one is ready to forsake classical logic. For now, however, let us restrict our attention to the epistemicist view and to what it commits us to.

4.2 Variations in the boundary

The epistemic conception of vagueness has been criticized on the ground that it severs the ontology of vagueness and the psychology of vagueness in a manner that appears too drastic (see Wright 1994, Schiffer 1999, Shapiro 2006). I sympathize with this line of criticism, but my opinion is that to make it compelling, it is necessary to articulate the tolerance principle and its negation in a way that makes its normative dimension explicit. So let us consider a sorites series of colors ranging from a clear red to a clear orange, where A is a unary predicate for "red" (we use *Red* where it is clearer). Let us assume it holds that $\exists n(A(n) \wedge \neg A(n+1))$. If so, this conclusion seems to entail that as a matter of fact, there is a shade n such that n *ought to* be judged red, and such that the consecutive shade $n+1$ ought to be judged not red. A weaker normative requirement might be that there is a shade n such that n ought to be judged red while shade $n+1$ ought *not* to be judged red. In what follows I shall focus on the former and stronger requirement, however, mostly for the sake of simplification. For the main part, however, our argument could directly be adapted to a discussion of the weaker requirement by appropriate adjustments (see fn.12).

The sense of *ought* I have in mind here means that subjects *rationally* ought to issue particular judgments. The formulation I used remains syntactically ambiguous, however. To sort it out, let us introduce an epistemic operator $\Box_s$ to mean "*s* judges that", and a deontic operator O to mean "it ought to be the case that". One possible normative understanding of the negation of the tolerance principle is the following:

$$(1)\ \forall s O \exists n \Box_s (A(n) \wedge \neg A(n+1))$$

This principle says that for every subject, there ought to be a shade n such that s judges that $A(n)$ and $\neg A(n+1)$. This principle is not implausible, for if we think of situations of forced march where subjects have to judge shades consecutively, the principle can be taken to mean that every subject that would judge $A(0)$ and $\neg A(k)$ logically ought to switch category at some point between 0 and k. This principle is weaker, in particular, than the following:

$$(2)\ \forall s \exists n O \Box_s (A(n) \wedge \neg A(n+1))$$

This says that for every subject, there is a shade n such that s ought to judge that it is red and its successor is not. Yet a stronger principle, finally, is the following:

$$(3)\ \exists n \forall s O \Box_s (A(n) \wedge \neg A(n+1))$$

This says that there a shade n such that every subject ought to judge that it is red and its successor isn't. [8]

When we judge the conclusion reached by the epistemicist exorbitant, I think that what we intuitively feel reluctant to accepting is primarily a principle such as (3). For (3) entails that subjects ought to draw boundaries between the categories of "red" and "non-red" at exactly the same point. But this does not sound right. Why cannot this be right?

---

[8] See Sweeney 2008, who draws a similar distinction between a *contextual* and an *acontextual* version of the affirmation of sharp boundaries in soritical series, depending on the scope of the quantifiers. On the contextual version, for every judgment context there is a cut-off, whose location can vary with the context; on the acontextual version, there is a cut-off, the same for every context.

One argument I can offer here rests on the consideration of Fisher's series. One characteristic of Fisher's series is that every figure is such that it can be perceived as a Man's face or as a Girl's face. Even if the likelihood or objective probability of that happening varies from one stimulus to the next, we saw that even the end figures in the series make room for this variation. Indeed, ambiguous figures are such that they can be conceptualized in opposite and mutually exclusive ways. As a result, all cards in Fisher's series are legitimate candidates for category shift. But at the same time, no card mandates a particular shift.

This fact suggests that even within a given subject, a weaker principle such as (2) remains too strong in the case of Fisher's series. Indeed, if we consider the 15 figures of Fisher's series, because all figures are such that they sustain either of the two percepts to some degree, no single figure seems to be such that a given subject ought to judge that it is A rather than not A, but also no figure is such that one ought not to judge it A or to judge it not A.

Interestingly, the particular configuration of Fisher's stimuli backs up a more general characterization of borderline cases that Wright puts forward in his defense of the permissibility of opposite verdicts for borderline cases (see Wright 1994: 139, Wright forthcoming, and Shapiro 2006). For Wright, borderline cases are cases for which competent speakers can judge in opposite ways. One reason to think so, on Wright's proposal, rests on the view that borderline cases are cases for which it has not yet been determined whether they are A or not A. I think Wright's characterization of borderline cases is entirely convincing. On the present account, however, the reason verdicts can go either way for borderline cases is grounded in the consideration that the stimulus itself sustains both interpretations even within a single subject, and already at the perceptual level.[9] This, in fact, is a far-reaching property of ambiguous figures and bistable stimuli: by definition, the categorization of such stimuli is response-dependent. There is no fact intrinsic to the stimulus that dictates that one interpretation should be absolutely preferred to the other.

On the epistemic conception of vagueness, on the other hand, if our discriminative capacities were more fine-grained than they actually are, then we would be able to locate an objective boundary between A and not A within a soritical series. In the specific case of a series of stimuli such as

---

[9] On a related view, see Schiffer 2009, who writes: "borderline applications aren't merely ones that fall between two stools; they are ones that bounce around between them because of the resemblance-based attraction each stool exerts".

Fisher's, such a view cannot be correct. For we should expect that even a subject with perfect discriminative capacities is likely to experience a phenomenon of Gestalt switch when confronted with any of the figures in the series. If indeed Fisher's series can be seen as revealing of the structure of sorites series more generally, this would suggest that the vagueness of the boundary in a soritical series is not wholly reducible to a phenomenon of imperfect *discrimination* (see Williamson 1994, to whom such a view might be imputed), but it is a phenomenon of ambivalence and shiftiness in *categorization* proper.

4.3 Discussion

As we pointed out earlier, however, Fisher's series may be highly specific in comparison to other soritical series. As a result several objections can be raised against our point. To articulate them, it may be worth repeating our argument in the following form:

1. In a Fisher series, category-shifting is permissible at every point in the series, and no figure mandates a particular shift.
2. One can establish a structural analogy between a Fisher series and the penumbral area of an arbitrary soritical series.
3. Therefore, in an arbitrary soritical series, category-shifting is permissible at every point in the penumbral area of the series, and no figure there mandates a particular shift.

In response to this, the epistemicist may object to premise 2. Or he may accept premise 2, but argue from the denial of 3 to the denial of 1, making use of the very same analogy. He may also grant the conclusion 3, finally, but argue that it leaves epistemicism unscathed.

In what follows I shall focus only on the first objection. The second objection is basically the idea that our modus ponens can be reverted into the epistemicist's modus tollens.[10] This is fair enough, but as we will see, the objection to premise 2 already has the seeds for simultaneously weakening premise 1 and conclusion 3 of our argument. Concerning the third objection, namely the idea that epistemicist can accept the argument but deny its impact, one way to articulate it is to say that even if boundaries between *perceptual* categories are indeed variable within and across sub-

---

[10] R. Cook and M. Werning both formulated this objection during a presentation of this paper at Kirchberg.

jects, boundaries between *linguistic* categories are determined by a complex process of aggregation of individual judgments, for which stronger normative principles such as (2) or (3) remain valid anyway. A discussion of this point would take us too far afield, however, and here too we will see that already from our discussion of premise 2 a point in favor of some mild form of epistemicism is conceivable.

So let us consider premise 2. First, one may object that the analogy we are suggesting is vacuous. Indeed, if really Fisher's stimuli are ambiguous all along, then one can argue that for such stimuli, the induction premise $\forall n(Man(n) \rightarrow Man(n+1))$ simply holds without exceptions, and likewise the induction premise $\forall n(Girl(n) \rightarrow Girl(n+1))$. More generally, the series supports $\forall n(Man(n) \wedge Girl(n))$, namely every figure represents both a Man and a Girl (irrespective of the degree to which they do so). Granted, because of the exclusiveness of the percepts, the series also supports $\forall n(\Box_s Man(n) \rightarrow \neg \Box_s Girl(n))$, and conversely, namely if I categorize shade n as representing a Man, then I do not categorize it as representing a Girl. But this shows nothing, our opponent should pursue, for in the case of a standard soritical series in which one starts from a non-ambiguous figure, for instance a clear red shade, until one reaches a clear non-red shade, then it is simply false that $\forall n(Red(n) \rightarrow Red(n+1))$, and assuming the logic to be classical it is also false that $\forall n(Red(n) \wedge \neg Red(n))$.

Another way to put the objection is that if indeed we could extend Fisher's series to the left and to the right, so that it starts out with a figure that has objective probability 1 of being perceived as a Girl's face, and finishes with a figure that has objective probability 1 of being perceived as a Man's face (and probability 0 of being perceived as a Girl), then the series would no longer support $\forall n(Man(n) \wedge Girl(n))$, and it would not support, in particular $\forall n(Girl(n) \rightarrow Girl(n+1))$. At any rate there ought to be a last non-ambiguous shade k such that $Girl(k) \wedge \neg Man(k)$, and a first ambiguous shade $k+1$ such that $Girl(k+1) \wedge Man(k+1)$.

The force of this objection is undeniable. What the objection urges us to acknowledge is that to the extent that one can establish a structural analogy between a Fisher series and the penumbral area of a soritical series, what this analogy shows is only, at best, that the penumbral area of a standard soritical series can be seen as one where contrary categories overlap and pattern ambiguously. But the analogy leaves open the possibility that there remains a sharp and objective cut-off between the last non-ambiguous stimulus and the first ambiguous one. For instance, there may be a range of shades in a color series from clear red to clear orange that are ambiguously red and orange. But on this account there must be a last non-ambiguously red shade.

Let us assume that there is such an objective and yet imperceptible demarcation. I think even so, the analogy we are drawing casts light on the nature of soritical series. Indeed, even if there is a sharp cut-off between the last non-ambiguous stimulus and the first ambiguous one, and we do not know where it is, it remains that the first ambiguous stimulus is one for which it will remain permissible to judge that it is A and permissible to judge that it is not A.

To justify this view, let us picture a soritical series of 8 color shades ranging from a clear red to a clear orange. Drawing inspiration from Fisher's series, we may suppose that each shade in the series comes with a different *potential* of being perceived as red or as orange. This potential should be seen as the extent to which the stimulus constrains perception and categorization (as reflected for instance in Fisher's survey, see Appendix, Table I). Mathematically, potentials can be described by means of prior probabilities $p(A(x))$ and $p(O(x))$ of perceiving shade x as red or as orange. In keeping with the idea of bistability, we make the assumption that each percept inhibits the other, so that $p(O(x)) = p(\neg A(x)) = 1-p(A(x))$. On the following figure, we are assuming that the first two shades have the same potential and can only be seen as red, while the last two have the same potential and can only be seen as orange. Each intermediate shade n is assumed to be such that its potential of being seen as red lies strictly between 0 and 1, and is less than for the previous shade.[11]

x	1	2	3	4	5	6	7	8
$p(A(x))$	1	1	α_3	α_4	α_5	α_6	0	0
$p(O(x))$	0	0	$1-\alpha_3$	$1-\alpha_4$	$1-\alpha_5$	$1-\alpha_6$	1	1

While shades come with different potentials of being categorized as red or orange, we are making the assumption that A and O are *true* of a shade whenever this potential is non-zero, and *false* whenever this potential is 0. Under this assumption, the series can be pictured by means of the following classical model, on which the O and A categories overlap, except for end shades (the two vertical bars delineate between ambiguous and unam-

---

[11] See Hampton 2007, MacFarlane 2008 and Lassiter 2009 for further discussions of probabilistic aspects of vagueness and categorization. See Lassiter 2009, in particular, for the idea that all vague predicates should be treated probabilistically.

biguous shades). The model now satisfies $\exists n(A(n) \wedge \neg A(n+1))$, since by assumption there is a first non-ambiguously orange shade:

A	A	A	A	A	A	$\neg A$	$\neg A$
$\neg O$	$\neg O$	O	O	O	O	O	O

Our main assumption, finally, is that a subject *ought to judge* $A(n)$ if and only if $p(A(n)) = 1$, and ought to judge $\neg A(n)$ if and only if $p(A(n)) = 0$. In other words, only shades that are non-ambiguous in their potential dictate a particular judgment.[12] Under those assumptions, an ideal and rational subject ought to start out judging the first two shades are red. But when reaching the third shade, the subject can go either way. The subject can judge the shade red or judge it orange, and therefore not red. Now assume several trials are performed. In principle an ideal subject whose judgments would obey exactly the shades' potentials should remain confident about the first two shades, but from the third shade onward, the subject is likely to switch her judgment, in accordance with the various probabilities that determine the saliency of O and A.

Obviously, the assignment of relative probabilities to A and O is reminiscent of degree-theoretic treatments of vagueness. But on our account, as soon as the potential of a predicate is non-zero, the predicate applies and is true *simpliciter*, and it is false *simpliciter* exactly when the potential is zero.[13] What is interesting regarding the distinctions we made earlier about normative judgments, however, is that such a structure would support both the following normative judgments:

(4) $\exists n O \square_y A(n)$
(5) $\exists n O \square_s \neg A(n)$

That is, there are shades that s ought to judge red, and other shades that he ought to judge not red, namely those for which the corresponding potential is 1 or 0 respectively. However, the crucial fact is that $\neg \exists n O \square_s (A(n) \wedge \neg A(n+1))$, that is, no shade is such that it ought to be judged red, while its successor ought to be judged not red, because no two

---

[12] Alternatively, for the case of wide scope negation, we could stipulate that a subject ought *not* to judge $A(n)$ exactly if $p(A(n)) = 0$.

[13] I do not see potentials as degrees of truth, but rather as the degree to which a property is expressed or salient in some stimulus. Nevertheless, the present discussion may easily be transposed to the degree-theoretic framework.

consecutive shades in the series are such that $p(A(x))$ goes directly from 1 to 0.[14] As a consequence, even when a series such as Fisher's is extended on both ends in a way that restores $\exists n(A(n) \wedge \neg A(n+1))$, normative principles like (2) and (3) need not follow. This, of course, should be seen as good news for the epistemicist. For what we have established is that from $\exists n(A(n) \wedge \neg A(n+1))$ it does not follow analytically that $\exists n O\square_s(A(n) \wedge \neg A(n+1))$ (contra principle (2) above).[15]

By way of consequence, this discussion also gives us a hint as to what an explicitly normative formulation of the tolerance principle might be. Here my conclusion will be exactly consonant with that of Raffman (2009), who distinguishes the false principle whereby small increments in a sorites series are ever insufficient to make a difference in the way we categorize consecutive individuals in the series, and the correct principle whereby small increments in a sorites series are "sufficiently small as to make any differential application of Φ as between them (either incorrect) or *arbitrary*."

As we suggested earlier, the tolerance principle has both a descriptive and a normative dimension. The descriptive dimension, on our account, corresponds to the idea that if the probability for a given stimulus n to be seen as A is α, then the probability for a sufficiently similar stimulus $n+1$ to be seen as A should be sufficiently close to α.[16] On this view, if two objects are very similar, then they are very likely to be categorized alike, although they need not be. The normative dimension of the principle, on the other hand, can be articulated from the negation of principle (2), which we take to be incorrect. Principle (2) is equivalent to $\exists n(O\square_s A(n) \wedge O\square_s \neg A(n+1))$. Its negation is equivalent to:

(6) $\forall n(O\square_s A(n) \rightarrow \neg O\square_s \neg A(n+1))$

---

[14] See Lassiter 2009, who makes exactly this point about probabilistic versions of the sorites more generally. Lassiter's observation is that a natural probabilistic understanding of the tolerance principle, for a vague predicate such as *tall*, is that there is usually no n such that the probability of judging $tall(x_n)$ is 0 while that of judging $tall(x_n)$ is 1.

[15] Of course, one may insist that where the potential switches from 0 to more than 0, one *ought to* make that distinction (a form of the higher-order vagueness problem). But on my view the corresponding sense for *ought* would be much too fine-grained.

[16] That is: if $d(x, y) \leq \varepsilon$, then $|p(A(x)) - p(A(y))| \leq \delta$ (for some specified $\delta \in \,]0,1[)$, namely: whenever two stimuli x and y are sufficiently similar given a suitable metric d, the probability of judging the second A must be close enough to the probability of judging the first A. Lassiter's constraint can be seen as a particular case of this constraint.

This says that if an individual ought to be judged A, then it is not the case that an individual that differs only very slightly ought to be judged not A.[17] Under suitable assumptions (see fn.12), this principle can be strengthened to:

$$(7)\ \forall n(O\Box_x A(n) \to \neg O\neg\Box_x A(n+1))$$

which says that if an individual n ought to be judged A, then it is *permissible* to judge an individual $n+1$ that differs only very slightly as A as well. Seen in Kantian terms, the resulting idea of tolerance is now expressed as a principle about *judgment*, and no longer directly as a standard induction principle constraining the category membership of *things in themselves*.[18] Thus, while we agree that the standard soritical premise cannot hold unrestrictedly in classical logic on pain of contradiction, the present discussion suggests that a safer view of the intent of this premise should be placed at the psychological rather than the strictly logical level.

5 CONCLUSIONS

Several claims have been made in this paper. The first is the idea that by reconsidering the relation between vagueness and ambiguity at the perceptual level, further insights can be gained for our understanding of soritical series. On our account, the penumbral area of a soritical series is primarily

---

[17] This version of the tolerance principle should be compared to the version proposed by Shapiro in terms of *competent judgment* (I am indebted to L. Horsten for this remark). For Shapiro, a tolerant predicate A is such that if one competently judges $A(n)$, then one cannot competently judge $\neg A(n+1)$ whenever n and $n+1$ "differ only marginally in the relevant respect" (see Shapiro 2006:8). If we equate *competent judging* with *ought to judge*, then (6) stands as a possible paraphrase for Shapiro's version of tolerance. This is no longer the case, however, if we define a *competent judge* as someone who never judges $\neg A(n)$ when $p(A(n)) = 1$, or $A(n)$ when $p(A(n)) = 0$. When $p(A(n))$ and $p(A(n+1))$ lie strictly between 0 and 1, then given our semantics one may competently judge both $A(n)$ and $\neg A(n+1)$. Prima facie, this makes room for more tolerance than Shapiro's principle. But this is also less tolerant, since when $p(A(n)) = 0.99$ and $p(A(n+1)) = 1$, one can competently judge $\neg A(n)$ by those standards, but one cannot competently judge $\neg A(n+1)$.

[18] See Shapiro 2006, chap. 1 for more on the centrality of the notion of judgment in the treatment of vagueness, following insights from Wright and Raffman in particular.

an area of competition, ambivalence and rivalry between overlapping categories. We are prone to judging that A and to judging that not A for borderline cases because those stimuli come with cues that support distinct representations, and ultimately opposite judgments. The hypothesis that borderline cases correspond to an area of overlap, where cues toward A-judgments coexist in different proportion with cues toward $\neg A$-judgments, needs further elaboration, but it presents several explanatory virtues. First it suggests that hysteresis effects in front of soritical series do not simply reflect pure judgment biases, but originate at the perceptual level, from the potential of a stimulus to elicit contrasting representations. Secondly, it supports a probabilistic theory of judgment, where those probabilities would express these various potentials of being perceived and categorized one way or the other. Finally, it suggests that borderline cases, as argued in particular by Wright, Schiffer, Raffman and Shapiro, are indeed adequately viewed as cases for which it is permissible to draw boundaries and categorize in variable and opposite ways, thereby affording us a clearer view of the tolerance principle. In agreement with epistemicism, some ignorance remains in the picture, in particular about the structure and amplitude of these potentials. But much of the error theory that goes with epistemicism is left behind.

ACKNOWLEDGMENTS

I am indebted to V. de Gardelle, R. Gregson, D. Pressnitzer, J-L. Schwartz, and J-M. Hupé for references and for enlightening discussions on the psychology of bistability and hysteresis phenomena, which sparked this research. Special thanks go to D. Raffman, S. Bromberger, S. Schiffer, and D. Lassiter, each of whose recent work on vagueness has been a source of insights and inspiration, and whom I thank for stimulating conversations. For helpful discussion and detailed comments, I am particularly grateful to D. Raffman, P. Schlenker, M. Cozic, and S. Bromberger and R. Dietz. Further thanks go to D. Bonnay, J. Chandler, R. Cook, W. Davies, I. Douwen, J. Dokic, L. Horsten, H. Rott, J. Sackur, B. Spector, J. Watanabe, M. Werning, and audiences at the Bistability Workshop held at the ENS in Paris in July 2008, at the 2008 Wittgenstein symposium in Kirchberg, at the Philosophy and Psychology of Vagueness Workshop held in Paris in November 2008, and at the Center for Logic and Analytic Philosophy in Leuven. This research was supported by the ANR project "Cognitive Origins of Vagueness" (ANR-07-JCJC-0070-01) and the ANR project "Multistap" (ANR-08-BLAN-0167-01), which are gratefully acknowledged.

REFERENCES

S. Bromberger (2008), Vagueness, Ambiguity and the "Sound" of Meaning, manuscript, MIT.

K. Fine (1975), Vagueness, Truth and Logic, *Synthese* 30, pp.265–300.

G. Fisher (1967), Measuring Ambiguity, *The American Journal of Psychology* 80 (4), pp.541–557.

R. Gregson (2004), Transitions between two pictorial attractors, *Nonlinear Dynamics, Psychology and Life Sciences* 8 (1), pp.41–63.

J. Hampton (2007), Typicality, Graded Membership and Vagueness, *Cognitive Science* 31, pp.355–384

H.S. Hock, J.A.S. Kelso, G. Schöner (1993), Bistability and Hysteresis in the Organization of Apparent Motion Patterns, *Journal of Experimental Psychology* 19 (1), pp.63–80.

H.S. Hock, L. Bukowski, D.F. Nichols, A. Huisman and M. Rivera (2004), Dynamical vs. judgmental comparison: hysteresis effects in motion perception, *Spatial Vision*, Vol.18, No.3, pp.317–335.

Keefe R. (2000), *Theories of Vagueness*, Cambridge UP.

J.A.S. Kelso (1995), *Dynamic Patterns*, MIT Press.

D. Lassiter (2009), Vagueness, Probability and Linguistic Representation, manuscript, NYU.

D. Lindsey, A. Brown and D. Raffman (2005), Hysteresis effects in a sorites series, manuscript, quoted in Raffman (2005) and Raffman (forthcoming).

John MacFarlane (2008), Fuzzy epistemicism, in R. Dietz & S. Moruzzi (eds), *Cuts and Clouds: Vagueness, Its Nature and Its Logic,* Oxford University Press.

M. Pinkal (1995), *Logic and Lexicon*, Kluwer.

D. Pressnitzer, J-M. Hupé (2006), Temporal dynamics of auditory and visual bistability reveal common principles of perceptual organization. *Current Biology* 16, pp.1351–1357.

D. Raffman (1994), Vagueness without Paradox, *The Philosophical Review* 103 (1), pp.41–74.

D. Raffman (2005), How to understand contextualism about vagueness, *Analysis* 65 (3), pp.244–248.

D. Raffman (2009), Tolerance and the Competent Use of Vague Words, chapter 5 in D. Raffman, *Unruly Words: A Study of Vague Language*, book in preparation.

M. Sainsbury (1990), Concepts witout Boundaries, repr. in R. Keefe and P. Smith, *Vagueness: a Reader*, MIT Press.

S. Schiffer (1999), The Epistemic Theory of Vagueness, *Noûs*, Vol.33, *Supplement: Philosophical Perspectives*, 13, *Epistemology*, pp.481–503.

S. Schiffer (2009), Vague Properties, forthcoming in R. Dietz and S. Moruzzi (eds.), *Cuts and Clouds: Vagueness, Its Nature and Its Logic*, Oxford University Press.

S. Shapiro (2006), *Vagueness in Context*, Oxford University Press.

R. Sorensen (2001), Vagueness and Contradiction, Oxford University Press.

P. Sweeney (2008), Contextual Intolerance, manuscript, University of St Andrews.

T. Williamson (1994), *Vagueness*, Routledge.

C. Wright (1976), Language-Mastery and the Sorites Paradox, in *Truth and Meaning*, G. Evans and J. McDowell eds, Oxford UP.

C. Wright (1994), The Epistemic Conception of Vagueness, in *Vagueness*, Spindel Conference 1994, T. Horgan ed., vol. XXXIII, *Supplement of the Southern Journal of Philosophy*.

C. Wright (forthcoming), On the Characterization of Borderline Cases, in *Meanings and Other Things: Essays on Stephen Schiffer*, edited by Gary Ostertag (MIT press).

APPENDIX

A. Fisher's "Gypsy and Girl" set of stimuli (from Fisher 1967: p.542, smaller reproduction)

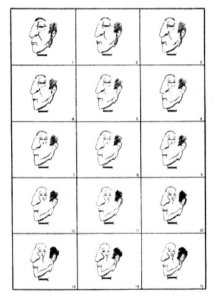

FIG. 1. THE 'GYPSY AND GIRL' SET OF AMBIGUOUS FIGURES

B. Fisher's results

Fisher's subjects were shown figures separately on a screen and asked to indicate the first aspect they saw on a piece of paper, "by writing an appropriate descriptive word, or phrase" (the descriptions "Gipsy" and "Girl" are from Fisher, who notes that subjects distinguished two percepts but varied in their descriptions, see p.544, fn.14). The following data, reproduced from Fisher's table I, report the number of responses (for 200 subjects) indicating the "Gypsy" as first aspect seen.

Figure	1	2	3	4	5	6	7	8	9	10	11	12	13	14	15
Responses	171	178	171	163	144	132	103	79	68	53	43	18	11	10	7

THE ELIMINATION OF MEANING IN COMPUTATIONAL THEORIES OF MIND

PAUL SCHWEIZER
University of Edinburgh

Abstract

According to the traditional conception of the mind, semantical content is perhaps the most important feature distinguishing mental from non-mental systems. And this traditional conception has been incorporated into the foundations of contemporary scientific approaches to the mind, insofar as the notion of 'mental representation' is adopted as a primary theoretical device. Symbolic representations are posited as the internal structures that carry the information utilized by intelligent systems, and they also comprise the formal elements over which cognitive computations are performed. But a fundamental tension is built into the picture – to the extent that symbolic 'representations' are formal elements of computation, their alleged content is completely gratuitous. I argue that the computational paradigm is thematically inconsistent with the search for content or its supposed 'vehicles'. Instead, the concern of computational models of cognition should be with the *processing structures* that yield the right kinds of input/output profiles, and with how these structures can be implemented in the brain.

1 THE COMPUTATIONAL PARADIGM

According to the traditional conception of the mind, semantical content is perhaps the most important feature distinguishing mental from non-mental systems. For example, in the scholastic tradition revived by Brentano (1874), the *essential* feature of mental states is their 'aboutness' or intrinsic representational aspect. And this traditional conception has been incorporated into the foundations of contemporary scientific approaches to the mind, insofar as the notion of 'mental representation' is adopted as a primary theoretical device. For example, in classical (e.g. Fodorian) cognitive science, Brentano's legacy is preserved in the view that the properly cognitive level is distinguished precisely by appeal to representational content. There are many different levels of description and explanation in the natural world, from quarks all the way to quasars, and according to Fodor, it is only when the states of a system are treated as representational that we are dealing with the genuinely cognitive level.

The classical paradigm in cognitive science derives from Turing's basic model of computation as rule governed transformations on a set of syntactical elements, and it has taken perhaps its most literal form of expression in terms of Fodor's Language of Thought hypothesis (Fodor 1975, 2008) (henceforward LOT), wherein mental processes are explicitly viewed as formal operations on a linguistically structured system of internal symbols. So in the present discussion I will use the LOT as a very clear exemplar of the classical approach, although the basic points generalize far beyond Fodor. According to the LOT, propositional attitude states, such as belief and desire, are treated as computational relations to sentences in an internal processing language, and where the LOT sentence serves to represent or encode the propositional content of the intentional state. Symbolic representations are thus posited as the internal structures that carry the information utilized by intelligent systems, and they also comprise the formal elements over which cognitive computations are performed. According to the traditional and widely accepted belief-desire framework of psychological explanation, an agent's actions are both *caused* and explained by intentional states such as belief and desire. And on the LOT model, these states are sustained via sentences in the head that are formally manipulated by the cognitive processes which lead to actions.

Fodor notes that particular tokens of these LOT sentences could well turn out to be specific neuronal configurations or brain states. The formal syntax of LOT thus plays a crucial triad of roles: it can represent meaning, it's the medium of cognitive computation, and it can be physically realized. So the syntax of LOT can in principle supply a link between the high level intentional description of a cognitive agent, and the actual neuronal process that enjoy causal power. This triad of roles allows content bearing states, such as propositional attitudes, to explain salient pieces of behavior, such as bodily motions, if the intermediary syntax is seen as realized in neurophysiological configurations of the brain. Because the tokens of LOT are semantically interpretable and physically realizable, they form a key theoretical bridge between content and causation. In this manner, a very elegant (possible) answer is supplied to the longstanding theoretical question of how mental states individuated in terms of their content, such as beliefs and desires, could be viewed as causes of actual behaviour, without violating fundamental conservation laws in physics.

So at first sight, this computational approach to cognition might seem to provide a compelling and harmonious theory of the mind/brain, potentially uniting the traditional notion of mental representation with the causally efficacious level of neural machinery. But alas, a fundamental tension is already built into the picture: a central purpose of the symbolic structures is to carry content, and yet, to the extent that they are formal elements of computation, their alleged content is completely gratuitous. Computation is essentially a series of manipulations performed on *uninterpreted* syntax, and formal structure alone is sufficient for all effective procedures. The specification and operation of such procedures makes no reference whatever to the intended meaning of the symbols involved. Indeed, it is precisely this limitation to syntactic *form* that has enabled computation to emerge as a mathematically rigorous discipline. If syntax alone is not sufficient, and additional understanding or interpretation is required, then the procedure in question is, by definition, *not* an effective one. But then the purported content of mental 'representations' is rendered superfluous to the computations that comprise the 'cognitive' processes of cognitive science. The intended interpretation of internal syntax makes absolutely no difference to the formal mechanics of mind.

2 THE CONNECTIONIST ALTERNATIVE

For a number of years now there has been a high profile struggle between opposing camps within the computational approach to the mind. In contrast to the classical paradigm derived from Turing, connectionist systems are based on networks of large numbers of simple but highly interconnected units that are brain-like in their inspiration. But according to Fodor (and Pylyshyn 1988), the brain-like architecture of connectionist networks tells us nothing about their suitability as models of *cognitive* processing, since it still leaves open the question of whether the mind is such a network at the *representational* level. He concedes that the connectionist approach may be the right type of architecture for the medium of implementation, which would mean that it characterizes a level below that of genuine mental structure. In view of the foregoing tension within the classical paradigm concerning formal syntax and the inefficacy of content, I would argue that Fodor is on the wrong track when he insists that, within a computational approach, the representational level is fundamental. Instead, I would argue that the internal processing structures yielding the salient input/output profiles are all that matter, whether or not these are thought of as content bearing. However, a number of connectionists have taken up Fodor's challenge and seek out ways of projecting representational content onto artificial neural networks.

One comparatively recent such attempt (Churchland 1988, Laakso, A. and G. Cottrell 2000, O'Brien, G. and J. Opie 2001) uses cluster analysis to locate 'vehicles' of representational content within artificial neural networks, where such clusters serve as surrogates for the classical notion of internal syntax. Along with serious difficulties in equating clusters with the syntax of traditional computation, I would contend that such attempts suffer from exactly the same built-in tension that afflicts the LOT model; namely, the purported content for which the clusters serve as vehicles does no work in the processing path leading from inputs to outputs. Just as in the classical case, the postulation of content within the connectionist framework is gratuitous, because it plays no role in the cognitive manipulation of inputs to yield the salient outputs. Indeed, if content weren't gratuitous, then computational versions of cognitive processing would be lamentably deficient in terms of their specification of the inputs. These are characterized solely in formal or syntactical terms, and content is entirely absent from the external stimuli recognized by the operations that can be defined within the model. If representational content were at all relevant, then cognitive systems would have to process content *itself*. But according to computational methods, content is not specified with the input, nor does it play any efficacious role in internal processing. So, from a perspective that takes computation as the theoretical foundation for cognition, it seems quite retrograde to posit content on top of the factors that do the actual work. Surely this is an ideal occasion for employing Ockham's razor.

3 THE CHINESE ROOM ARGUMENT

Of course, John Searle's (1980) celebrated Chinese Room Argument (henceforward CRA) runs the dialectic in exactly the reverse direction: rather than taking the formal, syntactic nature of computation as a reason for eschewing content in a properly naturalistic approach to the mind, Searle instead takes it as a reason for rejecting computation as the appropriate theory of the mental.

So, from the perspective of the present discussion, it is instructive to explicitly cast Searle's argument in terms of the separability of syntactical structure from its intended meaning. In what follows I will abstract away from the somewhat picturesque details of Searle's original version and express the logical core of the CRA via two premises and a conclusion:

(1) semantical content is an essential feature of the mind,
(2) syntactical manipulations cannot capture this content, therefore
(3) the mind cannot be reduced to a system of syntactical manipulations.

Premise (1) is an expression of the traditional conception of mentality, and is accepted by both Searle and by his opponents in orthodox cognitive science and AI. As stated above, classical cognitive science and AI view the mind according to the model of rule governed symbol manipulation, and premise (1) is embraced insofar as the manipulated symbols are supposed to possess representational content. Searle's dispute with cognitive science and AI centers on his rejection of the idea that internal computation can shed any real light on mental content, which leads to his conclusion (3), and to a concomitant dismissal of the research paradigm central to cognitive science and AI.

In response, a standard line for defenders of the paradigm is to try and defuse the CRA by arguing against premise (2), and claiming that the manipulated symbols really do possess some canonical meaning or privileged interpretation. However, I would urge that this is a strategic error for those who wish to defend the computational approach. As stated above, a distinguishing mathematical virtue of computational systems is precisely the fact that the formal calculus can be executed without any appeal to meaning. Not only is an interpretation intrinsically unnecessary to the operation of computational procedures, but furthermore, there is no unique interpretation determined by the computational syntax, and in general there are arbitrarily many distinct models for any given formal system.

Many classical *negative* results in mathematical logic stem from this separability between formal syntax and meaning. The various upward and downward Löwenheim-Skolem theorems show that formal systems cannot capture intended meaning with respect to infinite cardinalities. As another eminent example, Gödel's incompleteness theorems involve taking a formal system designed to be 'about' the natural numbers, and systematically reinterpreting it in terms of its own syntax and proof structure. As a consequence of this 'unintended' interpretation, Gödel is able to prove that arithmetical truth, an exemplary *semantical* notion, cannot, in principle, be captured by finitary proof-theoretic means.

Computational formalisms are syntactically closed systems, and in this regard it is fitting to view them in narrow or solipsistic terms. They are, by their very nature, independent of the 'external world' of their intended meaning and, as mentioned above, they are incapable of capturing a unique interpretation, since they cannot distinguish between any number of alternative models. This can be encapsulated in the observation that the relation between syntax and semantics is fundamentally *one-to-many*; any given formal system will have arbitrarily many different interpretations (in the very strongest case, a 'categorical' theory can determine its models up to isomorphism). And this intrinsically one-to-many character obviates the possibility of deriving or even attributing a unique semantical content merely on the basis of computational structure.

These (and a host of other) powerful results on the inherent limitations of syntactical methods would seem to cast a rather deflationary light on the project of explicating *mental content* within a computational framework. Indeed, they would seem to render such goals as providing a computational account of natural language semantics or propositional attitude states profoundly problematic. Non-standard models exist even for such rigorously defined domains as first-order arithmetic and fully axiomatized geometry. And if the precise, artificial system of first-order arithmetic cannot even impose isomorphism on its various models, how then could a *program*, designed to process a specific natural language, say Chinese, supply a basis for the claim that the units of Chinese syntax posses a *unique* meaning?

So I think that the advocates of computationalism make the wrong move by accepting Searle's bait and taking on board the seemingly intractable 'symbol grounding problem' that results. Instead I would accept Searle's negative premise (2) and agree that computation is too weak to underwrite any interesting version of (1). Hence I would concur with Searle's reasoning to the extent of accepting the salient *conditional* claim that *if* (1) is true *then* (3) is true as well. So the real crux of the issue lies in the truth-value of (1), without which the consequent of the *if-then* statement cannot be detached as a free-standing conclusion. Only by accepting the traditional, *a priori* notion of mentality assumed in premise (1), does (3) follow from the truth of (2). And it's here that I would diverge from the views of both Searle and orthodox cognitive science.

4 CONSCIOUS PRESENTATION

In explicating and defending his pivotal premise (1), Searle (1990, 1992) again follows Brentano, in claiming that the human mind possesses original intentionality because it can experience conscious presentations of the objects that its representational states are 'about'. Thus it is conscious experience that ultimately underwrites the intrinsic aboutness of genuine intentional states. So Searle holds that consciousness supplies the basis for the truth of premise (1), and he further believes that consciousness arises from the specific causal powers of the brain considered as a physical structure, rather than via the implementation of some abstract 'formal shadow', be it classical or connectionist. Hence intentionality is tethered to brain processes via consciousness, and Searle thereby attempts to naturalize the traditional notion of mentality, while at the same time discrediting the computational paradigm, since he argues that computation has nothing to do with consciousness.

And while I would again agree with Searle's view that consciousness arises from physical brain activities rather than from multiply realizable computational structure, I would nevertheless argue, contra Searle, that conscious experience, just like symbol manipulation, is too weak to underwrite any interesting version of tenet (1). With respect to the view that conscious experience is the cornerstone of intentionality, the CRA simply begs the question, because it presupposes that the homunculus Searle, replete with conscious presentations, *really does* understand English in some special way. Searle appeals to himself as the locus of genuine intentionality in the Chinese Room, and he would support this by citing the fact that he is consciously aware of the meanings of English expressions. For example, he can entertain a conscious image of the referent of the English string 'h-a-m-b-u-r-g-e-r', while for him the strings of Chinese characters are completely devoid of conscious meanings. Ostensibly, this special understanding of English enables him to follow the program and manipulate the 'meaningless' Chinese symbols. Hence lack of conscious presentation with respect to the semantics of Chinese constitutes the real asymmetry between the two languages, and this underlies Searle's claim that genuine understanding occurs in the case of one language and not the other.

But this line of thought is not particularly compelling, since one can easily concede that Searle has episodes of conscious awareness which attend his processing of English, while at the same time denying that these episodes are sufficient to establish intrinsic content, or to ground the semantics of natural language expressions. Indeed, the mere occurrence of conscious presentations is too weak to even establish that they themselves play a role in Searle's ability to follow the English instruction manual. Instead, I would argue that what consciousness actually provides is the foundation for the subjective *impression*, had by Searle and others, that the human mind enjoys some mysterious and seemingly magical form of intentionality with the power to uniquely determine representational content.

Thus when Searle contends that our mental states are 'really about' various external objects and states of affairs, this is merely an expression of the fact that, introspectively, it *seems to us* as if our mental states had some such special property. As argued in (Schweizer 1994), conscious experience is clearly sufficient to provide the source for this belief, since conscious experience intrinsic to how (some of) our mental states appear to us. But it cannot provide a basis for concluding that the belief is *true*, unless consciousness is something much more mysterious and powerful than the resources of natural science can allow. Brentano famously dismissed naturalism, and he thereby gave himself some room for the claim that consciousness underwrites the mind's essential intentionality. However, if one accepts naturalism and deems consciousness to be a phenomenon supported by, say, the causal properties of electrochemical reactions taking place inside the skull, then one should just bite the bullet and accept that it is too weak to support Brentano's thesis that intentionality is an essential feature of the mind.

It would be straying too far from the main goal of the article to expand on this latter claim at any great length, but considerations based on the 'narrow' status of consciousness should suffice to illustrate the central point. It is widely held by naturalistically inclined philosophers that psychological states and properties must supervene upon occurrent, *internal*, physical states and processes of organisms. This principle of 'psychological autonomy' should clearly apply to conscious states as well, and as a consequence, factors outside the boundaries of an organism cannot affect consciousness, unless they make some relevant impact on the occurrent, internal physical states and processes of that organism, most typically through inputs to the sensory mechanisms. But then the objection raised by Searle in the CRA against the computational paradigm comes back to undermine his own position: the intrinsic relation between consciousness and its object becomes one-to-many, just as the relation between computational syntax and its interpretation is one-to-many. Any number of different, nonstandard, causes can yield exactly the same conscious experience (by inducing exactly the same internal physical states and processes), just as a given formal system can have arbitrarily many distinct interpretations.

Therefore conscious experience is, by its very nature, too weak to determine a unique external object that one is conscious of. This problem is at the heart of Cartesian scepticism, and it still remains firmly entrenched within the narrow confines of naturalism. According to Descartes there could be any number of different 'causal' circumstances correlated with the same conscious state, and he therefore entertained a very radical version of the one-to-many problem, in which even a malignant demon could not be ruled out as a non-standard model. In a more contemporary guise, Putnam's (1981) celebrated brains-in-a-vat argument exploits this solipsistic feature to show that conscious psychological states are too weak to capture the semantics of natural language.

5 REPRESENTATION AS HEURISTICS

There have been a number of high profile positions advanced in negative reaction to 'traditional' cognitive science that take anti-representationalism as one their hallmarks, including dynamical systems theory (e.g Van Gelder 1996), behaviour based robotics (e.g. Brooks 1996), approaches utilizing sensory-motor affordances (e.g. Noë 2004), and some varieties of connectionism (that deliberately refuse Fodor's challenge). A common factor is that these views all advance some version of the slogan 'intelligence without representation'. In order to locate my position on the salient philosophical landscape, it is worth noting that it is *not* anti-representational in this sense. On my view, there could well be internal structures that play many of the roles that people would ordinarily expect of representations, and this is especially true at the level of perception, sensory-motor control and navigation. So I would be quite happy to accept things like spatial encodings, somatic emulators, internal mirrorings of relevant aspects of the external environment. Ultimately this boils down to questions that must be settled empirically in the case of biologically induced agents, but unlike the anti-representationalists, I do not deny that the most plausible form of cognitive architecture may well incorporate internal structures and stand-ins that many people would be tempted to *call* 'representations'.

But I would argue that this label should be construed purely in a weak, operational sense, and should not be conflated with the more robust traditional conception. To the extent that internal structures can encode, mirror or model external objects and states of affairs, they do so via their own causal and/or syntactic properties. And again, to the extent that they influence behaviour or the internal processing of inputs to yield outputs, they do this solely in virtue of their causal and/or syntactic attributes. There is nothing about these internal structures that could support Searle's or Brentano's notion of original intentionality, and there is no independent or objective fact of the matter regarding their 'real' content or meaning.

And similarly, my view is not eliminativist in the sense of Churchland (1981), because, just as in the case of low level activities such as sensation, navigation and motor control, so too in the case of higher level activities such as rational deliberation and the interaction of propositional attitudes – my position is not based on conjectures about the non-existence of various internal elements as revealed by future scientific research. Maybe it will turn out to be a theoretically fruitful level of description to view the brain as implementing a full blown system of recursive syntax. So, I would not deny, in advance of weighty empirical evidence, that there *may* even be processing structures that play the role of Fodor's belief and desire boxes, internal sentences, etc. (although I *would* find this rather surprising). So I would not at this point rule out the possibility that there may be some type of *operational* reduction of traditional psychological concepts to functional or neurophysiological states that could prove useful in predicting behaviour (see Schweizer 2001 for more discussion). Instead, my point is that even if there were such neural structures implementing an internal LOT, this still wouldn't ground traditional semantics and genuine aboutness. As will be argued in more detail in the next section, these structures would have the relevant causal/syntatctic properties but not the semantic ones.

So what I deny is not that there may be internal mechanisms that reflect external properties and states of affairs in systematic and biologically useful ways. Instead I would deny that there is anything *more* to this phenomenon than highly sensitive and evolved relations of calibration between the internal workings of an organism and its specialized environmental context. Evolutionary history can be invoked to yield interesting heuristics with respect to these mechanical relations of calibration, and perhaps support counterfactuals regarding their role in the organism's adaptive success. But evolution is based on random mutation, and natural 'selection' is an equally purposeless mechanism. Neither can provide the theoretical resources sufficient to ground the strong traditional notion of 'genuine aboutness'.

Thus if I had to coin a competing slogan to encapsulate my own position, it would be something like 'representation without intentionality'. If one is truly committed to naturalism, then there is only a difference of degree and complexity but not in kind between, say, the reflection of moonlight in a pond and the retinal image of the moon in some organism's visual system. Proponents of the orthodox view are inclined to think that a sufficient difference in degree and complexity somehow yields an esoteric difference in *kind*, a difference that allows us to cross the conceptual boundary from mere causal correlations to 'genuine aboutness'. But I would contend that naturalism itself supplies an asymptotic limit for this curve, and that the boundary can be crossed only by invoking non-natural factors.

6 BEHAVIOR VERSUS MEANING

The considerations presented so far have been motivated within the framework of a computational approach to the mind. But mental processes and natural language semantics clearly have many intimate philosophical connections, and the foregoing one-to-many relation underlying the symbol grounding problem has well known consequences for the linguistic theory of meaning. If one accepts the allied principle of psychological autonomy, then it follows that the mind is too weak to determine what its internal components are 'really about', and this extends to the case of expressions in natural language as well. The famed conclusion of Putnam's Twin Earth argument (Putnam 1975) is that "meanings ain't in the head", and this is because narrow psychological states are incapable of determining the reference relation for terms in our public languages. But rather than abandon natural language semantics in light of the problem, the externalist quite rightly abandons the traditional idea that the intentionality of mental states provides the foundation for linguistic reference.

Putnam's strategy is to directly invoke external circumstances in the characterization of meaning for natural languages. The externalist approach exploits direct, ostensive access to the world, thus circumventing the difficulty by relieving mental states of their referential burden. On such an approach, the object of reference can only be specified by indexical appeal to the object itself, and in principle it *cannot* be determined merely from the psychological states of the language user. Direct appeal to the actual environment and linguistic community in which the cognitive agent is situated then plays the principal role in determining the match-up between language and world. Putnam's strategy offers a viable account of linguistic reference *precisely because* it transgresses the boundaries of the mind intrinsic to the explanatory project of cognitive science. The externalist must invoke broad environmental factors, since nothing internal to a cognitive system is capable of uniquely capturing the purported 'content' of its representations and thereby semantically grounding its internal states. And from this it follows that original content is not a property of the representation *qua* cognitive structure, and hence it is not the cognitive structure itself that provides the theoretical basis for meaning. Indeed, outside factors then do the real work, and the purported *semantical* aspect of internal configurations is trivialized.

However, in normal, everyday practice, we continually use sentences of public language to ascribe various content bearing mental states, both to ourselves and others, and it is here that a potential confusion arises. A defender of the tradition might argue that the *truth* of such ascriptions shows that there is still a legitimate fact of the matter regarding mental content, and hence that there is an objective match-up problem remaining to be solved. When an agent is correctly attributed a given propositional attitude, such as the belief that φ, this captures an actual feature of their doxastic configuration and must be supported by some corresponding aspect of their internal make up.

At this point I do not wish to become embroiled in the 'Folk Psychology' debate, but in terms of the present discussion it is important to note that such a line of argument makes an unwarranted extrapolation from our common sense practices, because the age-old customs of folk psychology are independent of any assumptions about internal symbols, states or structures. Observable behavior and context are the relevant criteria, and the truth-conditions for such ascriptions are founded on external, macroscopic and operational considerations. As in everyday life, one can use behavioral and environmental factors to adduce that, say, Jones believes that lager quenches thirst, but this practice makes no assumptions about the nature or even existence of an internal representation encoding the propositional content of the belief. The attribution concerns Jones as an unanalyzed unit, a black box whose actions take place within a particular environmental and linguistic setting. It gives no handle whatever on postulating hidden internal cogs and levers that generate Jones' actions, and it's perfectly compatible with an agnostic disregard of such inner workings.

At this stage, an ardent representationalist is likely to invoke the belief-desire framework of psychological explanation to defend a realist account of internal meaning. As mentioned at the start of the paper, not only do we ascribe various content bearing states to ourselves and others, but furthermore we habitually *use* such ascriptions to explain and successfully predict behavior. According to this widely accepted framework, psychological states individuated in terms of their *content*, such as beliefs and desires, are *causally* responsible for a host of rational actions. Hence, it might be argued, the belief-desire framework can successfully predict behavior from the outside, precisely because it mirrors the internal processing structure that causes the behavior.

Thus when, from the outside, we justifiably ascribe to Jones the belief that lager quenches thirst, Fodor would have it that a token of some mentalese sentence, say 'n%^7 £#~ %&!+', which encodes the same semantical content as the English ascription, has been duly etched into her 'belief box'. This physical implementation of mentalese syntax is then poised to interact with other physically implemented tokens in her desire box to produce assorted forms of rational action, such as standing up and reaching for a pint. In this manner, the truth of propositional attitude ascriptions is directly correlated with salient internal configurations of the agent.

But this purported correlation breaks down at its most vital point – the level of semantical content. For the story to work, the sentences 'lager quenches thirst' and 'n%^7 £#~ %&!+' must both express the same proposition. Yet as a medium of classical computation, the LOT is just a scheme for rule governed symbol manipulation. Syntax churning within a formal system is fundamentally different from the operation of a public language, and it is a significant conflation to impute to the former the same semantical properties conventionally attributed to the latter. English is acquired and exercised in an inter-subjectively accessible context with which the entire sociolinguistic community has indexical contact. There are shared criteria for the correct use of natural language sentences and the rules under which various expressions are deployed, and there are direct, ostensive ties between publicly produced syntactic tokens and their referents. In vivid contrast, there are no such shared criteria nor public ties for the hidden, internal sentences of mentalese. The LOT serves as an extreme example of a *private* language (Wittgenstein, 1953), and as such it has no communal truth conditions nor standard semantic properties. Indeed, the LOT is so private it's even hidden from the introspective awareness of the individual agent, and it thereby also eludes Searle's traditional association of linguistic meaning with agent-based intentionality.

As elements in a formal system, there is no fact of the matter concerning what the internal sentences of mentalese 'really mean'. At best, these conjectured tokens of computational syntax would successfully govern our behavior in familiar surroundings, but they would fail to do so if we were placed in radically different circumstances. So they are merely calibrated with the environment in which they happened to develop, and this historical fact is not sufficient to imbue them with objective content. To the extent that these hypothetical symbols successfully govern behavior, they do so purely in terms of their formal, syntactical properties, and as noted before, there is no work left to be done by their intended interpretation. On a computational approach to the mind, it is processing structure and not semantics that is the cause of human action.

So at this point a wedge must be driven between two apparently related but nonetheless quite distinct theoretical projects. There is very significant difference between a theory of natural language semantics and a psychological theory regarding the internal states causally responsible for our input/output profiles. The former is an idealized and normative endeavor, concerned with articulating high level characterizations which reflect the socially agreed truth-conditions for sentences in a public language. As such, this endeavour has no direct bearing on an essentially descriptive account of the internal mechanisms responsible for processing cognitive inputs and yielding various behavioural outputs, even when we consider the production of *verbal* behaviour, or the common sense attribution of various propositional attitude states *using* natural language.

Hence I would diagnose the classical Fodorian effort to build semantical content into a computational theory of mind as an infelicitous failure to separate these two projects at exactly the point where they should *not* coalesce. The infelicity of this move is already apparent in *Psychosemantics*, where Fodor (1987) tries to address the notorious problems of wide versus narrow content introduced by Putnam and later Burge (1979). In an attempt to defend his narrow version of content against Twin Earth objections, Fodor is forced to claim that "... what my water-thoughts share with Twin 'water'-thoughts *isn't* content. Narrow content is radically inexpressible, because it's only content *potentially*;" (p. 50). But this sounds uncomfortably close to equivocation, and invites the question – why call it 'content' *at all*? Fodor goes on to say that "a narrow content is *essentially* a function from contexts onto truth conditions;" (p. 53), so that in the context of Earth this function yields thoughts about H_2O, and on Twin Earth it yields thoughts about XYZ. He states that this abstract function is implemented in the human brain, whereby it enjoys causal efficacy in the physical world. But it's crucial to note that the distinguishing characteristics of such abstruse functions are woefully underspecified by the brute facts of physical brain structure and natural selection. Mere terrestrial teleology is one thing, but how on earth could biological evolution select a function designed to yield XYZ thoughts on another planet?

This account appears to be a strained attempt to appropriate and internalize a normative, idealized position in the theory of natural language semantics, rather than to provide a naturalistically plausible story about cognitive processing. Instead of narrow 'content', what such Twins have in common is the same internal processing structure, and this produces the same outputs when given the same inputs, regardless of the input's distal source in the environment. In contrast to Fodor's claim quoted above concerning the essential nature of narrow content, the proper domain of the implemented cognitive function is *inputs* and *not contexts*, and this is precisely why individual cognitive systems cannot capture the semantics of public languages.

7 CONCLUSION

According to the position advocated herein, the traditional commitment to representational *content* constitutes a retrograde step within the context of naturalistic explanation. The crucial point to notice is that internal 'representations' do all their scientifically tangible *cognitive* work solely in virtue of their physical/formal/mathematical structure. There is nothing about them, qua efficacious elements of internal processing, that is 'about' anything else. Content is not an explicit component of the input, nor is it acted upon or transformed via cognitive computations. All that is explicitly present and causally relevant are computational structure plus supporting physical mechanisms, which is exactly what one would expect from a naturalistic account.

In order for cognitive structures to do their job, there is no need to posit some additional 'content', 'semantical value', or 'external referent'. Such representation talk may serve a useful heuristic role, but it remains a conventional, observer-relative ascription, and accordingly there's no independent fact of the matter, and so there isn't a sense in which it's possible to go wrong or be mistaken about what an internal configuration is 'really' about. Instead, representational content can be projected onto an internal structure when this type of gloss plays an opportune role in characterizing the overall processing activities which govern the system's interactions with its environment, and hence in predicting its salient input/output patterns. But it is simply a matter of convenience, convention and choice, and does not reveal an underlying fact of the matter nor any essential characteristics of the system.

From the point of view of the system, these internal structures are manipulated *directly*, and the notion that they are 'directed towards' something else plays no role in the pathways leading from cognitive inputs to intelligent outputs. Hence the symbol grounding problem is a red herring – it isn't necessary to quest after some elusive and mysterious layer of 'real' content, for which these internal structures serve as the mere syntactic vehicle. Syntactical and physical processes are all we have, and their efficacy is not affected by the purported presence or absence of meaning. I would argue that the computational paradigm is thematically inconsistent with the search for content or its supposed 'vehicles'. Instead, the concern of computational models of cognition should be with the internal *processing structures* that yield the right kinds of input/output profiles of a system embedded in a particular environmental context, and with how such processing structures are implemented in the system's physical machinery. These are the factors that do the work and are sufficient to explain all of the empirical data, and they do this using the normal theoretical resources of natural science. Indeed, the postulation of content as the essential feature distinguishing mental from non-mental systems should be seen as the last remaining vestige of Cartesian dualism, and, contra Fodor, naturalized cognition has no place for a semantical 'ghost in the machine'. When it comes to computation and content, only the vehicle is required, not the excess baggage.

REFERENCES

Brooks, R. 1996 "Intelligence without Representation" in *Mind Design II*, J. Haugeland (ed.), MIT Press.
Brentano, F. 1874 *Psychology from an Empirical Standpoint*.
Burge, T. 1979 "Individualism and the Mental", in French, P., Euhling, T., and Wettstein, H. (eds.), *Studies in Epistemology*, vol.4, *Midwest Studies in Philosophy*, University of Minnesota Press.

Churchland, P.M. 1981 "Eliminative Materialism and the Propositional Attitudes", *The Journal of Philosophy* 78: pp.67–90.

Churchland, P.M. 1998 "Conceptual Similarity Across Sensory and Neural Diversity: The Fodor/Lepore Challenge Answered", *Journal of Philosophy*, 96(1): pp.5–32.

Fodor, J. 1975 *The Language of Thought.* Harvester Press.

Fodor, J. 1987 *Psychosemantics,* MIT Press.

Fodor, J. 2008 LOT 2 *The Language of Thought Revisited,* Oxford University Press.

Fodor, J. and Z. Pylyshyn 1988 "Connectionism and Cognitive Architecture: A Critical Analysis", *Cognition,* 28: pp.3–71.

Laakso, A. and G. Cottrell 2000 "Content and Cluster Analysis: Assessing Representational Similarity in Neural Systems", *Philosophical Psychology,* 13(1): pp.47–76.

Noë, A. 2004 *Action in Perception,* MIT Press.

O'Brien, G. and J. Opie 2001 "Connectionist Vehicles, Structural Resemblance, and the Phenomenal Mind", *Communication and Cognition,* 34: pp.13–38.

Putnam, H. 1975 "The Meaning of 'Meaning'", in *Mind, Language and Reality,* Cambridge University Press.

Putnam, H. 1981 "Brains in a Vat", in *Reason, Truth and History,* Cambridge University Press.

Schweizer, P. 1994 "Intentionality, Qualia and Mind/Brain Identity", *Minds and Machines* 4: pp.259–282.

Schweizer, P. 2001 "Realization, Reduction and Psychological Autonomy" *Synthese* 126: pp.383–405.

Searle, J. 1980 "Minds, Brains and Programs", *Behavioral and Brain Sciences,* 3: pp.417–424.

Searle, J. 1990 "Consciousness, Explanatory Inversion and Cognitive Science", *Behavioral and Brain Sciences,* 13: pp.585–596.

Searle, J. 1992 *The Rediscovery of the Mind,* MIT Press.

Van Gelder, T. 1996 "Dynamics and Cognition" in *Mind Design II,* J. Haugeland (ed.), MIT Press.

Wittgenstein, L. 1953 *Philosophical Investigations.*

III.
... THE BRAIN

NEUROPSYCHOLOGICAL FOUNDATIONS OF PHILOSOPHY

PATRICK SUPPES
Stanford University

1 INTRODUCTION

It is over 200 years since the publication of Kant's *Critique of Pure Reason*. In spite of the many things that Kant understood, and above all, the problems that he saw into so deeply, it is generally recognized that, in any literal sense, the Kantian program is a dead one. There is not going to be, at any time in the future, a serious argument that there is a proper *a priori* synthetic foundation of science or even mathematics. The slow but steady accretion of the case for an empirical view of all human phenomena calls for a revision of much thinking in philosophy that still retains unfortunate remnants needing the kind of critique that Kant gave earlier, but now applied to a wider circle of philosophical ideas. The purpose of this lecture is not to make a systematic analysis of principles of a completely general kind, but rather to give four extended examples of problems that have often been thought of in philosophy, or in mathematics, as not being really empirical in nature. Here they will be presented as naturally so from a psychological and a neural standpoint. An approach to these problems that is purely rational or *a priori* seems, by today's standards of knowledge, mistaken.

It may be thought that what I am advancing as neuropsychological foundations of philosophy is something that is radical and new, but nothing could be further from the truth. In fact, what I have to say in this lecture is very much in the spirit of Aristotle. Let me give just one example to illustrate this point. If one looks for systematic psychological concepts in ancient times, the outstanding example, without any question, is Aristotle's *De Anima*. The treatment of problems of perception and of thinking have no match in any other text of the ancient world. Some credit, of course, must be given to Plato for an early beginning. The fundamental importance of the *De Anima* was fully recognized by many later commentators, including especially the detailed commentary of Aquinas; and the clarifying paraphrase of Themistius, written in the 4th century CE, widely read even in the Renaissance.

The thesis I am advancing is not meant to be universal in philosophy, but all the same wide ranging. The first example tries to bring out the empirical character of the ordinary use of the concept of truth, and how far the psychological methods by which the truth of ordinary empirical statements is assessed are from the theories of truth we have had in the past from philosophers and logicians.

The second example deals with beliefs, especially the special case of Bayesian priors. There has not been much philosophical discussion of prior beliefs with which I am taking issue, although there are some relevant aspects of epistemology. Instead, I am attacking the absence of deeper psychological considerations on the part of statisticians, economists, and others who believe that a Bayesian approach is a rational way to think about problems of uncertainty and statistical inference. I agree with much of what they have to say. But I find unsatisfactory the thinness of the psychological foundations that are provided, for example, by the forefathers of the modern Bayesian viewpoint, Frank Ramsey, Bruno de Finetti, and Jimmy Savage. They have important and insightful things to say about the foundation of statistics, but the psychological foundations of their Bayesian ideas are left in an undeveloped and primitive state. This is what I address in the second example.

The third example deals with problems of rational choice and rational thinking in general. In spite of having contributed myself in the past to the rational theory of preference, I find the empirical side of the theory weak. The deeper account of how choices are actually made is a matter of extended psychological development of concepts not usually brought to bear in rational-choice theory. What I have to say about choice here applies also, without more detailed consideration in the limited time available on the present occasion, to norms in general. I hold the same kind of empirical thesis about norms that I hold about rational choices.

Finally, in the fourth example, I set forth a psychological thesis about an important aspect of modern mathematics that is troublesome for many people. On the one hand, as part of the foundations of mathematics, there is a very well worked out formal theory of mathematical proof. It is recognized, on the other hand, by working mathematicians that almost all serious proofs in current mathematical research are, for good reasons, not formal proofs. So, the purpose of this example is to stress the psychological nature of verifying – mind you, not discovering, but verifying – the correctness of informal mathematical proofs. Here again I find much space for psychological thinking and analysis. Even if one might forecast that in the more distant future, an increasing part of mathematics will be checked in a formal way, informal methods will not disappear.

As yet I have said nothing about the brain. I leave the topic of neural phenomena, in particular neural computations, to the end, and will say no more at this point.

2 FOUR EXAMPLES

2.1. Computation of truth (Suppes and Béziau, 2003)

Philosophers discuss at length various theories of truth – coherence theory, correspondence theory, problem of direct reference, sense and denotation, and so on – but, curiously, do not give an account of how we actually perform truth computations, and even less why we are able to perform them so quickly. Philosophers who claim that "Paris is the capital of France" is true because Paris is the capital of France are generally not interested in explaining how we actually compute the answer. But, since such sentences are almost never remembered, or even previously encountered, a computation is necessary.

Logicians also do not solve these problems. If we want to describe how one answers a question like "Is 49+13 equal to 61?", it is certainly wrong to look at the logical foundation of arithmetic, whether it is proof-theoretical or model-theoretical. We answer such a question by using a series of small computational algorithms and tricks, not by looking for a formal proof from a set of axioms or by finding a model in which the axioms are true and 49+13 = 61 is false. In the case of a question like "Is Rome the capital of France?", it is even more doubtful that we are trying to deduce the truth or falsity of the sentence from a set of axioms, or by using a truth-table.

From my point of view it is misleading to say that we are making a *deduction* to arrive at the conclusion that "Rome is the capital of France" is false, unless we emphasize that deduction does not reduce to the narrow meaning of deduction in formal logic. To avoid misunderstanding, it is better to say that we are here trying to describe how we *compute* the truth or falsity of such a sentence.

In a recent book on computational semantics, the authors say:

> The book is devoted to introducing techniques for tackling the following two questions:
>
> 1. How can we automate the process of associating semantic representations with expressions of natural language?
>
> 2. How can we use logical representations of natural language expressions to automate the process of drawing inferences?
>
> (Blackburn and Bos, 2005, p.iii)

Their idea is to find some algorithms to translate natural language into the language of first-order logic to represent the meaning of natural-language sentences, and then to find some additional algorithms to make inferences with these first-order translations. The two steps seem wrong for our purpose. It is highly doubtful that our brains use first-order logic to compute empirical truths. Both AI researchers and computational linguists have been overly-influenced by formal logic. They do not deal directly with the problem of finding the obvious truth or falsity of atomic statements like "Rome is the capital of France".

The theory of the computation of such truths, i.e., the truths of ordinary empirical statements, is an important aspect of how the mind works. It is by no means anything like the whole story of the computations in which the mind, or the brain, is involved. Very much more is required in even the simplest computations of perception. Just think of the necessary computations to decide, perhaps incorrectly, that the image from a certain perspective of a person 200 meters away is indeed an image of your mother. What I shall have to say about computation will be much simpler than that of organizing such perceptual input to form beliefs about what I am seeing. Put another way, because of the great importance of perception in all our activities, we are continually forced to make a dazzling array of computations in processing stimulus input that actually reaches the cortex as electromagnetic signals, reflecting a marked degree of abstraction from the vivid language of ordinary talk about processes and things. It is mind-boggling when first thought about. Indeed, the electromagnetic signals that the cortex processes seem inherently more difficult to understand than the sensible forms of Aristotle's theory, as set forth in the *De Anima*.

In spite of my references to electromagnetic signals, discussion here will be at a still more abstract psychological level most of the time, but I will turn back on several occasions to the brain rather than the mind, because, historically, the literature on the mind is almost entirely absent any serious theory of computation. So, to continue this general point about computation and how the mind works, all the neurophysiological processes of perception that reduce observed features of things and processes to electromagnetic signals sent to the cortex are ignored in ordinary or philosophical talk about experience. And so modern philosophy of mind is not concerned with the details of how we learn about the ways in which phenomena in the world are connected.

I chose the last word deliberately. The approach to computation about such things and processes, characteristic of our minds, was well recognized by Hume, the godfather of the central mechanism of association, already foreshadowed by Aristotle. What I shall insist on here is the nearly universal role of association as the main method of computation in the brain at the system, but not cellular, level (and in the mind, if you will) in dealing with ordinary experience. The point is an important one, even if there is not space here to muster all the arguments that I think are relevant.

I will make the following general claim about computation. It is sometimes felt that a very clear criticism of behaviorism and connectionism in relation to much behavior is easily made. Rules play too central a role, it is held, to believe an associationist account could be correct. This, however, rests upon a deep mathematical misunderstanding of what can be done with quite simple methods of association or conditioning. It is evident from the many proofs that any computable function (and thus any rule) can be computed by a universal Turing machine, by a universal register machine, or by any of six or seven other devices. Very elementary primitive ideas are quite sufficient, once there is any method of recursion available, to prove that the basic device to do the computing can be quite simple in conception.

All of these remarks are a kind of prolegomena to what I have to say about the computation of the truth of ordinary empirical statements. One point I want to make is that I shall not, in this discussion of truth, distinguish between belief and truth. It is possible to be too zealous, from a philosophical standpoint, and not accept a discussion of the truth of ordinary statements, as opposed to 'Which ones do you believe to be true?' In fact, in much ordinary discourse, claims about belief are mainly used to express doubts about truth, not as a separate point of positive emphasis, for example, "Do you really believe what he said is true?"

Associative networks. Anyway, I want to give a sketch of a theory of how such ordinary computations of truth are made. In doing so, I draw on a recent article of mine with Jean-Yves Béziau (2003). The basic idea is that the computations are made by an associative network with brain representations of words being the nodes and the links between being the associations. More generally, auditory, visual, and other kinds of brain images can also be nodes.

In the initial state, not all nodes are linked, and there are, in this simple formulation, just two states, *quiescent* and *active*. No learning or forgetting is considered. It is assumed, without being formulated here, that, after a given utterance is responded to as being either true or false, all the activated states return to quiescent. The axioms, which are not stated here, are formulated just for the evaluation of a single sentence, not for giving an account of how the process works over a longer stretch of discourse. The way to think about the networks introduced is that a person is asked to say whether a sentence about familiar phenomena is true or false. It is very natural to ask, and not to have a quibble about 'Do you believe this, even though you don't know whether it is true?' I take examples that are so obvious everyone accepts them as true or false, as the case may be. Simple geography sentences are often used in experiments on these matters. Here is one: *Warsaw is not the capital of Austria.* This sentence input comes from outside the associative network in the brain. I will consider only spoken words forming a sentence, although what is said also applies to visual presentation, as well. So, as the sentence is spoken, the sound pressure image of each word that comes to the ear is drastically transformed by a sequence of auditory computations leading to the auditory nerve fibers which send electromagnetic signals to the cortex. Such signals are examples of those mentioned earlier. In previous work, I have been much concerned with seeing if we can identify such brain signals as brain representations of words. Some references are Suppes, Lu, and Han (1997) and Suppes, Han, Epelboim, and Lu (1999a, 1999b).

The brain activates quiescent states by using the energy for this activation from that brought into the cortex by the brain representation of the verbal stimulus input. With the activation of the brain representation of words by external stimuli, the associations, i.e., links, between activated brain representations are also activated.

Moreover, it is assumed in the theory that energy can be passed along from one associated node to another by a phenomenon characterized some decades ago in psychological research as *spreading activation* (a good reference is Collins and Loftus, 1975). For example, in a sentence about a city like Rome or Paris, some familiar properties are closely associated with these cities and the brain representation of these properties may well be activated shortly after the activation of the brain representations of the words *Rome* or *Paris*, even though the names of these properties, or verbal descriptions of them, did not occur in any current utterance. This is what goes under the heading of *spreading activation*. Some form of it is essential to activate the nodes and links needed in judging truth, for, often, we must depend upon a search for properties, which means, in terms of processing, a search for brain representations of properties, to settle a question of truth or falsity. A good instance of this, to be seen in the one example considered here, is the 1–1 property, characteristic of such a word as *capital: x is capital of y*, where here, *x* is ordinarily a city and *y* a country. There are some exceptions to this being 1–1, but they are quite rare and, in ordinary discourse, the 1–1 property is automatically assumed. But this is only one of many other examples, easily given, that arise in ordinary conversation.

One other notion introduced is the notion of the *associative core* of a sentence, in our notation, $c(S)$ of a sentence S. For example, in the kinds of geography sentences given in the experiments referenced above, where similar syntactic forms are given and the sentences are given about every four seconds, people apparently quickly learn to focus only on the key reference words, which vary in an otherwise fixed sentential context, or occur in a small number of such contexts. So, for example, the associative core of the sentence *Berlin is the capital of Germany* is a strongly linked core of three nodes, the brain representations of the three words *Berlin*, *capital* and *Germany*. For such a core I use the notation BERLIN/CAPITAL/GERMANY, with, obviously, the words in caps being used to denote the brain representations, i.e., the three nodes in the associative network. A more complicated concept is obviously needed for more general use.

In the initial state of the network associations are all quiescent, e.g., PARIS ~ CAPITAL, and after activation we use the notation PARIS ≈ CAPITAL. In the example itself we show only the activated associations and the activated nodes of the network. The steps of the associative computation are numbered temporally t_1, etc.

Example: *Rome is the capital of France.*

t_1.	ROME, CAPITAL, FRANCE	Activation
t_2.	PARIS, 1–1 Property	Spreading activation
t_3.	ROME $\approx$ CAPITAL, CAPITAL $\approx$ 1–1 Property	Activation
	CAPITAL $\approx$ FRANCE, PARIS $\approx$ CAPITAL	
	PARIS $\approx$ FRANCE	
t_4.	ITALY	Spreading activation
t_5.	PARIS / CAPITAL / FRANCE	Activation
	ROME / CAPITAL / ITALY	
t_6.	TRUE $\approx$ PARIS / CAPITAL / FRANCE	Spreading activation
	TRUE $\approx$ ROME / CAPITAL / ITALY	
t_7.	FALSE $\approx$ ROME / CAPITAL / FRANCE	Spreading activation

This sketch of an example, without stating the axioms and providing other technical details, is meant only to provide a limited intuitive sense of how the theory can be developed for simple empirical sentences. Most important, there is here no account of learning associations. Only an idealized performance setup is used.

But my point should be clear: such computations, or something like them, dominate ordinary discourse, and standard philosophical theories of truth are of little help in thinking about them. Detailed psychological theories of association are more useful.

2.2. Where do Bayesian priors come from? (Suppes, 2007)

Bayesian prior probabilities have had an important place in the theoretical and practical consideration of probabilistic and statistical methods since at least the middle of the twentieth century. In spite of this widespread interest in theoretically using Bayesian priors, and often empirically eliciting them, the analysis of where these priors come from and how are they formed has received little attention.

The absence of such consideration can be seen in the rather laconic views about prior probabilities themselves, as expressed by the three most important foundational thinkers on the Bayesian viewpoint in the twentieth century, namely, Ramsey, De Finetti and Savage. Quotations are omitted here, but supplied in the article referenced.

What is remarkable about the views of these three foundational thinkers is that none of them ventures very deeply into the psychological or common sense side of how, in fact, subjective probabilities are formed. If we are planning a scientific experiment and ask individuals for their prior beliefs about the design or outcome, almost everyone will agree to this summary of the situation. "Well, if this is an experiment in physics, it's likely that an experienced experimental physicist is going to have a much more interesting prior about the outcome of the experiment than will, for example, the most distinguished professor of philosophy or of English literature." Why is this so? Because we believe, well beyond any requirements of coherence or consistency, as it is sometimes called, there is the really much more important matter of the background experience which led to the formation of a given individual's prior.

It is reasonable to accept the lack of detailed psychological theory of the mechanisms by which prior probabilities are formed, but it is less excusable that there is an almost total absence of a detailed discussion of the highly differentiating nature of past experience in forming a prior applicable to a new experiment or, more generally, almost any action about to be undertaken. Note, of course, that the use of the term 'prior' is, in some sense, misleading. Of course, the partial beliefs we are eliciting in the case of an experiment or an action are prior to the experiment being conducted or the action being taken. But, they are not prior to experience relevant to the experiment or action. There is, in fact, usually much relevant prior experience. There is, if you wish, a beginning to the experience; we might say that we want to go back to the very beginning and consider only priors while still in some perfect state of ignorance. This is not a point worth quarreling about, but it is a point worth noting in terms of our linguistic usage. In fact, in talking about priors, we almost always accept that there has been experience prior to the elicitation of the prior. I will not return to this point, but I do think its consideration is badly missing in the usual discussion of priors. (This is an old point of mine about the obviously unsatisfactory character of many possible priors, Suppes, 1956, p.72.)

It is often said priors express, at least partly, differences in taste. We can agree that there will be differences in taste, even among experts. But it is also essential to make the point that we can properly and empirically assess whether or not the accuracy of priors of experts in a subject are better or worse than beginners and, in fact, who among the experts has a better record. Again, although this is a worthwhile topic, it is one for another occasion.

What I want to focus on here is what kind of account, even if necessarily schematic, can be given about the psychological mechanisms back of the formation of our Bayesian priors.

Nearly as common as our empirical statements, which are implicitly enunciated in such a way as to make clear that they are held, without any question, to be true, is our more tentative estimation of future events, or statements about past events, whose occurrence is uncertain in our minds. A familiar idiom of great importance, both in ordinary conversation and in the theory of probability, is the rich notion of expectation. So we speak of expecting to be home in 30 minutes, expecting to lose five pounds in the next two weeks on our current diet regime, or expecting to purchase a new car for less than we had anticipated, because of the highly competitive nature of the market. In all these cases, expectation is our way of dealing with events that are measured in terms of quantity. So, the outcome is not just a yes-or-no occurrence, but something to which is attached a quantitative measure – time measure, weight measure, money measure, etc. I will say more about expectations later.

At the moment, I will extend the analysis of the previous section by just considering events that occur or do not occur. Moreover, to simplify the formulation and discussion of examples, I restrict myself to events and their brain representations rather than consider sentences. This change is made for simplification, but also matches ordinary practice, which uses an event-formulation more than a statement-formulation as the basis for probability claims. This matches theoretical developments as well. The statement-formulation of probability, as in confirmation theory, developed mainly by philosophers, is not widely used, for many reasons, in systematic theoretical and scientific applications of probability theory. The set-theoretical framework of events is more common and useful for many familiar reasons, which I will not repeat here. (The foundations of this set-theoretical view, written in a way that is meant to be accessible to philosophers, is given in Chapter 5 of Suppes (2002).)

A second point about what I shall limit myself to doing here is that I will not generalize in complete form the axioms, referred to in the previous section dealing with the case of the truth of simple empirical statements, but only sketch their formal developments, which otherwise would require a much larger excursion into technical details than is appropriate. So, the remainder of the discussion will be at an informal level. I do give, in the article referred to (Suppes, 2007), a detailed example that represents a relatively simple restricted set of theoretical ideas that have also been extensively tested experimentally.

So, as we turn from truth to the estimation of probabilities, especially Bayesian priors, there are a number of observations with which I want to begin. The first is that such priors are based on a variety of experience, not on the sharp outcomes of well-planned experiments. The fundamental point is that we come to the design of experiments with such Bayesian priors well developed. It is they which guide, in many different ways, our thinking about the design of such experiments. It is, of course, a fundamental point about the design of experiments that we do not come to them with well-prepared algorithms, mechanically applicable, to hand us the design on a silver platter. It is not at all that way. Designing an experiment and executing that design are rather like designing a house and then building it. There are many practical decisions that must be taken along the way that are no part of any set of known algorithms and that are inescapable in actual work. Our prior knowledge and experience are the most helpful things we have. I emphasize experience rather than knowledge, because much of this experience is not consciously articulated – that marks the difference between amateur experimenters and experienced ones. Imagine turning an amateur loose in a modern physics laboratory. In almost any aspect of experiments now conducted in physics, from quantum entanglement to superconductivity, prior experience is the key to success. This kind of experience is gained from the kind of apprenticeship that is very similar to that found in any specialized work in ancient China, Egypt or Mesopotamia. More generally, this kind of prior experience is necessary in every aspect of ordinary affairs requiring some kind of learned competence, from driving a car to cooking a decent meal, or installing and using a photodetector.

Important in this formulation is the recognition that, by *Bayesian priors* we do not mean the beginning of the beginning, but the beginning of the end, in the sense that when we come to any of these tasks, we come with much developed skill and experience. The prior refers to our state of knowledge, skill and practical competence as we face the task at hand. The term *Bayesian prior* applies, of course, particularly to experiments, where we may be anxious to develop a body of knowledge into which the likely outcomes of the experiments will be accepted by all, or almost all, competent persons. This acceptance should lead to a modified posterior probability, which can, in turn, be taken as a future prior.

My theoretical point is that the basic mechanism of forming these priors, as in forming many other things, is that of association. I emphasize again the central principle that the mechanism of association is, if not universal, nearly universal, in the acquisition of knowledge and skill in animals and humans alike. It is not something special that is turned on for the purposes of acquiring a Bayesian prior, but is a deep mechanism of organisms from *Aplysia* to *Homo sapiens*. What is also apparent from what I have just said is that, though we may be hopeful of stating some general laws of association, the detailed analysis of the way associations are built up in everyday heterogeneous experience will not be practical in any detail. Just as in the external world, the testing of physical theories in heterogeneous experience scarcely occurs at all. As everyone knows who has thought about the problem for any length of time, it is impossible to consider writing down the differential or difference equations governing even the detailed motion of the leaves in the tree outside my study as I write these words. So, no apologies are needed for being able to find only partly systematic verification for the claims that are made for association, because this is no different from the claims that can be made for any general physical law. On the other hand, this is not to make the claim that the mechanisms of association are currently as well formulated and as well understood as the mechanisms postulated and tested in many parts of physics.

However we model things in particular, there are two general assumptions we need. The first is that, as we build up the strength of associations, there is an independence-of-path assumption that holds, at least approximately. This means that the exact historical path we followed in the experience of building up an associative connection does not strongly affect the strength of the association. The same strength can be reached by many other paths. The important point is that we do not need to know the detailed history of the past to infer the current intensity. This would, it seems plausible, impose an impossible burden on memory to require that we do indeed continue to keep track of each past increment to the intensities of associations. I think it is fair to say that the evidence is substantial that, in spite of the vast capacity of human and animal memories, brain computations based on such detailed histories would be too cumbersome for practical biological use.

The second approximate general assumption is the fading influence of the past, which means that our system of knowledge, skills and actions is nearly ergodic. In other words, the influence of the past fades away in some exponential fashion. What I have just said about memories would be an example of this. The accumulated experience of the past is kept in the relative intensities of association, but the memory of each increment, positive or negative, to these associations, is not kept. It is necessary, of course, to say that this ergodic property is approximate, because there are some salient memories that are remembered, but, compared to the total experience, their relative scarcity is evident.

Simple example. So, the mechanisms for estimating probabilities can be exemplified in a familiar example. Someone asks me the question 'Will it rain in Paris tomorrow morning?' I compute my answer by using the associative network of features and patterns of features in memory, activated by the brain representations of the words 'rain', 'Paris', and 'tomorrow morning'. This activation is now postulated to be more complicated than that of the previous section. In particular, it seems essential and fundamental that some concept of intensity be used to represent the varying strengths of associations. We shall do so using notation familiar in current work in neural networks by speaking of varying weights w_i, where w_i is meant to represent an intensity built up from past associations. The outcome, now, of computation in the associative network of the estimated probability can have in summary form, a simple representation:

$$\text{rain: } \sum w_i = r$$
$$\text{no rain: } \sum w_j = \bar{r}$$
$$\text{probability of rain } = \frac{r}{r + \bar{r}}$$

Of course, what I have shown here is the outcome of the computation, not how such a computation might actually be made by the brain.

More on representation and association. We can see from this simple example the main ways in which the assumptions considered in the previous section on truth must be extended and changed. First, there must be a clear mechanism for the build up of the intensity of activation in terms of change. Second, we must, explicitly, not consider just a given event, but, for the estimation of its probability in some form, the probability of the opposite happening. In some cases, there may be schemes for directly estimating only the probability of the event, but it is most natural, when weights are used, to determine probabilities from simple relationships between the weights, as in this example. Another important point of extension of the setup for truth, especially as we move on to the estimation of probability, is that it is necessary to think in terms of brain representations of other things than words. Words will continue to be important and they seem fundamental in much of our own mental activity. But, certainly, it is wrong to think just in terms of words as we move to nonhuman animals, where the brain representations of past experiences must obviously be nonverbal in form. But I see no problem with the representation in the brain of many different kinds of things – words, past events, past scenes that we have seen or things that we have heard. For example, the way in which passages of music, familiar from the past, generate brain representations that associate to a variety of emotional experiences is well known.

This remark may well raise a question in the minds of some, especially those oriented towards analytical philosophy or cognitive psychology: "But where are the concepts? Why speak of the brain representation of the word *rain* as opposed to the brain representation of the concept rain?" My answer to that is that we do not have direct brain representations of concepts, in the sense that we can physically identify events in the brain and say 'Ah, there is the concept of rain'. The events localized in time and space, so to speak, that we identify will be representations of concrete events, for example, instances of rain, or instances of words. As many readers will recognize, what I am upholding here is the exemplar theory of concepts. This is the theory that originates with Berkeley and Hume and is stated so elegantly in an early passage in Hume's *Treatise of Human Nature* (1739). This theory is also prominent among current theories of concepts. It stands more or less as a co-equal with the prototype theory and the classical definitional theory. (For a current account of psychological research on these three theories, see Murphy, 2002. But the most elegant exposition is given in the early pages of Hume's *Treatise*.) We need not be so sarcastic and sardonic as Berkeley, making fun of Locke's theory of abstract or general ideas, when we affirm there is much in the activity of the brain, as now understood, at least, to confirm Berkeley and Hume and the current exemplar theory. (For some detailed neural data on this point, see Suppes et al., 1999a.) For those who like their concepts clean and simple, there is much that is disturbing about the associative-network view I am proposing. Such networks have a natural inexhaustible complexity. William James puts the matter nicely in his chapter on association in the *Principles of Psychology*.

> The jungle of connections *thought of* can never be formulated simply. Every conceivable connection may be thought of – of coexistence, succession, resemblance, contrast, contradiction, cause and effect, means and end, genus and species, part and whole, substance and property, early and late, large and small,

landlord and tenant, master and servant, – Heaven knows what, for the list is literally inexhaustible.

… If pure thought runs all our trains, why should she run some so fast and some so slow, some through dull flats and some through gorgeous scenery, some to mountain-heights and jewelled mines, others through dismal swamps and darkness? – and run some off the track altogether, and into the wilderness of lunacy? Why do we spend years straining after a certain scientific or practical problem, but all in vain – thought refusing to evoke the solution we desire? And why, some day, walking in the street with our attention miles away from that quest, does the answer saunter into our minds as carelessly as if it had never been called for – suggested, possibly, by the flowers on the bonnet of the lady in front of us, or possibly by nothing that we can discover? If reason can give us relief then, why did she not do so earlier?

(James, 1890/1931, I, pp.551–552)

The patterns of association are rather like the patterns of railroad tracks built up over a century. Many are still used. Others are only barely visible and for some only the right-of-way can now be faintly seen. There is no sharp definition as to what the current state is, depending on use, on property rights, etc. And, so it is with associative networks. The main tracks we know well. They lead to the simple truths exemplified in the previous section. The common tracks for common talk about probabilities and expectations in everyday matters are of lesser strength in association but still quite manifest. The wilder reaches of association are another thing, still there and still important for some purposes, but seldom used. There is no drawing a line of any analytical precision as to where the associative network of a given concept ends and those of new ones begin. The line to be drawn is as arbitrary, if precision is insisted upon, as is that between the analytic and the synthetic.

2.3. Habits as the basis of the theory of rational choice (Suppes, 2003)

Unconscious nature of thinking. Our mental concept of ourselves is above all that of self-aware thinking beings. The pinnacle of rationality is systematic deliberation about ends and means for achieving those ends. From Aristotle to the present, practical reasoning has been a focus of attention in philosophy, but in spite of the acuity of much of what has been written, the complexity and sophistication of the kinds of problems considered as presenting issues for the application of practical reasoning have been limited. What has been especially missing has been attention to the large psychological literature on the nature of thinking, and in particular, the literature

151

concerned with the thinking processes involved in making serious and seemingly deliberate choices that involve major personal goals.

Contrary to much folklore psychology and the implicit assumptions of many philosophers, we are almost entirely unaware or unconscious of our detailed thinking processes. What we have excellent knowledge of is the results of thinking, often of partial results that constitute major steps in reaching a final decision about an important matter. Here is a relatively brief survey of the many kinds of experimental studies supporting these conclusions. They set scientific psychology in opposition to folklore psychology and numerous philosophical ideas and ideals about the rationality of practical reasoning. In fact, it is important not to imply a serious restriction to practical matters. The proper view of the unconscious nature of thinking processes applies to finding solutions to theoretical problems as well.

Two seminal articles on these matters are that of Nisbett and Wilson (1977), whose title is "Telling more than we can know: verbal reports on mental processes" and Wilson (1985), whose title is "Strangers to ourselves: the origins and accuracy of beliefs about one's own mental states." These articles survey in depth a number of experimental and nonexperimental empirical studies over many years, including their own work. I give a brief summary here.

In the first category I mention studies concerned with the inability of individuals to answer "why" questions. Gaudet (1955) found that respondents could not explain why they liked particular political candidates. Ranging far afield from this, Kornhauser and Lazarsfeld (1955) found that respondents could equally not explain why they liked certain detergents for laundering purposes. Lazarsfeld (1931) found that respondents could not explain why they chose a particular occupation and, in a similar vein, Davis (1964) found respondents could not explain why they chose to go to graduate school. Further back in time, Burt (1925) found respondents could not explain why they became juvenile delinquents or, in terms of more positive decisions, Goode (1956) found respondents could not explain in any reasonable way why they got married or divorced. Rossi (1955) found respondents unable to explain why they moved to a new home.

In discussing these examples on several different occasions, I have chosen to expand upon the example of buying a new house. This is a traumatic and difficult process for nearly everyone who has been involved in it. Almost without exception, explanation of the particular choice made is woefully inadequate. This does not mean that certain constraints do not obtain. Individuals are quite competent to state constraints, such as location from schools, overall cost, age of the house and other such factors contributing in a significant way to the final decision. It is just that no overall rationale for the decision taken is ordinarily given. The usual reason is that most individuals, or families, who are selecting a new home, make a very wide search for candidates. They end up with a smaller list with the property that no one dominates all the rest. Consequently, the final decision is based upon something different from the application of a final, solid constraint or a detailed, explicit computation.

Another class of studies, oriented toward theoretical rather than practical problems, concerns individuals' reports on problem-solving processes. Ghilesin (1952) collected data on creative problem solving, as he put it, from Picasso to Poincaré. He emphasizes that production by a process of purely conscious calculation seems never to occur. A classic study of Maier (1931) on combining extension cords on a ceiling for electrification purposes shows how unconscious problem-solvers usually are of their pursuit of a solution. In mathematics there is widespread recognition that theorem-proving of any difficulty depends upon imaginative leaps very similar to memory retrieval, but clearly computational in character. The key idea, just like that of retrieval of a memory, comes into consciousness with no trace at all of how it was arrived at. There are numerous famous anecdotes by scientists and mathematicians about this process. I shall not review them here, but almost everyone is aware of what Hadamard and Poincaré have claimed in this respect. I have never heard a serious mathematician deny that this important role of unconscious processes was in fact always at work in obtaining any significant mathematical result. Here is a short famous quotation from Hadamard (1945).

> One phenomenon is certain and I can vouch for its absolute certainty: the sudden and immediate appearance of a solution at the moment of sudden awakening. On being very abruptly awakened by an external noise, a solution long searched for appeared to me at once without the slightest instant of reflection on my part – the fact was remarkable enough to have struck me unforgettably – and in a quite different direction from any of those which I had previously tried to follow. (Hadamard, 1945, p.8)

The attempts to explain this lack of awareness have produced a large number of new experiments, hypotheses and theoretical analyses from psychologists. Let me just summarize some of the reasons given for why we are unaware of our unawareness. The first is a confusion of content and process. This is not a separation usually made in ordinary talk about decision making, why we have chosen a certain goal or adopted certain means for achieving a certain goal. Second, we have detailed private knowledge of ourselves that is obviously not accessible to anyone else. We can confuse this information with the processes of thinking, because these processes are naturally intertwined with the data that are more or less private for every person. Each of us knows private historical facts about his own thought and action that can affect his thinking processes. Moreover, an individual can tell you his focus of attention at any given moment, which is in itself something quite different from an account of his thinking processes, but is natural to confuse with those processes. Still another factor is private, intermittent awareness of various sensations. We can be aware of seeing a car in the distance or a person nearby missing a step. Recording these observed objects or events can be mistaken for the process of thinking about them.

Perhaps most important, almost all of us are capable of describing coarse intermediate steps in complex problem solving. Good examples are the many steps taken in buying a house, from surveying various neighborhoods, calling an agent, making an escrow deposit, closing the bank loan, to the final dramatic act of moving in. These intermediate steps are intermediate results, easily externally described, but not so for the associated thinking processes. Moreover, such results are at the same time easily confused with the processes themselves, because we do not naturally separate our successive processes of thinking from our successive intermediate results.

What I want to emphasize is this. A theory of rationality that is posited on some exemplary style of rational deliberation, conscious, measured and complete, is utterly mistaken as a psychological account of how any of us go about making decisions about practical problems or solving theoretical ones.

Fantasies of expected utility computations. It is not just the philosophers of practical reasoning that have been mistaken, but it is also the economists and statisticians who have bought into the image of endless rational computations. The further the reach of the computations, the greater the sin of psychological omission in formulating the theoretical ideas. Perhaps the most excessive brand of this is Savage's (1954, p.14) famous fantasy of utility functions over possible states of the world, and the related and intertwined fantasy of de Finetti (1937/1964, p.146) that once we have a probability distribution, all future revisions of thought processes will be by

154

conditioning only, that is, strictly in the sense of probability theory. Of course, they were both too smart to hold that these fantasies could be realized.

For reasons too numerous to enumerate here, the number of actual long-run calculations ever made is negligible. Keynes had it right. The important fact about the long run is that in the long run we are all dead.

The actual computations we do are fragmentary, occasional, contextual, driven by associations internal and external. A much better guide to thought than the utilitarian principle of maximization taken in its raw form is William James's account of the stream of thought in chapter IX of his *Principles of Psychology* (1890/1931). Here is one passage.

> Now we are seeing, now hearing; now reasoning, now willing; now recollecting, now expecting; now loving, now hating; and in a hundred other ways we know our minds to be alternately engaged. But all these are complex states. (James, 1890/1931, I, p.230)

As I will argue shortly, our computations are built up from myriads of associations, intertwined with our past in ways that we can no more understand in detail now than we can explain how we retrieve a familiar name or a well-known fact from memory. It is why I like to say that when it comes to human computations, fragmentary and associative in character, Proust is a better guide than Turing. Here is a quotation that illustrates this well, from *Time Regained: In Search of Lost Time*, the last part of Proust's extraordinary novel (1927/1999).

> All day long, in that slightly too countrified house which seemed no more than a place for a rest between walks or during a sudden downpour, one of those houses in which all the sitting-rooms look like arbours and, on the wall-paper in the bedrooms, here the roses from the garden, there the birds from the trees outside join you and keep you company, isolated from the world – for it was old wall-paper on which every rose was so distinct that, had it been alive, you could have picked it, every bird you could have put in a cage and tamed, quite different from those grandiose bedroom decorations of today where, on a silver background, all the apple-trees of Normandy display their outlines in the Japanese style to hallucinate the hours you spend in bed – all day long I remained in my room which looked over the fine greenery of the park and the lilacs at the entrance, over the green leaves of the tall trees by the edge of the lake, sparkling in the sun, and the forest of Méséglise. Yet I looked at all this with pleasure only because I said to myself: "How nice to be able to see so much greenery from my bedroom window," until the moment when, in the vast verdant picture, I recognised, painted in a contrasting dark blue simply because it was further

away, the steeple of Combray church. Not a representation of the steeple, but the steeple itself, which, putting in visible form a distance of miles and of years, had come, intruding its discordant tone into the midst of the luminous verdure – a tone so colourless that it seemed little more than a preliminary sketch – and engraved itself upon my windowpane. And if I left my room for a moment, I saw at the end of the corridor, in a little sitting-room which faced in another direction, what seemed to be a band of scarlet – for this room was hung with a plain silk, but a red one, ready to burst into flames if a ray of sun fell upon it. (Proust, 1927/1999, pp.9–10)

This long passage from Proust shows why he is a better guide to human computation than Turing. The true complexity of much, if not most, human computing is to be found in perception. The human visual system may be the most complicated system in the universe, after the brain itself. And our continual attention to vision, seen from an unusual angle, in Proust's highly particular perceptions and associations, is characteristic of much of our waking hours, even if we do not usually focus on what we see as intently as in Proust's account. This primacy of perception is testimony to the relative ease of building digital computers compared to the great difficulty of constructing artificial visual systems. The gap between the richness and complexity of perception and thought, so well described by James and Proust, compared to the crude oversimplifications characteristic of any attempt at direct expected utility computations over possible states of the world is an important source of skepticism about the latter.

Habits. There is a scent of *tabula rasa* about the approach to rational choice via maximizing expected utility. It is as if the organism has a simple, uncomplicated structure, whose behavior can be maximized in the way that a simple physics problem can be solved by finding a maximum or minimum of an appropriate quantity. For biological organisms, beginning even with the simplest, nothing could be further from a sensible way of thinking about their behavior. The complexities that can be invoked at this point are much too numerous to be pursued in any detail, but there is one class of phenomena that may be seen not only in mankind but in animals up and down the hierarchy of evolution or complexity. These are the effects of learning on the long-term behavior of an animal. There is, however, a better term, older, and also very much a part of folklore psychology, although not well developed. This is the concept of a *habit*. Some things that we call habits are undoubtedly purely instinctual, that is, are unlearned and encoded in the genes somewhere in the DNA. Most things, however, that we call habits represent an interaction between the genetic structure of an animal and the environment in which it develops and continues to exist. Habits are superb examples of learning, but I want to put the emphasis here on the results of learning, rather than on the learning itself.

Before I say more about habits, let me put my cards face up on the table, so that it will be clear how I am using the concept of habits to help characterize rationality. Habits constitute restraints, in the standard mathematical sense of constraints, on the choices we make. We do not consciously think of our habits in making choices, but concentrate, so far as we exercise conscious discrimination at all, in choosing one thing rather than another, in such a way as to satisfy the appropriate constraints. For example, I am at the stage of my life where I very much prefer wine to beer. At an ordinary dinner in a restaurant, faced with a menu, I only think about the choice of wine, and almost never consider beer. I do not go through any deliberate, rational analysis of the virtues of wine over beer, because of the constraint already established by long-settled habits. I accept the constraint without even thinking or being conscious of it. I can, of course, at another time and for another purpose, make myself conscious of having this constraint. But the important point is that in the act of choosing itself, we do not ordinarily pay conscious attention to the habits we have.

This is not to say that such conscious occasions can never occur. It is the stuff of family drama and the essence of many good novels for a person, real or fictitious, to face up to habits that must be broken, in order to make a choice that is much more important and meaningful to the person than any casual breaking of habits of old. But this is the exceptional situation – one that we can, of course, describe. Yet it is important to get the usual regime of choosing properly thought out. In fact, in the context of this article, I will not attempt to give a serious discussion of when we want to breach our constraints, that is, our habits, and go for something unusual, challenging or even frightening. This is an important topic, but one that can be left to the side, because of the low frequency of such choices, and the necessity of having a much better view of the usual kind of choices we make, from the dramatic ones of buying houses to the trivial ones of choosing glasses of wine.

So, I emphasize, the habits of a lifetime, as the saying goes, present constraints that are ordinarily satisfied. But the constraints do not fix the choice. My strong constraint of always choosing wine, and never beer, does not in any way determine the particular choice of wine on a given occasion.

You may think that I am next going to say that we have come upon the proper role for maximization, namely, to maximize our choices subject to the constraints of habits. But I will not even accept the traditional theory of maximizing expected utility in this reduced role. To anticipate what I will say later, and to give you a sense of the organization of the ideas about rationality I am presenting, the next step after habits is to let the associations of the moment make the choice as freely and as easily as possible. I will not say more about these associations yet, but this is a prelude to what is to replace, not just maximization, but even satisficing, the central concept of Simon's (1955) well-known theory of bounded rationality.

Now back to habits. Much of what I want to say in the context of the present article about habits is said better and in more detail in chapter IV of James's *Principles of Psychology*. I shall not attempt a faithful summary of his ideas, but only emphasize points that are relevant to the characterization of rationality, and I do not claim that what I say is anything like a faithful paraphrase of his thoughts.

The first point is that habits are really physical and already present in nonanimate matter. What we ordinarily think of as certain material properties correspond to what we would call habits in animals. But particle or animal, the habit should be thought of as something physically embodied in the nervous system, and in the muscles, where appropriate. The only real difference on this score between animals and inanimate objects is the much greater mutability of habits in animals. James has a wonderful quote from someone else about the many ways in which matter itself is not immutable. The examples are particularly from designed objects, which have a special property. This is the second point: such objects function better the more they are used. Engines, locks, hinges on doors and the like improve with age, up to a point of course. Let me quote James (1890/1931, p.112), "habit simplifies the movements required to achieve a given result, makes them more accurate and diminishes fatigue." The ironic thing about this aspect of habit is to recognize the importance of efficiency and yet to realize how little it is ever given its pride of place in the discussion of such matters by utilitarians. Habits, indeed, are themselves utilitarian in the deepest sense of that word, namely, in their clearly useful contribution to doing things.

The third property to be mentioned, one of importance in connection with mistaken notions of rational deliberation, is that habits diminish the conscious attention with which acts are performed. In more domains of experience than can be named, only the inept, the awkward and the untrained are conscious of their performances. The accomplished, the gifted and the

158

well trained are not. And so it is with choices. The final process of choosing is one that is properly left unconscious, once the first round of constraints that are either habitual, or deliberately modified for application to a new situation, have been satisfied. The final reduced choice set should be one worthy of unconscious contemplation and free association. Now many will think that my phrase 'unconscious contemplation' is really overdoing it. Only the mindless choose this way. The data show otherwise. Only the inept are mindful of their final choices, to put the matter in the most controversial way, but one about which I am all the same utterly serious.

Finally, I cannot forego one more quotation from James about the important social role of habits. This topic lies somewhat outside my main focus here, which is on individuals, but a theory of rationality that ignores the social framework, of one kind or another, in which all of us live, is a Robinson-Crusoe view that is clearly a reductive absurdity.

> Habit is thus the enormous fly-wheel of society, its most precious conservative agent. It alone is what keeps us all within the bounds of ordinance, and saves the children of fortune from the envious uprisings of the poor. It alone prevents the hardest and most repulsive walks of life from being deserted by those brought up to tread therein. It keeps the fisherman and the deck-hand at sea through the winter; it holds the miner in his darkness, and nails the countryman to his log-cabin and his lonely farm through all the months of snow; it protects us from invasion by the natives of the desert and the frozen zone. It dooms us all to fight out the battle of life upon the lines of our nurture or our early choice, and to make the best of a pursuit that disagrees, because there is no other for which we are fitted, and it is too late to begin again. (James, 1890/1931, p.121)

We don't have to accept or use all of James's examples. We can easily write new ones, suitable for our own age and technology, but his point is understandable without any changes needed.

Entropy and free associations. A habit that is deterministic will, of course, have an entropy rate of zero. In my familiar example of usually choosing wine over beer in a restaurant, the entropy rate of my responses, at the concrete level of the kind of wine, vintage and winemaker selected, will not be zero. Notice that the level of abstraction selected will vary the entropy rate. It is also part of my philosophy of these matters that there is no ultimate concrete specification, so that any level selected reflects some kind of abstraction. As we eliminate vintage, say, first, then winemaker, and then kind of wine, we expect the entropy rate to decrease, so that finally, if we have only the choice of beer, wine or soft drink, as the three possible choices, my entropy rate is close to zero. (An interesting question for consumer-behavior studies is what level of abstraction is of the most interest in calculating entropy rate.)

There is a deeper question and one I am not yet entirely clear about, but fundamental to the ideas I am working on. This is what is the proper level of abstraction, in terms of what is represented mentally (or in the brain). So, after making some determination of habit, if the entropy rate is not zero, room is left for free associations. It is especially the free associations that we expect to be malleable and therefore subject to transient changes in stimulation; such expectations are also characteristic of firms that vie for shelf space to advertise their products.

My tentative answer to the level of abstraction of the associations is that it just depends on the strength of resemblance or similarity between the mental (or brain) images, on the one hand, and the stimuli on the other. And, in fact, it is a mistake of mine to introduce the misleading idea of abstraction. It is better to introduce different relations of similarity, which we can use to make corresponding, but more psychologically realistic, claims. In other words, any use of abstraction should be backed up by a working concept of similarity or isomorphism to define the particular level of abstraction.

Both the concepts of habit and of free association can be applied with varying definitions of similarity or isomorphism. Note that the two, habit and free association, must go together, if we want to complete the study of choice. For example, to use again my familiar example, if we consider just my standard choice of wine over beer, habit completely accounts for my choice at this level and there is no room left for free association. But if we make the isomorphic or similarity relation more detailed, there is. In fact, in the present formulation of ideas, whenever the level of characterization of a habit has nonzero entropy, the remaining nontrivial choice set leaves room for free associations.

This remark leads to the natural question of how to distinguish between habits and free associations. Can we just define a relation of isomorphism or similarity at any level and thereby mark a distinction, so that we distinguish only relative to such a relation? In some ways this seems a good choice, for after all, according to the ideas being advanced here, association or the special case of conditioning, is also at the basis of habit, except possibly for some small part that is genetic in character. Is such a complete relativization of the distinction between habit and free association a satisfactory answer? I do not think so. For, it seems to me, it is important also to separate the ephemeral quality of free associations from the lasting quality of habits. This separation can be made by introducing further distinctions among the similarity relations used, based on their temporal character. I do not pursue the formal details here.

Associations as natural computations. From a philosophical standpoint, the great opposition to the fundamental mechanisms of the mind being just associative computation and memory is the Kantian line of transcendental idealism grounded in the *a priori* synthetic. But it is important to note that Kant thought that Hume was right in what he claimed empirically for association (*Critique of Pure Reason*, 1781/1997, A100). It is just that he did not accept that Humean empiricism was ultimately enough as a foundation for science, especially for Newtonian mechanics and mathematics.

Writing a hundred years later, William James is an enthusiastic critic of Kant's grounding of science with necessary *a priori* synthetic principles. Here is a passage expressing his thought well.

> ... The eternal verities which the very structure of our mind lays hold of do not necessarily themselves lay hold on extra-mental being, nor have they as Kant pretended later a legislating character even for all possible experience. They are primarily interesting only as subjective facts. They stand waiting in the mind, forming a beautiful ideal network; and the most we can say is that we *hope* to discover outer realities over which the network may be flung so that ideal and real may coincide. (James, 1890/1931, I, pp.664–665)

The passage comes nearly at the end of the 2nd volume of James's deep and majestic survey of 19th-century psychology. But it is not an isolated few lines. James attacks again and again Kant's transcendental idealism and his attempted *a priori* grounding of knowledge.

Moving ahead to more recent developments in psychology, the special case of association that is important, in the first half of the twentieth century in the development of psychology, is, of course, conditioning. The concept of conditioning dominated thinking about almost all aspects of psychology from the first decade of the twentieth century to the second half of the century. It ended only with the linguistic revolution of Chomsky and others, and the subsequent development of a cognitive psychology that, to a large extent, has emphasized the role of rules over associations as the basis for thought. This regime, which was prominent from about 1965 to 1980, has had, as its hallmark, the replacement of nonsymbolic by symbolic thought. The decline of this line of theory began around 1980 with the introduction of nonsymbolic computational processes, so characteristic of modern neural networks. More than two centuries after the death of David Hume in 1776 we again find ourselves returning to associations, now often in the form of neural networks. Currently they occupy the dominant place in the conception of the mechanisms of thought. Not everyone will agree with the formulation I have just given. Many will claim that it is still just too strong to say this, that there are other modes of thinking that remain of great importance. I am skeptical of that. I am happy to push the thesis that those other modes are themselves splendid examples of conditioning, for example, the mental computations of arithmetic, the algorithmic rules we all learn early. If we turn from such algorithms with the contempt with which many cognitive scientists and some mathematicians do, then the response is even better. Surely the evidence is that the best and hardest mathematical proofs arise, not from some linear, nicely formulated line of explicit reasons, but from random, scattered, jumbled associations of the kind mentioned in the passage from James and the one from Hadamard. Only later is an orderly exposition of justification found.

To push these ideas further, in 1969 I gave a clear mathematical proof that, just from ideas of stimulus and response, we could generate finite automata (Suppes, 1969). In a later article (Suppes, 1977), I showed how to extend these ideas to an arbitrary Turing machine, all operating by conditioning, that is, by special cases of association. The argument is amplified in Suppes (2002, ch.8). From a psychological standpoint, these constructions of finite automata or simulated Turing machines are too simple. No doubt the actual computational processes in the brain using associations extensively are more devious and complicated. Moreover, we do not begin language learning with a mind that is a *tabula rasa*. Much structure and related processing is constrained by our common genetic inheritance. It is then above all association or conditioning that shapes the further development.

There is one additional point I want to make to those who remain skeptical about association. Think about your own methods of memory retrieval, and then try to give a theory that does not deeply involve processes of association.

Freedom of association. As some may note, the title of this section is meant as a double entendre. On the one hand, I have in mind associations in the brain, and on the other, the great historic libertarian demand of freedom of association for the individual. But it is the brain about which I am serious at this point. Let me be explicit about what I want to mean by *free-*

dom of association. I have in mind a hierarchical conception of how we make rational choices. To begin with, we must satisfy our habits. With satisfaction of the constraints given by habits or some specific computations, we are then left with an unresolved set of choices. How should we choose from this set? The classical utilitarian method is by maximizing utility. The classic algebraic theory I consider a hopeless enterprise, for reasons already given. The rational individual, who satisfies the constraints of habit, is one who is freely associating and choosing that one of the remaining available set of options that seems most attractive, based on past associations that are brought up, as can be the case in buying a house, or, in other instances, by the association to anticipated events. Often, a glimpse at something attractive nearby sets off the train of associations. Belief in the relatively high frequency of this last case is a fundamental tenet of advertising.

The immediate reaction of some readers may be to challenge this probabilistic mechanism of choice as normal. They may recall (perhaps I should say, *associate*) their earlier encounter with the literature of psychoanalysis and its emphasis on the central role of free association in interpreting dreams or analyzing repressions, slips of the tongue and many other phenomena. But the central role of association in our mental life was not a Freudian discovery. It goes back at least to Aristotle. Here is Freud describing the associations arising from the interpretation of a dream:

> And next, we obtain these associations. What they bring us is of the most various kinds: memories from the day before, the 'dream-day', and from times long past, reflections, discussions, with arguments for and against, confessions and enquiries. Some of them the patient pours out; when he comes to others he is held up for a time. Most of them show a clear connection to some element of the dream; no wonder, since those elements were their starting-point. (Freud, 1971, p.11)

It does not sound much different from one of the earliest references to associations in various passages of Aristotle's *On Memory and Recollection*. For example,

> It often happens that one cannot recollect at the moment, but can do so by searching, and finds what he wants. This occurs by his initiating many impulses, until at last he initiates one such that it will lead to the object of his search. For remembering consists in the potential existence in the mind of the effective stimulus; and this, as has been said, in such a way that the subject is stimulated from himself, and from the stimuli which he contains within him.

But one must secure a starting-point. This is why some people seem, in recollecting, to proceed from *loci*. The reason for this is that they pass rapidly from one step to the next; for instance from milk to white, from white to air, from air to damp; from which one remembers autumn, if this is the season that he is trying to recall. ...

If one is not moving along an old path, one's movement tends towards the more customary; for custom now takes the place of nature. Hence we remember quickly things which are often in our thoughts; for as in nature one thing follows another, so also in the actualization of these stimuli; and the frequency has the effect of nature. ...

That the experience is in some sense physical, and that recollection is the search for a mental picture in the physical sphere, is proved by the annoyance which some men show when in spite of great concentration they cannot remember, and which persists even when they have abandoned the attempt to recollect, ...

(Aristotle, 1975, pp.303–311)

In the last part of this passage, especially with the reference to frequency, Aristotle is distinguishing between natural and customary associations. Earlier in the passage, when he mentions *loci* he is referring to the ancient "artificial" art of memory by associating, for example, people with given places. Ancient and medieval texts are full of a wonderful range of examples of such use of spatial places as an aid to memory. Aristotle does not use a Greek term for association, but it is implied in phrases such as "pass rapidly from one step to the next" or when he says slightly earlier than the quoted passage "Arts of recollection occur when one impulse naturally succeeds another" (p.301). Finally a few lines later on the same page he describes what are sometimes called his three laws of association.

This is why we follow the trail in order, starting in thought from the present, or some other concept, and from something similar or contrary to, or closely connected with, what we seek. (Aristotle, 1975, p.301)

Here similarity is just like Hume's resemblance, and "closely connected" with contiguity.

The maxims and heuristics of the ancient art of artificial memory were aimed at the facilitation of memory, but the associations used, often with an emphasis on vivid and striking images, are not far removed from those Freud encountered in the free associations of his patients. (For the history of the art of memory, see Yates, 1966.)

To make another point, I want to say something more explicit about what I mean by *free* associations, since the general theory of associations covers a large part of executing practical activities. In such activities the associations are not free, but conditioned in a fixed sequence to accomplish the task at hand. As the standard phrase goes, they have become automatic. Free associations are of a different sort, consciously used in memory searches, for example, when automatic retrieval is not working. Free associations are more characteristic during moments of meditation or reverie, but also as unexpected intrusions of images unrelated to the task at hand, prompted by any of a great variety of possibilities.

The message I am trumpeting is that of learning to recognize the guidance and the help we can get from such associations, and perhaps even more, from those that do not rise to consciousness, but that are expressed in action by our actual choices. We often describe such choices as instinctual, as "the one I liked but I can't say why," or as "the one that seemed familiar but I can't explain it."

Free associations are a mixed bag, some come with positive affect and some not. A good example of "not" is to be found in the early pages of Joyce's *Ulysses* (1934, pp.7–11) as Stephen Daedalus ruminates about the death of his mother following Buck Mulligan's remark that he killed her by his stubborn refusal to kneel and pray at her bedside as she lay dying. Such inward-turning ruminations can interfere with the quality of associations and thus of choices. Experimental confirmation of this claim is to be found in Wilson and Schooler (1991) and related studies referred to there.

The variety of empirical studies that I would classify as relevant to the understanding of free associations is very large. But there are two broad, not quite orthogonal, classifications of the most importance. One is the distinction between those having positive or negative affect, and the other is between being inward or outward directed. The connections between ruminative, negative-affect associations and psychological depression have been much studied. The detailed complex conclusions cannot be summarized here, but a good overview is to be found in Nolen-Hoeksema (1991).

Even though I am persuaded that the theory of rationality, or of freedom for that matter, in the fullest sense should include the psychological concepts and problems mentioned in the preceding paragraph, it is not feasible to go further here. I do think there has been far too much separation between the conceptual approaches to choice behavior of economists, on the one hand, and social or personality psychologists, on the other. Only in the empirical studies of consumer behavior have we as yet seen a real reduction of this separation.

A formal remark on utility. Even though I am, as already expressed, skeptical of the grander schemes of how expected utility is maximized in the choices of ideally rational persons, there is a natural connection between the probabilistic phenomena of free associations in choice and random utility models. Much of the current literature on choice in the social sciences, especially economics, uses random utility functions (e.g., McFadden & Train, 2000). A strict derivation of such utility models from basic assumptions about momentary mental associations is straightforward. We sketch the mathematical argument here. We define the momentary random utility of a choice response r at time t by the sum of the strengths of momentary associations of the brain image of r to brain images of scenes, pictures, persons, and so forth at t. The decision rule is now that a choice response r is made at time t if its momentary random utility at t is the maximum among choice responses available. In other words, among the possible choice responses, the probability of choice response r occurring is just the probability that at time t the momentary associative strength of the brain image of r is the largest. The essential connection of utility to free associations is made by using fluctuating random utility functions, which literally change from moment to moment, as advertisers realize and depend on to promote their products.

2.4. Psychological nature of the verification of informal mathematical proofs (Suppes, 2005)

Even less than what was said in the first example on truth computations can be easily said about the intuitive steps, without explicit formal verification, in informal proofs. But I would defend the proposition that in such proofs we continually use patterns of associations that are more complicated and subtle than those needed in my truth examples. Yet I suggest, it is a feasible psychological project to survey the main features of such patterns in the informal proofs that occur in a given area of mathematics. Memory of many such patterns is undoubtedly a mark of being an expert in a given domain. Perhaps even more important is having a feeling of how to judge correctly the similarity of a prior pattern, widely held to be valid, to a new one being evaluated. Such experienced judgments of similarity are not at all special to proofs, but occur in every area of experience from case studies of the law to athletic skills of every variety. The content is special to the domain, but the general empirical character is not. (For an introduction to the formal aspects of the large psychological literature on similarity, often an intransitive relation due to thresholds, see Chapter 14 on proximity spaces and Chapter 16 on representations and thresholds of Suppes, Krantz, Luce, and Tversky (1989), which also contains extensive references.)

What I have said is too general, but can quickly be extended to more specific considerations by examining some examples of informal proofs. For reasons of space, I restrict myself to two.

Example 1. Proof of an Archimedean axiom, taken from Royden (1963). The axiom C referred to in the proof is the standard completeness axiom: every nonempty set S of real numbers which has an upper bound has a least upper bound. Here is the theorem and informal proof, as given by Royden:

> **Axiom of Archimedes**: *Given any real number x, there is an integer n such that x < n.*
>
> *Proof:* Let S be the set of integers k such that $k \leq x$. Since S has the upper bound x, it has a least upper bound y by axiom C. Since y is the least upper bound for S, $y - \frac{1}{2}$ cannot be an upper bound for S, and so there is a $k \in S$ such that $k > y - \frac{1}{2}$. But $k + 1 > y + \frac{1}{2} > y$, and so $(k + 1) \notin S$. Since $k + 1$ is an integer not in S, we must have $k + 1$ greater than x by the definition of S.
>
> (Royden, 1963, p.25)

As expected, there is no filling out of obvious simple arguments. For example, "$y - \frac{1}{2}$ cannot be an upper bound for S." The formal expansion is obvious but tedious. What is important here, and critical for informal proofs, is the power of ordinary language along with a minimum of notation to describe the argument that could easily be written as an algorithm. In saying this I am not claiming that we know how to write general algorithms for any such gaps. In general form they may not exist, because of well-known undecidability results, or high lower bounds on such decision procedures as Tarski's for the first-order theory of real closed fields. The last sentence of the proof exhibits a similar use of ordinary language to summarize informally the argument.

Example 2. This one concerns equivalents of the axiom of choice. I take the example from my own book on axiomatic set theory (Suppes, 1960/1972). A useful maximal principle, due independently to Teichmüller (1939) and Tukey (1940), is characterized by defining when a set is of *finite character*, which is true of a set A if and only if

(i) A is a nonempty set of sets,
(ii) every finite subset of a member of A is also a member of A.

The intuitive idea behind this formulation is that a property is of finite character if a set has the property when and only when all of its finite subsets have the property.

Teichmüller-Tukey Lemma: T. *Any set of finite character has a maximal element.*

The theorem of interest is:

Theorem: *The Teichmüller-Tukey Lemma* T *is equivalent to Zorn's Lemma* Z.

Recall that Zorn's Lemma states that if $A \neq 0$ and if the sum of each nonempty chain which is a subset of A is in A, then A has a maximal element, where A is a chain if and only if A is a set of sets and for any two sets B and C in A either $B \subseteq C$ or $C \subseteq B$.

> *Proof*: We prove only the first half, namely, that Zorn's Lemma (Z) implies the Teichmüller-Tukey Lemma.
>
> Let A be a set of finite character, and let C be any chain which is a subset of A. To apply Z we need to prove that $\cup\, C \in A$. Let F be a finite subset of $\cup\, C$. Then F is a subset of the union of a finite collection D of members of C, for each element of F must belong to some member of C and there are only a finite number of elements in F. Now since D is finite and is a subset of the chain C, it has a largest member, say E; and F must be a subset of E, for otherwise C would not be a chain. $E \in A$, whence since A is a set of finite character, $F \in A$; but then also $\cup\, C \in A$. The hypothesis of Z is thus satisfied by A and by virtue of Z, A has a maximal element.
>
> (Suppes, 1960/1972, p.249)

A first rough comparison to the length of this informal proof to formal ones that assumed the same background of prior theorems may be made using empirical data in Suppes and Sheehan (1981, p.79) on the length of nine formal proofs made by students in a course I taught for many years on set theory, for which a computer-based proof checker was developed and then regularly used. (Details are in the article just cited.) The mean length, is terms of number of lines with explicit inference rules, was 41.8, with the min = 25 and the max = 61. As expected, the informal proof given above is much shorter.

The central characteristic of this informal proof, like the previous one, is the use of ordinary English sentences with some embedded mathematical symbols to summarize intuitively individual arguments, each of which correspond approximately to a number of steps in a formal proof.

A psychological point about this linguistic feature of many informal written proofs is the implication for understanding such sentences. Undoubtedly the problem of being satisfied with a personal verification of an informal proof is quite dependent on the intuitive mathematical clarity of the written form of the informal proof. So, often it is not the overall structure of the proof, but the difficulty of comprehending individual sentences. To comprehend such sentences the reader often needs to be able to build a mathematical model satisfying the sentence, and often some other sentences as well as visual graphs and the like, at least in sufficient detail to feel the model is enough. Mathematicians are good at this. It is an essential part of what they have learned. Intellectually, this differs from algorithmic checking in a way that is parallel to the difference between model theory and proof theory.

From a broader perspective, the contrast between formal and informal proofs is striking. A formal proof manipulates symbols, and to check such a proof a computer program needs to have no understanding at all of the symbols to make an evaluation of correctness. A corresponding informal proof ordinarily does not mention mathematical symbols or language of any sort, but only mathematical objects, numbers, not numerals, operations on sets, not the notation for the operations, etc. The linguistic demand, in this case, is semantically driven, not syntactically. Understanding of the informal language used to talk about nonlinguistic mathematical objects is necessary.

Finally, I want to emphasize that the model sketches, as I am calling them, used to check informal proofs, are special to mathematicians only in part, not in their general psychological features, which are surely shared by architects, builders, and designers of all kinds who rely on a variety of images, externalized on paper or on a computer screen, but also images of the imagination, to facilitate thinking about whatever problem is current.

On the basis of the sound methodological principle that properties of the mind are really properties of the brain, it is useful to see what can be said about informal proofs from the standpoint of brain activity, even though it is obvious we have at present many mental concepts we cannot characterize in terms of what we know about the brain.

The first observation is one that brings us back to formal proofs. It is widely recognized by almost everyone working on the subject that all computations are physical computations. In other words, any actual computations require a physical embodiment. This does not mean that digital computers are in any sense the universal model of how computations are made. Natural computations in the biological world have an endless variety of physical embodiments. The computational nature of DNA as the genetic code is probably the greatest single scientific discovery of the second half of the twentieth century. But the problems of understanding the physical computations of the seemingly simple motions of the thousands of insect species are overwhelming in their complexity and diversity. How, for example, does an ordinary house fly compute its escape route of flight from a detected predator?

Formal proofs are certainly recognized as having relatively easy implementation as physical computations on a digital computer. Whatever abstract talk there is about the meaning and implications of a formal proof, the verification of the proof is a recursive physical process, painfully explicit in its details, as emphasized earlier from a different perspective.

Something similar has to be true of informal proofs, with brain computations replacing digital ones. A much too simple model of such brain computations was given earlier in the analysis of how the truth is computed of ordinary empirical statements about highly familiar matters, such as the most obvious sort of geographic or demographic facts. At the psychological level, the method of computation proposed is that of association. Informal proofs are a triumphant application. At least until recently, many psychologists unfamiliar with the detailed analysis of mechanisms of computations were inclined to be skeptical of such a claim. But the general complexity analogy with digital computers is too obvious to tolerate any wholesale rejection of association as the primary basis of the brain's computations. Yet, as I have already stated, it is a long way from Minsky's simple universal Turing machine (1967) with four symbols and seven internal states to the complexity of a digital computer with programs able to defeat the best human chess players, for example, or make a trillion computations to predict the weather. So it is with the brain, from the simple associations of small invertebrates like *Aplysia* to the most intricate mathematical proofs.

I have introduced, in these last paragraphs, many inadequately developed ideas about how the brain works. Full details are available nowhere, but will undoubtedly be a subject of intense research for many years to come. There is not space to try to say in a careful way what I think we do, at the present, know. So I will end with two remarks, one speculative and one empirical.

The first remark concerns meaning. It is a standard complaint of many years that Hilbert's formal systems for the foundations of mathematics turn mathematics into a meaningless game. The arithmetic of numerals, as opposed to numbers, has nothing like the rich content of genuine number theory or geometry, a source of endless intuitions and meaningful relations. The new home of Hilbert-style formalisms is, of course, in computer science, and much more broadly, the programming efforts throughout the world to use formal languages to write computer programs, which implement solutions to a vast array of tasks and problems. There is no additional sense or meaning given to the computer as part of these programs. It is formalism all the way down, but with physical embodiment. Moreover, it is hard to think of its being any other way.

Detailed thinking about the brain moves in the same direction. There is no mysterious Fregean sense lurking somewhere in the cortex, ready to supply meaning as needed. The meaning of a word, a phrase or a sentence, like the meaning of a perceptual image, is to be found in a welter of associations, or, to put it more soberly, in associative networks that are, in humans, if not in *Aplysia*, of great complexity. Of course, to put it this way is too bald and simple, as if reference to complexity were sufficient to explain how a predictive model of the weather computes an estimate of what the weather will be like the day after tomorrow. It helps not at all, in concrete terms, to say the program uses a terabyte of memory and computes at the rate of two terabits a second. Sustained research will be required for the indefinite future to untangle just how the brain is computing any important task, but the associative nature of the computations is, on present evidence, a reasonable conjecture.

Displacing the Aristotelian and Cartesian conceptions of mind, attractive and empirically sound as they were in many respects, will, when fully accomplished be comparable in intellectual importance to the displacement of Ptolemaic astronomy by that of Copernicus, Kepler and Newton. This philosophical and scientific revolution of the mind was given a big boost by Hume's *Treatise of Human Nature* (1739/1888). Moreover, the claim that the workings of mind reflect above all the workings of collections of synchronized neurons linked in a complex associative network is broadly accepted already in neuroscience, and much of psychology, but by no means to the same extent in philosophy.

The second and final remark is more down to earth and empirical. An early question that arises in thinking about how the brain processes ordinary language, including that used in informal proofs, is, how does the brain process linguistic input, i.e., language for listeners? (The question of linguistic output, i.e., speech production, is even more complicated.) Here I have in mind the relatively simple question of just what can we say about the initial brain processing of words and sentences heard. (I consider here only spoken language, but most of what I have to say applies just as well to the visual process of reading.) Now the analysis of sentences as finite sequences of words, and the analysis of words as sequences of syllables, and, at the more detailed level, sequences of phonemes, is widely accepted as being approximately correct. In addition, for many reasons, it is a sensible hypothesis to expect that the methods of brain computation are likely to preserve approximately the temporal order of words in sentences, syllables in words, and so forth.

To test this idea in brain data is to test a hypothesis of structural isomorphism between spoken sentences and their brain representations. I summarize some unpublished work with my younger colleagues (Suppes, Perreau-Guimaraes, and Wong, In press). Sentences are presented auditorily or visually, one word at a time on a computer screen, at the temporal pace of the auditory recordings. Electric waves in the cortex, time-locked to the presentation of each sentence, are recorded for each subject using standard electroencephalography (EEG) techniques. Various linear models, such as those based on Fourier transforms and filters, or one-layer neural networks, are used to eliminate noise and find an approximately invariant signal (Wong, Perreau-Guimaraes, Uy, and Suppes, 2004). The measure of success at the first level is being able to classify correctly a significant number of test trials not used in estimating the parameters of the model being evaluated. The sentences were of the geographic type mentioned earlier, and the subjects were asked to judge each one as true or false, and so indicate by typing '1' for true and '2' for false. Good, but far from perfect, recognition results were obtained by sets of sentences of size 24, 48 or

100. We also isolated in the temporal sequence of presentation, individual words to which the same models were applied.

Let f be a one-one function mapping each sentence s to its brain representation $f(s)$. Let g be a corresponding function for words. Then our test of structural isomorphism is whether or not we can find empirical support for the structural equation, where $s = w_1 w_2 \ldots w_n$,

$$f(w_1 w_2 \ldots w_n) = g(w_1) g(w_2) \ldots g(w_n).$$

It perhaps seems too obvious that this equation should hold, just by asking how else could the brain process sentences. But already at the level of speech such precise identification is not always easy, so it is a serious problem whether or not such results can be substantiated in the brain. We have good support, but not as good as our recognition of sentences, which is not surprising, since this same relation of relative difficulty holds for speech.

Finding support for such a natural isomorphism seems necessary to get started, but it is clearly a long journey of further results to get to such questions as how informal proofs are processed in the brain. In this case, much more than the initial isomorphism of recognition is needed. Semantic computation in the spirit of the associative networks and model sketches mentioned earlier are essential. Still, at a certain level the task is well-defined, and I see, at the present, no alternative conception that is more promising. Whatever empirical route does prove successful, I find it unimaginable that there can be a fully satisfactory theory of the verification of informal proofs that is *a priori* and devoid of psychological, and ultimately neural, concepts and data.

ACKNOWLEDGMENTS

Earlier versions of this paper were given at the College de France in Paris and at the Department of History and Philosophy of Science, Indiana University, Bloomington, Indiana. I have made extensive revisions based on comments made on these earlier occasions and most recently at the 31st Wittgenstein Symposium in Kirchberg, Austria.

173

REFERENCES

Aristotle (1975). On memory and recollection. In G.P. Goold, ed., *On the Soul [De Anima], Parva Naturalia, On Breath*, pp.287–315. Cambridge, MA: Harvard University Press, 4th edn. English translation by W.S. Hett. First published in 1936.

Blackburn, P. and J. Bos (2005). *Representation and Inference for Natural Language: A First Course in Computational Semantics*. Stanford, CA: CSLI Publication.

Burt, C.L. (1925). *The Young Delinquent*, 4th edn., London: University of Toronto Press.

Collins, A.M. and E. Loftus (1975). A Spreading Activation Theory of Semantic Processing. *Psychological Review*, 82, pp.407–428.

Davis, J. A. (1964). *Great Aspirations: The Graduate School Plans of America's College Students*. Chicago: Aldine.

de Finetti, B. (1937/1964). La prévision: ses lois logiques, ses sources subjectives. *Annales de l'Institut Henri Poincaré*, 7, pp.1–68. Translation in Kyburg and Smokler (1964).

Freud, S. (1971). New Introductory Lectures on Psycho-analysis, and Other Works. In J. Strachey, ed., *The Standard Edition of the Complete Psychological Works of Sigmund Freud, Vol.XXII*, p.11. London: Hogarth Press. First published in 1964.

Gaudet, H. (1955). A Model for Assessing Changes in Voting Intention. In P.F. Lazarsfeld and M. Rosenberg, eds., *The Language of Social Research*. New York: Free Press of Glencoe.

Ghilesin, B. (1952). *The Creative Process*. New York: Mentor.

Goode, W.J. (1956). *After Divorce*. New York: Free Press of Glencoe.

Hadamard, J. (1945). *The Psychology of Invention in the Mathematical Field*. Princeton: Princeton University Press.

Hume, D. (1739/1888). *A Treatise of Human Nature*. Oxford: Oxford University Press. Selby-Bigge edition.

James, W. (1890/1931). *Principles of Psychology*, Vol.I. New York: Henry Holt.

Joyce, J. (1934). *Ulysses*. New York: Random House.

Kant, I. (1781/1997). *Critique of Pure Reason*. Translated by P. Guyer and A.W. Wood. New York: Cambridge University Press.

Kornhauser, A. and P.F. Lazarsfeld (1955). The Analysis of Consumer Actions. In P.F. Lazarsfeld and M. Rosenberg, eds., *The Language of Social Research*. Glencoe, IL: Free Press.

Lazarsfeld, P.F., ed., (1931). *Jugend und Beruf*. Jena, Germany: Fischer.

Maier, N.R.F. (1931). Reasoning in Humans: II. The Solution of a Problem and its Appearance in Consciousness. *Journal of Comparative Psychology*, 12, pp.181–194.

McFadden, D. and K. Train (2000). Mixed MNL Models for Discrete Response. *Journal of Applied Econometrics*, 15, pp.447–470.

Minsky, M.L., (1967). *Computation: Finite and Infinite Machines*. Englewood Cliffs, N.J.: Prentice-Hall.

Murphy, G.L. (2002). *The Big Book of Concepts*. Cambridge, MA: MIT Press.

Nisbett, R.E. and T.D. Wilson (1977). Telling More Than We Can Know: Verbal Reports on Mental Processes. *Psychological Review*, 84, pp.231–259.

Nolen-Hoeksema, S. (1991). Responses to Depression and their Effects on the Duration of Depressive Episodes. *Journal of Abnormal Psychology*, 100, pp.569–582.

Proust, M. (1927/1999). *Time Regained: In Search of Lost Time*. Translated by A. Mayor and T. Kilmartin. New York: Modern Library.

Rossi, P.H. (1955). *Why Families Move: A Study in the Social Psychology of Urban Residential Mobility*. New York: Free Press of Glencoe.

Royden, H.L. (1963). *Real Analysis*. New York: The Macmillan Company.

Savage, L.J. (1954). *Foundations of Statistics*. New York: Wiley.

Simon, H. (1955), A Behavioral Theory of Rational Choice, *Quarterly Journal of Economics*, 69, pp.99–118.

Suppes, P. (1956). The Role of Subjective Pprobability and Utility in Decision-making. *Proceedings of the Third Berkeley Symposium on Mathematical Statistics and Probability, 1954–1955*, 5, p.72.

Suppes, P. (1960/1972). *Axiomatic Set Theory*. New York: Van Nostrand, slightly revised edition published by Dover, New York, 1972.

Suppes, P. (1969). Stimulus-response Theory of Finite Automata. *Journal of Mathematical Psychology*, 6, pp.327–355.

Suppes, P. (1977). Learning Theory for Probabilistic Automata and Register Machines. In H. Spada and W.F. Kempf, eds., *Structural Models of Thinking and Learning*, pp.57–79. Bern: Hans Huber Publisher.

Suppes, P. (2002). *Representation and Invariance of Scientific Structures*. Stanford, CA: CSLI Publications.

Suppes, P. (2003) Rationality, Habits and Freedom. In N. Dimitri, M. Basili and I. Gilboa, eds., *Cognitive Processes and Economic Behavior*. Proceedings of the Conference held at Certosa di Pontignano, Siena, Italy, July 3–8, 2001, pp.137–167. Routledge Siena Studies in Political Economy. New York: Routledge.

Suppes, P. (2005). Psychological Nature of Verification of Informal Mathematical Proofs. In S. Artemov, H. Barringer, A.S. d'Avila Garcez, L.C. Lamb, and J. Woods, eds., *We Will Show Them: Essays in Honour of Dov Gabbay, Vol.2*, pp.693–712. London: College Publications.

Suppes, P. (2007). Where do Bayesian Priors Come from? *Synthese*, 156, pp.441–471.

Suppes, P. and J.-Y. Béziau (2003). Semantic Computations of Truth, Based on Associations already Learned. *Journal of Applied Logic*, 2,pp. 457–467.

Suppes, P., B. Han, J. Epelboim, and Z.-L. Lu (1999a). Invariance between Subjects of Brain-wave Representations of Language. *Proceedings National Academy of Sciences*, 96, 12953–12958.

Suppes, P., B. Han, J. Epelboim, and Z.-L. Lu (1999b). Invariance of Brain-wave Representations of Simple Visual Images and their Names. *Proceedings National Academy of Sciences*, 96, 14658–14663.

Suppes, P., D.H. Krantz, R.D. Luce, and A. Tversky (1989). *Foundations of Measurement, Vol.II. Geometrical, Threshold and Probabilistic Representations.* New York: Academic Press.

Suppes, P., Z.-L. Lu, and B. Han (1997). Brain-wave Recognition of Words. *Proceedings National Academy of Sciences*, 94, 14965–14969.

Suppes, P., M. Perreau-Guimaraes, and D.K. Wong (In press, Neural Computation). Partial Orders of Similarity Differences Invariant between EEG-recorded Brain and Perceptual Representations of Language.

Suppes, P. and J. Sheehan (1981). CAI Course in Axiomatic Set Theory. In P. Suppes, ed., *University-level Computer-assisted Instruction at Stanford: 1968–1980*, pp.3–80. Stanford, CA: Stanford University, Institute for Mathematical Studies in the Social Sciences.

Teichmüller, O. (1939). Braucht der Algebraiker das Auswahlaxiom? *Deutsche Mathhematik*, Vol.4, pp.567–577.

Themistius (1966). *On Aristotle's "On the Soul".* Translated by Robert B. Todd. New York: Cornell University Press.

Tukey, J.W. (1940). *Convergence and Uniformity in Topology.* Annals of Math. Studies, No.2, Princeton.

Wilson, T.D. (1985). Strangers to Ourselves: The Origins and Accuracy of Beliefs about One's Own Mental States. In J.H. Harvey and G. Weary, eds., *Attribution: Basic Issues and Applications*, pp.9–36. Orlando, FLA: Academic Press.

Wilson, T.D. and J.W. Schooler (1991). Thinking too much: Introspection Can Reduce the Quality of Preferences and Decisions. *Journal of Personality and Social Psychology*, 60, pp.181–192.

Wong, D.K., M.P. Guimaraes, E.T. Uy, and P. Suppes (2004). Classification of Individual Trials Based on the Best Independent Component of EEG-recorded Sentences. *Neurocomputing,* 61, pp.479–484.

Yates, F.A. (1966). *The Art of Memory.* Chicago: University of Chicago Press.

DECOMPOSING, RECOMPOSING, AND SITUATING CIRCADIAN MECHANISMS: THREE TASKS IN DEVELOPING MECHANISTIC EXPLANATIONS

WILLIAM BECHTEL and ADELE ABRAHAMSEN
University of California, San Diego

Reductionist inquiry, which involves decomposing a mechanism into its parts and operations, is only one of the tasks of mechanistic research. A second task (which may be undertaken largely simultaneously) is recomposing it – conceptually reassembling the parts and operations into an organized arrangement that constitutes the mechanism. Other tasks include determining how multiple operations are orchestrated in real time, and investigating how the mechanism interacts with the environment in which it is situated.

Accordingly, explaining how a mechanism generates a phenomenon requires integrating research from at least two levels of organization – one involving the parts and their operations and another involving the mechanism as a whole. Sometimes additional levels are so salient that they too must be incorporated into the account. Researchers may come to recognize, for example, that the target mechanism is itself part of a larger integrated system (a higher-level mechanism) that confronts its own environment, and that operations within the target mechanism may be affected as the larger system confronts varying environmental conditions. Choosing mechanistic explanation as the preferred framework for pursuing questions of reduction both illuminates the importance of reductionistic inquiry and reveals that it must be complemented by other kinds of explanatory work.

Although the modern pursuit of mechanistic explanation has a history spanning several centuries in the life sciences, it is only recently that certain philosophers focused on biology have subjected this pursuit to systematic analysis. The new mechanistic philosophy of science that has emerged from that endeavor remains unfamiliar to many other philosophers. Accordingly, we begin with a brief account of mechanistic explanation and the roles of decomposition and recomposition in developing such explanations. We then illustrate these two tasks of mechanistic research by examining their interplay in research on circadian rhythms. After briefly introducing the phenomena of circadian rhythms, we present highlights of the attempts to decompose the responsible mechanisms – research that began in the 1970s and has advanced rapidly since the early 1990s. We then address how the very success of this research has prompted new inquiries into how the parts and operations are integrated so as to constitute a mechanism and how those operations are orchestrated. Finally, we add another level of analysis by considering how that mechanism is situated in and affected by a higher-level mechanism.

The account we offer here stands in sharp contrast to a common philosophical characterization of reduction according to which the reducing science (e.g., molecular biology) explains all of the phenomena originally explained by the reduced science (e.g., neurophysiology), which thereby loses its autonomy (Churchland, 1986; Bickle, 2003). On that view, the reduced science at best provides shorthand accounts for the more complete accounts offered in the reducing science. Accordingly, a primary line of argument for opponents of reduction (e.g., Fodor, 1974) has been that the reducing science cannot account for certain important regularities (laws) in the sciences to be reduced. Since these regularities therefore remain in the province of an autonomous, unreduced science, the attempt at reduction is said to have failed. It is important to note that this characterization of reduction and the counterarguments against it are tied specifically to the deductive-nomological (D-N) account of explanation. As characterized by Hempel (1965), explanation involves deriving statements describing phenomena to be explained from statements of laws and initial conditions. In the hands of philosophers of science such as Nagel (1961), this led to the theory-reduction account of science, according to which reduction explains the laws in the earlier (reduced) theory by deriving them from the laws of a more basic science (the reducing theory) together with bridge principles and boundary conditions (for historical review and critical discussion, see Bechtel & Hamilton, 2007). This account is especially problematic when applied to the life sciences, where explanations invoke laws infrequently (if laws are even available), but appeal to mechanisms regularly. Mechanistic explanations, as we will see, require integrating processes at different levels and do not invite supplanting accounts at one level with those from a different level.

1 MECHANISTIC EXPLANATION AND NEW PERSPECTIVES ON REDUCTION

A mechanistic explanation starts with a phenomenon produced by some system across a certain range of conditions. The phenomenon is explained by construing the system as a mechanism and describing how that mechanism works. In a previous paper, we characterized a mechanism as "a structure performing a function in virtue of its component parts, component operations, and their organization" (Bechtel & Abrahamsen, 2005; for related accounts, see Bechtel & Richardson, 1993; Glennan, 2002; Machamer, Darden, & Craver, 2000). In order to develop a mechanistic explanation it is necessary to decompose the mechanism into parts and/or the operations they perform. Doing so often requires specialized instruments and techniques since naturally functioning systems typically conceal their parts and operations. Many of the advances in modern biology have stemmed from the development of particularly effective means for decomposing particular classes of biological systems. Scientists have not *explained* a phenomenon, however, until they have recomposed the mechanism – determined how it is organized and interacts with its environment. As challenging as is decomposition, recomposition often is even more difficult. Parts and operations are often highly integrated with one another so that as one part of the mechanism changes, numerous other parts are affected and change their operations. If the organization involves cycles, the effects of a part's operations may feed back (positively or negatively) on it, affecting operations on the next cycle. Ambitious modeling projects, sometimes using the available tools for analyzing dynamical systems, often are required to understand the consequences of organization and particularly the orchestration of multiple operations in real time (Bechtel & Abrahamsen, in press).

Many scientists regard the process of decomposition as *reductionistic*, but it is important to recognize how their conception of reduction differs from the philosophical conception described above. The goal of decomposition is to determine what parts and operations together make a functioning mechanism. The operations performed by the parts are quite unlike the activity of the whole mechanism. (For example, the valves in a heart open and close, but the heart itself pumps blood.) The components must be appropriately organized and the mechanism situated in an appropriate environment to realize the phenomenon (valves and chambers of the heart have a proper spatial organization, their operations have proper temporal organization, and the heart must be properly localized, supported, and connected to veins and arteries). To figure out the organization within the mechanism, scientists must recompose what they have decomposed. We will illustrate these two complementary tasks by examining their interplay in research on circadian rhythms. First, though, we will delineate the phenomena to be explained.

2 Delineating Circadian Phenomena

The ability of organisms to keep track of the time of day and respond appropriately to it, even when deprived of external cues such as exposure to sunlight, has fascinated investigators since ancient times. (Androsthenes of Thasus, a captain in Alexander's fleet, recorded the daily movement of the leaves of the tamarind tree, while Hippocrates and Galen both observed how body temperature in patients with fevers varied with time of day). Subsequently, circadian rhythms have been found in a wide variety of living organisms, from cyanobacteria to plants, fungi, and a variety of animals including *Drosophila*, mice, and humans. They affect biochemical processes (e.g. protein synthesis), physiological functions (e.g., digestion), behavioral phenomena (e.g., locomotor activity), and cognitive performance (e.g., reaction times). Systematic study of these rhythms – incorporating experimental methods in addition to finer-grained description – began only in the middle of the 20th century and yielded a richer characterization of the phenomena. In particular, early experiments maintaining organisms in regulated conditions (constant darkness, or light exposure limited to certain hours) demonstrated that these rhythms (1) are endogenously controlled, (2) are entrainable by Zeitgebers (environmental cues such as onset of daylight or temperature changes), and (3) are temperature compensated (the period of oscillation remains nearly the same across a wide range of temperatures). Halberg (1959) termed these rhythms *circadian* (*circa* = about + *dies* = day) because when Zeitgebers are removed, the periods are regular but with periods varying slightly from 24 hours.

3 Decomposing and Recomposing the Circadian System

We will primarily focus on the quest to explain how animals maintain rhythms endogenously. Investigations in the 1970s, some focusing on mammals and some on fruit flies (*Drosophila*), began to provide clues as

180

to the mechanisms underlying circadian rhythms. First, mammalian researchers traced the maintenance of these rhythms to a specific region of the brain – the suprachiasmatic nucleus (SCN) – which is regarded as the central clock.[1] The SCN is a bilateral structure located just above the optic chiasm, where projections from the two eyes come together, with each side comprising approximately 8,000 to 10,000 neurons. Evidence that the SCN serves as a central clock came from demonstrations that (1) it receives appropriate projections from the eyes for entrainment by light; (2) damage to it eliminates endogenous rhythms; and (3) it can sustain its own rhythms (Inouye & Kawamura, 1979).

The mammalian research identified the locus of the central clock, but not how it worked. The task of decomposing the mechanism into its component parts and operations was begun by going inside individual *Drosophila* neurons to determine how they sustained oscillations. The first breakthrough was Konopka and Benzer's (1971) identification of a specific gene – *period* (*per*) – in which mutations yielded arrhythmic flies or ones with significantly shortened or lengthened rhythms. Rosbash and his colleagues cloned *per* in the 1980s, enabling them to determine that concentrations of both *per* mRNA and PER (the protein synthesized from *per*) exhibited circadian oscillations (Hardin, Hall, & Rosbash, 1990). At this point they could begin to coordinate decomposition with recomposition (figuring out spatial and temporal organization of the parts and operations). One clue was that peaks and valleys in concentrations of PER lagged behind those of *per* mRNA by approximately 8 hours. Moreover, since PER was detected not only in cytoplasm (where it is synthesized) but also in the nucleus, they proposed a mechanism incorporating a negative feedback loop to explain circadian oscillations in *Drosophila*. Its parts, operations, and organization are illustrated in Figure 1. On this account, synthesis of the protein PER is initiated by the transcription of *per* into *per* mRNA, which must be transported to the cytoplasm to be translated into PER. Several hours thereafter PER is transported back into the nucleus, where it slows synthesis of additional PER by somehow inhibiting *per* transcription. (Though not shown, *per* eventually is released from inhibition by the breakdown of nuclear PER, allowing a new turn of the 24-hour cycle to begin.)

---

[1] The determination that a specific set of neurons in *Drosophila*, the lateral neurons, comprised its central clock was not made until much later (Helfrich-Förster, 1996).

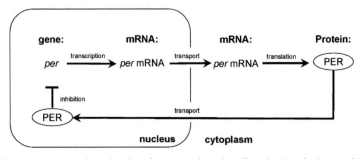

Figure 1: Proposed mechanism for generating circadian rhythms in *Drosophila* (Hardin, Hall, & Rosbash, 1990).

Hardin et al.'s proposal generated a host of additional questions. Why do concentrations of PER lag behind those of *per* mRNA? What determines when it is transported into the nucleus? Precisely how does PER inhibit *per* transcription? Over the next 15 years, research addressing these questions brought discovery of a host of additional genes and proteins and determination of how they are involved in the feedback loop whereby PER inhibits *per*. For example, it was found that after PER is synthesized it forms a compound with another protein, TIMELESS (TIM), and that only as part of the compound does it enter the nucleus. Moreover, the ability of the PER:TIM compound to inhibit *per* transcription involves it acting on another compound formed from a third protein (CLOCK) and fourth protein (CYCLE). This interaction inhibits the ability of CLOCK:CYCLE to bind to the promoter site on *per* and *tim* DNA and hence to activate their transcription. Entrainment was found to involve an additional protein, CRYPTOCHROME (CRY), which in response to light serves to degrade TIM, and thus to release CLOCK:CYCLE from inhibition by PER:TIM (for details, see Bechtel, in press-b). Figure 2 shows how these components fit into the mechanism sketched in Figure 1. As a result of these and other discoveries, the number of components and the range of operations in the clock increased dramatically.

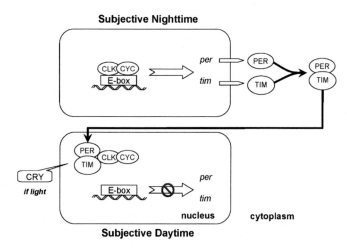

Subjective Nighttime

Subjective Daytime

Figure 2. A fuller account of the feedback mechanism that maintains circadian rhythms in *Drosophila*. It includes component parts and operations that were discovered in the late 1990s and shows how the mechanism's dynamics differ between nighttime and daytime. The large open arrow indicates whether or not gene transcription is activated. The smaller open arrows represent the operations of gene expression (transcription, transport, and translation) that were separately indicated in Figure 1.

Most of these advances stemmed directly from research on *Drosophila*, but the discovery of CLOCK actually resulted from mammalian researchers seeking mutations that affected mammalian circadian rhythms. A homolog of the mammalian gene was then found in *Drosophila*. Subsequently, homologues of several *Drosophila* genes were found in mammals. The circadian clock, like many biological mechanisms, is largely conserved through phylogeny. Phylogenetic conservation is not perfect, however; often key components are retained but significantly modified. CRY, for example, subserves entrainment in *Drosophila*. In mammals it no longer performs that role, but replaces TIM in forming a compound with PER. This discovery prompted a search for a protein that could replace CRY in subserving entrainment in mammals, culminating in the identification of melanopsin. But the way in which these molecules subserve entrainment was found to differ: melanopsin (in mammals) promotes *per* transcription, whereas CRY (in *Drosophila*) indirectly releases it from inhibition by degrading TIM. The assumption of conservation thus served as a discovery heuristic both when direct homologues of genes in one order of animals were found in another and when differences were uncovered (Bechtel, in press-c). While additional parts and operations undoubtedly remain to be identified, these efforts to decompose the circadian clock have yielded an extensive catalog of clock parts and operations in both *Drosophila* and mammals and confidence that the basic component parts and operations in the clock are now known.

4 ORCHESTRATING AND SITUATING THE CIRCADIAN SYSTEM

The scientists discussed successfully executed their task of decomposition, identifying a number of genes and proteins in the circadian clock and the operations they perform. They were similarly successful in their complementary task of recomposition, offering a well-supported account of how these component parts and operations were organized. A different group of scientists could now use computational modeling to explore how the operations were orchestrated so as to produce sustained periodic oscillations. In addition to the negative feedback loop shown in Figure 1 through which PER serves to inhibit its own transcription, there is a positive feedback loop involved in the generation of CLOCK. The combination of positive and negative feedback loops and the nonlinear nature of the various reactions render it impossible to determine simply through mental simulations whether periodic oscillations will result and can be sustained rather than dampen. Using differential equations for quantifying and relating the various operations, Goldbetter (1995; Leloup & Goldbeter, 1998) developed a model that showed that with biologically plausible values for key parameters, such a mechanism would exhibit sustained periodic oscillations. (For details, and discussion of other contributions of computational modeling to understanding the orchestration of circadian mechanisms, see Bechtel, in press-a.)

The importance of situating the intracellular mechanisms in a larger context was recognized when Welsh, Logothetis, Meister, and Reppert (1995) found that individual SCN neurons dispersed in culture exhibited a large range of variation (21.25 to 26.25 hours) and standard deviation (1.2 hours) in their oscillations. This finding indicated that the close to 24-hour rhythms exhibited in the circadian controlled activities in whole organisms depends on synchronization between SCN cells. Although several mechanisms have been considered, evidence points to synchronization being achieved via the release and uptake of hormones such as vasoactive intestinal polypeptide (Aton, Colwell, Harmar, Waschek, & Herzog, 2005). Such synchronization involves individual oscillators modifying their behavior as a result of the signals they receive from other oscillators to which they are coupled. As in the case of relating the operations of parts within cells, researchers turned to computational modeling to understand conditions under which synchronization can be achieved.

Other research points to the need to situate the entire central clock (SCN in mammals) within a yet larger system. In order to be entrained by Zeitgebers (via the mechanism involving genes and proteins within neurons as described above), the SCN must have inputs from sensory organs. Moreover, the SCN must send signals to other (peripheral) organs of the body if it is to affect their activity. In the early stages of research, investigators assumed a linear arrangement of signals from sensory organs to the central clock and from the central clock to peripheral organs. This assumed arrangement, however, has been severely challenged as a result of further investigation. There is evidence that photoreceptive proteins are themselves modified by the SCN, so that the SCN is modulating its own entrainment system (Roenneberg, Daan, & Merrow, 2003). Further, already in the 1990s it became apparent that cells in the output organs contain the same clock genes and proteins as the SCN and that cells in peripheral organs of the body exhibit oscillations in clock proteins when they receive input from the SCN. Since these oscillations appeared to dampen when peripheral cells did not receive SCN inputs, the peripheral oscillators initially were viewed as slaves. However, there are now findings that suggest the apparent dampening of peripheral oscillators may be due to desynchronization, not to cessation of oscillation (Welsh, Yoo, Liu, Takahashi, & Kay, 2004). Moreover, some of the peripheral oscillators have their own Zeitgebers (e.g., liver oscillators respond to the period of feeding). They also seem capable themselves of altering oscillation within the SCN (Panda & Hogenesch, 2004). Increasingly, as researchers situate the central clock (SCN) mechanism in a larger system responsible for circadian oscillations, they realize that there are extensive feedback connections rendering it a highly integrated system, as illustrated in Figure 3.

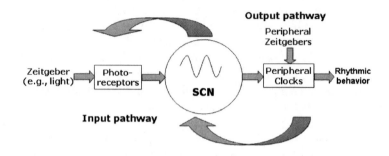

Figure 3. Feedback (curved arrows) help integrate components of the overall system responsible for circadian rhythms. Previously these components were construed as forming a linear system (straight arrows).

Although it was possible to investigate experimentally how individual SCN neurons functioned when isolated from other components, and this provided enormous insight into the parts and operations within them, a full understanding of how circadian behavior is produced requires conceptually recomposing the whole mechanism within these neurons and situating it in relation to other SCN neurons and also other organs of the body. Studies of individual SCN neurons in isolation resulted only in a first approximation – in recomposing and situating the mechanism, researchers must modify their initial accounts to incorporate what is learned about how component parts and operations are, in part, altered by activities occurring in the broader environment.

5 CAUSATION AT MULTIPLE LEVELS WITHOUT ELIMINATION OR INTERLEVEL CAUSATION

The account of research on circadian rhythms we have presented supports a very different perspective on reduction than that commonly encountered in philosophy. Reductionist inquiry involved decomposing the central clock into component genes and proteins within each of its neurons. To understand how these components constituted a clock, however, investigators had to recompose the mechanism – ascertain that these components were organized into a feedback loop in which a clock gene, *per*, is expressed in a protein which then serves to inhibit its own expression. Further pursuit of this inquiry identified a host of additional genes and proteins. The discovery of these parts and their operations did not end the explanatory endeavor, however, as recomposition was required to understand their contribution to the overall mechanism. Moreover, the individual neurons are constituents of a larger system (the SCN), and the way they are coordinated within that system affects their individual behavior. As well, that system functions as part of a yet larger integrated system involving sensory inputs and peripheral oscillators, and these affect the behavior of genes and proteins within the central clock mechanism. The accounts of these higher-level systems were not obtained by deriving them from what is known of the genes and proteins within individual cells. Rather, they had to be discovered (and are still being discovered) by using investigatory tools appropriate for the level at which the entities of current interest are interacting. There is no possibility of eliminating the account of these higher-level processes in favor of accounts of lower-level processes, since what is learned at the lower level does not provide a complete account of the phenomenon.

When speaking of decomposing a mechanism into its parts or recomposing the whole, it is natural to speak, as we have, of the parts residing at a lower level than the mechanism as a whole (and the mechanism as at a lower level than any system of which it is a constituent). This introduction of levels into the account of mechanisms, however, is highly circumcised as it is dependent on the decomposition of particular mechanisms. The level down from the mechanism as a whole consists of those parts whose operations contribute to the functioning of that mechanism. They are not necessarily of the same size – they are related only insofar as their operations are coordinated to produce the phenomenon of interest. Moreover, if researchers take any two components of a mechanism apart, there is no basis for determining whether these yet lower-level components all reside at one common level (Craver, 2007).

In accounting for the behavior of a mechanism, reductionist researchers seek to determine how the parts interact with each other causally. When parts perform their operations, the mechanism as a whole is affected, and this can result in the mechanism functioning differently in its environment. Also, the causal engagement of the mechanism with entities in its environment affects the way its parts operate. The notions of bottom-up and top-down causation are sometimes invoked to characterize these relations, but Craver and Bechtel (2007) have argued against extending causation to the interlevel context on grounds that this leads to unnecessary conceptual problems. For example, causes usually precede their effects, but something happening at one level does not precede the corresponding change at another level – when a part of a mechanism is altered, the mechanism as a whole is altered simultaneously, and vice versa. Instead of extending the notion of causation to interlevel contexts, Craver and Bechtel advocated characterizing interlevel relations in terms of constitution (i.e., part-whole relations in the mechanism). They emphasized that any changes to the whole mechanism are also changes to at least one of its parts, and changes to a part are also changes to the whole. If the change to the part is brought about by interaction with other parts, then that is the level at which causation is identified. If, on the other hand, the mechanism as a whole is changed by interactions with other mechanisms, then the causal relation is between those mechanisms. By combining intralevel causal analysis at multiple levels with interlevel constitution relations, one can account for the phenomena for which others invoke the notions of bottom-up and top-down causation without unnecessary conceptual problems.

The idea that reductionistic research can eliminate the need for higher-level accounts stems in part from the assumption that there is a lowest level at which all causal processes can be described. The account of levels just sketched does not require us to embrace the idea of a lowest level of entities out of which all higher-level entities are built. And even more emphatically, it does not support the idea that a comprehensive causal account can be provided at the lowest level. Rather, the mechanistic project starts with identifying a phenomenon that one wants to explain. Researchers posit that the phenomenon is due to a mechanism behaving in a certain way under specified conditions. Successful mechanistic inquiry reveals how it is that the mechanism is able to exhibit the behavior under those conditions (by identifying the parts, operations, and organization, and orchestration within a mechanism), but it does not itself explain how those conditions arise. In the course of mechanistic inquiry researchers may discover other conditions that impact the mechanism and affect whether it exhibits the behavior. These causal relations are not explained by the account identifying the parts and operations within the mechanism and their organization – they are viewed as additional factors that are included in the full mechanistic explanation of the phenomenon. The reductionist (decompositional) task of mechanistic research provides part, but only part, of the overall endeavor of mechanistic explanation.

REFERENCES

Aton, S.J., Colwell, C.S., Harmar, A.J., Waschek, J., & Herzog, E.D. (2005). Vasoactive Intestinal Polypeptide Mediates Circadian Rhythmicity and Synchrony in Mammalian Clock Neurons. *Nature Neuroscience*, 8, pp.476–483.

Bechtel, W. (in press-a). Computational Modeling and Mechanistic Explanation: Understanding Circadian Rhythms. *Studies in History and Philosophy of Science Part A*.

Bechtel, W. (in press-b). The Downs and Ups of Mechanistic Research: Circadian Rhythm Research as an Exemplar. *Erkenntnis*.

Bechtel, W. (in press-c). Generalization and Discovery through Conserved Mechanisms: Cross Species Research on Circadian Oscillators. *Philosophy of Science*.

Bechtel, W., & Abrahamsen, A. (2005). Explanation: A Mechanist Alternative. *Studies in History and Philosophy of Biological and Biomedical Sciences*, 36, pp.421–441.

Bechtel, W., & Abrahamsen, A. (in press). Complex Biological Mechanisms: Cyclic, Oscillatory, and Autonomous. In C.A. Hooker (Ed.), *Philosophy of Complex Systems. Handbook of the Philosophy of Science, Volume 10*. New York: Elsevier.

Bechtel, W., & Hamilton, A. (2007). Reduction, Integration, and the Unity of Science: Natural, Behavioral, and Social Sciences and the Humanities. In T. Kuipers (Ed.), *Philosophy of Science: Focal Issues*. New York: Elsevier.

Bechtel, W., & Richardson, R. C. (1993). *Discovering Complexity: Decomposition and Localization as Strategies in Scientific Research*. Princeton, NJ: Princeton University Press.

Bickle, J. (2003). *Philosophy and Neuroscience: A Ruthlessly Reductive Account*. Dordrecht: Kluwer.

Churchland, P. S. (1986). *Neurophilosophy: Toward a Unified Theory of Mind-brain*. Cambridge, MA: MIT Press.

Craver, C. (2007). *Explaining the Brain: What a Science of the Mind-brain Could Be*. New York: Oxford University Press.

Craver, C., & Bechtel, W. (2007). Top-down Causation without Top-down Causes. *Biology and Philosophy*, 22, pp.547–563.

Fodor, J. A. (1974). Special Sciences (or: the Disunity of Science as a Working Hypothesis). *Synthese*, 28, pp.97–115.

Glennan, S. (2002). Rethinking Mechanistic Explanation. *Philosophy of Science*, 69, S342–S353.

Goldbeter, A. (1995). A Model for Circadian Oscillations in the *Drosophila* Period Protein (PER). *Proceedings of the Royal Society of London. B: Biological Sciences*, 261(1362), pp.319–324.

Halberg, F. (1959). Physiologic 24-hour Periodicity: General and Procedural Considerations with Reference to the Adrenal Cycle. *Zeitschrift für Vitamin-, Hormon- und Fermentforschung*, 10, pp.225–296.

Hardin, P.E., Hall, J.C., & Rosbash, M. (1990). Feedback of the *Drosophila period* Gene Product on Circadian Cycling of its Messenger RNA Levels. *Nature*, 343(6258), pp.536–540.

Helfrich-Förster, C. (1996). Drosophila Rhythms: From Brain to Behavior. *Seminars in Cell & Developmental Biology*, 7(6), pp.791–802.

Hempel, C.G. (1965). Aspects of Scientific Explanation. In C.G. Hempel (Ed.), *Aspects of Scientific Explanation and Other Essays in the Philosophy of Science* (pp.331–496). New York: Macmillan.

Inouye, S.-I.T., & Kawamura, H. (1979). Persistence of Circadian Rhythmicity in a Mammalian Hypothalamic "Island" Containing the Suprachiasmatic Nucleus. *Proceedings of the National Academy of Sciences (USA)*, 76, pp.5962–5966.

Konopka, R.J., & Benzer, S. (1971). Clock Mutants of *Drosophila melanogaster*. *Proceedings of the National Academy of Sciences (USA)*, 89, pp.2112–2116.

Leloup, J.-C., & Goldbeter, A. (1998). A Model for Circadian Rhythms in *Drosophila* Incorporating the Formation of a Complex between the PER and TIM Proteins. *Journal of Biological Rhythms*, 13(1), pp.70–87.

Machamer, P., Darden, L., & Craver, C. (2000). Thinking about Mechanisms. *Philosophy of Science*, 67, pp.1–25.

Nagel, E. (1961). *The Structure of Science*. New York: Harcourt, Brace.

Panda, S., & Hogenesch, J.B. (2004). It's all in the Timing: Many Clocks, many Outputs. *Journal of Biological Rhythms*, 19(5), pp.374–387.

Roenneberg, T., Daan, S., & Merrow, M. (2003). The Art of Entrainment. *Journal of Biological Rhythms*, 18(3), pp.183–194.

Welsh, D.K., Logothetis, D.E., Meister, M., & Reppert, S.M. (1995). Individual Neurons Dissociated from Rat Suprachiasmatic Nucleus Express Independently Phased Circadian Firing Rhythms. *Neuron*, 14(4), pp.697–706.

Welsh, D.K., Yoo, S.-H., Liu, A.C., Takahashi, J.S., & Kay, S.A. (2004). Bioluminescence Imaging of Individual Fibroblasts Reveals Persistent, Independently Phased Circadian Rhythms of Clock Gene Expression. *Current Biology*, 14(24), pp.2289–2295.

ADAPTIVE CONTROL LOOPS AS AN INTERMEDIATE MIND-BRAIN REDUCTION BASIS

JOËLLE PROUST
Institut Jean-Nicod (EHESS-ENS), Paris[1]

Abstract
Jaegwon Kim has proposed that the proper way to reduce mental to physical events and properties is to apply the *causal inheritance-as-identity principle:* "*M* is the property of having a property with such-and-such causal potentials, and it turns out that property *P* is exactly the property that fits the causal specification. And this grounds the identification of *M* with *P*". It is argued that this principle should require further that the connection between properties *M* and *P* be dynamically intelligible (that is, compatible with the evolutionary and developmental features of mind-brains), and nomologically grounded. It is claimed that an adequate 'causal inheritance-as-identity principle' requires an intermediate level of reduction between mind and brain, in terms of adaptive control structures. It is further argued that this level provides dynamical intelligibility of the *P-M* connections, and provides nomological explanations for how physical and mental properties must develop jointly.

1 MULTIPLE REALIZATION, CAUSAL INHERITANCE AND PROPERTY IDENTITY

The so-called "mind-body problem" arises from the difficulty of understanding how mental states and events (endowed as they are with intentional and phenomenal properties) are related to brain states and events. Cartesian dualism is a traditional answer to the problem; it has been found wanting on many accounts; in particular dualism has trouble explaining how two different substances can be made to interact causally. Reductionism is the view that the mind is identical with a set of brain processes (Place, 1956). Reductionism holds that there is only one type of causation, physical causation, holding between individual physical events. This view of causation is called "physicalism": only physical entities are able to pro-

---

[1] Institut Jean-Nicod, Department of Cognitive Studies, Ecole Normale Supérieure, 29 rue d'Ulm, 75005 Paris, France.

duce changes in the material and in the mental domains. While physicalism remains the dominant view concerning causation, the metaphysics of reductionism has been rejected by most philosophers. Types of mental states cannot be taken to be identical with types of neural states. Before we come to the main argument for this claim, let us agree first on the type of argument that simply *does not* apply. What is at stake here is not what the terms "mind" (mental state, pain, etc.) or "brain" (cerebral state, firing neurons) *mean*, but whether they can be shown to be identical through empirical research, i.e. theory construction.[2] Thus the idea *is not* to reject mind-brain identity on the basis of the fact that people fail to know how pain is realized, but are still aware of what pain is. The main objection to reductionism has rather to do with the multirealizability thesis (MT), which was first stated by Putnam (1967).

In a nutshell, here is Putnam's argument. Let us represent mental activity using an analogy with a Turing Machine whose states (including motor dispositions) are probabilistically related, and are able to combine and to influence output. What are the relevant mental states in such a probabilistic Machine? Taking a physically characterized state of this machine, (or a neural state) as providing the basis or the condition of an identity between two tokens of mental states would involve two important mistakes. First, one would tend to misdescribe two states from two different systems as identical, on the superficial evidence of their having the same physical realizer, even though they may belong to different machine tables,[3] and have, e.g. different probabilistic connections with other states. Conversely, one would fail to track the functional analogy of two different organisms which happen to have a different realization for the same function. Pain, for example, does not seem to be nomologically associated with a given physical realization, for we have no idea how many possible physical realizers for pain there may be in nature. On this "functionalist" view, what makes a mental state a state of pain consists rather in the "transition probabilities" to avoidance behavior, to a certain set of self-directed emotions, to a disposition to classify certain stimuli as having a common valence, etc. *The multirealizability thesis claims that what makes a functional compo-*

---

[2] See U.T. Place (1956), Putnam (1967), p.433.

[3] A machine table describes the rules allowing the transitions between a current state (q_i), a symbol currently read, and specific actions: i) erase or write a symbol; ii) then move the head to the left, to the right, or stay in the same place; iii) then go to prescribed state (q_n).

nent the mental type it is, is its role in relating inputs to outputs and its relations to other functional components.

MT, however, is compatible with physicalism (even though it does not entail it as reductionism does). The kind of physicalism that is compatible with MT is "token physicalism", according to which having a mental state *supervenes on* some physical state or other – a human brain state, or possibly some non-human brain state, or even some circuit state in a computer. More generally, properties that are causally involved in the special sciences, such as psychology, economics, etc., *supervene* on physical properties, but cannot be reduced to them. The laws of physics are not contradicted by the laws of the special sciences, but the latter have their own vocabulary, and their own regularities, which cannot be couched in physical terms. What makes this physicalism "non reductive" is that two properties in the special sciences may be identical while having a different physical realization. In other words, mental states may be functionally identical, but fail to be realized by the same type of brain state.

However, as Kim observed, supervenience baptizes a difficulty rather than solving it. There is a variety of ways in which supervenience itself can be explained. The way in which MT explains supervenience consists in invoking the relation between the mental state and its physical basis as one in which a second-order property M, (such as the property of having such and such a functional role) is related to a first-order property P that "realizes" M. In Kim's terms: "Having M is having a property with causal specification D, and in systems like S, P is the property meeting specification D." (Kim, 1998, p.24). Many authors have taken this "realization" relation to relate two different types of properties, physical or neural, on the one hand, and mental or psychological, on the other. On such a view, mental properties, although they are necessarily physically realized, are not reducible to their realizers. This non-reductive interpretation of the "realization" relation, however, has been questioned. It raises the old worry of causal overdetermination; if there are two different properties, then why should we attribute any causal role to the mental property, once it is admitted that it has a physical realization? To prevent causal pre-emption of the physical over the mental, Kim offers three arguments in favor of a different view of "realization", in which the two properties are actually identical. First, he observes that, pace Putnam, multirealizability is not an obstacle to having "local reductions", i.e. species or structure-specific bridge-laws.[4] Second, reduction seems to be the best way of explaining why a mental state *M* correlates with a given brain state. How can mere "bridge-laws", such as those that correlate mental and physical properties, be themselves accounted for if not in terms of identity? "If *M* and *P* are both intrinsic properties and the bridge-law connecting them is contingent, there is no hope of identifying them. I think that we must try to provide positive reasons for saying that things that appear to be distinct are in fact one and the same." (98). Third, reduction offers an ontological simplification that contrasts with a non-reductive approach (in which entities proliferate). It is only when bridge-laws correlating the mental and the physical are "enhanced into identities" that we obtain the ontological simplification that is needed.

We can conclude with Kim that "functionalization" – a characterization of mental states through their functional roles – is compatible with reductionism, *at least if* we are able to provide a way of enhancing the relations derived from bridge-laws into identities. The method recommended in this endeavor, however, is itself fundamentally flawed, if it only consists in a purely nominal or a priori move. For as we have seen, identity of a mental and a physical state is a consequence of how the real world turns out to be. Kim's own strategy is to include the contingent dependency of the mental on the physical as the ground of the *M-P* identity in the following way:

(1) The causal inheritance-as-identity principle (CIIP): "*M* is the property of having a property with such-and-such causal potentials, and it turns out that property *P* is exactly the property that fits the causal specification. And this grounds the identification of *M* with *P*" (p.98)[5].

"Turning out to fit a causal specification" is a contingent property: what realizes *M* changes from world to world, and the identity *M = P* is both metaphysically contingent, and nomologically necessary: in all the worlds nomologically similar to ours, *M* will be identical with *P*. The identity of *M* and *P* as formulated in (1) has the interest of avoiding the kind of objection derived from Kripke's idea that an identity is necessary when *M* and *P* rigidly designate their referents. Here, *M* only refers non-rigidly to the property to be reduced; it is only defined relationally, through the set of its causal potentials at the psychological level.

---

[4] On the difficulties of claiming that local reduction does not present a problem for reductionism, see Kistler (1999).
[5] See also p.111–112.

As a consequence of (1), and given that functionalization (i.e. the pattern of causal dispositions which constitutes M) is not species- or structure-specific, there are as many different realizers for one and the same functionally defined M as there are species (on the assumption that no two species are alike in their physical realizers or neural structures). Actually, neuroscientific research has collected evidence showing that no two individual subjects are alike in their neural structure either, a fact that provides still further reason to embrace (1). Multirealizability therefore obtains, in the sense that at a certain level of description of the pattern of causal relations constituting M, there are several realizers that are identical to M depending on the species, or the individual structure considered.

Although conceptually correct in the nominal sense, the problem for the mind-body theorist is to convert this nominal identity into a real identity; that is, an identity that can be shown to be instantiated in our actual psychological dispositions. We must offer evidence that we are in a world in which (1) is satisfied (let us call this demonstration "the CIIP (Causal Inheritance-as-identity principle) satisfaction condition". Why should CIIP be argued for, rather than taken for granted? The reason is that we have assumed, right from the start, that two sets of causal descriptions hold at a world. We started with two different, heterogeneous[6] ways of characterizing causation, one at the psychological, the other at the physical (including neural) level, and discussed the possibility of having the first realized via the second. If, however, it is contingent that there is one property P such that it "fits the causal specification", as (1) requires, then we must show how it can be the case that it does, that is: what the physical properties are that are involved in mental causation, and through which processes they come to have this surprising "fit" with psychological functions. Otherwise, (1) simply holds in a set of worlds in which mental states turn out to be identical to physical states, but we don't know whether it holds in our world. In other words, "the property of having a property with such-and-such causal potentials" again *describes* a solution to the mind-body problem, rather than providing one.

In summary, CIIP needs to be shown to work in a given world, by explaining how, given the nomological regularities in that world, information and physical structure are related in a way that instantiates CIIP in it.

---

[6] When the reduced theory contains terms or concepts that do not appear in the reducing theory the reduction is said to be "heterogeneous". (Nagel, 1961) By extension, the causal regularities that hold at each level can be called "heterogeneous" too.

Otherwise, causal inheritance as property identity is postulated *ad hoc* rather than justified.

2 THE SPECIFICS OF MENTAL CAUSATION

How can we offer a more specific explanation of how M and P are in fact one and the same causal property? Two features need to be present for such an explanation to be adequate. First, to be explanatory, the connection between mental and physical properties, or rather between the functional characterization of a mental property and the physical causal network that realizes it, must be *nomologically necessary* (in the sense of being not only compatible with, but necessitated by the laws of physics given the biological constraints that apply to psychological properties).[7] One obstacle here is that the metaphysical debate about mental causation does not rely on a scientific understanding of what a psychological function, and a psychological property, are in their essences. It relies, rather, on folk psychology, and merely assumes that common parlance on the mental captures the psychological properties that are causally relevant in perceiving, learning and acting. Note, in addition that there is no agreed scientific definition of what a psychological property is, nor of a psychological function.[8] Most theorists agree that psychology involves representations.[9] What representations are, however, how they are acquired, and how they combine, are still controversial, open issues.

A second required feature of the connection is that it should *be dynamically intelligible*. The picture of the mind shared by most philosophers engaged in metaphysics is under the joint influence of the computer metaphor, (mental states are Turing machine "table states") and the linguistic characterization of mental contents. This view is a convenient simplification, which was initially the source of important insights about intentionality and mental content. Indeed mapping a set of structurally specified states to what they are about is helpful when our job is to understand interpretation and communication. When metaphysical questions are being raised, however, the exercise is no longer to identify shared contents, but to actu-

---

[7] This requirement is articulated by Kim: "We may know that B determines A (or A supervenes on B) without having any idea why this is so. Can we explain why something has M in terms of its having P?" (Kim, 1998, p.18).

[8] For a proposal concerning a definition for mental function, see Proust (2009).

[9] With the notable exception of Gibson and his followers.

ally characterize the causal processes through which mental properties represent world properties, i.e. acquire the function of carrying information about them. Here, the 'static' view of the mind is clearly inadequate, for unstable patterns of activation can also have causal efficacy, a fact that is much more easily accounted for in terms of attractors in connectionist networks than in terms of symbolically articulated mental states.[10] A causally adequate account of psychological properties should thus explain, not only what their global relations are with inputs, outputs, and other states, as stipulated by the functional definition (where "mental states" are roughly characterized, through their recurrent input-output interactions), but why they are *developing, dynamic* entities: why can they be (or not be) acquired, how easily? How resiliently? With how much inertia? How do some subsets of them determine the dynamics of others? Obviously, these important characterizations are only partially available given the present state of science. But adequacy conditions, if they are shown to be relevant, are meant to drive research, rather than follow it. Research on the dynamics of the mental, however inchoate, already exists on three types of time scale, which as we will see, are the most relevant to understanding what psychological properties "actually" are.

The first is the *phylogenetic level*. On a Darwinian view of Evolution, organisms are selected, by and large, as a result of their capacity to adjust flexibly to a changing environment. The study of the plasticity of minds over evolutionary time is thus a goldmine for those attempting to understand mental causation and to identify psychological properties in terms of this evolution.[11] Mental causation develops, at this dynamic scale, under the influence of two main evolutionary types of selection; one is the

---

[10] See Cleeremans & Jimenez, 1999, p.151: "Such patterns are no less representational than stable ones: the entire activation space at each layer of a connectionist network is thus both representational and causally efficacious". Unstable states however are present at all the dynamic levels that jointly constitute mental causation.

[11] Here are two prominent examples of how such a study can be conducted. Behavioral Ecology – the study of the ecological and evolutionary basis for animal behavior – takes phylogenetic constraints and adaptive significance to be the structuring causes of any organism's behavior. Similarly, Evolutionary Psychology hypothesizes that human behavior is generated by psychological adaptations; the latter were selected (on the basis of prior adaptations) to solve recurrent problems in human ancestral environments. (See, inter alia, Gintis et al., 2007, p.613. These two types of research can offer fruitful ways of framing the metaphysical question we are interested in, concerning the nature of mental causation. For a general discussion, see Sterelny (2000, 2003) and Proust (2006, 2009).

phenotype, the other is the group. Cooperation is associated with within-group beneficial behaviors and the suppression of internal competition, which in turn influences evolutionary dynamics. The dynamics of primate mental evolution should then be studied both at the genetic and at the cultural level, taking into account both the physical and the (group-level) institutional environments.

The second is the *ontogenetic level*. Scientists now fully appreciate that genes are expressed as a result of their interactions with physical and social environments. The connection of genes to cognitive competences is currently hotly debated. While evolutionary psychologists tend to favor the view that genes directly drive the development of highly specialized cognitive modules, neuroconstructivists argue that genes regulate low-level processes, such as motor coordination and detection of contingencies, rather than macro-adaptations such as linguistic competence or theory of mind (more on this below).

The third time scale is that of the dynamics of *individual learning*. Granting that a given organism has inherited a set of genes as well as an ecological niche which will structure its development, the way it uses its mental capacities will dynamically retro-act on them. Exercising a function (whether perception, memory, empathy or action planning) does not leave a mind unchanged. As evidenced in brain imagery and in experimental psychology, cognitive exercise on a task modifies both the individual's neural connectivity and his/her "behavioral output" in a way that is tightly constrained by temporal and dynamical factors. This evolution-sensitive aspect of individual psychological organization and brain "realization" is again an indication for the mental being dynamically coupled with a temporally developing environment.

Let us note that a complex interactive pattern among the three types of selection is at play at any given time. Learning indeed is primarily made possible by specific developmental patterns and pre-adaptations, which seem to be present in all animate organisms, in the most primitive and enduring forms of habituation and sensitization.[12] Which specific contents are learned, however, does not depend on evolution and development alone; it depends on the changing organism's environment – which itself retroacts, as we saw, on the genes' influence on development. Similarly, learning partly drives development; learning how to focus on individual contents is a precondition for most acquisition relevant to developing capacities, such

---

[12] See Hawkins & Kandel (1984).

as linguistic, motor or social capacities. Individuals with a similar genetic endowment and similar ontogenetic development may still present considerable differences in the ways they use their cognitive capacities if their environment provides them with different tasks and motivations. We need therefore to make room for a distinctive causal level for individual learning, in order to account for the fact that even genetically similar individuals have differently shaped mental dispositions.

3 FROM STANDARD FUNCTIONALISM TO DYNAMIC FUNCTIONALIZATION

The notion of mental causation that is used in standard functionalism ignores the previous distinction between the dynamic levels at which causation operates. The mind is taken to be essentially constituted by a recurring, single-layer causal structure, characterized from a snapshot viewpoint. When a mental state is identified with its causal network comprising inputs, outputs, and other states, the dynamics through which it acquires these various dispositions is deemed irrelevant. This snapshot view, however, fails to keep track of the phylogenetic, developmental, and learning constraints that causally explain how the mind forms and uses representations as it does; it ignores the fact that a mind is a flexible set of dispositions, and that flexibility in structure (neural plasticity) and in use (learning ability) constitute, in combination, fundamental conditions for mind-brain identity.

Cognitive scientists might object that, where the philosopher Jaegwon Kim merely contrasts a higher-order with a lower-order type of causation, at which the physical realizers perform the actual causal work, the psychologist of vision David Marr offers a more complex theory of the functional organization of the mind, which allows one to account for the different dynamic layers contrasted above.[13] According to Marr, a functional device needs first to be characterized at the most abstract level of what it does, and why it does it. For example, an adding machine is performing addition, characterizable by a set of formal properties. This he calls the "computational theory", which provides the rationale that accounts for the device being present. The *computational, or program, level* describes in the most general terms what the cognitive task is, and why this particular device is adaptive, i.e. fulfills its constraints. Thus the computa-

---

[13] See Marr (1982), p.22 sqq.

tional theory offers a response to the evolutionary query above. The second *"algorithmic" level* spells out the specific representations that the process uses, as well as the algorithm that transforms inputs into outputs. This level cashes out the higher-level characterization in terms of causal-representational processes, which may well differ from one individual to the next (either because they belong to different species, or because they have had different developmental stories, or different learning processes). The third level, as in Kim's model, *"implements"* the representations and their algorithmic relations in specific hardware structures, whether neurons or silicon chips. This third level, again, offers the theorist a chance to take into account the various constraints explaining why a particular individual uses idiosyncratic realizers for his/her representational and computational needs (for example, why an adult will use her fingers to add).

While acknowledging that there seems to be a theoretical duality between starting with mental states to reconstruct the dynamics that generated them, and starting with dynamic facts to reconstruct mental states, the dynamicist might insist, in response, that such a duality has merely conceptual rather than methodological relevance. For only a dynamical functionalization will have the two features that a proper connection between M and P events requires, namely nomological necessity and dynamical intelligibility. Each mind-brain can only be explained, in the ways required, if its structure as well as its functional organization are accounted for in terms of its evolution, its ontogenesis and its learning environment. If these dynamic properties are actually what shape minds, then state stability is a curious exception. Most probably, one state can only be considered to be the same state as another (prior in time in the same individual, or in another individual of the same species) if one adopts, for the sake of interpretation, a simplificatory method by which a mental state is characterized non-structurally. One might for example consider that an organism does "the same task" insofar as the same linguistic description can be offered for it, a standard way of speaking in experimental psychology. But if what is at stake is the mind-body problem, we cannot help ourselves to these linguistic descriptions of cognitive contents, because they do not respect Kim's restriction on causal inheritance as structure-bound.

If these observations are on the right track, then the proper way of functionalizing mental facts should be to look at them as constituted by the various co-evolving systems that determine, at each moment, the patterns of sensitivity and reactivity of a particular organism. Let us use the term "D-functionalism" for an approach to the mind in which the causal connectivity of interest is not that among individual mental states, but among individual developing cognitive dynamics. D-functionalization requires looking at how the mind-brain develops; the idea behind it is that an approach to mental events through D-functional organization is the only one able to satisfy our two explanatory constraints, which in turn suggests that neural dynamics is the relevant level at which nomological explanations can be offered for why a system does what it does, or does not do what other systems do. Looking at mental states as static, recurrently activated nodes in a causal network, in contrast, would fail to offer these kinds of explanations; it would, that is, block insight into prior dynamical conditions and further evolutions.

4 D-FUNCTIONALISM: LEARNING AND BRAIN CHANGE

D-functionalism, in contrast with standard functionalism, aims to account for how a given neural substrate gains a specific functional role – for how it comes to be recruited in the performance of such and such a mental task. In order to understand the relationship between the mind and its "realization", we must figure out which types of process this notion of "realization" (which in standard functionalism is a purely conceptual one) refers to in our world, for a given cognitive organism, and how it is in fact instantiated. One way of fulfilling this aim is to explain how brain growth relates to learning. Two types of responses have been offered to these questions. For *neural selectionism*, also called "brain Darwinism", brain development drives learning under genetic influence[14]. A neuronal competition occurs, and selection among the fittest is operated in interaction with environmental demands: neurons that are more often used outlive the others. For *neural constructivism*, learning is what stimulates and guides brain growth, by inducing changes in the brain structures involved in learning.[15]

Within both schools of neural growth theorists, there is a large consensus *against* standard functionalism, and the way it frames the relationship between the functional and the physical levels. Not that they embrace eliminativism: the brain is a "representational device" (*representation* here being taken to mean that neural events and properties are correlated with

---

[14] Representatives of this view include Edelman (1987) and Changeux & Dehaene (1989).
[15] Representatives of this view include Karmiloff-Smith (1992), Thelen & Smith (1994), Quartz & Sejnowski (1997), Christensen & Hooker (2000).

world events and properties, about which they carry information).[16] Brain development, however, is seen as the indispensable process which generates the constitutive link between cell growth, on the one hand, and informational uptake and monitoring, on the other. Research on learning, for example, shows that specific representations do not develop in a linear way. Representational development in ontogeny is, rather, characterized by "U shaped" patterns, in which children begin by performing well, then undergo a period of failure, by overgeneralizing their earlier knowledge, until they finally come up with a new stable, more robust, and extensive ability. As the neuroconstructivist Annette Karmiloff-Smith has documented,[17] later representational stages are not mere refinements of earlier stages, but involve large-scale reorganizations. This suggests that the brain is *nonstationary* – its statistical properties vary with time, which means in turn that the structures underlying acquisition change over time. Distal feedback from neural activity helps regulate these reorganizations. In other words, the neural vehicle of a given set of representations is dynamically shaped by the very processes through which mental representations are constructed. Here, then, is a major contrast with standard functionalism: *mental functions and representations cannot be identified independently of how their neural vehicles develop.* Let us explain why in more detail.

Marr's trichotomy is not rejected, but it is reinterpreted by selectionist theories in a connectionist spirit, as levels of organization *within the nervous system.* At the most basic level is the single cell, with its functional differentiation between axon, dendrite and synapse. At that level, the function of the neuron can already be deemed 'cognitive': it is to transform input into output, in virtue of specific patterns of electrical and chemical properties that carry information. A single neuron is already performing a computational task (at Marr's "program level"); it is following an algorithmic process, and does so according to specific physical properties (molecular properties of the synapse and the membrane). There is, therefore, no "ontological" autonomy of any one task-level, as standard functionalists claim, but a relation of "*co-dependence*" among levels. The characteristics of the synapse and the membrane determine, in part, which computations can be performed, as well as which kind of goal they can serve. Reciprocally, serving a goal modulates both the computational and the physical

---

[16] Is it important to observe here that concepts can be represented non-linguistically, as partitions in a multi-dimensional vector space. See Churchland & Sejnowski, (1992).

[17] See Karmiloff-Smith, (1992).

levels, and helps stabilize the physical properties of the cell. A second anatomical layer encompasses "circuits", i.e. neuronal assemblies of thousands of cells organized in well-defined structures, i.e. presenting task-dependent synchronous firings. A third layer is constituted by "metacircuits", i.e. relations of neuronal assemblies. Finally the traditional mental faculties are taken to roughly correspond to various groupings of these metacircuits.

In contrast to standard functionalism, the question of how such an organization emerges can now be raised and answered. The response offered by selectionists is that a recurrent two-phase process is responsible for brain organization and learning. An initial exuberant, genetically driven, growth of neural structure, leading to an overproduction of synapses, is followed by a selective pruning back of connections. There are successive waves of this sort of growth and selection from birth to puberty, each wave presenting in succession "transient redundancy and selective stabilization". A metaphor used by Changeux is that the system is informed (in the sense of being organized) by the 'instructions' delivered by the environment."[18] Indeed neural growth consists in stabilizing those dynamic patterns that have high predictive value, while suppressing those that have low value, as a function of *the environment in which development is taking place.* Bouts of learning can accordingly be analyzed through some version of Herbert Simon's "generate and test" procedure. Neural proliferation produces variety; neural pruning selects those variants that have been more often activated through feedback from the environment. The observed mind-brain organization results, on this view, from a generalized and hierarchical stabilizing effect of "generate and test" procedures with re-entrant feedback loops within larger populations of neurons.

The Neural Constructivists' response to how organization emerges offers a more prominent role to development than Neural Darwinists allow. On their view, dendrite growth (and diversity) is exclusively controlled by the environment, rather than dually by genetic and exogenous influences. Furthermore, they speculate that individual dendritic segments could be the brain's "basic computational units".[19] The central contrast with the selectionists is that they take an immature cortex to be initially equipotent. The actual functional organization of the mature brain – and, for example, the brain structure of perceptual areas – is supposed to depend entirely on the external constraints that the brain needs to internalize: "It is the differing

---

[18] Changeux (1985), p.249.
[19] Quartz & Sejnowski (1997), p.549.

pattern of afferent activity, reflective of different sensory modalities, that confers area-specific properties onto the cortex – not predispositions that are somehow embedded in the recipient cortical structure".[20] While neural suppression plays (on their view) a minor role in brain development, the structuring force consists rather in neural connections being created under the influence of incoming stimuli. The mechanisms that are hypothesized to generate brain tissue growth and, more specifically, dendritic arborization, seem to involve local releases of neurotrophins, i.e. feedback signals that are delivered post-synaptically and are thus activity-dependent signals.[21] As a consequence of these constructive, bottom-up mechanisms, the cortex is "enslaved", that is, fully controlled, by the periphery. Representational capacities thus consist primarily in types of "enslavability": they involve the production of flexible, adapted responses to varying environmental constraints as well as to changing body size. Hierarchical representations result from cascades of environmental influences working from cells to assemblies onto circuits, thus building representations of increasing complexity.[22]

In summary, the two neurocognitive theories under review agree on the dynamics of development and its cascading effects on brain structure and function. They disagree, however, on the relations of brain and environment. Selectionists see the brain as imposing structure, through its own innate "biasing" agenda, on an unstructured world. Neural constructivists reciprocally see the world as enslaving the brain by imposing on it spatio-temporal patterns of reactivity and sets of representations.

---

[20] Quartz & Sejnowski (1997), p.552. Constructivists defend, against selectionists, the view that the so-called Darwinian algorithms (cheater detection, snake detection, etc.) which are claimed to constitute modern minds, are actually the outcome of domain-general learning mechanisms, which have turned out to be more often used for specific inputs: *domain-relevant* mechanisms are thus progressively turned into *domain-specific* mechanisms, as a result of their particular developmental history (Karmiloff-Smith, 1992).

[21] For a clear analysis of these mechanisms in the visual cortex, see Katz & Shatz, 1996.

[22] Quartz & Sejnowski (1997) p.550. Several interesting principles are used to explain the mature brain's functional organization; one is the so-called "geometric principle" through which information is collected in a topological way, spatially or conceptually related representations being realized in neighboring physical structures; the other is the "clustering" principle, through which related inputs onto dendritic segments result in a pattern of termination that mirrors the informational structure of the input. (ibid, p.549)

5 MIND-BRAINS AS SELF-REGULATING AND SELF-ORGANIZING CONTROL ARCHITECTURES

Let us take stock. In Section 1, we presented Kim's interesting proposal: functionalization offers the conditions for mental states to be seen as inheriting the causal properties of brain states, and, from this, as being identical to the latter. Section 2 raised two problems with this reductionist project: two additional requirements should be fulfilled for the proposed account to go through. One is that the functional characterization should be nomologically necessary under some description. The other is that it should be dynamically intelligible. Sections 3 and 4 focus on the latter problem. Section 3 examines how functionalization needs to be modified to be made dynamic, resulting in what is called here "D-functionalization". Section 4 reviews two classes of theories which aim to explore the dynamics generated by the gene-environment-phenotype interaction, and come up, in this process, with a specific view on D-functionalization.

Thus, as we saw, there are two conditions that need to be fulfilled for a reductionist account to be adequate. Being a *dynamic* account is one, being a *nomological* account is another. While they address the first worry, our two theories are silent on the second. Not only because the exact mechanisms for the interaction between genes and information from the environment are not yet known; but also because, were these mechanisms known, they would still fail to be directly derived from physical laws. Our task in this section is to try to determine what the proper reduction basis of the mental would be, one that would fulfill the nomological condition as well as the dynamic one.

The two versions of how neurons develop might each capture one part of the picture: regressive and constructive mechanisms might in fact concurrently be engaged in development, as evidence piles up for each type of process.[23] What we are interested in at present, is not so much adjudicating between them (which obviously would go beyond a philosopher's competence), as looking for the underlying ontology which both views are implicitly appealing to. Our strategy here will involve two steps. In the present section, we defend the view that mind-brains are, as far as their causal structure goes, dynamically shaped by their having a specific

---

[23] Katz & Shatz, 1996, p. 1137, Hurford et al. (1997), p. 567, Dehaene-Lambertz & Dehaene (1997).

205

kind of control structure, which we will try to specify. In the next and final section, we will claim that mathematical models of dynamic control offer nomological constraints on mind-brain development.

The causal structure of the mind-brain is an adaptive control structure.

Four ontologically relevant claims are made in both theories of neural growth, which, to anticipate a little, point to the fact that causal efficacy is gained by mental states in virtue of their being embedded in physically realized adaptive control structures. On the basis of these claims, a preliminary rough characterization of the ontology of mental states may be achieved.

1.   The brain develops over time and reorganizes itself as a consequence of being an adaptive control system.
2.   Regulation and reorganization take place as a consequence of environmental feedback.
3.   Environmental feedback drives representational success both through informational capture and attainment or failure of the current goal.
4.   There are many different levels of regulation and reorganization, which are generatively entrenched and interdependent. For example, the way in which propagation of activation occurs at the neural cell level imposes limits on how fast one can compute or retrieve a memory.

5.1. The mind-brain is, in its essence, an adaptive control system.

Self-organization is the ability of a system to acquire and modify its structure on the basis of its own behavior in an uncertain, changing environment, by extracting signals that statistically correlate with preferred outputs. Self-regulation is a capacity that is necessary, but not sufficient for self-organization. In self-regulated systems, a controller manipulates the inputs in order to obtain some desired effect as an output. For this to be possible, an arbitrary number of loops mediate the causal interaction of the device with its environment (given the role of feedback, it is called a "closed-loop control system"). In top-down flow, a command is selected and sent to an effector; in bottom-up flow, reafferences (i.e. feedback generated by the selected command) are compared to stored values. Usually, a feedback loop uses negative feedback: the sensed value is subtracted from the desired value to create the error signal, which is conveyed to the controller. Such comparators help the system decide whether the command was successfully carried out or should be revised.

Describing a mind in terms of control imposes no arbitrary reshuffling of mental functions, but rather allows us to make inner-outer interactions more explicit. From a dynamic control viewpoint, perceptual organs have as a major function that of filling in the data to be used by comparators, by providing feedback, i.e. patterns and intensities to be stored or extracted; in other words, they help select cues that are relevant to monitoring the efficiency of a given command.[24] Comparators, in turn, guide current and subsequent control decisions.

While control can sometimes rely on predetermined parameters (think of thermostats, and thermoregulation), mental activity usually does more than adjust itself to pre-established parameters; it can also autonomously create or change its regulation parameters on the basis of the feedback received (from the environment, and from the interactions between its states). As recognized by Neural Darwinists and Neural Constructivists alike, brain plasticity and mental plasticity depend on the evolution of devices subserving close-loop construction over phylogenetic time. The fact that a mind-brain is an adaptive control system, however, should not be taken as a mere brute empirical fact about how our minds develop. It may rather be seen as a result of nomological constraints being exerted on coupled dynamical systems (see section 6).

5.2. Regulation and reorganization are conducted as a consequence of environmental feedback.

A classical worry about control and regulation is that these concepts seem to involve a teleological, i.e. a design interpretation. The selection of commands as well as natural phenomena such as the propagation of light, follow a principle of extremum, (for example the principle of least action) which was long taken to be an expression of divine Providence. As Providentialists, including Leibniz, Maupertuis and Euler, were eager to claim, a

---

[24] For a similar view of the mind, see Grush (2004) & Hurley (2008), The grain of truth in enactive theories of perception (Noe, 2004) is that perception is functionally engaged in the control and monitoring of action. On the present view, it has evolved to extract cues for potential action goals and compare new cue patterns with stored ones.

variational constraint can and should only be explained by an agent's intention. This speculation was made redundant, however, when it was found that variational constraints depend on certain invariant characteristics of the underlying mechanical system and its dynamics. A proper theory of extremum "principles" should rather explain the propagation of light through space on the basis of the symmetry properties of the underlying physical system,[25] and an agent's intention through the variational constraints on the control system that constitutes this agent.

In the particular case of the mind-brain, development, regulation and reorganization are based on the retroaction of the environment on brain activity. In Changeux & Dehaene's theory, the brain develops by pruning the dendrites that are not involved in stable connections; the activity of the postsynaptic cell retroacts on the stability of the synapse, through various molecular mechanisms that cannot be discussed here.[26] In Quartz & Sejnowski's theory, as we have seen, feedback signals – delivered postsynaptically – are hypothesized to generate brain tissue growth through the release of neurotrophins. On their view, the cortex is "enslaved", that is, fully controlled, by the periphery.

The ontological consequences of such a constructivist view have been articulated as the "Extended Mind" hypothesis (Clark & Chalmers, 1998). The crucial idea is the following: Being a dynamic system coupled with a specific environment in which it continuously evolves, a mind cannot be taken as being contained in the skull, namely: as being independent from the structuring, contentful contribution of the environment which drives its evolution. The present article follows a similar route to understanding mind-brain relations. On the extended mind view, the environment is constantly reshaping the brain as well as the mind; both reflect its affordances and its constraints; both dynamically adapt to the speed of environmental change and its amount of diversity. If mental content and brain organization are acquired in the very process through which an organism as a whole is coupled with its environment, then mental dynamics (learning) is determined both by neural growth and by environmental dynamics.

---

[25] This is a direct consequence of Emily Noether's theorem.
[26] See Changeux & Dehaene, (1989), pp.79–80.

5.3. Environmental feedback drives representational success both through informational capture and current goal achievement or failure.

What then is the role that accrues to information in generating mental representations from feedback? In simpler forms of regulators, such as thermostats or Watts' flyball governors, the physical organization of a mechanical device allows unwanted perturbations to be neutralized, and brings the system back to a desired state as a function of the environmental condition. Information plays no role in any particular activation of the mechanism; it plays a role, however, by constituting an adequacy condition on the design itself: a thermostat will only fulfill its role if the thermosensitive device reliably tracks room temperature. Granting, however, that the causal structure of the physical interactions is designed so as to map the values to be compared, information plays no further role in these simple control systems; they are called "slave control systems" because the range of their "responses", given a particular input, is strictly and inflexibly determined by the machine design; these systems cannot learn and cannot change their goals.

In Adaptive control systems, in contrast, control parameters need to be constantly updated, expanded or replaced. Informational capture now seems to have a causal role in making such dynamic coupling possible. Is flexible control a sufficient reason to include information among the causal factors that drive such systems? A common intuition is that information, namely the converse relation of a causal relation, is involved in the stabilization of given commands. For example, if my receptors spot a red traffic light, (as a consequence of the causal effect of that light on my perceptual receptors), the information so collected, "red light", will cause me to apply the brakes: the red light means that there is an injunction to stop the car. This red light was itself selected as a signal for this particular injunction because it can be easily detected by the majority of drivers, who have a strong personal interest in following some coordination rule or other. The same causal process, *mutatis mutandis*, explains sexual coloration as having coordinative value in mating. In both cases, a selection process occurs, in virtue of which the signal is used in a certain way. But did the fact that the signal carries conventional information actively contribute to shaping the agent's behavior? Or is the agent responding, rather, in virtue of the causal properties of the vehicle carrying that information?

Here is an eliminativist view of adaptive control: it is a set of procedures that have been selected because they were more efficient than their competitors, just as neural Darwinism would predict, and some Neural constructivists as well. It need not involve any kind of informational resources. Adaptive control is a sophisticated selectionist machine, that blindly reproduces what has worked, under pressure exerted by the environment. Just as conditioning can be exhibited in animals without representational abilities, such as *aplysia*, adaptive control can occur without the need to attach meaning to the sequences of neuron firings that are being selected for their beneficial effects.

Eliminativism concerning the role of information in adaptive control, however, results from intuitions concerning the selection of basic types of behavior, such as walking, or adjusting posture to gravity.[27] When it comes to processes that objectively require the integration of information from various sources, information seems to have a necessary role to play: a control vehicle will be selected now not only because it has been successful in the past in bringing about some result, but in virtue of its being able to have certain representational properties, i.e. because of the information that it carries. A vehicle now has a double function: that of directly implementing a command, and that of representing that command, or representing a class of other commands similar from a certain control viewpoint.

This double usage of vehicles, both as executers of commands, and as representations of commands, is actually borne out by an important formal finding. Classic control theory theorizes that, in order to reach optimal efficiency, control systems must have internal models available, able to dynamically represent the dynamic facts in the domain they control. How is this dynamic representation best achieved? According to Roger Conant and W. Ross Ashby, the most accurate and flexible way of controlling a system consists in taking the system itself as a representational medium. In an optimal control system, therefore, the regulator's actions are "merely the system's actions as seen through a specific mapping".[28] This means, in other words, that a system that needs to control, say, an army, should be able to represent the space of action for that army, using its own agentive capacity as a model for army movements. Similarly, a system, such as the brain, that also needs to control itself, should be able to simulate itself in the possible behaviors that need to be controlled. Planning to do something is best achieved by using the vehicles engaged in execution to represent themselves, i.e. by using them "off-line", in a simulatory way.

---

[27] See, for example, Thelen & Smith, (1994).
[28] See Conant & Ashby, (1970).

210

5.4. There are many different levels of control, which tend to be hierarchically organized and interdependent.

Granting that the brain dynamically develops on the basis of its preceding acquisitions, both theories allow for the fact that there are multiple levels of regulation and self-organization. This notion of level has been defined by Kim as an organization of elements that has a distinctive causal power (for example, microphysics and macrophysics refer to different levels of organization). Kim's notion of order, on the other hand, refers to the distinction between a causally efficacious property, and its abstract functional description (for example acetylsalicylic acid is a first-order substance that satisfies the second-order description of being an analgesic).[29]

In contrast with Kim's mereological definition, the notion of "level" relevant to adaptive control reflects the notion of a progressive evolution and development of the mind-brain, with earlier forms of control being re-used and expanded in more recently evolved forms. This architectural constraint, called "generative entrenchment",[30] may be fatal if the environment has changed so as to make the first forms of control obsolete; but in most cases, it turns out to be an economical and efficient way of building on prior acquisitions. Various levels of control thus typically include a subordination of prior mechanisms to more recent ones, for tasks of growing difficulty. What a Control "level" means is that, at that level, constraints of a given type are used in selecting a given command, which are not present in lower levels, but which will be inherited at the higher levels. The relevant constraints for the notion of a control level are usually of a temporal nature: the farther in time the constraints involved are, the higher the level considered. For example, Etienne Koechlin has shown, using fMRI, that the control of action is mediated by spatially distinct regions along the rostro–caudal axis of the Prefrontal cortex, with immediate sensory control as the lowest level (supported by premotor cortex), episodic control being the highest, and contextual control being an intermediate structure. In a cascade of this sort, information is asymmetrically inherited in the sense that a higher level combines more constraints into a command than a lower level; cascade also involves enslavement, in the sense that lower forms of control are automatically used by higher forms.[31]

---

[29] Kim (1998), pp.80 sqq.
[30] On this concept, see Wimsatt (1986) & Griffiths (1996).
[31] Does adaptive control entail a form of downward causation? Craver and Bechtel (2007) argue that the relevant downward relationship is not causal, but constitutive.

6 THE NOMOLOGICAL CONSTRAINTS ON MIND-BRAIN EVOLUTION AND DEVELOPMENT

What we have described in the preceding section can be more economically presented in mathematical terms, as two clauses which define adaptive control:

(1) $dx/dt = f(x(t), u(t))$
(2) $u(t) \in U(x(t))$

The first clause describes an input-output system, where x stands for a state variable, and u a regulation variable. It states that the velocity of state x at time t is a function of the state at this time and of the control available at this time, which itself depends upon the state at time t (as defined in 2). Clause (2) states that the control activated at time t must belong to the class of controls available at that state (be included in the space of regulation).

A general theory of how these differential equations can have solutions (in what is called "differential inclusions", i.e. differential equations with a set-value on the right-hand side) offers us a descriptively adequate, and highly predictive view of how adaptive control systems can or cannot adjust to an environment. Describing the dynamic laws that apply to such systems is the goal of a mathematical theory called "Viability theory" (Frankowska et al., 1990, Aubin, 2001, 2003, henceforth: VT).[32] Viability theory sets itself the task of describing how dynamic systems evolve as a consequence of a non-deterministic control device's having to meet spe-

---

Kistler (in press) acknowledges the possibility of downward causation through a non-causal, and non-constitutive, interpretation of system-level constraints. Dretske's concept of a "structuring cause" seems to offer a third possibility, which is explored here. Lack of space prevents discussing this important question.

[32] Let us briefly justify the introduction of a mathematical theory into our "intermediate reduction" account. A mathematical theory can receive various interpretations. VT has been used to model various phenomena in the areas of economics and biology, where dynamic coupling of sets of events must be described. This does not prevent this same mathematical theory from being relevant to the domain of mind-brain relations. As we have seen in earlier sections, the relations of mind-brains to their environments instantiates dynamic coupling. Indeed, the brain internalizes world constraints through self-regulation and self-organization. If this assumption is granted, we are justified in assuming that Viability Theory, which describes the possible dynamics through which such coupling occurs, adequately characterizes our target domain.

cific constraints (both endogenous and environmental). Given one such system, and the constraints of a task in a given environment, are there one or more viable evolutionary paths for that system? The aim of the theory might also be used to describe a central function of a mind: "to discover the feedbacks that associate a viable control to any state". When some of the evolutionary routes are not viable, (because they fail to satisfy the constraints in a finite time), VT aims at determining the *viability core*, i.e. the set of initial conditions from which at least one evolutionary path can start such that either

a) it remains in the constrained set for ever;
or
b) it reaches the target in a finite time (without violating the constraints).

The set of initial states that satisfies condition *b* only is called the "viable capture-basin" of the target.

The present hypothesis can now be articulated as the following set of claims. As claimed in section 1, a reduction of mental to physical states or properties cannot be directly obtained, for lack of bridge-laws accounting for how a neural structure or neural activation accounts for the existence of a psychological function or mental content. It is possible, however, to express such a reduction using an intermediate level of reduction, where functionalization and "implementation" coincide. At that level, we can explain how both mental and neural events occur, how mental and neural properties are acquired, as parts of dynamic control structures, which explain their respective growth and development as physical and as mental events and properties.

This theory can further be used to articulate an alternative to Kim's proposal, discussed in section 1. Remember Kim's *Causal inheritance-as-identity principle (CIIP), stating* "*M* is the property of having a property with such-and-such causal potentials, and *it turns out* that property *P* is exactly the property that fits the causal specification. And this grounds the identification of *M* with *P*". The problem we had with this formulation was that "turning out" was a contingent property that we had no reason to think was holding in our actual (or some other, possible) world. Now consider the alternative formulation which I will defend in this section:

"*M* is the property of having a property with such-and-such causal-dynamic potentials. A neural property with an identical causal-dynamic potential exists, which exactly fits the causal specification, in virtue of the regulation laws and the feedback laws which apply to neural-environmental interactions; these two sets of laws jointly explain why a given neural structure P was selected in a given M function. And this grounds the identification of M with P".

The alternative CIIP formula includes some of the claims that were made earlier: that M is D-functionalizable was argued for in section 3. The claim that a neural property fitting the causal specification for each M-state is an outcome of the neural growth theory exposed in 4. A sketch for how this claim can be articulated as a result of a control structure relating brain states and environment is drawn in section 5, where vehicles are seen to acquire a double content, as implementing a command, and as representing the fact that they do, in virtue of their control properties. What we need to argue for, now, is that such control structures necessarily operate under laws. These make the connection of D-functionalization to physical states (neural and environmental) a nomological one.

My suggestion will, I think, appear obvious. There are mathematical laws which are necessarily true of adaptive filters; these laws describe the capacity of a system to converge on a solution given the dynamic properties of the system itself and of the statistical environment to which it is coupled, i.e. the linear or non-linear characteristics of the signal and noise statistics in that environment. Among the mathematical theories for adaptive filters, Viability Theory, being in the business of extracting the universal constraints that allow a system to evolve in a viable way, provides us with lawful regularities concerning the dynamics of viable systems. According to VT, dynamic control trajectories necessarily fall under *regulation* and *feedback laws*. Regulation laws associate with a given state and command a certain rate of evolution. Feedback laws determine what portion of the regulation space is accessible to an organism with a given control history. We will concentrate on these two sets of laws, constituting as they do nomological constraints for a mind-brain with viable trajectories. Let us examine each type of regularity in turn, in order to see whether and how it provides us with a potential nomological account for our mind-brain evolutionary-developmental trajectories.

Regulation laws: These regulation laws, intuitively, tell us that cellular development, or mental activity, could not have developed in environments whose rate of change exceeds the rate at which the system can track or select adaptive solutions. Regulation laws can predict viability crises, and the kinds of transitions that can restore viability. More to the present point, they provide adequate mathematical models for explaining the evolution described by brain growth/mental development theorists.

Three types of regulation laws will illustrate our point. The first attaches to stationary environments (where statistics are stable). In such a case, there is an optimum command that an adaptive filter can converge on in a finite amount of time.[33] In nonstationary conditions, however, there must be a given kind of relation between the system and the rate of change in the environment for adaptive control to be possible: the system can only track adaptive types of feedback if its adaptation rate is faster than the rate of objective statistical change in the world. A third regulation law has to do with inertia, i.e. the rate at which a system will change its regulation parameters or routines. Granting resource limitation constraints, viability theory translates the "principle of inertia" into functional terms: controls evolve only when viability is at stake. Biological and cognitive evolutions tend to exhibit a hysteresis effect, or time lag, when confronted with the need for strategic change. "Punctuated equilibrium" illustrates this principle in evolutionary biology: most species experience little change for most of their history; when evolution occurs, it is localized in rare, rapid events of branching speciation. "Resistance to change" expresses the same dynamic phenomenon in belief, behavior or institutional revision.[34]

Feedback laws: Intuitively, a developing cognitive system cannot master complex forms of learning before mastering their components. Feedback laws deal with the constraints applying to strategy selection (i.e. choice of a given set of commands at a given time) as a function of the present and past history of the control system. In other terms, feedback laws describe the evolution of the regulation space over time. Feedback laws explain the relationship between exploration and exploitation as the two main functions in learning. They also explain the existence of control cascades.

7 CONCLUSION

Let us summarize what this section contributes to our initial problem. Although at present there is no bridge-law showing how these two types of dynamic laws apply in the general domain of cognitive development, the

---

[33] See Zaknich (2005), p.4.
[34] A negative attitude to change is thus seen as having a dynamic distal cause.

existence of viable trajectories in a developing mind-brain entails that there is a regulation map for such a system, which obeys dynamic laws of the two kinds discussed above. The present point is that this level of analysis should allow us to identify the parameters that allow certain regulations to emerge, and causally explain why the regulations in operation develop, and why they may be kept, conservatively, even when alternative regulations would allow their targets to be attained more efficiently.

In the light of the mathematical model of evolution sketched above, one can explain cascade effects in development and in evolution as the selection of a sequence of capture-basins, achieved on the basis of prior feedback, that will minimize a trajectory to a target control. VT thus provides, given initial conditions on a dynamic system, an explanation for why development follows such and such patterns, and why dedicated brain structures exchange information in the way they do so as to control behavior in the most flexible way available.

Finally, and surprisingly, the mathematics of control also accounts for why representational functions were selected, and why representations are constantly acquired and updated: homomorphic representations of the dynamic changes in the world are formed and memorized by mental systems because they are conditions for flexible control: this is an optimum that a variational system had to converge on. That is so because neural vehicles acquire their double function – that of directly implementing commands, and that of representing these or other potential commands, as a consequence of the structure of regulation spaces.

What causal role does this account leave for information? From Conant & Ashby's theorem, one can infer that information is a constraint on a control device to be flexibly adaptive. This idea can be articulated on the basis of Dretske's useful distinction between "structuring" and "triggering" causes.[35] Informational properties (such that the fact that quick/reliable information can be carried by certain color patterns or neuro-chemical properties) have a "structuring role", in that they help stabilize certain regulations; for example, the fact that this external object is represented by that neural network is in part caused by the informational constraints attached to the regulations involving that object. Triggering properties, however, do not belong to "purely mental" representations, but to their vehicles. "Purely mental" representations do not have a specific causal roles; rather, the physical realizers of the control system to which they belong have them;

---

[35] Dretske (1988).

216

they do not have additional causal power, as Kim (1993) has convincingly shown (the present contribution is a dynamical variant of Kim's theory of psychological causation). Information is not what triggers neural pruning or growing. What triggers these is the differential production of neurotrophins (and other mechanisms resulting from dendritic activity as a consequence of adaptive control). Information is a constraint on the optimal design of a device meant to be flexibly adaptive. This constraint works as a structuring, not a triggering cause. Information is the causal dimension enabling optimal learning structures and learning conditions to be selected. As Dretske has taught us, it is because a property G always follows property F (because, say, F causes G as a law of nature), that G carries information about F. The temporal succession of physical events thus carries statistical information, which is then used as a constraint for finding predictors for G. This is what adaptive filters are meant to do. The enterprise of reducing mental properties to cerebral events needs to use adaptive filters as a mechanism providing the ontological common ground allowing reduction to be performed in a way that preserves the properties of the reduced entities.

ACKNOWLEDGMENTS

I am deeply grateful to Dick Carter for his comments, questions, and linguistic suggestions. I thank Jean-Pierre Aubin and Hélène Frankowska, for helpful discussions on Viability theory. I also thank Max Kistler, Reynaldo Bernal, and the participants of the 2008 Kirchberg Symposium for their critical comments on a prior version.This article was written as part of the European Science Foundation EUROCORES Programme CNCC, and was supported by funds from CNRS and the EC Sixth Framework Programme under Contract no. ERAS-CT-2003-980409.

REFERENCES

Aubin, J.P. & Frankowska, H. 1990. *Set-Valued Analysis.* Basel: Birkhäuser.
Bickle, J. 1995. "Psychoneural Reduction of the Genuinely Cognitive: Some Accomplished Facts", *Philosophical Psychology,* 8:3, pp.265–285
Churchland P. & Sejnowski, T. 1992, *The Computational Brain.* Cambridge: MIT Press.

Changeux, J.P. & Dehaene, S. 1989. "Neuronal Models of Cognitive Function". *Cognition*, 33, pp.63–109.

Christensen, W.D. & Hooker, C.A. 2000. "An Interactivist-Constructivist Approach to Intelligence: Self-Directed Anticipative Learning", *Philosophical Psychology*, 13:1, pp.5–45.

Clark, A. & Chalmers, D.J. 1998. "The Extended Mind", *Analysis*, 58, pp.10–23, 1998. Reprinted in (P. Grim, ed.) *The Philosopher's Annual*, XXI, 1998.

Cleeremans, A. & Jimenez, L. 1999. "Stability and Explicitness: In Defense of Implicit Representation", *Behavioral and Brain Sciences*, 22:1, pp.151–152.

Conant, R.C. & Ashby, W.R. (1970). "Every Good Regulator of a System must be a Model of that System", *International Journal of Systems Science*, 1, pp.89–97.

Cosmides, L. & Tooby, J. 1994. "Beyond Intuition and Instinct Blindness: Toward an Evolutionarily Rigorous Cognitive Science", *Cognition*, 50, pp.41–77.

Craver, C.F. & Bechtel, W. 2007. "Top-down Causation without Top-down Causes", *Biology and Philosophy*, 22, pp.547–563.

Dehaene-Lambertz G. & Dehaene, S. 1997. "In Defense of Learning by Selection: Neurobiological and Behavioral Evidence Revisited", *Behavioral and Brain Sciences,* 20:4, pp.560–561.

Dretske, F. 1988. *Explaining Behavior*. Cambridge, Mass: MIT Press.

Duncan, J. 2001. "An Adaptive Coding Model of Neural Function in Prefrontal Cortex". *Nature Neuroscience Reviews*, 2, pp.820–829.

Edelman, G.M. 1987. *Neural Darwinism: the Theory of Neuronal Group Selection*. New York: Basic Books.

Grush, R. 2004. "The Emulation Theory of Representation: Motor Control, Imagery, and Perception". *Behavioral and Brain Sciences,* 27, pp.377–442.

Hall, B.K. 1992. *Evolutionary Developmental Biology*. New York : Chapman & Hall.

Hawkins, R.D. & Kandel, E.R. 1984. "Is there a Cell Biological Alphabet for Simple Forms of Learning", *Psychological Review*, 91, pp.375–391.

Jaenisch R. & Bird, A., 2003. "Epigenetic Regulation of Gene Expression: how the Genome Integrates Intrinsic and Environmental Signals". *Nature Genetics* 33, pp.245–254.

Gintis, H., Bowles, S. Boyd, R. & Fehr, E. 2007. "Explaining Altruistic Behaviour in Humans", in R.I.M Dunbar & L. Barrett (eds). *Oxford Handbook of Evolutionary Psychology*, 2007, Oxford: Oxford University Press, pp.605–619.

Griffith, P.E. 1996. "Darwinism, Process Structuralism and Natural Kinds". *Philosophy of Science*, 63, pp.1–9.

Hurford, J., Joseph, S., Kirby, S. & Reid, A. 1997. "Evolution might Select Constructivism". *Behavioral and Brain Sciences,* 20:4, pp.567–8.

Hurley, S. 2008. "The Shared Circuits Model: How Control, Mirroring, and Simulation can Enable Imitation, Deliberation, and Mindreading". *Behavioral and Brain Sciences,* 31, pp.1–58.

Karmiloff-Smith, A. 1992. *Beyond Modularity*. Cambridge, Mass.: MIT Press.

Karmiloff-Smith, A. 2006. "Ontogeny, Genetics and Evolution: A Perspective from Developmental Cognitive Neuroscience". *Biological Theory,* 1:1, pp.44–51.

218

Katz, L.C. & Shatz, C.J. 1996. "Synaptic Activity and the Construction of Cortical circuits". *Science*, 274. p.1133–1138.

Kim, J., 1993. *Supervenience and Mind.* Cambridge: Cambridge University Press.

Kim, J., 1998. *Mind in a Physical World*, Cambridge, Mass.: MIT Press.

Kistler, M. 1999. "Multiple Realization, Reduction, and Mental Properties", *International Studies in the Philosophy of Science 13*, 2, 135–149.

Kistler, M. In press. Mechanisms and Downward Causation, *Philosophical Psychology*

Koechlin, E., Ody, C. & Kouneiher, F. 2003. "The Architecture of Cognitive Control in the Human Prefrontal Cortex". *Science* 14 November 2003: Vol.302. no.5648, pp.1181–1185.

Marr, D. 1982. *Vision.* New York: W.H. Freeman and Co.

Nagel, E. 1961. *The Structure of Science.* London: Routledge and Kegan Paul.

Noe, A. 2004. *Action in Perception.* Cambridge, Mass.: MIT Press.

Place, U.T. [1956] 1990. "Is Consciousness a Brain Process?" Reprinted in W.G. Lycan (ed.) *Mind and Action, A Reader*, Oxford: Blackwell, pp.29–36.

Proust, J. 2006[a] "Agency in Schizophrenics from a Control Theory Viewpoint", in W. Prinz & N. Sebanz (eds.), *Disorders of volition*, Cambridge, Mass.: MIT Press, 2006, pp.87–118

Proust, J. 2006[b]. "Rationality and Metacognition in Non-human Animals", in S. Hurley & M. Nudds (eds.), *Rational Animals?* Oxford: Oxford University Press, 2006.

Proust, J. 2009. "What is a Mental Function?" in: A. Brenner & J. Gayon (eds.), French Studies in the Philosophy of Science. Contemporary Research in France, *Boston Studies in the Philosophy of Science, 276*: pp.227–253. New York: Springer.

Putnam, H. [1967] 1975. "The Nature of Mental States". In *Mind, Language and Reality, Philosophical papers* Cambridge: Cambridge University Press, vol. 2, pp.429–440.

Quartz, S.R. & Sejnowski, T.J. 1997. "The Neuronal Basis of Cognitive Development: a Constructivist Manifesto". *Behavioral and Brain Sciences, 20*, pp.537–596.

Sterelny, K. 2000. "Development, Evolution and Adaptation", *Philosophy of Science*, 67, pp.369–387.

Sterelny, K. 2003. *Thought in a Hostile World, The Evolution of Human Cognition,* Oxford: Blackwell.

Thelen, E. & Smith, L.B. 1994. *A Dynamic Systems Approach to the Development of Cognition and Action,* Cambridge, Mass.: MIT Press.

Wimsatt, W.C. 1986. "Developmental Constraints, Generative Entrenchment, and the Innate-acquired Distinction", in W. Bechtel, ed., *Integrating Scientific Disciplines*, Dordrecht: Martinus Nijhoff, 1986, pp.185–208.

Zaknich, A. 2005. *Principles of Aadaptive Filters and Self-learning Systems,* London: Springer.

ontos
verlag

Volume 1

TIME AND HISTORY

Friedrich Stadler and Michael Stöltzner (Eds)
Time and History
Proceedings of the 28. International Ludwig
Wittgenstein Symposium, 2005
ISBN 978-3-938793-17-6
621 pp., Hardcover € 79,00

Renowned scientists and scholars address the issue of time from a variety of disciplinary and cross-disciplinary perspectives in four sections: philosophy of time, time in the physical sciences, time in the social and cultural sciences, temporal logic, time in history/history of time, and Wittgenstein on time. Questions discussed include general relativity and cosmology, the physical basis of the arrow of time, the linguistics of temporal expressions, temporal logic, time in the social sciences, time in culture and the arts. Outside the natural sciences, time typically appears as history and in historiography in different forms, like a history of our conceptions of time. The first chapter of the book is dedicated to the major positions in contemporary philosophy of time. The importance of Wittgenstein for present-day philosophy notwithstanding, his ideas about time have hitherto received only little attention. The final chapter, for the first time, provides an extensive discussion of his respective views.

Volume 2

WITTGENSTEIN:
THE PHILOSOPHER
AND HIS WORKS

Alois Pichler, Simo Säätelä (Eds.)
Wittgenstein:
The Philosopher and his Works
ISBN 978-3-938793-28-2
461pp., Hardcover € 98,00

This wide-ranging collection of essays contains eighteen original articles by authors representing some of the most important recent work on Wittgenstein. It deals with questions pertaining to both the interpretation and application of Wittgenstein's thought and the editing of his works. Regarding the latter, it also addresses issues concerning scholarly electronic publishing. The collection is accompanied by a comprehensive introduction which lays out the content and arguments of each contribution.

Volume 3

Cultures
Conflict - Analysis - Dialogue

Christian Kanzian, Edmund Runggaldier (Eds.)
Cultures. Conflict - Analysis - Dialogue
Proceedings of the 29th International
Ludwig Wittgenstein-Symposium 2006
ISBN 978-3-938793-66-4
431pp., Hardcover € 59,00

What can systematic philosophy contribute to come from conflict between cultures to a substantial dialogue? – This question was the general theme of the 29th international symposium of the Austrian Ludwig Wittgenstein Society in Kirchberg. Worldwide leading philosophers accepted the invitation to come to the conference, whose results are published in this volume, edited by Christian Kanzian & Edmund Runggaldier. The sections are dedicated to the philosophy of Wittgenstein, Logics and Philosophy of Language, Decision- and Action Theory, Ethical Aspects of the Intercultural Dialogue, Intercultural Dialogue, and last not least to Social Ontology.

ontos
verlag

Frankfurt • Paris • Lancaster • New Brunswick
P.O. Box 1541 • D-63133 Heusenstamm bei Frankfurt
www.ontosverlag.com • info@ontosverlag.com
Tel. ++49-6104-66 57 33 • Fax ++49-6104-66 57 34

ontos verlag

Publications of the
Austrian Ludwig Wittgenstein Society. New Series

Volume 3

Christian Kanzian, Edmund Runggaldier (Eds.)
Cultures. Conflict - Analysis - Dialogue
Proceedings of the 29th International Ludwig Wittgenstein-Symposium in
Kirchberg, Austria.
ISBN 978-3-938793-66-4
431pp., Hardcover, EUR 59,00

What can systematic philosophy contribute to come from conflict between cultures to a substantial dialogue? – This question was the general theme of the 29th international symposium of the Austrian Ludwig Wittgenstein Society in Kirchberg. Worldwide leading philosophers accepted the invitation to come to the conference, whose results are published in this volume, edited by Christian Kanzian & Edmund Runggaldier. The sections are dedicated to the philosophy of Wittgenstein, Logics and Philosophy of Language, Decision- and Action Theory, Ethical Aspects of the Intercultural Dialogue, Intercultural Dialogue, and last not least to Social Ontology. Our edition include (among others) contributions authored by Peter Hacker, Jennifer Hornsby, John Hyman, Michael Kober, Richard Rorty, Hans Rott, Gerhard Schurz, Barry Smith, Pirmin Stekeler-Weithofer, Franz Wimmer, and Kwasi Wiredu.

Volume 4

Georg Gasser (Ed.)
How Successful is Naturalism?
ISBN 13: 978-938793-67-1
ca. 300pp., Hardcover, EUR 69,00

Naturalism is the reigning creed in analytic philosophy. Naturalists claim that natural science provides a complete account of all forms of existence. According to the naturalistic credo there are no aspects of human existence which transcend methods and explanations of science. Our concepts of the self, the mind, subjectivity, human freedom or responsibility is to be defined in terms of established sciences. The aim of the present volume is to draw the balance of naturalism's success so far. Unlike other volumes it does not contain a collection of papers which unanimously reject naturalism. Naturalists and anti-naturalists alike unfold their positions discussing the success or failure of naturalistic approaches. "How successful is naturalism?" shows where the lines of agreement and disagreement between naturalists and their critics are to be located in contemporary philosophical discussion.

Volume 5

Christian Kanzian, Muhammad Legenhausen (Eds.)
Substance and Attribute
Western and Islamic Traditions in Dialogue
ISBN 13: 978-3-938793-68-8
ca. 250pp., Hardcover, EUR 69,00

The aim of this volume is to investigate the topic of *Substance and Attribute*. The way leading to this aim is a dialogue between Islamic and Western Philosophy. Our project is motivated by the observation that the historical roots of Islamic and of Western Philosophy are very similar. Thus some of the articles in this volume are dedicated to the history of philosophy, in Islamic thinking as well as in Western traditions. But the dialogue between Islamic and Western Philosophy is not only an historical issue, it has also systematic relevance for actual philosophical questions. The topic *Substance and Attribute* particularly has an important history in both traditions; and it has systematic relevance for the actual ontological debate.
The volume includes contributions (among others) by Hans Burkhardt, Hans Kraml, Muhammad Legenhausen, Michal Loux, Pedro Schmechtig, Muhammad Shomali, Erwin Tegtmeier, and Daniel von Wachter.

ontos verlag

Frankfurt • Paris • Lancaster • New Brunswick
P.O. Box 1541 • D-63133 Heusenstamm bei Frankfurt
www.ontosverlag.com • info@ontosverlag.com
Tel. ++49-6104-66 57 33 • Fax ++49-6104-66 57 34

Publications of the
Austrian Ludwig Wittgenstein Society. New Series

Volume 6

Alois Pichler, Herbert Hrachovec (Eds.)
Wittgenstein and the Philosophy of Information
Proceedings of the 30th International Ludwig Wittgenstein-Symposium in
Kirchberg, Volume 1
ISBN 978-3-86838-001-9
356pp., Hardcover, EUR 79,00

This is the first of two volumes of the proceedings from the 30th International Wittgenstein
Symposium in Kirchberg, August 2007. In addition to new contributions to Wittgenstein
research (by N. Garver, M. Kross, St. Majetschak, K. Neumer, V. Rodych, L. M. Valdés-
Villanueva), the book contains articles with a special focus on digital Wittgenstein research
and Wittgenstein's role for the understanding of the digital turn (by L. Bazzocchi, A.
Biletzki, J. de Mul, P. Keicher, D. Köhler, K. Mayr, D. G. Stern), as also discussions - not
necessarily from a Wittgensteinian perspective - of issues in the philosophy of information,
incl. computational ontologies (by D. Apollon, G. Chaitin, F. Dretske, L. Floridi, Y.
Okamoto, M. Pasin and E. Motta).

Volume 7

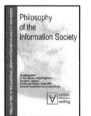

Herbert Hrachovec, Alois Pichler (Eds.)
Philosophy of the Information Society
Proceedings of the 30th International Ludwig Wittgenstein-Symposium in
Kirchberg, Volume 2
ISBN 978-3-86838-002-6
326pp., Hardcover, EUR 79,00

This is the second of two volumes of the proceedings from the 30th
International Wittgenstein Symposium in Kirchberg, August 2007. It contains selected
contributions on the Philosophy of media, Philosophy of the Internet, on Ethics and the
political economy of information society. Also included are papers presented in a
workshop on electronic philosophy resources and open source/open access.

Volume 8

Jesús Padilla Gálvez (Ed.)
Phenomenology as Grammar
ISBN 978-3-938793-91-6
224pp., Hardcover, EUR 59,00

This volume gathers papers, which were read at the congress held at the University of
Castilla-La Mancha in Toledo (Spain), in September 2007, under the general subject of
phenomenology. The book is devoted to Wittgenstein's thoughts on phenomenology. One
of its aims is to consider and examine the lasting importance of phenomenology for
philosophic discussion. For E. Husserl phenomenology was a discipline that endeavoured
to describe how the world is constituted and experienced through a series of conscious
acts. His fundamental concept was that of intentional consciousness. What did drag
Wittgenstein into working on phenomenology? In his "middle period" work, Wittgenstein
used the headline "Phenomenology is Grammar". These cornerstones can be signalled by
notions like language, grammar, rule, visual space *versus* Euclidean space, *minima
visibilia* and colours. L. Wittgenstein's main interest takes the form of a research on
language.

Frankfurt • Paris • Lancaster • New Brunswick
P.O. Box 1541 • D-63133 Heusenstamm bei Frankfurt
www.ontosverlag.com • info@ontosverlag.com
Tel. ++49-6104-66 57 33 • Fax ++49-6104-66 57 34

ontos
verlag

PublicationsOfTheAustrianLudwigWittgensteinSociety
NewSeries

Vol. 1 Friedrich Stadler and Michael Stöltzner
Time and History
Proceedings of the 28. International
Ludwig Wittgenstein Symposium, 2005
ISBN 978-3-938793-17-6
621 pp., Hardcover € 79,00

Vol. 2 Alois Pichler, Simo Säätelä (Eds.)
Wittgenstein:
The Philosopher and his Works
ISBN 978-3-938793-28-2
461pp., Hardcover € 98,00

Vol. 3 Christian Kanzian,
Edmund Runggaldier (Eds.)
Cultures. Conflict - Analysis -
Dialogue
Proceedings of the 29th International
Ludwig Wittgenstein-Symposium 2006
ISBN 978-3-938793-66-4
431pp., Hardcover € 59,00

Vol. 4 Georg Gasser (Ed.)
How Successful is Naturalism?
ISBN 978-3-938793-67-1
300pp., Hardcover € 69,00

Vol. 5 Christian Kanzian,
Muhammad Legenhausen (Eds.)
Substance and Attribute
ISBN 978-3-938793-68-8
248pp., Hardcover, 69,00

Vol. 6 Alois Pichler, Herbert Hrachovec
Wittgenstein and the
Philosophy of Information
Proceedings of the 30th International
Ludwig Wittgenstein-Symposium, 2007,
Volume 1
ISBN 978-3-86838-001-9
356pp., Hardcover,€ 79,00

Vol. 7 Herbert Hrachovec, Alois Pichler
Philosophy of the Information
Society
Proceedings of the 30th International
Ludwig Wittgenstein-Symposium, 2007,
Volume 2
ISBN 978-3-86838-002-6
326pp., Hardcover, EUR 79,00

Vol. 8 Jesús Padilla Gálvez (Ed.)
Phenomenology as Grammar
ISBN 978-3-938793-91-6
224 pp., Hardcover, EUR 59,00

Vol. 9 Wulf Kellerwessel
Wittgensteins Sprachphilosophie in
den „Philosophischen
Untersuchungen"
Eine kommentierende Ersteinführung
ISBN 978-3-86838-032-3
330 pp., Paperback EUR 39.90

Vol. 10 John Edelman (Ed.)
Sense and Reality
Essays out of Swansea
ISBN 978-3-86838-041-5
235 pp., Hardcover EUR 89.00

Vol. 11 Alexander Hieke, Hannes Leitgeb
Reduction – Abstraction – Analysis
Proceedings of the 31th International
Ludwig Wittgenstein-Symposium in
Kirchberg, 2008
ISBN 978-3-86838-047-7
414pp., Hardcover, EUR 79,00

Vol. 12 Alexander Hieke, Hannes Leitgeb
Reduction
Between the Mind and the Brain
ISBN 978-3-86838-046-0
216pp., Hardback, EUR 69,00

ontos
verlag
Frankfurt • Paris • Lancaster • New Brunswick
P.O. Box 1541 • D-63133 Heusenstamm bei Frankfurt
www.ontosverlag.com • info@ontosverlag.com
Tel. ++49-6104-66 57 33 • Fax ++49-6104-66 57 34